A Mortal Likeness

A MORTAL LIKENESS

A VICTORIAN MYSTERY

———◆•❈•◆———

Laura Joh Rowland

CROOKED
LANE

NEW YORK

Copyright © 2018 by Laura Joh Rowland

Published in the United States by Crooked Lane Books, an imprint of The Quick Brown Fox & Company LLC.

Crooked Lane Books and its logo are trademarks of The Quick Brown Fox & Company LLC.

Library of Congress Catalog-in-Publication data available upon request.

ISBN (hardcover): 978-1-68331-447-9
ISBN (ePub): 978-1-68331-448-6
ISBN (ePDF): 978-1-68331-449-3

Cover design by Melanie Sun
Book design by Jennifer Canzone

Printed in the United States.

www.crookedlanebooks.com

Crooked Lane Books
34 West 27th St., 10th Floor
New York, NY 10001

First Edition: January 2018

10 9 8 7 6 5 4 3 2 1

To the Queens Mystery Writers Group
Nancy Bilyeau
Mariah Fredericks
Jennifer Kitses
Shizuka Otake
Triss Stein
for their friendship and support

LONDON,
APRIL 1889

1

The train thunders along the track, through rain, fog, and smoke. In my seat by the window, I fidget with the camera and leather satchel on my lap. Beside me, Hugh pages through a newspaper he's already read twice since we left Victoria station at ten this morning. He checks his pocket watch; it's twelve fifteen now.

"Where the devil is he going?" Hugh whispers.

We behold the man seated across the aisle two rows up. I've been staring at him for so long, I've memorized his black derby, the auburn hair curling under the brim, his gray wool coat, and the masculine curve of his jaw. "Heaven only knows."

"Heaven and the woman he's secretly meeting," Hugh says.

"The woman we hope he's meeting."

"Sarah, his wife is certain he's having an affair. A rich elderly widow goes to a seaside resort and falls in love with a young bellhop? Of course Noel Vaughn only married her for her money, and he's unfaithful."

"But we've been spying on him for two weeks, and we haven't caught him."

Five months ago, Hugh and I formed a private inquiry service. We placed advertisements in the newspapers: *Experienced detectives will conduct investigations of any kind. Discreet, confidential service. Reasonable rates.* Alas, all our cases have been small and the fees low. Not many people want to hire a photographer who was evicted from her studio in seedy Whitechapel or an aristocrat who'd never worked a day in his life. So far Hugh and I have found missing cats who'd taken up residence at neighbors' houses and a diamond bracelet thought stolen but actually dropped behind a bed. We were also hired to lurk in a notions store and catch shoplifters. Yet the one major investigation that gives us the right to call ourselves "experienced" is one that we must keep secret. In the meantime, Mrs. Vaughn is our biggest client to date, our hope of better work later.

"We'll catch him if we stick with it long enough," Hugh says, "and we need the money."

When I was evicted from my studio, where I also lived, I couldn't afford to rent a new place. Hugh came to my rescue. He had become estranged from his wealthy noble family when they learned that he's a homosexual, but his father, the Marquis of Ravenswood, gave him an allowance and a house to live in for a year while he establishes himself in a profession, and he invited me to move in. Although it's improper for me to reside with a man I'm not married to, we're the best of friends and I've nowhere else to go. Now the year is half gone, Hugh's allowance isn't enough to support both of us, and we're unqualified for ordinary jobs. Our private inquiry service is our only hedge against a looming uncertain future.

We contemplate Noel Vaughn. He didn't notice us when we boarded the train behind him and hasn't turned around once. If he did look in our direction, he would see a strikingly handsome blond-haired man who wears a coat, hat, and trousers suitable for a shop clerk. Vaughn wouldn't notice me. A thin, plain spinster of thirty-three in a modest gray coat and bonnet, I'm unremarkable at best and invisible when with Hugh, who outshines everyone around him. Two young ladies across the aisle are trying to catch his eye. He is oblivious.

"We must be halfway to Antarctica," he says. The train has crossed the Thames and is now carrying us through London's southern suburbs. "Is Vaughn ever going to get off the train?"

I'm patient, accustomed to taking many pictures of customers in my studio and waiting hours in the field for the right light, but patience is not among Hugh's many virtues. He taps the front page of his newspaper. "Now *this* is the kind of case I'd like."

The headline reads, "Baby Robin Still Missing. Police Pursuing New Leads." Robin Mariner was kidnapped on the eighth of April— eleven days ago— from his family's estate on Hampstead Heath. His father is Sir Gerald Mariner, one of the wealthiest men in England, and his mother is Alexandra Lyle, the famous former actress. The picture, which has appeared in every newspaper and on posters and handbills all over town, is an engraving from a photograph of Lady Alexandra holding Robin. Her hair is an upswept mass of fair ringlets, her bosom swells the bodice of her lace-trimmed frock, and her beautiful, sensuous face wears the smile that once lit up the West End stages. Dark-haired Robin, aged twenty months and dressed in a sailor suit, blends into the shadows. His kidnapping is a national sensation that has diverted the public's attention from Jack the Ripper.

The killer known by that nickname killed six women during last August, September, and November. The police's search for him is still ongoing, his identity known to only a few persons. Hugh and I are among the fewer who know the truth about the murders and why London need fear the Ripper no longer.

"The reward's been upped to five thousand pounds," Hugh says. Sir Gerald has offered to pay for information leading to Robin's rescue and the kidnapper's capture. "We should be looking for Robin."

"Half of London already is." I too have eagerly followed the story; I've a personal interest in cases that involve missing persons. The papers report that the police are swamped with tips about sightings, none of which have panned out. The Special Kidnapping Squad, composed of officers from all the police jurisdictions, hasn't been able to pick up Robin's trail.

"We might get lucky." Hugh is more optimistic than I. It was his idea to start a private detective agency.

The train slows with a grinding sound of brakes. Through the window I glimpse a huge redbrick station topped by conical turrets. It looks unexpectedly familiar. As I try to remember when I've seen it before, the station swallows up the train, which shudders to a halt. Noel Vaughn gathers his umbrella and rises.

"It's about time," Hugh says.

Following Vaughn down the aisle, I carry my satchel and Hugh my camera, which is enclosed in a square wooden case twelve inches high. It's bulkier and heavier than my miniature camera, but it takes better photographs. Also burdened by umbrellas, we step onto the platform in the cold, smoky train shed. I didn't see the sign for the station; I don't know where we are.

As Vaughn strides through a door, Hugh whispers, "Hang back. Don't let him spot us."

We descend stairs to an underground passage. White brick pillars flare at the top into broad, circular capitals decorated with orange and white bricks in geometric patterns. My sense of familiarity is stronger, a weight in my stomach. When I was nine years old, my father began teaching me photography, taking me on expeditions to practice. This was one of the places we went. Benjamin Bain, my father, disappeared in 1866 when I was ten. He is the reason that Robin Mariner's kidnapping and other cases that involve missing persons touch a nerve in me. The wound caused by his departure is still raw, painful. I'm always glad when a buried memory of him resurfaces, but a disturbing sense of unfinished business gnaws at me. For twenty-four years, I thought my father was dead. Last autumn I learned that he might still be alive. The possibility has been constantly on my mind, but I've yet to explore it, for I'm too afraid of what I might discover.

Hugh tugs my arm as I stand immobile. "Come on, Sarah! He's getting away."

More and more often, thoughts about my father stop me cold, disrupt my daily life. Sooner or later I must find out the truth despite my fear—for better or worse.

We press forward as Vaughn's tall figure recedes between the pillars. Two police constables appear in front of us. My heart lurches; I freeze in my tracks. I've had a terror of police since childhood. My father organized laborers to march in demonstrations and demand better pay and working conditions. It put him at odds with the police, who deemed him a rabble-rouser. They barged into our house, ransacked it, and shouted threats at my father while I hid and cried. The memory resurges whenever I see police, and I have bad memories from my own clashes with them last autumn.

A constable accosts Hugh and me. "May I have a word?"

"We're in a bit of a hurry." Hugh has reason to fear the police himself, and Vaughn has vanished from sight.

The constable blocks our path. "Not so fast."

Last autumn, Hugh and I and some friends of ours did something that we considered right and necessary but that the police would call a crime. We live in fear that they'll find out and hold us accountable. Maybe this is the day.

"Very well." Hugh masks his own anxiety with his most charming, debonair manner. "What seems to be the problem, Officer?"

"I'll ask the questions. What's your name?"

"Lord Hugh Staunton, at your service." Hugh doffs his hat and bows.

The constable turns his unfriendly gaze on me. "And you?"

I square my shoulders and look him in the eye. "Sarah Bain." Our experiences magnified my fear of the police but also instilled a bedrock of courage in me. Facing death and surviving does that.

"What are you doing here?"

"We came to take photographs." Hugh holds up my camera. "See?"

"You picked a bad day. It's raining."

"I'm a fool for my favorite hobby," Hugh says with a self-deprecating smile. "What's yours? Darts?"

His uncanny ability to read people is as impressive as his ability to charm. The constable smiles and says, "I do like a good game. Sorry to bother you, sir, but we've had a tip. Somebody reported seeing a man and woman at this station yesterday. They had a baby with them, and they acted nervous. It could've been the kidnappers and Robin Mariner."

Now I notice the other constable questioning a mother and father with a toddler. Hugh says, "It wasn't us. We weren't here yesterday. And we didn't kidnap Robin."

The constable nods; he believes Hugh. "Well, we have to investigate every tip. I'd love to be the chap who puts that little boy back in his mum's arms."

Released, Hugh and I hurry to the end of the passage, through a doorway, and up a flight of stairs. We emerge in a vast building like a giant conservatory, its walls and high arched ceiling made from glass panes divided by iron bars. People roam around statues on pedestals under potted trees. Chatter and laughter reverberate.

"The Crystal Palace," Hugh and I exclaim simultaneously.

The Crystal Palace is a giant museum on Sydenham Hill. Built some thirty years ago, it contains exhibits of art and industry and objects of scientific, historical, and national import. It's not as popular a landmark as in its heyday, when thousands of people flocked in daily. I've seen it many times in pictures, so I don't know whether I recognize it from them or from memories of being here.

"I came here with my nanny when I was a boy," Hugh says as he buys tickets for us at the booth. "I wandered off, and it took her all day to find me." He looks around anxiously. "If we don't lay eyes on Vaughn soon . . ."

A tinkling noise draws my attention to a large fountain, some twenty feet high, entirely made of glass. Water cascades down a central column, which resembles a glittery splinter of an iceberg, into an enormous crystal basin. Among the folks admiring the fountain stands Vaughn.

"There he is!" As I point, a young woman wearing a dark-green coat and a black straw hat decorated with a chartreuse feather joins him. Her pouf of hair is a shiny, coppery red. She has a full bosom and tiny waist, huge eyes fringed with blackened lashes, and a little bee-stung mouth. A black beauty mark dots her creamy cheek. Many men would find her attractive. Vaughn certainly does. Even from a distance, I can see his face suffuse with lust.

Hugh pushes the camera into my hands. I move nearer to the couple and pretend I'm photographing the fountain. As I peer at them through the viewfinder, the woman leans close to Vaughn and whispers. Her tongue flicks inside his ear. The dim daylight from the glass ceiling illuminates their sly, furtive expressions. It's a perfect shot that spells "adultery." But as I press the shutter control, someone jostles the camera.

"Of all the rotten luck," Hugh mutters.

The couple turns and walks away. Hugh and I follow them out of the Crystal Palace. Rain pelts the terrace that fronts the length of the glass building. Marble balustrades and statues drip water. Vaughn holds his umbrella over his lady as they walk down a broad flight of granite steps. I struggle to open my umbrella and keep my camera dry. Hugh motions me to hurry.

"There are so few other people out here," I say in a loud whisper. "They'll notice us."

"We'll have to take the chance."

Below the terrace, a wide avenue bisects the park that spreads down the hill. We skirt a huge circular basin that I know—from pictures or memory?—once had fountains that sent sprays of water sky-high. The fountains aren't working today. The water in the basin is flat and murky, the rusty iron piping like half-submerged serpents. Down a flight of cracked steps, the avenue continues between overgrown lawns and flower beds. The paramours are thirty feet ahead of us, partially hidden beneath their umbrella.

"We can't just run in front of them and tell them to pose for us.'" Hugh belatedly opens his umbrella; his hat and coat are beaded with raindrops. "Let's see where they go. Maybe a better opportunity will present itself."

We trail our quarries down the hillside. Paths branch off the avenue into dense coppices of trees. I glance backward at the palace, whose glass structure looks like an elongated block of gray ice melting on top of the hill. Nobody else has ventured this far from it. As we lag farther behind the couple, the woman's laughter drifts in the cold, damp air. The bottom of the park is a virtual wilderness. Vaughn and the woman lead us along a path that winds through the woods. All dimness and dripping water, puddles underfoot and mist in the air, the woods are like a primeval forest. Strange birds chitter, and monkey-puzzle trees spread branches studded with spiny green fingers.

The woman shrieks.

Hugh and I freeze. She and Vaughn stop on the path as she points at something in the woods. I aim my camera, but they laugh and quickly move on. We follow and see what they saw—two great winged beasts, each with the body of a lizard, a serpent's neck, and a beak full of sharp teeth, perched atop a jagged stone wall, ready to swoop down.

"This is the exhibit of antediluvian monsters. They're models of dinosaurs," I whisper, elated because I remember coming here with my father. We photographed the dinosaurs. None of the photographs remain. My mother burned them and most of my father's other work after he disappeared.

"When I was a boy, I thought they were real." Hugh chuckles. "Scared me half to death."

The passage of twenty-three years has been cruel to the dinosaurs. Many of their yellow ceramic scales have fallen off, revealing plaster underneath. We shadow Vaughn and his lady as they skirt an irregularly shaped lake. Dinosaur models resembling crocodiles with birds' bills and snakes with dolphins' bodies and flippers are placed as if they're crawling up out of the water. Islands in the lake are inhabited by more dinosaurs—ponderous creatures with heavy bellies, clawed toes, and eyes the size of dinner plates. The couple pauses to look. Hugh and I hide behind a stone sculpture of a palm tree. Vaughn embraces the woman and bends his head.

"Now!" Hugh whispers.

They passionately kiss. I aim my camera, center them in the viewfinder, and take a photograph before they stroll down the path. "I'm afraid it'll be too dark."

Sometimes I think there's a mischievous god who delights in thwarting photographers. Today everything goes wrong. Exposures are too short; while changing glass negative plates, I drop and break two; rain spatters the camera's lens. Soon we're drenched, defeated, and miserable.

"God, this is sordid," Hugh says.

"And we're not even good at it," I say. We're both remembering that we solved the Jack the Ripper case via a combination of mishaps, wild ideas, and luck. So much for our daydreams of solving other murders or rescuing a famous kidnapped baby. Our glory days are over.

"Mrs. Vaughn will have to take our word for it that her husband is cheating," I say.

"Our word's not enough," Hugh says. "We need proof."

We glumly watch Vaughn and his lady pick their way through mud and weeds to the largest dinosaur model, about thirty feet from where we're hiding behind a pine tree. The scaly green creature, more than ten feet high with jagged hackles on its back, resembles a fat dragon with a horn on its nose. Its glass eyes glare. A big hole in its side reveals a hollow interior and the bricks and iron skeleton from which it's constructed. Nearby, a wooden scaffold, buckets, and a wheelbarrow full of tools indicate that the dinosaur is undergoing renovation. Vaughn boosts his lady into the hole as she giggles.

"Are they doing what I think they're doing?" Hugh asks.

Moans emanating from within the dinosaur are our answer. A blush heats my cheeks. I'm not a prude; rather, I'm thinking of the things I've done that no respectable unmarried woman does. The memory is arousing and guilt-inducing.

"Much as I hate to be a voyeur, we need this photo," Hugh says. "Shall I?"

"Yes, please." I would be mortified if anyone photographed me during my most private, uninhibited moments. I hand Hugh the camera.

Hugh tiptoes to the dinosaur, aims the camera inside the hole, and opens the shutter. Praying that the lovers don't see him or move too vigorously, I count off the seconds. Hugh turns to look at me, and I nod. He closes the shutter and hurries toward me with a triumphant grin. I sigh in relief. Then his foot catches on an exposed tree root. He trips, flails his arms in an attempt to regain his balance. The camera drops; Hugh sprawls on hands and knees. I gasp.

"Damn!" Hugh says.

The moans within the dinosaur abruptly stop. Vaughn puts his head out of the hole and sees Hugh scrambling to his feet, grabbing the camera. "Hey! Are you spying on us?"

As Hugh and I run, Vaughn shouts, "Peeping Tom! Pervert!"

2

Three hours later, Hugh and I trudge from St. Pancras station through Bloomsbury. The afternoon fades into a premature twilight as smoke from the trains blends with the thickening fog. Men are lighting the gas lamps along the streets that surround the central garden in Argyle Square. Horse-drawn carriages rattle past the terraced brick houses that repose behind black iron fences. Machinery in nearby factories pounds and clangs.

"What a day," Hugh says. "I need a drink."

I need a cup of hot tea and a hot bath. The rain has stopped, but my clothes are still damp from our adventure at the dinosaur park, and I shiver in the chill.

"I'm sorry I dropped your camera," Hugh apologizes for the tenth time. He knows my cameras are my dearest possessions.

"Never mind; it wasn't broken, and neither was the negative plate. Let's just hope the photograph turns out all right."

We come upon our next-door neighbor, a lawyer. He nods a cold, silent greeting as he enters his gate. None of the neighbors like us. They know who Hugh is; they're aware he's a homosexual. It seems that virtually everyone in London is aware. He was exposed in a newspaper story that ignited a blaze of scandal. Our neighbors erroneously think I'm a former prostitute he took in. I know this because I've overheard them gossiping. That we're not welcome here is all the more reason we wish our private inquiry service to be a success—so we can move. But I fear there's nowhere we could go that Hugh's reputation won't follow and our secret won't catch up with us someday.

As we walk up our front steps, the door opens, and a thin, lanky boy with red hair and freckles appears. "Thought you'd never get home."

Hugh smiles. "Hello, Mick. This is a nice surprise."

Mick is a former street urchin I befriended last autumn. He lived in a sewer tunnel and eked out a precarious existence by scavenging, working odd jobs, and stealing until I convinced him to go into St. Vincent's orphanage. There, he's fed, clothed, educated, and safe.

In the foyer, as Hugh and I shed camera and umbrellas, wet hats and coats, I say, "Mick, why aren't you at St. Vincent's?"

"I ran away."

"Oh, dear."

"Orphanages are for babies," Mick says. "I'm thirteen."

Indeed, he's grown two inches since we first met, his voice cracks, and many youths his age are working men. "But what are you going to do?" I ask.

"I thought I could live here."

"That's a capital idea!" Hugh loves company, and we have none except our few close friends. Although he was once among the most popular bachelors in town, his high-society acquaintances have dropped him. He's lonely, and Mick doesn't hold his homosexuality against him. I too would love to give Mick a home, but we can't.

Mick sees my frown and says, "I ain't a freeloader. I'll work for my keep. I could help you with investigations like I did before."

He helped us solve the Ripper case, but I've realized that we did Mick a disservice by letting him. It rendered him unfit for the orphanage, where he's treated like an ordinary boy and strictly disciplined by the nuns. Hugh and I mustn't expose him to more dangers.

"Let's talk about it at dinner," Hugh says. "I'm starved."

"Me too." Mick casts a beseeching glance at me, then accompanies Hugh to the dining room.

The savory odor of food whets my own appetite, but I hesitate because I see Fitzmorris—the third member of our household—hovering in the passage. A thin, gray-haired, somber fellow, he wears a white apron, and his shirtsleeves are rolled up. He's officially Hugh's valet, but he and I share the cooking, cleaning, and other housework.

"The creditors are demanding payment again," he says.

We owe money to the grocer, the bakery, the launderer, the coal deliveryman, and everyone else who provides us goods or services. Hugh doesn't know how to run a household on a tight budget, and Fitzmorris and I conspire to shield him from reality as much as possible.

"Can't you ask for another extension?" We've already used up my savings.

"They can't wait any longer, and unless we pay up, they'll cut us off." Fitzmorris doesn't mention that he hasn't been paid since January. "The biggest bill is the tailor's."

Hugh has been overspending on clothes again, and I must curtail him. I dread the talk with Hugh. Despite his cheerful nature and his determination to make the best of bad circumstances, I know that losing his family, friends, and social status was a terrible blow, and he suffers spells of black depression. He once tried to commit suicide, and I'm afraid that any straw will be the last and that he'll try again and succeed.

"Hugh will have to ask his father to increase his allowance," I say with great reluctance. He's already done so twice, and on each occasion, his father lectured him about his spendthrift habits and moral laxness. Each occasion sent him into a black spell.

Fitzmorris looks grave; he shares my concern about Hugh. "I overheard your conversation with Mick. I like the lad, but we can't afford to feed another mouth."

The dilemma weighs heavily on me. "I know. I'll have to tell him he can't stay."

We go in to dinner. After Fitzmorris serves the soup, Hugh pours wine into our glasses. "Mick is going to live with us. Let's drink a toast!"

Mick beams. Hugh has given him permission to stay, and I can't retract it. Fitzmorris and I try to hide our consternation as we clink glasses. After we finish the soup, I say to Hugh, "Help me fetch the next course."

In the kitchen, dishing up lamb stew, I say, "You shouldn't have said yes."

"How could I not?" Hugh is chastened yet defiant. "After what he did for us?"

If not for Mick, we would both be dead. "But if we take him in, we'll have to put him out when the year is up, your allowance ends, and we have to leave this house. That would be cruel." I don't mention that I'll be homeless too.

"Maybe we won't have to put him out. We're just wrapping up our most lucrative case. Things are looking up."

"Things will have to look up a lot more if we're to support Mick." If they don't, I'll have to find work someplace and lodgings for myself. As much as it would upset me to give up photography and my dream of having my own studio again, leaving Hugh would be worse. He's become my family. "And I'm not sure the orphanage will take Mick back later."

"Have a little faith, Sarah," Hugh says with affectionate exasperation.

We bring the stew to the table. As we eat, Hugh tells Mick about our surveillance at the dinosaur park. Mick laughs and says, "I wish I'd been there!"

I contemplate what his living with us will involve. Although Mick thinks himself grown up, and Hugh and I have treated him as if he were, we must now act as parents. When dinner is over, I say, "I need to develop the photographs we took today. Mick, will you help?"

My darkroom is on the ground floor, in a room off the kitchen intended for a maid, whose walls and window I painted black. My enlarger sits on a battered table I bought at a flea market, and an old cupboard holds my supplies. The room is cold, airless, and damp. My biggest camera and tripod are jammed in the corner, and there's no running water. Mick mixes chemical solutions in the kitchen and pours them into trays. He's learned how by watching me. I feel sad because he knows I have qualms about taking him in, and he's trying to show me how useful he can be.

"Mick, I'm glad to have you here," I say, and it's true. "But we need to set some conditions."

"Sure," he says cheerfully.

"First, no stealing or roaming the streets after dark." I improvise as I go along. "No breaking and entering or fighting." I wince because these are all things he's done for my benefit in the past.

Mick lifts an eyebrow at me; he hasn't forgotten. "Sure."

"And you have to go to school."

"I had enough school already." Mick hates sitting still in a classroom. "I know how to read and write and do my sums."

It isn't enough. The world is changing fast—good jobs require more education, and Mick deserves better than manual labor that will wear him out before he's forty. "Either you go to school, or you go back to St. Vincent's."

"Well, if you put it that way . . ." Mick carries the trays to the darkroom.

There, I lay out the flat cases containing the glass negative plates. Mick closes the door and stuffs rags under it to keep out the light. Working by touch in the pitch-black darkness, I slip a plate into the tray of developing solution.

"You seen the Lipskys lately?" Mick asks.

Mr. and Mrs. Lipsky are a Jewish butcher and his wife, our good friends. They too were involved in the events associated with the Ripper case. "Not since the Sabbath dinner we took you to at their house two weeks ago."

"What about Catherine?" Mick's tone is deliberately nonchalant.

"Not for a while." Catherine Price, also a party to the events, is a beautiful, young fledgling actress. Aware that Mick has an unrequited crush on her, I reluctantly say, "She's engaged to a man she met at the theater. He owns a factory."

"Oh."

I sense Mick's hope that the engagement won't last and he'll grow up and Catherine will fall in love with him before she marries someone else. He's silent for a moment, then he says, "You won't be sorry you took me in, Miss Sarah. I promise."

#

It's ten thirty at night by the time the negatives are developed, the plates dried, and the photographs printed. Hugh, Mick, and I examine the enlarged prints hanging from clothes pegs on a string stretched above the kitchen sink.

"They're worse than I thought," I say unhappily.

The shot I took inside the Crystal Palace is an off-kilter view of strangers admiring the glass fountain. The others are underexposed, the couple dwarfed by trees and dinosaur models or blurred by motion. So much for my thirteen years as a professional photographer; these pictures look as if they were taken by an amateur.

"They're good enough," Hugh says. "It's obvious that Vaughn and the woman aren't just friends. And this takes the whole sordid cake." He indicates his photograph of them inside the dinosaur model.

It's too dark with shadows, blurry, and devoid of context to show where the photograph was taken, but it's obvious who they are and what they're doing. The woman lies on her back, Vaughn on top of her, both fully clothed. Her skirts are up, her knees hugging his waist. Their profiles touch, eyes closed, mouths gaping.

"Criminy!" Mick says.

I experience more qualms about involving him in our work; it's not fit for a thirteen-year-old. "Mick, time for bed." Fitzmorris has prepared the guest room for him, and earlier I discovered that Mick brought his possessions with him from the orphanage. He correctly assumed he'd be staying. "You have to get up early for school tomorrow."

"Aw!" He starts to argue, then remembers the rules and goes.

I take a last look at the pictures. Sometimes the camera captures things I don't notice until after the photographs are developed. In one of the prints, the two lovers stroll along the path through the woods. The big dragon-like dinosaur looms in the background. I thought that and Hugh and I and the lovers were the only people in the park, but I was wrong.

"What is it?" Hugh scrutinizes the photograph. "Oh, I see—there's a man in the woods."

The old man stands between the dinosaur and the photograph's right-hand edge, gazing at something outside the frame. He wears a mackintosh, his figure is stocky, and he has a white beard. His face, shaded by a brimmed cap, is too small to see clearly. His hands are raised, forefingers and thumbs extended with the tips pointing at each other to form a rectangle, the other fingers curled into his palms. An eerie sensation creeps through me.

"What's he doing?" Hugh asks.

"He's composing a photograph. He's making a view-finder with his hands." I'm suddenly breathless, thinking of the last time I saw that gesture. My vision goes dark at the edges, I sway, and Hugh grasps my arm, steadying me.

"Sarah, you look like you've seen a ghost."

"My father used to do that." As I imitate the gesture, I can feel my father's hands arranging mine in position, showing me how to see the world as though I were a camera.

Hugh looks startled; I've told him all about my father. "You think that's your father in the picture?"

"It could be!" I speak through a welter of hope, wonder, and confusion. It's as if my thoughts of my father conjured him up from thin air. "He took me to the dinosaur park when I was a child. I just remembered today."

"But what are the chances that he would return there after twenty-four years on the very same day as you? Isn't that a whopping coincidence?"

"Yes, but if he's alive . . ." I'm dizzy with exhilaration. My father's resurrection from the ranks of the presumed dead was proof that miracles happen. Why shouldn't a second miracle be possible?

Hugh hesitates, reluctant to rain on my parade yet not wanting to encourage unrealistically high hopes. "Does the man look like him?"

I fetch a magnifying glass, lay the damp print on the kitchen table, and hold the glass over it. The man's face is just a larger blur. "My father didn't have a beard. But of course he would look different now." My exhilaration fades even as I make the excuse. "Of course it's not him." I sigh and drop into a chair. "It's just wishful thinking."

Hugh's eyes narrow in thought. "Maybe we shouldn't rule out the possibility that the man is your father and the two of you did accidentally cross paths today. Stranger things have happened." That we, aided by Mick, Catherine, and the Lipskys, dispatched Jack the Ripper is indeed stranger. Hugh taps the photograph. "Do you know what this means, Sarah?"

I shake my head, but my heart begins to thud, pumping apprehension through my veins.

"It means you have to look for your father."

Trepidation vies with my need to know his fate. If he's in London, why has he never gotten in touch with me? I wouldn't have been impossible to find. For ten years, I operated a studio that bore my father's surname, and London is like a conglomeration of gossipy small towns; someone could have told him where I was. And when I moved in with Hugh five months ago, I left my forwarding address with the post office.

"I'm not ready."

"Listen, Sarah." Hugh sits beside me. "Until you look for the truth and find it, you'll always be wondering. You'll never have peace."

Look for the truth. It's what my father often told me while he was teaching me photography. *"Look for the truth under the surface of what's before your eyes. It's what makes a good picture."*

"How do I know the truth when I see it?" I would ask.

"Your heart will beat faster."

Although I'm rarely sure I've captured the truth in a photograph, I realize Hugh is right. I've learned to trust my heart, and it's beating faster. "But I don't know where to start looking."

"Yes, you do," Hugh says gently.

#

I'm seated in an armchair in the parlor. Light from the lamp on the table shimmers in the glass of brandy that Hugh poured for me. The only sound is the ticking of the clock. Hugh, Mick, and Fitzmorris are asleep. My hands tremble as I untie the white strings around the brown cardboard letter case in my lap and remove the contents—folded sheets of lined paper, yellow with age. They're from my father's police file, obtained several months ago. Since then, they've been entombed in the back of a drawer. I've tried to forget them, but while I'm asleep, they flutter through my dreams like ghostly birds.

Once I know what's in the papers, I can never return to a state of ignorance. I unfold them, draw a deep breath, and look at the first page.

METROPOLITAN POLICE is printed above the hand-written date "23 April 1866" and the title "Murder of Ellen Casey, age 14, Clerkenwell." The text below, written in the same hand, reads,

> *The body of a girl was found on Gough Street at 7 AM*
> *by Lewis Morton, a laborer. 7:45 AM: Body examined by*

Dr. Philips, who pronounced life extinct and estimated that she had been dead 18 hours. Bruises on her neck indicated death by strangulation. Blood on her undergarments and thighs suggested rape.

I'm puzzled because this report doesn't mention my father. Then my mouth drops in astonishment. *I remember Ellen Casey!* She lived on my street, a freckle-faced girl with red braids. I vaguely recollect that she died. I didn't know exactly how; my parents wouldn't tell me, and people talking about it always stopped when I came near. Now my heart begins to pound an ominous cadence as I turn to the next report. It's dated 29 April 1866 and titled, "Rape and Murder of Ellen Casey. Interview with Benjamin Bain."

Suspect was the last person to see Ellen Casey alive. PC Oliver and I (PC Evans) interrogated him in his home at 21 Clerkenwell Close. Suspect admitted that he photographed Ellen in his studio the day she disappeared. He claims she went home afterward and he did not see her again. He claims he has no knowledge about her death. We searched his house and found no incriminating evidence.

Horror deluges me in a black, nauseating flood. *Suspect. Rape. Murder.* The words pound in my head like an iron mallet striking an anvil. *It can't be!* My father was a good, kind, decent man who never harmed anyone. He never spanked me or raised his voice in anger. At the protest demonstrations he organized, he tried to keep order and prevent brawls when the workers marched through the streets carrying effigies, signs, and burning torches. He couldn't have killed Ellen Casey. But I also remember the day the police came to our house; it must have been the occasion described in the report. My mother and I hid in the bedroom and clung to each other as the police shouted at my father and his loud protests weakened

into frightened whimpers. My mother said they were scold-
ing him because he tried to help poor people, and I believed
her. It's as though for twenty-four years I've been looking at a
photograph that was taken from one angle, and now I've been
shown another photograph of the same scene taken from a dif
ferent angle that tells a new, terrible story.

There's a bad taste in my mouth, as if I'm going to vomit.
I gulp brandy, and the strong, sweet liquor burns down my
throat. I read the other pages, desperate to find something to
indicate that my father was wrongly accused. Three reports,
dated from 1864 to 1865, detail Benjamin Bain's arrests at
demonstrations. My father was a rabble-rouser; the police
must have wanted to quash him. Why not frame him for a
murder? I feel better until I read this report:

7 May 1866. Interrogation of Benjamin Bain,
primary suspect in the murder of Ellen Casey. Arrested
8:35 PM and brought to Newgate Prison. Interrogated by
PC Evans and PC Oliver. Suspect persisted in his claim
that he is innocent. He was released for lack of evidence on
8 May at 9:50 AM and ordered not to leave the vicinity.

A cruel light shines into my memory of a time when my
father was gone overnight and came home the next morning
bruised and bloody. My mother said he'd been to a march, a
riot had started, and he'd been beaten by the police. But now
it seems he was in jail while the police tried to make him
admit he'd killed Ellen Casey. In spite of his denials, they considered him their prime suspect. I, ten years old at the time,
had no idea.

The last report concerns the disappearance of Benjamin
Bain. It lists places where the police looked for him in vain
and possible sightings by witnesses. The last sighting was on
11 May 1866 near the London docks. The police speculated
that he had left the country.

I stuff the pages in the letter case and tie the strings. Numb from shock, I finish the brandy and realize that my father's police file has raised more questions than it answered.

Was my father a murderer?

What really happened in 1866?

If my father is alive, where has he been for twenty-four years, and was he the man in the dinosaur park?

I wrap my arms around myself as the landscape of my past becomes unrecognizable alien territory.

3

Troubled and sleepless, I lie awake in bed until I hear the morning sounds of carriage wheels outside and Fitzmorris lugging coal up from the cellar, filling the teakettle, and clattering pans. My head aches and my eyes burn, but I can't leave all the work to him. I force myself to get up, wash, and dress, then open Mick's door.

"Mick, time to get up."

The blanket-covered lump in the bed stirs. I go downstairs and help Fitzmorris prepare toast, eggs, bacon, and tea. Hugh comes down in his dressing gown, unshaven and yawning. While he and Mick and Fitzmorris eat, I only sip tea; I've no appetite.

When we're done, Fitzmorris carries dishes to the kitchen, and Hugh says to me, "We'll deliver the photos to Mrs. Vaughn today."

"Can I come with you?" Mick asks.

"No, you're going to school," I say.

"He can start tomorrow," Hugh says.

Hugh and I need to have a talk. Tired, distressed by what I've learned about my father, and in no mood for argument, I snap at Mick, "We had a deal. You're going to school, and you're going today."

Mick and Hugh exchange glances. I'm usually sedate, but I have a temper, and they know to beware when it surfaces. Mick says, "I better go get ready," and leaves the room.

Hugh bends his perceptive scrutiny on me. "Did you find something disturbing in your father's police file?"

When I tell him, his eyes darken with compassion. "I'm so sorry. But the police were wrong about your father. He didn't do it."

"How do you know? You never met him."

"I know you, Sarah. You're not the daughter of a man who would kill a little girl."

I appreciate Hugh's confidence, but he's hardly objective. "I keep remembering things. After the night my father spent in jail, my mother and I suddenly lost all our friends. I never understood why. But now . . ." Now that I've learned my father was accused of rape and murder, it makes perfect sense that they thought him guilty and ostracized his family.

"We both know the police aren't above railroading an innocent man," Hugh says, "and people believe things that aren't true. They believe Jack the Ripper is still at large."

I'm still torn between my desire to believe my father is innocent and my fear that he's guilty. Hugh says, "The police reports are one side of the story. You need to hear the other before you make up your mind."

I knew that reading his police file would be only the first step in my search for the truth about my father. My mother died fifteen years ago, so he's the only person who can tell me the other side of his story. "After I enroll Mick at school and we deliver the pictures to Mrs. Vaughn, I'll go back to the Crystal Palace and look for the man I photographed."

"No, *I'll* enroll Mick at school and deliver the pictures. You go back to the Crystal Palace now, before your father's trail gets any colder."

#

The Crystal Palace shines atop the hill like a diamond in the rays of sunshine that pierce the clouds. People flock to the terraces, enjoying the first warm spring day. In the vast grounds, crocuses, hyacinths, and daffodils have bloomed overnight. I weave through strolling crowds along the avenue toward the dinosaur park. My satchel contains my miniature camera and the photograph of the man. Maybe my father wants to photograph the dinosaurs and didn't bring his camera yesterday because the weather was bad. I'm afraid as well as hopeful that he's there now. Do I really want to know whether he killed Ellen Casey? Didn't he love me enough to tell me why he disappeared, no matter how much it might hurt?

Maybe the man in the photograph isn't my father after all and I'm hunting a stranger.

At first, I'm too preoccupied to notice that all the other folks are hurrying in the same direction as me. They crane their necks, chattering excitedly. Police constables block the path to the dinosaur park and hold back a crowd. I'm dismayed because something must have happened inside the park and I won't be allowed to enter.

People from the crowd scatter and sneak into the park through the woods. "Stop!" the constables yell, chasing the trespassers.

My fear of the police is no match for the sudden gut conviction that I need to see what's happened. I plunge into the woods, slipping on fallen leaves wet from yesterday's rain. My satchel snags on a bush. As I yank it loose, more constables join the pursuit. I run and see the lake ahead. Voices drift from the distance. Men are talking beyond the point where the lake curves, hidden from my view by the islands and dinosaurs.

"Who are they?" The deep voice is gruff, as if from too much smoking.

"We don't know, sir." The second voice belongs to a younger man. "There's no identification on them."

My pace slows as I glimpse the men. They're wearing civilian clothes, standing with three uniformed constables near the big dragon-dinosaur. I hide behind a bush. They're gazing at a human figure that lies motionless on the ground. Alarm sucks in my breath so hard I almost choke. There's been a murder. That's why the police are here. A nightmarish sense of déjà vu washes through me. This isn't my first murder scene. A previous one was Polly Nichols—the Ripper's second victim last August. Is that why there are so many police—because they think the Ripper has struck again?

I could tell them he hasn't and never will.

Bracing myself for the sight of death, I look at the body. It's a woman, her legs crumpled under her skirts and dark-green coat, her arms bent. With her coppery red hair and the chartreuse feather trimming her black straw hat, she's a bright splash of color. Her glassy blue eyes protrude; her made-up face is bloated, her tongue caught between her teeth. I see the round black mole on her cheek. A shock of recognition increases my horror.

It's Noel Vaughn's mistress.

"Bruises on her neck," says the older plainclothes officer. He's stout with a gray beard. He points at the purplish marks on the woman's white skin. "She was strangled. Probably after he killed the man."

Now I see, sprawled facedown near the woman, a body clad in Noel Vaughn's gray wool coat. His black derby rests on the mud. The back of his head is a caved-in mass of hair, clotted blood, and pulp.

"That's the murder weapon." The younger officer, tall and fair, points at a crowbar lying on the grass, the end darkened. His gaze shifts to the tools by the dinosaur model. "It must've come from over there."

My mind reels with disbelief and confusion. Yesterday I photographed Noel Vaughn and his lady; now they're both dead. Why would two murders obviously unrelated to the Ripper case bring out the law in full force?

A police surgeon carrying a black medical bag approaches and greets the officers, then crouches to examine the bodies. "They've been dead for about twenty-four hours."

I cover my mouth with my hand as fresh shock stuns me. They never left the park yesterday. They must have been killed soon after Hugh and I departed.

"The victims could be the kidnappers." The younger officer sounds excited, hopeful.

I'm astonished that the murder case seems connected with the kidnapping of Robin Mariner. That's why there are so many policemen. They must be the Special Kidnapping Squad.

"If they're the kidnappers, where is the ransom money?" the older officer asks. "Sir Gerald said it was left in a briefcase inside that hollow tree, according to the instructions. It's not there now, and it's not with the victims."

The Mariner family must have received a ransom note that said to leave money in exchange for Robin's return. Unbeknown to Hugh and me yesterday, we were on a collision course with the police. And my search for my father has become entwined with the kidnapping investigation.

"Sir Gerald should have called us the minute he got the note," the older officer says. "Now there's no Robin, no directions to his whereabouts, and Sir Gerald is out a thousand pounds. That's what he gets for cooperating with crooks."

I surmise that the ransom note told the Mariners not to notify the police, and Sir Gerald did so only after something went wrong.

"If these two were the kidnappers, their deaths would explain why Robin hasn't been returned," says the younger officer. "Maybe this was a mugging—someone killed them and stole the money."

But Hugh and I followed Noel Vaughn for two weeks and never saw any sign that he had possession of Robin Mariner. Nor did Vaughn and the woman seem to have any purpose here except lovemaking.

"The only thing we can be sure of is that there's more to this than meets the eye," the older officer says.

Much more happened here yesterday than met Hugh's and my eyes. We didn't see the man I hope is my father until after I developed the photographs. What else didn't we see?

"The chief should be here soon," the older officer says. "We'd better start looking for witnesses. You and Jones go up to the Crystal Palace. Ask the employees to describe every visitor they saw."

I'm a witness, and so is Hugh. I could aid the police by identifying Noel Vaughn and explaining what he and the woman were doing in the park, but we may have been the last people to see them alive, which would also make us suspects in the murders, and we're already on bad terms with the police—one in particular. Seeking a quick escape, fighting panic, I steal through the woods. Constables are everywhere.

"Hey, you! No more playing nosey parker. Time to go."

The irate, familiar voice stabs fear deep into my stomach. I bolt too late. Inspector Reid, the officer I wanted most to avoid, grabs my arm. According to the newspapers, he's been removed from the Ripper case and appointed chief of the Special Kidnapping Squad. His nose is sharper than I remember; his hair, mustache, and beard are grayer than when I last saw him six months ago. New lines crinkle the skin around his cold, deep-set brown eyes. His hunt for the Ripper has aged him. As he recognizes me, his pink complexion turns red with anger.

"Sarah Bain, as I live and breathe."

Reid has a grudge against me because he thinks I obstructed the Ripper investigation. He's right. He thinks that I'm hiding something important I know about the Ripper and that I'm to blame for some trouble he got into with his superiors. He's right on those scores too, and he's sworn to get revenge.

"What the hell are you doing here?" Reid demands.

I'm afraid of him, but I'm angry too. Reid isn't the only one with a grudge. He tried to send my friend Mr. Lipsky to the gallows. I wrench my arm free. My anger makes me bold, defiant.

"I'm taking photographs." I open my satchel, remove my miniature camera, and aim the lens at him. "Shall I take yours?"

"Put that thing away, or I'll break it."

I shouldn't provoke Reid. My precious miniature camera cost a fortune, and I can't afford to replace it, but fear and daring have always been intertwined for me. When confronted with someone or something dangerous, it's as if I've come upon a sleeping wolf, and I feel an urge to poke it and wake it up. I suppose that's one reason I'm looking for my father: the truth about him is another sleeping wolf I can't let lie. As I tuck my camera inside my satchel, my fingers touch the photograph concealed there. Once again, I have something to hide from Reid.

"Here you are, smack in the middle of another high-profile investigation," Reid says. "Don't tell me it's a coincidence."

I'm already regretting my decision to look for my father. It's put me back in Reid's sights.

"What do you know about these murders?" Reid asks.

Although my nerves tighten with alarm, I look him in the eye. "Nothing." It's true that I don't know who killed Noel Vaughn and his girlfriend or why.

Suspicion turns Reid's gaze colder. "Were you here yesterday?"

"No." But inside my satchel is proof that I was here, and proof that this isn't the first time I've seen the victims.

Reid shakes his head; he doesn't believe me. "How long have you been here?"

"A few minutes."

"Long enough for you figure out that the murders are connected to the kidnapping of Robin Mariner." Reid inflects his words as a statement, not a question.

I press my lips together. I know from experience that it's best to say as little as possible to Reid, who will seize a mile when given an inch.

"Here's the deal, Miss Bain," Reid says. "This isn't the time for whatever game you're playing. There's a child missing and a desperate family. If you withhold information, you're helping the kidnapper avoid getting caught."

I feel wretched because Reid's points have hit home. Anything observed in the dinosaur park yesterday might provide a clue to the kidnapper's identity and Robin's whereabouts. Every day that Robin is gone must be agony for the Mariners and increases the risk that he'll come to harm. But I didn't observe anything relevant to the kidnapping, and I can't tell Reid about yesterday. Hugh was with me, and I can't expose him to the police. Last autumn, he was beaten by the police when the vice squad raided a party attended by homosexuals. He wasn't caught in a lewd act, arrested, or convicted of any crime, but the story in the newspaper ruined his reputation and made him an outcast. The police wouldn't treat him kindlier now, and Hugh isn't the only other person I must protect. If the man in the photograph is my father, he's wanted for Ellen Casey's murder. I can't let Reid find him and arrest him before I determine whether he's guilty or innocent.

"I'm not withholding information." My conscience is as heavy as lead. "I have none."

As Reid glares at me, a constable approaches. "Guv, there's a mob of reporters outside the park. If we don't give them an official statement, they'll print all kinds of hogwash."

"All right, I'm coming." Reid jabs his finger at my face. "I still owe you for sabotaging the Ripper investigation. Your friends Hugh Staunton, Mick O'Reilly, Catherine Price, and the Lipskys too. If you sabotage this one, by God, you'll all wish you'd never been born."

4

I postpone my search for my father because the Crystal Palace and the surrounding area are overrun with police. If I show people the photograph and ask them about the man, word could get back to Inspector Reid. The police need to know there may be a witness to the murders and the ransom exchange, but I can't tell them. My hands are tied with regard to advancing either the kidnapping investigation or the search for my father. It's a most frustrating dilemma.

When I return to Argyle Square in the early afternoon, fog has obliterated the sun. I spy a constable leaning on the iron fence, and my heart thumps with more than my usual fear of the police. Then he smiles at me and tips his helmet. He's toughly handsome with unruly black hair and dark stubble on his cheeks and jaws. It's Police Constable Thomas Barrett. Fear yields to delight. Smiling, I hasten to Barrett.

"I didn't think I would see you until Saturday."

"I was working in the neighborhood. I just stopped by for a minute."

We met last autumn when Barrett was assigned to the Ripper case. Subsequent events bound us in an alliance that can be broken only by his death or mine. Since then Barrett has been— I still cannot entirely believe it—courting me.

"Working here?" I'm surprised because his usual beat is the East End. "How come?"

"I've been assigned to the Special Kidnapping Squad." Barrett beams with pride.

It's a prestigious position. Barrett is eager to distinguish himself and move up in the world, and I'm happy for him, but my troubles have just multiplied. "That's wonderful."

Barrett doesn't notice my lack of enthusiasm. "I'm investigating tips. There are hundreds coming in." His speech is carefully proper; in hopes of making a good impression on his superiors and the public, he tries to disguise his humble East End origins. "This tip was from Bloomsbury. A woman at a lodging house heard a baby crying. The other lodgers don't have children, and she thought they'd kidnapped Robin Mariner and hidden him in the house. It turned out to be a stray cat trapped in the attic." Barrett chuckles. "But next time, who knows? Maybe I'll find Robin."

If he did, then he would receive the promotion we both want for him, but right now the only certainty is the rift I see opening between us like a black chasm. I kept secrets from him in the past. He forgave me. Now I can't tell him that there's been a double murder at the Crystal Palace that appears connected to the Mariner kidnapping or that I know the identity of one victim. I can't show him the photograph and say I think the man in it is my father. Barrett would be duty-bound to report all of it to Inspector Reid. Withholding important information from Barrett would be bad enough even if I hadn't done it before. If he finds out I'm doing it again in connection with the case he hopes will make his career, will he forgive me this time?

Barrett isn't just the only suitor I've ever had. I'm in love with him, so I have much more to lose than when I kept secrets from him last time.

"So where've you been?" Barrett asks. "On a new investigation for your detective business?"

I evade answering. "We shouldn't talk here." Two neighbor women are standing across the street, watching us with disapproval. "Why didn't you go inside the house?"

"Nobody answered the door."

"Oh, it's Fitzmorris's day off." I'd forgotten. "He always visits his family." We enter a quiet, empty house. "Hugh must be out somewhere, and Mick is at school."

"Mick is living with you?" Barrett hangs his helmet on the hat rack.

I explain while shedding my coat, hat, and satchel. Barrett and I look at each other. "Nobody's home," we say in unison.

We fly together so fast, I don't know who made the first move. His mouth is on mine, his hands clasping my face. My hands clutch his back through the rough wool of his uniform as he presses against me. Intoxicated by the taste of his kiss and the earthy, clean male scent of him, I close my eyes. We're suddenly on fire, and the fire is no less hot than on previous occasions. We break apart and stumble, gasping, up the stairs. This is a rare opportunity not to be wasted.

We have so little privacy. Barrett lives in a police barracks, and although Hugh and Fitzmorris like him and I don't think they would censure me for having relations with him in the house, I would be ashamed to do it while they're here. And it would be cruel to Hugh, like rubbing his nose in the fact that I can legally make love to a man, but he can't because homosexual acts are a crime.

In my room, Barrett unbuttons my frock. I peel it down to my waist, and I loosen the lacings on my corset. We're breathless, clumsy. I slip my chemise off my shoulders, baring my breasts, while he unfastens his trousers, then we fall onto the bed. We don't undress entirely in case we're interrupted. We kiss and caress frantically. My nipples tingle, and I grow wet under Barrett's touch. The size and pulse of him while I stroke him is as exciting as the first time. He climbs on top of me, his trousers down, my skirts and petticoats up, and my knickers open. We thrust, hardness against slickness, faster and faster. Barrett doesn't enter me; I'm afraid of getting with child. But the release is an enormous, completely satisfying pleasure. I yell as he shudders and groans.

Exhausted, after we're fully dressed again, we lie side by side on our backs, listening. If we hear the front door open, Barrett will rush down the back stairs. I turn my head to look at him. I never thought I would have a lover, would experience this pleasure with a man. I still can't believe my desire is requited. I don't know whether my love is.

Barrett is tense; he gazes at the ceiling. Does he know I'm hiding something from him, or is there another cause for my sudden uneasiness? I'm two years older than he is; he could get a younger, prettier woman, and he's made no promise to be faithful. Because of my past, love and loss are entangled in my mind. Is this the day he tells me it's over?

"Is something wrong?" I ask.

Barrett doesn't look at me. My uneasiness turns to fear. He says in a somber voice, "I'm tired of playing instead of—well, you know."

I thought it was as pleasurable for him as it is for me. I thought he didn't mind restraining himself to protect me, but I should have realized he wouldn't be satisfied with half measures forever.

"And I'm tired of sneaking around as if our relationship is something shameful."

He's breaking it off. Pride won't let me cry in front of him or beg him to stay. I sit up, muster my dignity, and say, "I'm sorry I can't give you what you need, and I understand that you want to be free." My father's disappearance taught me that men leave, and I should have known Barrett would.

"Hey, wait a minute! That's not what I want." Barrett sits up and puts his arm around me. "I'm not good at talking about things like this. What I mean is, I love you. I want to be with you properly, and all the time. I want to let the whole world know we're together."

As I stare, dumbfounded, he laughs self-deprecatingly. "I know this isn't the kind of proposal a girl wants, but . . ." He looks into my eyes. His eyes are keen and clear, bright gray like river agates in the sunlight. "Sarah Bain, will you marry me?"

This is the proposal I never thought I would receive, from the one man I could accept. Joy makes me so giddy that I could float up from the bed. I see my own smile reflected on Barrett's face.

"Is that a yes?" he asks.

I want to be with him legally, publicly, and permanently, but sudden misgivings render me cautious. "This is so sudden."

"We've known each other for eight months."

"We don't know each other very well."

"We know everything we need to know."

We're both remembering that night in the slaughterhouse. I doubt there's a moment when it's not somewhere on our minds. It's the thing that binds us more tightly than love. It's also the thing that, should we marry, would color every day of our life together.

"You know I'm capable of killing." No matter that I didn't deliver the fatal blow myself.

"You're capable of doing what's right even when it's against the law," Barrett says, "and you know I am too."

If he weren't, I would be dead now—and so would Hugh, Mick, Catherine, and Mr. Lipsky—and the Ripper would still be carrying out his ghastly crimes. I owe Barrett my hand in marriage and whatever else he wants, but my feet are getting colder.

"Where would we live?" I ask, stalling for time.

"We can rent a flat. I've been saving money since I joined the police force." He smiles, proud of the fact that he can provide for me.

I envision living with Barrett, going to bed with him every night and waking up with him every morning in a home of our own. Cooking his meals, washing his clothes, and cleaning house. Having his child. This normal, desirable prospect daunts me. When my father disappeared, my mother and I went to work in a factory and lived in cheap lodgings. A charity school provided my education. Barrett knows my history, but this is what I've never told anyone: all my imaginings about marriage end with my husband leaving me and our child to a similar fate.

"If we married, you would have to tell Inspector Reid," I say.

Reid is Barrett's superior, and there's as much bad blood between the two of them as between Reid and myself. For that reason, Barrett and I have kept our relationship secret. Reid knows we're acquainted but not that we've become lovers.

"I've had it with tiptoeing around Reid," Barrett says. "I'm not going to let him control me. If he doesn't like my choice of a wife, that's his problem."

But I'm afraid Reid will lash out against both of us, and how can I accept Barrett's proposal while hiding information that I know he would consider important? I realize that I must pass on some of what I know before he hears it from Reid.

"By the way, I ran into Reid today." I tell him about the murders at the dinosaur park, but I don't reveal why I was there or confess that Hugh and I were there yesterday and explain what we were doing. I simply say I went to photograph the Crystal Palace this morning. The photograph in my satchel downstairs tugs at my conscience as I tell him about the conversation I overheard between the two policemen.

Barrett listens with concern. "I knew the ransom had gone wrong. It was the big news at the station this morning. But maybe these murders will provide a lead to the kidnapper."

"Reid wasn't happy to see me." I say not a word about the man in the photograph who may be my father.

"I'll bet." Barrett looks worried about the possible consequences of my run-in with Reid. "I'm sorry you happened into another murder case. At least you're not mixed up in this one."

If he only knew.

"I have to get back to work," Barrett says. "About my proposal—what do you say?"

I avert my gaze from his eager smile. "There's my photography. And my private inquiry business."

"You can still do photography after we're married. And you won't need to work."

He doesn't understand that my photography is an art, not a hobby, and I haven't given up my dream of earning a livelihood and a reputation from it. "But I can't quit on Hugh." It would be unfair to leave him to his own devices just because I've found someone to support me.

"Your business doesn't earn much money, and Hugh will have to find something else to do anyway." Barrett frowns. "You keep coming up with excuses. Does that mean you don't love me?"

"No, of course not."

"You've never said it."

I've never said it to any man except my father. If I don't say it now, I'll lose Barrett. I draw a deep breath, meet his expectant gaze, and whisper, "I love you."

His face relaxes into a smile; he perceives my sincerity. "I know it's a big decision. You don't have to answer yet. Take some time to think it over."

#

After Barrett departs, I sit on my bed and quake with nerves. Barrett knows my father had a police file—he's the one who gave it to me. Maybe I should tell him about the photograph and ask him to keep it secret. He's kept big secrets for me in the past. But this time a baby's life is at stake, and I doubt Barrett would agree to withhold information about a potential witness from the Special Kidnapping Squad. Maybe I can find my father and determine whether he murdered Ellen Casey, whether he was at the dinosaur park yesterday and observed anything germane to the ransom exchange. If he's not guilty and not a witness, I've no obligation to share information about him with the police, and I needn't make Barrett choose between his loyalty to me and his professional duty.

The weight on my conscience lightens, but there's still the problem of how to locate my father. I rise, open the drawer of my bureau, and take out the police reports. Perusing them for clues I missed last night, I notice something on the back of the one that details my father's night at Newgate Prison, written in fresh black ink:

George Albert, 245 Cheyne Walk, Chelsea.

5

I'm in the kitchen, peeling potatoes for supper, when Mick comes home. "How was school?"

"I got sent to the headmaster's office."

"*What?*" He's been there one day, and he's already in trouble. "Why?"

He drops his books on the table. "I punched some boys and knocked them down."

"Mick, we agreed: no fighting."

"They started it. I had to defend myself, didn't I?"

"What was the fight about?" I want the whole story before I explode.

"They teased me about how I talk. They called me an Irish cockney bastard. They shoved me around."

I should have known that the children from this middle-class neighborhood would look down on Mick.

"But I showed them. Nobody'll mess with me again," Mick says proudly.

I haven't the heart to scold him. "Well, try to keep out of trouble from now on."

"The lessons are easy, though. I could teach myself by reading books at home at night and work during the day," Mick says.

I ignore the hint. While we eat supper, I decide not to tell him about the murders, my father, or the police file because if I did, he would want to be involved in whatever happens next. I would have to tell him no, and he would feel left out.

That night, after Mick has gone to bed, I wait in the parlor for Hugh. He's left no word as to where he went, but it's not the first time he's stayed out late. I surmise that he's meeting men in taverns, clubs, or parks frequented by homosexuals and that he'll go to a hotel with one of them. I worry because it's dangerous—he could be robbed by an unscrupulous lover, attacked by ruffians who hate men of his kind, or arrested by the police. We don't talk about it. Hugh never mentions who he's been with; I gather it's a different man each time. I wish he could find someone to love, who would love him, and they could have a life together, but either he's not meeting the right kind of person or he's afraid to risk more scandal and punishment.

That's another reason I'm reluctant to marry Barrett. When the year is up and Hugh loses his allowance and his home, he'll be completely alone.

#

By midnight, Hugh still isn't back, so I go to bed. He returns while I'm asleep, and the next morning, the door to his room is shut. When he finally comes downstairs at noon, he looks pale, sick from the aftereffects of heavy drinking, and ashamed; he still smells of liquor. When I offer him breakfast, he says, "Just tea, thanks."

His hands tremble as lifts the cup to his mouth. By tomorrow he'll be his usual cheerful self, but I feel so sorry for him. To distract him from his unhappiness, I tell him about the murders in the dinosaur park.

A glimmer of interest awakens in his bloodshot eyes. "When I delivered the photographs to Mrs. Vaughn yesterday, she was upset because her husband hadn't come home. She thought he'd left her for the other woman. I never imagined they'd been murdered."

"Listen to the rest of the story." I tell him about the ransom money and my clash with Inspector Reid.

"So the kidnapper came to the park to get the cash. He had to get rid of anybody who'd seen him. That's why he killed Vaughn and the lady." Excited by my discovery, Hugh seems revitalized, on the mend. "I see why you didn't tell Inspector Reid, but we can't just do nothing. We have to solve the murders and rescue Robin Mariner ourselves."

I don't balk at his grandiose thinking. Grandiose thinking enabled us to put Jack the Ripper out of action, and I welcome a chance to get in on the kidnapping investigation. "But we haven't any information to go on—unless you saw something at the park?"

"I didn't, but there's someone else who may have," Hugh says. "The man you think is your father."

Here is another reason to look for him. He could be the witness who leads us to the man who killed Vaughn and his lady and kidnapped Robin Mariner. Here is my chance to combine my search for him with the search for Robin—two birds, one stone. "I have a new clue," I say and tell Hugh about the note written on the police report. "Maybe this George Albert recently sighted my father and has clues to his whereabouts."

"Splendid! You should go to Chelsea right away."

I resist. "Maybe my father is there, but he wasn't the man in the park. Or maybe he was the man, but he's not in Chelsea."

"You won't know unless you go."

"All right. But even if I find him and he did see the kidnapper, that's a long way from discovering where Robin is hidden. I feel bad about keeping the information secret."

"Maybe we don't have to keep it secret. We could tell Sir Gerald Mariner."

"Are you serious?"

"Very. We could get the reward. Five thousand pounds," Hugh exults. "Sarah, this is the opportunity we've been waiting for. We can offer our detective services to the Mariner family. This case could put us on the road to success."

"There have been hundreds of tips. Why would Sir Gerald think ours is genuine when so many are false?"

"I've a connection. His bank manages my family's finances." Hugh's expression turns sober and apprehensive. "I'll ask my father for a favor—an introduction to Sir Gerald."

#

That afternoon, I find myself in Cheyne Walk. Tall, stately brick townhouses face across the green toward the Chelsea Embankment. Beyond ornate gas lamps mounted on a low stone wall, I see the Thames bracketed by the Albert Bridge to the east and the Battersea Bridge to the west. Barges, ships, and ferries glide along the river. From a rift in the gray mist and smoke in the sky, a sheet of pale sunlight beams down. The brown water gleams like a dragon's scales. But I'm too nervous to appreciate the beautiful view, remove my miniature camera from my satchel, and take a photograph. I turn away from the river and face the house, which stands behind a black iron fence, its gate flanked by pillars topped with marble urns. White marble flagstones pave the path below marble steps that lead to the marble facade of the first floor. All this gleaming stone testifies to the owner's wealth. An iron-railed balcony overhangs a turquoise door. When I tilt my head back to look up at the three tiers of arched windows and the dormers set into the roof, I feel dizzy. Hunting down Jack the Ripper gave me confidence as a detective, but this investigation is personal. My legs wobble as I push open the gate, climb the steps, and knock on the door.

A young woman wearing a white apron over a gray dress and a white cap over her hair greets me. "Good morning, ma'am. May I help you?" Her enunciation places her among the better class of servants.

I take a second look at her, and I see, as if in a mirror, a startling version of myself. Some ten years younger, she has the same slim figure, square jaw, and deep-set hazel eyes. My mouth opens, but I can't speak.

This is my half sister. I know—without proof but with absolute certainty—that after his disappearance, my father begot another child. I'd thought that all my features except my eyes had come from my mother, but some happenstance has made my father's two daughters by different women virtual look-alikes.

Confusion wrinkles her smooth brow. She's reacting to the astonishment on my face; she doesn't seem to notice our resemblance. My trained photographer's eye notices our differences: her hair, visible beneath her cap, is more golden than mine, her features softer. She's not only younger; she's prettier than I am.

A stab of jealousy, like a knife to my viscera, jolts words from me. "I'm looking for George Albert." I suddenly realize who George Albert is—not a stranger who sighted my father and reported it to the police but my father himself. "Is he here?"

Her smooth skin pales, her hazel eyes widen, and her lips part. A short older woman in a black dress, white apron, and white cap—evidently the housekeeper—appears in the hall behind her. "Sally, who's there?"

My half sister turns to her. "Oh, Mother!" Gesturing at me, she says, "She's asking for Father."

The woman and I stare at each other in mutual shock. *This is my father's second wife.* She's in her forties, with a full bosom and small waist. Despite the gray streaks in the brown hair coiled atop her head and the lines in her oval face, she's prettier than my mother ever was. She must have been much younger than my father when they married. Her hand presses her throat as she sees the resemblance between her daughter and me.

"My God," she whispers. "Who are you?"

She and her daughter are servants, meaning my father isn't rich and this isn't his house. But my resentment swells, for they've had him all these years while he's neglected me. "Good day, Mrs. Albert. My name is Sarah Bain. Your husband is my father. His real name is Benjamin Bain."

"No!" Sally responds with horrified disbelief. "That can't be!"

Mrs. Albert's shock contains resignation, as if the news isn't entirely unexpected. "We shouldn't talk here. You'd better come in."

"Mother, she's lying!" Sally says. "Make her go away."

But when I pass her to enter the house, she doesn't try to stop me. Mrs. Albert leads me up the back stairs to an attic partitioned into servants' quarters. Sally trails us, huffing in indignation. We gather in a small room where we have to stoop under the slanted ceiling, crowded among two iron cots, a wooden chair, and a washstand. Everything is neat and spotless. Mrs. Albert motions me to the chair, perches on a bed, and says, "Sally, go and get Miss Bain a cup of tea."

Sally frowns, then flounces off. I drop into the chair, dazed into speechlessness while a thousand questions rattle in my mind.

"I didn't know about you." Mrs. Albert speaks quickly, trying to finish before Sally returns. "But I knew he had a past. He wouldn't talk about it. And I suspected that 'George Albert' wasn't his real name. His camera case had the initials 'B. B.' carved on it. He said he'd bought it at a pawnshop. How did you find us?"

"It doesn't matter."

"Your mother. Is she . . . ?"

"She died in 1874. So you needn't worry about being the wife of a bigamist."

Mrs. Albert flinches. Her expression shows puzzlement, then a hostility that matches mine. "When did he leave?"

"In 1866."

"Well, I didn't meet him until 1868. He was working as a photographer for the Oxford University Press and living on his own. I'm not the reason he left. If your mother had a sharp tongue like yours, maybe that's the reason."

I could tell her about Ellen Cascy and knock the spiteful expression off her face, but I cut to the chase. "Where is my father?"

"You seem prosperous enough," Mrs. Albert says, as if to deflect my question. Her gaze rakes me over, observes the lack of a wedding ring on my hand. "A spinster, I see. Where do you live? How do you keep yourself?"

"I live in Argyle Square, Bloomsbury. I'm a photographer. Where is my father?"

"Ah, a chip off the old block. Well, lucky for you. You're not in service like Sally and me."

I've gotten on the wrong side of this woman from whom I need information.

"We don't know where he is." Sally speaks from the doorway, holding a cup of tea. "He disappeared. We've not seen him in ten years."

"*Disappeared?*" Not once but twice. I'm shocked to the core. "How?"

Sally's eyes shine with tears. "One night he just never came home."

"Is that how it happened to you?" Mrs. Albert smiles; she can read the answer on my face. "Does that make you feel better? That he did it to us too?"

It's the disaster from my childhood, visited on my half sister at approximately the same age as I was. "Why?" I ask Sally and her mother. "Why did he leave you?"

Mrs. Albert laughs bitterly. "He was a drifter and a dreamer. He liked roaming around the country taking pictures. I should have known he would get tired of us."

"He didn't!" Sally sets the cup on the washstand with a thump that sloshes tea into the saucer. Tears spill down her cheeks; the pain of her loss is more recent than mine. "He wouldn't have. He loved us!"

Mrs. Albert rises, puts her arm around Sally, and dabs her daughter's tears with her apron. "Of course he loved us, but some men just aren't cut out to be husbands or fathers."

At least she didn't pretend he was dead, but her explanation is terrible food for thought. Has he married a series of wives, begotten a series of children, and cut them all loose? The idea, on top of his being a suspect in Ellen Casey's murder, makes me feel physically ill.

"He wouldn't have chosen to go away. Something bad must have happened to him," Sally insists.

"It's in the past." Mrs. Albert's curt tone reminds me of my mother. "Best not to dwell on it." She says to me, "Sally and I must be getting back to work."

I'm far from ready to end the conversation. "Have you heard from him? Received a letter, perhaps?"

"No," Mrs. Albert says.

I belatedly remember my photograph of the man in the dinosaur park. When I packed it in my satchel earlier this morning, I hoped to show it to "George Albert," whom I surmised to be a former friend or acquaintance of my father's. I never imagined having an opportunity to show it to people who'd known my father as well as I had—and much more recently. Now I bring out the photograph, hold it up for Mrs. Albert and Sally to see, and point to the man.

"Is this him?" I ask.

Sally gasps. Her complexion turns gray, as if she's about to faint.

"That picture is so blurry," Mrs. Albert says. "That man could be anyone." But her daughter's reaction, and her own suddenly tremulous manner, have told me what I need to know. "I'll see you out." She advances on me, compelling me to rise and move toward the door.

On my way down the stairs, with her and Sally close behind me, I call over my shoulder, "Did you ever look for him? Did you go to the police and report him missing?"

"No more talk, Miss Bain. You've already upset my daughter enough."

At the front door, I face her and Sally. "Have you any idea where he went?"

"Please go." Mrs. Albert holds the door open, her expression stony. Sally hovers, wringing her hands and looking sick.

"I'm his daughter! I have a right to know!"

"You have no rights as far as Sally and I are concerned. You're nothing to us," Mrs. Albert snaps. "If you don't leave now, I'll fetch the butler to throw you out."

6

"Now I know why my father didn't come back or get in touch with me." I'm at home in the parlor with Hugh. Fitzmorris is preparing dinner in the kitchen while Mick keeps him company. "It wasn't because he was afraid the police would find him and he would be hanged for Ellen Casey's murder." I thought I'd cried all my tears for my father long ago, but my face is awash in tears that burn with anger as well as grief. "It was because he had a new family!"

I wonder if my mother knew. That would explain why she spoke bitterly of him after he disappeared, why she destroyed his photographs—not because he was the primary suspect in a murder, but because he'd made a fresh start and replaced us. She pretended he was dead because the truth was so humiliating.

Hugh hands me a glass of brandy. "Your father wouldn't have just washed his hands of you. There must have been extenuating circumstances."

He sees people in the best light, even after what happened to him. For most of his life, he was his parents' adored, pampered golden boy despite the fact that he's the youngest son, not the heir. In contrast, my mother was critical, unloving, and harsh toward me, and she taught me her habit of distrusting other people. I suppose the difference between our pasts explains why Hugh is ready to give my father the benefit of the doubt.

"It must have been strange to meet a half sister and step-mother you didn't know you had," Hugh says. "Are you going to see Sally and Mrs. Albert again?"

I shake my head, torn between contradictory, complicated feelings. I didn't like Mrs. Albert; I can't think of her as my stepmother, but I want to know whatever she could tell me about my father. I feel drawn to Sally despite my jealousy. She's my only living kin.

"Aren't you curious?"

"They wouldn't welcome me back with open arms." Their treatment of me was hurtful, and I have neither the desire nor the courage to risk another rejection. "I wish I'd never started looking for my father." Once my camera had a tear in its bellows, and light leaked in and overexposed the negative plates. I feel as if the harsh light of a new day has seeped into me.

"At least we now know he really is the man in the photograph. Even if Mrs. Albert and Sally didn't actually identify him in so many words." Hugh regards me with sympathetic concern. "But I'm sorry I put you up to looking for him and it turned out like this. If you really want to stop looking before you discover anything worse . . ."

I sigh and bow my head. "I can't stop. My father was in the dinosaur park. He could have witnessed the kidnapper taking the money and killing Noel Vaughn and the woman. I have to keep looking."

"That's very brave of you." Hugh smiles with admiration and relief that I'm not going to quit. "By the way, I spoke with my father today. He's agreed to introduce us to Sir Gerald tomorrow."

#

The Mariner Bank is a palatial building constructed from white stone, located in Bishopsgate on a corner in the heart of London's financial district. Tall Corinthian columns separate the high arched windows on the first floor. Statues crown the roofline. Among them, I see St. George and the Dragon, Britannia holding a wreath and shield, Galileo with his telescope, and a goddess with a cornucopia of fruits. The largest statue is a ship in full sail above the main entrance, which is set in an archway in the building's curved corner. The bank itself resembles a ship ready to sail across the city and sea in pursuit of wealth.

Hugh and I arrive at nine o'clock on Tuesday morning, 22 April. "I heard that Sir Gerald started as a cabin boy on a merchant ship out of Liverpool that carried cargo to and from Africa and the Americas." Hugh is in high spirits, eager for our big day. "He eventually bought his own fleet of ships and made a fortune before he switched to banking. And then he made another fortune by taking over other banks and investing money all over the world."

As Hugh opens the door for me, I grip my satchel in hands damp with cold sweat. I'm afraid Sir Gerald will think our information is useless. My first sight of the bank's vast interior doesn't relieve my anxiety. It's like a Venetian cathedral, with marble columns and floors illuminated by three large, domed, stained-glass skylights. Bank tellers behind brass grilles wait on fashionably dressed customers. I'm wearing my best dark-blue frock with white lace jabot and cuffs, but I feel outclassed, intimidated.

"Here comes my father," Hugh says.

Lord Staunton, Marquis of Ravenswood, is in his late sixties, tall and lean, white-haired, and expensively tailored; he's an older, haughty version of Hugh. "Good. You're on time," he says. His cold manner conveys his unspoken meaning: promptness is about the only thing he thinks is good about Hugh, who disgraced their family and wheedled this favor that Lord Staunton is reluctant to provide.

Hugh's spirits visibly deflate, and I feel sorry for him, the golden son no longer. I know how much he misses and looks up to his father, and his situation is in some ways worse than mine. Although it hurt to discover that my father had a second family, I've had twenty-four years to get used to his absence. Hugh's estrangement from his father is still fresh.

"Father, may I introduce Miss Sarah Bain," Hugh says.

Lord Staunton casts a brief glance at me. I bow awkwardly. It's obvious that he thinks me immoral for living with a man—a homosexual at that. I'm angry on Hugh's behalf. Hugh is the same clever, good-natured, kind person he was before his family learned his secret, yet Lord Staunton treats him like an abomination.

Lord Staunton glances around, as if he's afraid someone will recognize Hugh and see them together. "Are you sure this information of yours is important?"

"Positive." Hugh speaks without his usual confidence.

Lord Staunton obviously doubts Hugh, and I wonder why he agreed to introduce us to Sir Gerald. "I wish you would tell me what it is and allow me to give it to him for you."

"Something might get lost in the translation," Hugh says.

A sleekly groomed young man approaches us. "Lord Staunton? Sir Gerald will see you now."

We follow him up the marble staircase into a big noisy room full of clicking telegraph machines. Clerks labor beneath green-shaded lamps at rows of desks, writing in ledgers, poring over documents. Sir Gerald's office is smaller than I expected, enclosed by paneled walls and shelves of books with worn bindings. His massive wooden desk takes up most of the space. Behind it, Sir Gerald sits in a simple leather-backed chair while a subordinate hands him letters to sign. He looks about sixty years old, his stoutness emphasized by the double-breasted waistcoat of his black suit. His body appears to be all muscle, no fat. His thick, coarse dark hair and beard are streaked with gray and neatly trimmed, his broad features swarthy and toughened from exposure to the elements. He gives orders of which all I can understand are the names of foreign countries and huge sums of money. His voice is rough with a Northern accent. The former cabin boy from Liverpool, unlike Barrett, doesn't try to disguise his humble origins.

I feel guilty as I think about Barrett, who would be upset if he knew I was here and why.

The subordinate lays telegrams on Sir Gerald's desk. "The President of the United States, the Emperor of Japan, and the Pope send their sympathies and hope that your son comes home safely."

Sir Gerald looks up at us. His eyes are deep brown, opaque, and watchful. He dismisses his subordinate and our escort, then rises, extending his hand to Lord Staunton. "Hello, Richard."

He's taller than Hugh and his father, who stand almost six feet high. He radiates power, confidence, and ruthlessness. Whatever emotions he feels about his missing son are under tight control. The lone painting in the room, hung above his desk, depicts a ship in a storm at sea. Sir Gerald is a man who doesn't desert the helm of his business empire, no matter what.

Lord Staunton introduces Hugh and me. He addresses Sir Gerald in a manner that combines condescension and obsequiousness. He's a hereditary peer while Sir Gerald earned his title, but Hugh told me that although the Mariner Bank works for his father, Sir Gerald could afford to buy and sell the Marquis of Ravenswood a thousand times. "My son and his, er, detective partner think they have information pertaining to Robin's kidnapping."

"So you said in the message you sent me yesterday." Sir Gerald's dark eyes take Hugh's measure first, then mine.

He's one of few people who's ever studied me with such interest. My heartbeat quickens, to my surprise. The sensation I feel is disconcertingly like attraction.

"Since they wouldn't tell me what it is, I can't vouch for its value," Lord Staunton says, "but I thought I'd better bring it to your attention just in case—"

"Thank you, Richard," Sir Gerald says. "I won't keep you any longer. Lord Hugh, Miss Bain, have a seat." He gestures at two chairs facing the desk. His hands are brawny, as weathered as his face. The left bears a gold wedding band. I regard him with more than my usual interest in a new acquaintance, and somehow I don't think it's only because he's rich, powerful, and famous.

Lord Staunton blinks, taken aback by the cursory dismissal. As he reluctantly departs, he gives Hugh a look that's completely at odds with the way he treats his son. It says that he loves Hugh in spite of everything and wants him to make good.

Hugh and I sit, both stiff with uneasiness.

"Let's get one thing out of the way," Sir Gerald says to Hugh. "I know about you."

Hugh looks mortified. He didn't tell me so, but I knew he was afraid Sir Gerald had heard of his scandal.

"Never mind," Sir Gerald says. "I judge men on their own merit, not what other people think of them. If you can help me get my son back, I don't care who you bed. Pardon my language, Miss Bain."

Somehow his bluntness and vulgarity don't put me off, even though they would if coming from any other man. He gives me a brief smile that lights his dark eyes and shows he can be charming when he wishes. I involuntarily smile back.

"Now let's hear what you've got," Sir Gerald says.

Dumb struck, Hugh has lost his usual poise; he looks helplessly at me. I'm also flustered, confused by my reactions to Sir Gerald. Unprepared to do the talking, I stammer, quail under his impatient stare, then take the photograph from my satchel and hand it to him. "We were in the dinosaur park the day of the ransom. I took this photograph."

Sir Gerald studies it intently. "That's the man and woman who were murdered." He must have been informed by the police. He doesn't ask why we photographed the couple; that detail must seem extraneous to him. He points to the man in the woods. "Who's this?"

Hugh finds his voice. "We don't know."

Yesterday we decided not to tell Sir Gerald that I believe it's my father. Sir Gerald wants to rescue his baby, and he's liable to use any information we give him to serve that aim, which might include reporting it to the police. Although I'm hurt that my father abandoned me for a new family, I don't want him hunted down and punished for killing Ellen Casey if he didn't do it. Love and loyalty are stubbornly persistent. I'm scared that Sir Gerald will know Hugh is lying even though Hugh is a good liar. He's one of the scariest men I've ever met, and that's saying a lot.

"This man could be the kidnapper?" Sir Gerald suggests.

That's another reason we decided not to tell him about my father. We anticipated that he would jump to the logical conclusion that a man lurking in the woods at the site of the ransom exchange is the kidnapper come to fetch the money, and then my father would be on the hook for Robin's kidnapping as well as Ellen Casey's murder.

"We don't think so," Hugh says. "The kidnapper wouldn't have stood around making a viewfinder with his hands when other people were there. It's more likely that he's a possible witness who saw the kidnapper take the ransom money."

Sir Gerald contemplates the photograph for a moment, then turns his scrutiny on us. My pulse quickens; my hands are cold, but I'm as much attracted to danger as frightened by it. This is the same quirk in my nature that inclines me to poke wolves. But somehow I don't think that all the sensations Sir Gerald has aroused in me are due to that particular quirk of mine.

Sir Gerald hands me the photograph. I'm disappointed because he apparently thinks our tip is worthless; he's going to dismiss us, and we'll never earn the reward.

"I'm going to offer you a job," Sir Gerald says. "You investigate the kidnapping. I pay you a thousand pounds up front as a retainer, plus expenses. If you find Robin, you get the five thousand pounds' reward. If you turn in the kidnapper, you get a bonus of another thousand pounds."

Hugh and I gape in disbelief. "You're hiring us, just like that?" Hugh asks.

"Just like that."

Excitement spurs my heartbeat to a gallop. I muster the courage to ask, "Why?"

"Because I don't trust the police. In two weeks, they've accomplished nothing. You have a fresh angle on the case, and you've turned up the first solid lead."

"But you just met us," Hugh says.

"I'm a good judge of people," Sir Gerald says, "and I didn't get where I am by dragging my feet while opportunities pass me by."

I wonder if he has an extra sense that perceives hidden truths beneath appearances. Does he intuit that Hugh and I are more successful at solving crimes than our reputation would suggest? It's one reason I can think of that would explain why he would take a chance on amateurs without even asking for references. The other possibility is that he's chosen us for a purpose he's keeping secret.

"We can't guarantee we'll find Robin," Hugh says.

"If you said you could guarantee it, I'd call you a braggart and throw you out of my office," Sir Gerald says. "Do we have a deal?"

Things are going so much better than we expected. The retainer is enough to live on for a long time, and Hugh and I are so gleeful that we don't bother driving a harder bargain. "Yes," we say in unison.

"First you'll have to sign this." Sir Gerald places a sheet of paper in front of us.

Confidentiality Agreement

I accept employment with Mariner Enterprises under the condition that I will keep all information related to my work strictly confidential and not disclose it to anyone except Sir Gerald Mariner unless he authorizes me to do so. I understand that should I violate the terms of this agreement, I will be subject to retribution including but not limited to fines, lawsuits, and criminal prosecution.

Signature _____ Date _____

Hugh's face wears the same conflicted expression I feel on my own. If we take on this case, we'll have to keep our investigation and discoveries secret from everyone we know. I'd hoped to come clean with Barrett at some point, but signing this agreement will make that impossible. Sir Gerald has already said he doesn't trust the police. We won't be able to tell Mick either. Then I think of our unpaid bills, the few months until Hugh loses his allowance and house, and the uncertain future.

"I haven't got all day." Sir Gerald tosses a silver fountain pen onto the paper. "If you don't want the job, tell me now."

Hugh and I look at each other, afraid of what Sir Gerald will do to us if we fail to rescue Robin. Too timid to ask, loathe to lose our biggest case, we sign the agreement.

"Good." Sir Gerald speaks like a man accustomed to getting his way. "Now I'm going to give you some information. It's for you only. Understood?"

Hugh and I nod. I feel the barrier of secrecy enclosing us like the walls of a fortress.

"I agree that your mystery man in the woods isn't the kidnapper," Sir Gerald says, "because I think the kidnapper is someone in my family."

We stare, surprised. "The newspapers didn't mention that," Hugh says.

"Not everything is printed in the newspapers. Nobody else knows about my suspicions."

"Why do you think it's an inside job?" Hugh asks.

"Because of this." Sir Gerald opens a drawer in his desk, removes a small object, and sets it before Hugh and me.

It's a little toy rabbit with white plush fur and pink glass eyes. The fur is grubby and bedraggled.

"This is Robin's favorite toy," Sir Gerald says. "He sleeps with it, and it was in his crib when he was kidnapped. I know because I tucked it in with him that night." His gaze softens with a mist of tears that's gone so fast, I'm not sure I saw it, but he suddenly seems more paternal, more human. He notices me studying him; I blush and lower my gaze.

"After Robin was kidnapped, I found his rabbit on the back stairs. Here's what I think happened: the kidnapper wrapped Robin in his blanket with the rabbit. When he carried Robin down the stairs, the rabbit fell out."

"I thought the kidnapper came up a ladder and in through the window, then carried Robin out the same way," I say. The newspapers printed a picture of the ladder leaning against the ivy-covered brick wall.

"The ladder was planted to make it look like an intruder broke in and took Robin." Sir Gerald sounds sure. "The kidnapper was already inside the house."

"The servants—?" Hugh begins.

"Servants are always the first to be blamed when anything goes wrong," Sir Gerald says disdainfully. "The police have been all over them. They have alibis; they've been cleared. What a waste of time. I don't hire crooks."

But he thinks there's a crook within his own family. For the first time, I feel more pity than fear for Sir Gerald.

"You'll move into my house tomorrow morning," he says. "A carriage will meet you at Hampstead Heath station at nine sharp."

"*Move into your house*?" Hugh asks.

"Yes," Sir Gerald says impatiently. "To spy on my family. I'll tell them I hired you to investigate the kidnapping because the police aren't getting anywhere. I won't tell them you're investigating *them*." He adds, "If you're not there around the clock, you might miss something important."

I'm breathless, caught up in events beyond my control. I've signed my freedom away. Now I'm committed to looking for my father. He could be the witness on whom our success depends, our best chance of rescuing Robin and avoiding Sir Gerald's wrath. Tomorrow I'll have to move into the Mariner house, which will create hazards that I'm only beginning to fathom.

7

In a cab, riding past the banks, taverns, and shops on Bishopsgate Street, Hugh says, "Did we just make a gigantic mistake?"

"I hope not." Now that we've won the coveted job and Sir Gerald has transferred a thousand pounds to Hugh's bank account, I'm less happy than I would have expected.

I'm trying to understand the strange sensations Sir Gerald has aroused in me. The possibility of romantic infatuation is puzzling as well as disturbing. He's old, I don't think he's handsome, and I'm not usually drawn to wealthy, powerful, famous men. Then again, he's the first I've ever met.

"There's nothing like walking blindfolded into a jungle," Hugh says. "Do you realize that if someone in the Mariner family really is the kidnapper, we'll be sleeping under the same roof as the person who killed Noel Vaughn and his lady friend?"

"We should have asked Sir Gerald some questions about his family so we would know who we're up against," I say, vexed by my lack of foresight.

"He didn't exactly give us a chance to ask questions."

I voice the idea that's been on my mind: "I don't believe he hired us just because we brought him a new lead."

"Neither do I," Hugh says. "If I were the father of a kidnapped baby, *I* wouldn't hire us. What do you think his real motive is?"

"I hope he's not up to anything illegal."

"Illegal, no problem," Hugh says with false lightness. "We've been down that road before."

But we barely survived, and we're still living in fear that our past will catch up to us someday. I'm disturbed to realize that the money and rescuing Robin aren't the only reasons I took the job. The other is that I want to see Sir Gerald again. "We won't be able to investigate the murders at the dinosaur park, and we can't even tell Mrs. Vaughn what we think happened to her husband."

"Solving the kidnapping will solve the murders," Hugh points out. "Then we can come clean with Mrs. Vaughn."

"I feel bad about putting a new client ahead of an old one." I also fear that my feelings about Sir Gerald have tipped Hugh and me into water that's over our heads.

"So do I, but there's nothing to be done about it. What should we pack for our stay with the Mariners? Maybe I'd better ask Fitzmorris to sharpen some knives."

"Speaking of Fitzmorris, what are we going to tell him? And Mick?"

"Haven't the foggiest. I'd trust them with my life, but it would be bad form to violate a confidentiality agreement on the day we signed it."

I haven't time to think of something to tell Barrett because when Hugh and I arrive at home, he's waiting for me in the parlor, dozing on the faded yellow chaise longue. As I halt in surprise, he wakes up and scrambles to his feet.

"Hello." He smiles at me. "You look nice. Where've you been, all dressed up?"

"We had business at the bank this morning," Hugh says quickly.

To forestall more questions from Barrett, I say, "I thought you were busy with the Special Kidnapping Squad. What brings you here?"

"I've been working around the clock since Sunday night." Barrett yawns and stretches. "I've got the afternoon off."

"That's nice." At any other time, I would be delighted to have an afternoon with him, but I wish he hadn't come.

"I'll give you some time to yourselves," Hugh says and goes upstairs.

"I've been assigned to investigate the murders in the dinosaur park," Barrett says.

My legs give out. I sink onto the sofa.

Barrett sits beside me. "I've identified the victims. People at the Crystal Palace knew them. Their names are Noel Vaughn and Ethel Norris."

I can barely keep the horror off my face. It's only a matter of time before Barrett tracks down Vaughn's wife and connects her to Hugh and me. Then he'll know I withheld from him that we were spying on Mr. Vaughn and Miss Norris. And it's already too late to confess without making him angry.

Barrett scrutinizes me. "Is something wrong?"

I steer the conversation to even riskier ground. "I won't be able to see you for a while. I—I have to go away."

Barrett frowns in surprise; I'm not in the habit of traveling. "Go away where?"

"To Nottingham, to see a friend." I'm too flustered to think of a better lie, and Nottingham is far enough that Barrett couldn't take time off work to visit me.

"I didn't know you knew anyone in Nottingham."

"It's an old friend from school. I haven't seen her in years, but we've kept in touch. She wrote to say she's very ill."

Barrett's face takes on the expression of distrustful suspicion that it wore so often last autumn. "When are you leaving?"

"Tomorrow morning."

"How long will you be gone?"

"I don't know." Guilt makes me wretched. So does my eagerness to begin working for Sir Gerald. It makes me feel unfaithful to Barrett.

"Will you write to me?"

"Yes, of course." It's another lie. I can't mail him a letter from Hampstead; he'll wonder why it's not postmarked

Nottingham. I'm glad he didn't ask for my nonexistent friend's address; if I made one up and he wrote to me, his letter would be returned. But I feel worse knowing why he's letting the issue go. He doesn't want to catch me in a lie. He loves me too much to risk the consequences.

"Well. Have a good trip."

Barrett doesn't stay long after that. When we kiss good-bye, his lips are tense. As he walks away, I fight the urge to run after him, for I have a terrible premonition that when we meet again, nothing will be the same.

8

"I still feel bad about Mick," Hugh says as we lug my photography equipment and our trunks out of Hampstead Heath station the next morning.

"So do I."

We packed while Mick was asleep last night and left after he went to school. We had to tell Fitzmorris we were going away, and he was upset because we wouldn't tell him where. My story about a sick friend wouldn't hold water with Fitzmorris or Mick, so it seemed better to say as little as possible.

"Mick will be all right until we wind this up," Hugh says.

Outside the station, we breathe air that's colder and fresher than at home; we're only about four miles away but higher up and distant from the factories. Hampstead is like a village, with shops along the high street and a green down the block. A brisk wind blows puffy white clouds across a blue sky; London proper is a dirty smudge of smoke and fog in the south. Before we can look for the carriage that Sir Gerald said he would send, people flock around us.

"Read the latest about the kidnapping!" cries a newsboy with a stack of papers.

"See where it happened!" A man wearing a sandwich board that reads, *Guided Tours to the Mariner Estate, 3 p.*, beckons us toward the cabs waiting in a line by the green. Vendors selling tea, sausage rolls, and eel pies from pushcarts hawk their wares. The bakery, the grocery, and other shop windows display the newspaper photograph of Robin and his mother.

"The kidnapping has become a cottage industry for the locals," Hugh remarks.

A large black carriage, drawn by two black horses, stops before us. The driver climbs down from the box, tips his cap, and says, "Lord Hugh Staunton. Miss Bain." Apparently Sir Gerald gave him our descriptions. The driver has rugged features, a muscular physique, and the same Liverpool accent as Sir Gerald. "At your service."

He stows our bags and helps me into the carriage; Hugh climbs in beside me. We ride quickly out of the town and along a wide, level road that runs between fences and hedgerows. Beyond these spreads Hampstead Heath—moors interspersed with woods, seemingly without limit. It's beautiful, but I have a disturbing fancy that we're leaving all that's dear, and I can't imagine what awaits us. As the road ascends a hillside, the sunlit moorland gives way to dense, dark forest, the air grows colder, and unease creeps into our mood. The only sounds besides the clatter of the carriage wheels and horses' hooves are birdsong and the wind. The heath is too quiet for our comfort.

"We can still change our minds." Hugh's tone is half joking, half serious.

I'm still feeling guilty because of Barrett, and I have yet to tell Hugh about Barrett's proposal. I feel under pressure because the future of our detective agency hinges on this case. "I won't if you won't."

The carriage turns onto a narrower road that zigzags higher up the hill. At the summit, I glimpse chimneys and pointed rooftops above the trees. The carriage stops on a flat, paved expanse of ground where other carriages are parked outside the high brick wall that surrounds the Mariner estate. A crowd loiters by the black iron gates. A group of ladies listens to a tour guide lecturing, "The original house was built in 1806. Sir Gerald Mariner bought it in 1879 and enlarged it. He's got a whole room full of hunting trophies—wild animals he's shot."

Reporters armed with notebooks and pencils rush to our carriage, calling, "Who are you? Have you any news about the kidnapping investigation?"

Police constables are among the crowd. I sink down in my seat. The driver cracks his whip, someone opens the gates, and as the carriage rolls through, Hugh says, "Abandon hope all ye who enter here."

The grounds, where trees arch over carpets of bluebells, are more welcoming than Dante's hell. The carriage stops on a semicircular drive in front of the mansion—three stories of ivy-covered red brick with perpendicular wings at either end, white trim, dormers studding the slate roof, and countless gleaming windows. The whole thing is as long as several city blocks. I feel like an intruder in a world high above my station.

Even Hugh is impressed. "This puts my family's pile to shame."

The man who opens the door under the columned portico is the same rugged, muscular type as the carriage driver; they seem less servants than guards. He verifies our names, ushers us into the mansion, and carries our bags. The foyer is two stories high, with a huge crystal gas chandelier suspended from a carved plaster ceiling and a gallery on the second story. Our footsteps clatter on white marble and green malachite tiles. Statues I'm too intimidated to examine stand in niches. Open doors lead to vast, opulent rooms. Perhaps his wealth really is the attraction that Sir Gerald holds for me.

Another guard helps the first carry our baggage up a grand marble staircase, and we're left alone in the foyer. Hugh murmurs, "How many of those chaps do you think there are?"

"Welcome to Mariner House."

Hugh and I whirl, surprised by the speaker's soundless approach. The man is of medium height, in his late forties, with a lean, wiry build and rust-colored hair. His complexion is sunburned, roughened, and marred by freckles and old scars.

His clothes are as expensively tailored as Hugh's but not the latest fashion, designed to deflect rather than attract attention.

"I'm John Pierce, Sir Gerald's chief aide." His voice is hushed like an undertaker's, with an accent I can't place. His sharp features could have been attractive if they had showed humor instead of wary caution.

Hugh introduces us. Shaking hands with Pierce, I feel strength in his sinewy fingers, his callused palm. His narrow eyes are a blazing blue, the inner lids around them red.

"Is Sir Gerald here?" Hugh asks.

"He's at his bank. He'll be back for dinner. I'm to get you settled in." Pierce gestures at the staircase. "This way to your rooms."

I'm disappointed not to see Sir Gerald. As Hugh and I climb the stairs, I sense Pierce's stare on my back, but I can't hear his footsteps behind us. He moves like a ghost. A shiver runs through me. He escorts us along the gallery, then down a wide passage where gas lamps illuminate framed oil paintings that hang on walls covered with gilt paper. We pass many closed doors. Carved tables stand at intervals along the walls, displaying art objects. We round a corner into a similar passage.

"This is the north wing," Pierce says. "Sir Gerald and his family live in the south wing."

"And you?" Hugh asks.

"My room is in the south wing too."

Pierce must count as a suspect, although he's not a family member. He opens a door and says, "Miss Bain, you'll be staying in the Chinese Room."

We step into a chamber saturated with brilliant red. It has scarlet wallpaper patterned with scenes of an Oriental palace, red-and-gold brocade curtains, and a plush rug like a crimson pond afloat with deep-pink lotus blossoms. The only relief comes from the white silk quilt and a white canopy on the black sleigh bed, which looks ready for an emperor to despoil a concubine. My trunk, satchel, and photography equipment look shabby placed among the antique furniture and knick-knacks. Although the room is three times bigger than my room at home, I feel closed in, oppressed. I hasten to the window, crank it open, and breathe as I take in the view of a topiary garden, the hillside below, and distant marshes and woods. The faint sound of carnival music drifts from the Hampstead Heath fairground. I feel small and forlorn in this alien world.

Pierce opens an adjoining door and says to Hugh, "Here's your room. You can lock this door if you want."

The door connecting my room with Hugh's isn't the one that worries me. As Hugh inspects his quarters, I glance at my door to the passage. A key protrudes from the lock. I wonder who has a master key.

Hugh returns. "Did Sir Gerald tell you who we are and why we're here?" he asks Pierce.

"He said you're private detectives who are supposed to rescue Robin and catch the kidnapper." Contempt for us shades Pierce's tone.

"Who else besides Lady Alexandra is in the family?" Hugh asks.

"Sir Gerald's older son, Tristan, and daughter, Olivia."

I didn't know Sir Gerald had other children; I don't recall the newspapers mentioning them. Hugh asks, "How old are they?"

"Tristan is twenty-nine. Olivia, seventeen. There's also Tabitha Jenkins. She's Lady Alexandra's sister." Pierce says, "There'll be a cold luncheon set out in the dining room at noon. Dinner is at seven. Is there anything else you need?"

"Can you introduce us to the family?" Hugh asks.

"Tristan and Olivia have gone out. Lady Alexandra is indisposed, and Miss Jenkins is with her." Pierce sounds pleased to disappoint us.

"In that case, can you show us the crime scene?" Hugh says.

"The police already went over it with a fine-tooth comb."

"A fresh set of eyes can't hurt," I say.

"Very well." Pierce condescends to humor us in what he clearly thinks a waste of time.

I unpack my camera and then Pierce leads us outside the mansion to a garden landscaped like a scene from a neoclassical painting by Poussin. Marble statues of Greek gods and goddesses pose amid cypress trees. Pierce points upward at the mansion.

"There's Robin's nursery."

I photograph the high, ivy-covered brick wall and the mullioned window on the second floor. Hugh asks, "Do the police have the ladder that was found after Robin went missing?"

"They examined it for clues and didn't find any. They gave it back."

I doubt that Hugh and I could find any either, but I say, "May we see it?"

"It's in the toolshed." Pierce leads us down steps to the lower level of the garden, to a small stone building, and opens the door.

Hugh raises an eyebrow at me, noting that the door was unlocked and anyone from the house had access to the shed. Pierce drags the ladder out. It's old and dirty, two sections of rough wooden beams and slats joined by metal hinges. Hugh carries the ladder up to the mansion, extends it to its full length, and positions it below the nursery window.

"May I?" Hugh says.

"If you insist," Pierce says.

Hugh climbs the ladder, pushes open the window, and disappears inside. Pierce directs his sardonic gaze at me. Compelled to prove I'm a bona fide detective, I set my camera on the ground, grasp the ladder with one hand, lift my skirts above my ankles, and climb. The ladder wobbles so much that I'm afraid I'll fall. Glancing over my shoulder, I see that Pierce has vanished, and so has my camera. At the top, I pull myself over the windowsill and tumble into the room.

Hugh helps me to my feet. "Here's one piece of evidence to support Sir Gerald's theory. It was hard enough to climb up that ladder and get in here in broad daylight. At night it would be even harder."

"And almost impossible to climb down while carrying a baby." I look around the room. It's as big and lavishly appointed as mine. The rosewood crib—with its turned rails and four posts, the ship resembling the statue on the Mariner Bank carved on the headboard, its white lace canopy, white eider-down mattress, and white lace skirt—is fit for a Prince Royal. Armoire and bureau, chairs upholstered in striped blue silk, and washstand are similarly ornate. Shelves display enough tin soldiers, stuffed animals, jack-in-the-boxes, picture books, and other items to stock a toy store. In a corner are a painted rocking horse, a child-sized table and chairs, and a train set. All the toys look expensive and new.

"Have you seen enough?" Pierce enters the room and hands me my camera.

Again we didn't hear him coming. How did he get here so fast?

"Is everything the same as it was the night of the kidnapping?" Hugh asks.

"Yes," Pierce says. "Sir Gerald's orders."

Hugh points at dirty footprints on the blue carpet. "Whose are those?"

"Probably the police's. It was raining that night. They tracked mud all over the house and likely obliterated whatever prints the kidnapper left."

If the kidnapper was someone from inside the house, he wouldn't have left any. While I photograph the crib, Hugh says to Pierce, "Have you spent time in America?"

"I was born there."

So that's the source of his accent.

"Whereabouts?"

"Virginia."

"Ah, the Confederacy."

"Not since the Civil War ended in '65."

I observe no signs of a trespasser, a struggle, or any other clues, but I take more photographs in case something shows up in them that my eyes miss. Hugh looks inside the armoire and bureau while asking Pierce if his family owned a cotton plantation.

"Tobacco," Pierce says.

"You're a long way from home. Why'd you leave?"

"My father lost the plantation in a card game."

We glance at him to see if he's joking, but his face is as expressionless as I imagine it would be if we asked him point-blank whether he kidnapped Robin.

After Hugh elicits from Pierce that he had gone to sea on merchant ships that traveled to South America, the West Indies, and Africa, I ask, "How did you come to work for Sir Gerald?"

"I met him in Jamaica. The first mate on his ship had just quit. Shouldn't you be looking for the kidnapper?"

"Right," Hugh says cheerfully. "Maybe you can help us with that. Did you see or hear anything the night of the kidnapping?"

"No. I was asleep. My room is downstairs at the other end of the wing."

"The newspaper stories said that Robin was kidnapped between eleven thirty and midnight," I say. "Is that correct?"

"Yes. The afternoon nurse quit her shift a half hour early. She had a headache and went to bed. When the night nurse came on duty, she discovered the empty crib and raised the alarm. The afternoon nurse has been fired." Pierce says, "If you're finished here, I'll show you back to your rooms."

Hugh and I need some information that we neglected to get from Sir Gerald. "Who put the ransom money in the dinosaur park?"

"I did." Pierce herds us out of the nursery. "In case you're going to ask me if I saw who took it, the answer is no." He closes and locks the door.

"We'll find our way back after we have a look around the estate," Hugh says.

"Suit yourselves." Pierce laughs, a brief, raspy, mirthless chuckle. "You two don't have a chance in hell of finding Robin, and you know it. You're here to swindle Sir Gerald."

"Not true," Hugh says smoothly. "If there's anything we know, it's that swindling Sir Gerald would be even harder than finding Robin."

Pierce's feverish, hostile blue eyes stare us down. "I deal with people who make trouble for Sir Gerald. Those I've dealt with in the past would tell you I'm not gentle—the ones who are still able to talk, that is. If you're smart, you'll resign."

He turns, walks noiselessly down the passage, and vanishes into a room. Hugh and I look at each other. "He's scared," Hugh says. "He must know we think he's a suspect."

A dangerous man who's scared is even more dangerous. "I'm certain he knows. I just wonder whether he realizes we got the idea from Sir Gerald."

"He hasn't an alibi for Robin's kidnapping," Hugh points out. "He was in the dinosaur park. He could have killed Noel Vaughn and Ethel Norris."

I wonder if my father saw the murder or if Mrs. Albert and Sally know anything that could help me find him. "Let's go outside and look for clues the police missed."

As we walk toward the back staircase, following the trail that Sir Gerald thinks the kidnapper took that night, Hugh tries the knobs on the doors along the passage; they're all locked. I hear muted voices, their words and location obscured by echoes. I have an uncomfortable feeling that hidden lurkers are watching and listening to us. I pause at a table set against the wall. It holds a tall Chinese vase, a figurine of a dancing man with many arms, and a large photograph in a gold frame. The photograph is of Robin, wearing his sailor suit and sitting on Lady Alexandra's lap; it's the original image from which the engraving in the newspapers was made. The fine nuances of tone, from white through shades of gray to black, are clearly visible, whereas in the engraving, they're converted to patterns of inked lines. My photographer's eye perceives a difference that disturbs me.

"There's something wrong with this," I say.

"It looks fine to me," Hugh says.

"Robin is twenty months old, but in this picture he must be at least six months younger."

"So he's small for his age."

"It's not just his small size. I've photographed many children, and I know how they are at different ages. Look in the shadows behind Robin." I've noticed something that wasn't visible in the newspaper images. "Lady Alexandra's hand is supporting his head. At twenty months, a child can hold his head up by himself."

"But why would the Mariners give an old photograph to the press? A recent one would be more likely to help the public spot Robin."

Lady Alexandra's famous smile seems strained, and when I cover it with my hand, her eyes look haunted. Robin's eyes are half closed. My heart contracts as I think of another possible reason Robin couldn't sit up by himself.

"What is it?" Hugh asks.

"This looks like a postmortem photograph."

It's common for parents to pose with deceased children who are propped up to look as though they're alive. Sometimes the parents are too poor to afford the luxury of photographs, but when their child dies, they somehow find the money, and a picture of their child dead is better than no picture at all. Other times they just want one final memento. They can seldom completely hide their distress from the camera. Postmortem photography is a staple of any studio, and I've done it. Is this photograph a likeness of Robin in death rather than in life? Now Hugh's face reflects my dismay as he catches my meaning.

"If you're right, then Robin wasn't kidnapped sixteen days ago," Hugh says. "He's been dead for six months."

9

We spend that afternoon exploring the estate. Its grounds contain some ten acres of gardens and outbuildings. Five gates in the brick wall give access to the wooded hillside, which is riddled with trails. Below the hill, the heath covers a vast area, and around it are miles of streets leading to all points distant. It's far more territory than Hugh and I can search thoroughly. We return to the mansion at twilight, cold, dirty, hungry, and tired, having found no sign of Robin or the kidnapper.

"If there was no kidnapping, that would explain why there are no clues," Hugh calls.

We're in our rooms with the connecting door open while I braid my hair at the lacquered Chinese vanity and Hugh shaves in his bathroom. I've already bathed in the huge claw-footed tub in my own bathroom, and I'm wearing my best dark-blue frock, which was ironed by the maid who unpacked my clothes and hung them in the teak wardrobe. I locked my door before I left, but now I know that at least one other person has a key.

"If Robin died six months ago, why would the Mariners pretend he was kidnapped?" I say. The gas lamps in my room are brass dragons holding translucent glass globes in their mouths. The red walls, carpet, and curtains give my reflection in the mirror a rosy tint, as if my skin and hair are suffused with blood. "Why would Sir Gerald hire us?"

"Good questions." Hugh, sleekly groomed in black evening coat and trousers and white silk shirt, accompanies me out of our rooms and down the grand staircase.

The idea that Sir Gerald could be deceiving us troubles me. I find that I don't want to think badly of him even though I know I shouldn't rule out any possibility at this early stage.

Voices emanate from the immense drawing room, where gold columns along the walls flare into ribbed vaults beneath the arched ceiling and a fire smolders in a hearth big enough to roast a deer. The room is a museum of treasures—medieval tapestries, dark gilt-framed oil paintings, and glass cases of taxidermy birds. Near the sofas and armchairs in front of the hearth, Sir Gerald, a woman, and another man stand by a table arrayed with bottles and glasses. As Hugh and I walk toward them across soft Turkish carpets, I feel the same quickening of my pulse as I did in Sir Gerald's office. The other man and the woman are facing away from us. The man is tall, well built, and dressed in black; his thick black hair curls over his nape. The woman is a petite brunette in a brilliant-yellow frock. She must be Sir Gerald's daughter Olivia, and the man her brother Tristan. Hearing our footsteps, they turn.

Hugh is the handsomest man I've ever seen, but Tristan Mariner is his equal. Deep, intelligent black eyes burn in a tanned face with chiseled features and a strong jaw. Many women must consider him attractive, but his haughty air puts me off. Then I notice his white collar. Tristan Mariner is a priest.

He and his sister regard us with surprise. Olivia Mariner is pretty rather than beautiful. Her bold brown eyes, inherited from Sir Gerald, are too big for her heart-shaped face, as is her wide mouth. She has a full bust, arms like slender twigs in the tight sleeves of her silk frock, and a tiny waist. Her hair is a cloud of loose ringlets tinged with auburn. She seems at once younger and more mature than her seventeen years.

"Here are our guests." Sir Gerald performs the introductions.

Tristan bows to me. "It's a pleasure to make your acquaintance, Miss Bain." His voice is a cultured baritone, his manner somberly courteous.

I murmur a reply. Olivia squeezes my fingers with her small, delicate ones before pouncing on Hugh. "My lord! How delightful!" she says in a husky, breathless tone. She dimples as she offers him her hand.

"The delight is mine." Hugh kisses her hand and smiles into her eyes. He's an expert at flirting with women; he's done it all his life in order to disguise his true nature.

Olivia casts a mischievous glance at her father, as if daring him to scold her for her pertness, but Sir Gerald is watching Tristan shake hands with Hugh. Antagonism flares as the two men size each other up. It's more than the rivalry of proud male animals who think that the jungle isn't big enough for both of them. Tristan's glowering expression suggests that he knows about Hugh. Hugh's face is rigid with dislike as they exchange terse greetings, and I think I know why. Soon after Hugh was exposed as a homosexual, the pastor from his church—a lifelong friend—ranted at Hugh, calling him a disgrace to God. The sense of betrayal plunged Hugh into a black depression, and he hasn't been to church since. He must see every clergyman as a personification of the Church's disgust toward him. Now he and Tristan step back from each other like fighters retreating to their corners of the ring.

While Sir Gerald serves us sherry, Olivia divides her attention into a big share for Hugh and a smidgen for me. "Are you friends of Daddy's?"

"They're private detectives," Sir Gerald says. "I hired them to investigate the kidnapping and find Robin."

A loud gasp comes from the shadows by the fireplace. There, in a red-and-gold damask armchair, sits a woman with her mouth open. She has faded blonde hair styled in tightly crimped curls and wears a gray frock over her dumpy figure.

As she sees everyone staring at her, dismay fills her pale eyes. She shuts her mouth and clasps her hands to her bosom.

"Tabitha," Sir Gerald says. "I didn't know you were there."

I suspect she's often overlooked. Tabitha Jenkins is older than Lady Alexandra, with none of her famous sister's beauty. I'm disconcerted that I didn't notice her. The mansion is uncharted territory, and I'll have to be more observant.

"Come and meet Miss Bain and Lord Hugh," Sir Gerald says.

Tabitha obeys reluctantly. Tristan pours her a glass of sherry. She whispers, "Thank you," and gulps the liquor as if for courage.

I've behaved similarly myself, due to shyness, but could it be guilt that's made her so anxious? Did this meek, mousy woman kidnap her sister's child? She seems no more likely a culprit than do Tristan the priest and seventeen-year-old Olivia. I also can't picture any of them murdering Noel Vaughn and Ethel Norris. For now, my money is on the absent John Pierce.

"Why hire private detectives?" Tristan asks Sir Gerald. If he fears what Hugh and I might discover, the look he gives us contains nothing but repugnance. "The police are doing everything possible to find Robin."

"Not in my opinion," Sir Gerald says.

"But what fun!" Olivia turns an enraptured gaze on Hugh. "I've never met a detective before."

"What sort of experience do you have?" Tristan asks Hugh.

I feel Hugh's hackles rise. "Surveillance," Hugh says. "Recovering lost property."

Tristan eyes Hugh as if reading his origins in his speech, clothes, and manner. "You should have called in Pinkerton's," he tells Sir Gerald. "Not a dilettante who's set himself up in the private inquiry business because he's bored with society balls."

Hugh flushes with humiliation. Sir Gerald says calmly, "Lord Hugh and Miss Bain will be staying in the house. Everybody is to cooperate with their investigation."

"They're staying in the house?" Tristan looks as appalled as if we're vermin.

"Can I watch?" Olivia asks Hugh. "Oh, please say yes!"

Hugh forces a smile. "Of course."

"Father, you're usually so careful about who you employ," Tristan says. "This isn't normal for you. What's going on?"

"This isn't a normal situation." Sir Gerald says abruptly, "Let's go in to dinner."

Olivia seizes Hugh by the arm and sashays toward the dining room with him. Tristan, visibly frustrated by his father's evasion, ignores me and escorts Tabitha. His rudeness stings, and I dislike him on my own account as well as Hugh's.

Sir Gerald draws my arm through his, smiles, and says, "The honor is mine."

His arm is like steel. I feel as much dominated as flattered and as giddy as a girl asked to dance for the first time at her debut. I'm ashamed of my silliness, but I can't help wondering what it's like to be married to such a man, who could give his wife all the luxuries, status, and security that money can buy. I think of Barrett and the modest life we'll have together if we marry, and I feel even guiltier toward him and more ashamed. I begin to resent Sir Gerald because his money has, in effect, bought me, and he's the source of these discomposing, inexplicable feelings. Then I recall how his gaze softened when he spoke of Robin. He deserves my compassion even though I suspect, more strongly than ever, that he's not been entirely frank with Hugh and me.

Olivia glances over her shoulder. The look she gives me could cut granite.

In the dining room, white plaster swags border gray-green walls. A ceiling like a huge white doily molded from stucco soars overhead. A crystal chandelier hangs above a long, linen-covered table with mahogany chairs for twenty people but set for six. Nude marble statues, wearing fig leaves for modesty, stand frozen in niches. From what I've seen of Mariner House, I think it must contain the most lavish, costly examples of every style of decor. Sir Gerald sits at the head of the table with me on his right and Hugh on his left. Olivia is next to Hugh, Tristan beside me. Tabitha sits on Tristan's other side, somehow apart from the rest of us. A manservant pours wine into crystal goblets. A maid serves soup in porcelain dishes embellished with the Mariner ship in blue and gold. There are so many pieces of silverware that I have to watch Hugh to see which spoon he chooses before I pick up mine. The soup is a rich, creamy lobster bisque. Sulfur fumes waft from the gas chandelier, and its flames flicker in drafts that flow in invisible currents. The room is cold despite the fires in the two hearths. I feel as if we're dining in a Roman mausoleum.

"So where is your parish, Father Mariner?" Hugh addresses Tristan with a touch of belligerence.

Tristan pauses before deigning to answer. "I don't have one. I'm a missionary in India."

"You could have had your own parish. You still can," Sir Gerald says. "A little talk with the bishop, a nice donation to the Church—"

"I don't want you to buy a living for me," Tristan says through gritted teeth.

"Why not?" Hugh asks. "Are you too holy to benefit from nepotism?"

Tristan glowers. Hugh smiles as if happy to give insult for insult. Although I know he can be snappish when hurt or angered, I'm shocked by his rudeness.

Sir Gerald seems more displeased with Tristan than offended by Hugh. "My son is too pigheaded to accept help."

"I'm following my calling." Tristan's anger is glacial. "It's my duty to God."

Olivia whispers loudly to Hugh, "Daddy and Tristan don't get along. This is Tristan's first visit home in two years. He's been here a month, and they've been at each other's throats the whole time."

I wonder if it's mere coincidence that Robin was kidnapped while Tristan was home. Did his bad blood with his father drive Tristan to take revenge on his innocent brother? Not all priests are virtuous. At my boarding school, the minister waxed at length on the sins of the Roman Catholic clergy. His favorite example was a medieval Borgia pope who'd had mistresses, fathered children with them, and murdered his rivals.

"Your calling is just an excuse to neglect your duty to your family," Sir Gerald tells Tristan. "You belong in business with me."

"Father thinks he's God," Olivia whispers.

I don't like Tristan, but I also don't like the way Sir Gerald treats him. I'm surprised that I care.

"Please pass the bread, Olivia," Tristan says.

Olivia complies, smiling innocently at him. "My dear half brother would rather nurse lepers than make money." She sees the quizzical look on my face and explains, "Tristan and I have different mothers. His was Daddy's first wife—a textile mill heiress from Yorkshire. Mine was an Italian opera singer."

I can see where she acquired her tempestuous personality.

"Tristan's mother died after falling off a cliff. Mine killed herself with poison," Olivia says brightly. "Lady Alexandra is wife number three. I wonder who'll be number four?" She flashes a merry, malicious glance at me.

I've done nothing to warrant her hint that I've set my cap at her father, but I blush. Sir Gerald regards her as if she's a gnat buzzing around his head. She scowls, disappointed because she failed to get a rise out of him. The next course is rare roasted beef, enough for twenty people, with mushroom gravy and asparagus pudding. It's the best meal I've ever been served, but I'm so tense that I can't swallow much. Hugh washes his food down with wine. Sir Gerald eats hungrily, Tristan sparingly.

"By the way, where is Lady Alexandra tonight?" Olivia asks, gobbling her meat.

"She has a headache," Tabitha says, joining the conversation for the first time.

Olivia snorts. "More likely she's entertaining the friends or reporters who've been fawning over her since Robin was kidnapped."

Sir Gerald ignores Olivia and tells Hugh and me, "Visitors are a comfort to my wife. She's very upset about Robin."

"She wallows in the attention like a pig," Olivia says.

So Olivia is possessive of her father, jealous of her stepmother and any other woman who comes near him. That's why she doesn't like me. Did her jealousy extend to Robin, the new, favored baby of Sir Gerald's family? I picture her lifting Robin out of his crib and carrying him down the back stairs.

"My secretary has found a new finishing school for you, Olivia," Sir Gerald says. "The sooner you're gone, the better."

Tabitha murmurs, "Excuse me," and scurries out of the room before things get uglier.

Olivia's huge eyes shine with tears. She smiles through them at Hugh. "I was expelled from my last finishing school."

"I'm sorry to hear that," Hugh says politely.

"I stabbed the dance teacher with my nail file," Olivia explains. "He tried to ravish me. He said I led him on. The headmistress took his side."

Tristan has been watching Olivia with grave concern. "Olivia, you'd better learn to control yourself, or you'll seriously hurt someone."

"You're a fine one to talk." Olivia says to Hugh, "Tristan was thrown out of the army because he killed a man during a boxing match."

Tristan's face turns crimson with anger under his tan. "It was an accident."

"Better your opponent dead than you." Sir Gerald seems prouder of Tristan for killing a man than for his charity toward the poor.

"Is that why you're a missionary?" Hugh asks Tristan. "To atone for your sin?"

Tristan shoves back his chair and stalks off.

Olivia bursts into tinkling laughter. "You should come hunting with me, Lord Hugh. You're an excellent shot."

Hugh preens himself. "I may take you up on your invitation after I find Robin."

"Oh, don't waste your time looking for Robin," Olivia scoffs. "He's probably dead."

Sir Gerald's expression turns menacing. "Olivia!" His outburst rattles the crystal on the table.

Gratified because she's finally provoked a reaction, Olivia feigns wide-eyed, puzzled innocence. "Well, he must be. It would explain why the kidnapper took the ransom money but didn't give him back."

Hugh and I look at each other, sharing the suspicion that Olivia has reason to know that Robin won't be found alive.

"Go to your room," Sir Gerald says.

Olivia rises and says to Hugh and me, "We Mariners have a taste for violence. Did you know that Daddy started out as a slave trader? It was against the law, but he didn't let that stand in the way of making money. When the Africans on his ship rebelled, he shot them. You'd better watch your step." She flounces away.

I don't like the way Sir Gerald treats Olivia, even though she asked for it. But his relations with his children are none of my business except as they relate to my investigation. The maid removes our dinner plates and serves fragrant chocolate sponge cake with whipped cream. The food I've already eaten sits in my stomach like lead.

"Now you see why I suspect my family," Sir Gerald says. "There's no love lost between my children and me."

I think their love has been damaged by strife and unfulfilled expectations but not necessarily lost. My love for my father persists despite my feelings of hurt, anger, and betrayal. But damaged love could well be a motive for attacking Sir Gerald through Robin.

"Any news on the mystery witness since yesterday?" Sir Gerald asks.

Hugh doesn't answer. He looks stunned, as if something has hit him and he doesn't know what. I clear my throat and say, "We've come to a dead end." I can't reveal the shameful, incriminating facts about my father. We promised to keep Sir Gerald's business secret; he didn't promise the same for ours.

Sir Gerald changes the subject, as if he hasn't time to waste on leads that didn't pan out. "What's your impression so far? Any idea who took Robin?"

"It's too early to jump to conclusions." I don't want to believe my father is guilty of murder, and I doubt that Sir Gerald really wants to believe one of his children is guilty of Robin's kidnapping. "We haven't had a chance to talk to Miss Jenkins or Lady Alexandra."

Sir Gerald tosses his napkin on the table and stands. Before he can leave, I ask, "Where were your family members when Robin was kidnapped?"

"That's for you to figure out."

He didn't ask his family. I'm surprised to discover that this bold, powerful man is afraid to confront them, afraid of the truth. "Why did you spring Lord Hugh and me on your children and Miss Jenkins tonight?"

A crafty smile makes Sir Gerald look wicked. "Throw a cat among pigeons, and watch the feathers fly." He says in parting, "I'll be in the City tomorrow. I'll expect a report when I get home."

After he leaves, Hugh emerges from his daze and says, "His trick might panic somebody into doing something to reveal that he—or she—is the culprit." He stands up. "Let's go spy on Tristan, Olivia, and Tabitha."

"Wait." At the moment, I'm more concerned about him. "You shouldn't have been so rude to Tristan."

"Why not? The good priest might challenge me to a boxing match and knock my block off?"

His habit of being flippant at the wrong times irritates me, especially now. "That's not what I meant. Tristan is our client's son. Antagonize him, and you'll antagonize Sir Gerald."

"Tristan and Sir Gerald do a fine job antagonizing each other. But you're right." Hugh rubs his eyes. "I'm sorry. I shouldn't have let him get to me. I'll be more careful."

I'm afraid to think about exactly in what way Tristan has gotten to Hugh. "Sir Gerald left before I could ask him who he thinks is the culprit."

"And before we could ask about the old photograph of Robin," Hugh adds.

"I still think it looks like a postmortem photograph, but I can't picture the family hiding the secret that Robin died six months ago and conspiring to pretend he was kidnapped."

"Maybe they're not all in on the secret."

The maid comes to remove our empty plates. We're silent until she's gone, in case she's a spy who'll report our conversation to Sir Gerald. I glance out the window and see one of his guards, as I can't help thinking of them, walk across the terrace. "I wish I could trust Sir Gerald."

"You and me both. I feel like we're blind puppets in a show he's directing, and we're groping in the dark instead of finding Robin."

My inclination to trust Sir Gerald is about something else besides finding Robin, although I don't know what. "I wonder what role he really brought us here to play."

"One thing's for certain," Hugh says as we exit the room. "This is no ordinary family. These people are dangerous. We'd better watch our backs."

10

After dinner, we explore the house, meeting no one except Sir Gerald's guards and finding nothing of significance. That night, before climbing into my canopied bed, I wedge a chair under the doorknob. I awaken at seven AM to the sounds of footsteps on stairs, doors opening and closing, distant voices, and the rush of water in pipes. I have a troubling sense that there was activity in the night that I missed hearing.

Washed and dressed, I meet Hugh in the passage. As we walk to the staircase, maids go into rooms, carrying tea trays. "There must be other guests," Hugh says. I'm uneasy because I was oblivious to the presence of strangers while I slept.

In the dining room, some dozen guests are serving themselves from chafing dishes on the sideboard. The only familiar face is John Pierce. Hugh greets him and asks, "Who are all these people?"

Pierce doesn't look happy to see us. "Lady Alexandra's entourage."

They're mostly men—handsome young ones in smart clothes and a corpulent, white-haired gent in striped trousers and a red waistcoat who looks like Humpty Dumpty. The several women are dressed in the height of elegant, expensive fashion.

"Where are Lady Alexandra and Miss Jenkins?" I ask Pierce.

"They take breakfast in Lady Alexandra's room."

"Where are Tristan and Olivia?" Hugh asks.

"They caught the early train to town." Pierce smiles at our disappointment, then carries his full plate to the table.

"I suppose Tristan wants to avoid us and persuaded her to fly the coop with him," I remark to Hugh. "It makes me wonder whether they have something to hide."

"We might as well eat," Hugh says. "Then we'll pay a visit to Lady Alexandra."

The enormous repast consists of boiled eggs, scrambled eggs, omelets, kippers, bacon, sausages, smoked salmon, crumpets, marmalade and toast, and coffee and tea. We eat at the end of the table by ourselves while the other guests chat together. Outside the French doors, beyond the veranda, a terrace gives way to a double, curved, stone staircase that leads down to the garden. There, marble urns on flagstone pavement surround a fountain in a rectangular pond. Flowerbeds and topiary trees pruned into cones and spheres decorate the green lawns. Three figures emerge from the mist—two of Sir Gerald's guards dragging a smaller person who kicks, struggles, and yells, "Lemme go!"

I choke on my coffee as I recognize the voice. Hugh says, "Oh, God."

We rush out the French doors, across the veranda, and down the staircase. The guards stop by the pond, and Mick sees us. "Hugh! Miss Sarah!"

An irate voice calls, "What the hell is going on?"

I turn to see Sir Gerald standing on the balcony outside a second-floor room. My heart flutters.

"We caught him trespassing," says one of the guards. That may not be their official title, but providing security for the estate and the people in it is clearly their function.

"Mick, what are you doing here?" I ask.

"I skipped school yesterday, and while I was hangin' around the street, I saw you go by in a cab. I jumped onto the back of it and followed you on the train, and then to the house, and climbed over the wall."

"You spent the night outside?"

"Yeah." Mick seems relieved to see us but unhappy, defiant.

"I should have known we couldn't pull the wool over his eyes," Hugh says, crestfallen.

"You know this boy?" Sir Gerald says.

"He's a friend," I explain.

"This is where that baby was kidnapped," Mick says to Hugh and me. "Are you workin' on the case?"

Hugh and I are silent, remembering the confidentiality agreement.

"I don't pay you to sleep on the job," Sir Gerald says to the guards.

"Sorry, boss. It won't happen again," says one of the guards, and they start to drag Mick away.

On the verge of tears, Mick appeals to Hugh and me. "Please, don't let 'em!"

I feel bad, but I say, "You should go home for your own good."

"Wait a minute." Hugh calls to Sir Gerald, "He's our assistant. He's been instrumental in solving our cases. We could use his help now. May he stay?"

Sir Gerald turns his shrewd gaze on Mick. "What's your name?"

Mick stands at attention. "Mick O'Reilly, sir."

"How old are you?"

"Almost fourteen." Mick's fourteenth birthday is eight months away, but he looks Sir Gerald straight in the eye.

"Why should I let you work for me?" Sir Gerald asks.

"Because I'm clever and a hard worker."

Sir Gerald strokes his chin, perhaps to hide a smile. "Do you know how to keep your mouth shut?"

"Yes, sir." Mick runs his finger across his lips.

"You're hired," Sir Gerald says.

Maybe he sees his young self, the cabin boy, in Mick. Maybe he has secret motives concerning Mick as well as Hugh and myself, but I can't help feeling glad that Mick made a good impression on Sir Gerald.

"Let him go," Sir Gerald orders his guards.

They obey. Mick smirks at them. Sir Gerald says to Pierce, who's materialized beside me, "Find someplace for him to stay." He tells Hugh and me, "The boy is bound by your confidentiality agreement. See that he understands it." Then he disappears into the house.

"I can bunk with the servants," Mick says.

Pierce regards him with distrust and says, "Very well," before silently departing.

Mick sticks his thumbs under his lapels and grins, proud of his coup. "If there's anybody knows what goes on in a house, it's the servants. I'll pump 'em about the kidnapping."

"A capital idea," Hugh says as we walk toward the mansion.

The servants belong to Mick's own class, and they may talk to him even if they didn't to Sir Gerald or the police. But I say, "Mick, you shouldn't have followed us or trespassed." This isn't the time to scold him for skipping school. "You might have been hurt."

"But you left without telling me." Anguish darkens Mick's blue gaze. "I thought you wasn't coming back."

Hugh affectionately punches Mick on the shoulder. "You idiot, we wouldn't just up and leave you forever."

But now I understand how it must have seemed to Mick. It was awful when my father disappeared without a word. We're Mick's family, and I'm furious at myself for doing such a cruel thing to him. "I'm sorry," I say and explain the confidentiality agreement.

He nods, but I see that he's not sure Hugh and I won't disappear on him again. There's a new rift between us, and I fear for his safety. I'm also uneasy about what the impulsive, unpredictable Mick might do.

"I'll get to work right away," Mick says, determined to prove he's worthy of his new job.

"Let's get you some breakfast first," Hugh says.

Mick cheers up. "Won't say no to that."

#

Later that morning, while Mick passes the time in the kitchen and befriends the servants, Hugh and I locate Lady Alexandra in the library on the main floor. The library walls are covered with two tiers of bookshelves rising to the paneled ceiling, and a spiral staircase leads to the upper gallery. The smell of old paper and leather exudes from volumes in gilded bindings. Pedestals hold large dictionaries, atlases, and a giant antique globe. Servants are moving leather sofas and armchairs across the parquet floor.

"Put them against the bookshelves," orders a tall, dark, willowy man dressed in black.

The fat, white-haired Humpty Dumpty man I saw at breakfast sits at the grand piano in the corner, playing a tune full of dramatic flourishes, while a matronly woman dressed in emerald satin sings in a powerful soprano voice. People stand waiting by the windows. It's as if they're actors and we've wandered onto the stage before a performance. One figure is Tabitha Jenkins. The woman at their center is Lady Alexandra.

She hurries gracefully toward us. The bouffant skirts of her amethyst gown rustle. Even without stage lights or makeup, she's striking. Tall and slim but full-bosomed, she must be thirty years younger than her husband. Her beautiful features are bold enough to be visible from the back balcony of a theater. Her famous smile is so radiant that everyone else fades into the background. I've never seen her act, but I can imagine her enthralling effect on her audiences, and I'm relieved to find that I'm not jealous of her on Sir Gerald's account, which I surely would be if I were romantically infatuated with him.

Perhaps my feeling for him is merely kinship—we both have missing family members.

"You must be Gerald's detectives." Although her voice isn't loud, it's so clear, melodious, and resonant that it fills the room and mutes the sounds of the piano, the singing, and the dark man saying, "Move that table here." Up close, I can see the hollowness of her violet-blue eyes, the shadows under them, and the tension lines that age her face. Robin's kidnapping has taken its toll on his mother.

Hugh introduces me and himself. "It's an honor to meet you. I saw you play Lady Macbeth. You were marvelous."

"You're too kind." Lady Alexandra extends her clasped hands to us. "Can you bring my Robin back to me?" Her voice quavers, and her hollow eyes sparkle with tears.

"We'll do everything in our power," Hugh says. He's not immune to a damsel in distress, and his sympathy toward Lady Alexandra is genuine even though she's a suspect. "You can help us by providing some information."

"Whatever you want to know, just ask."

"Did you see or hear anything unusual when Robin was kidnapped?"

"No. I was ill with one of my terrible headaches."

"Was anyone with you?"

"Tabitha. She nursed me through it."

I note that she's provided herself and Tabitha with alibis. I glance at Tabitha. Her anxious gaze follows the dark man as he moves chairs.

Lady Alexandra sobs. "If only I'd been with Robin! This never would have happened!"

Her devastation seems genuine, but she's one of England's most brilliant actresses, and her emotions as well as her alibi could be false.

"Sarah has a question for you," Hugh says.

My muscles tense; I'm nervous with strangers, and Lady Alexandra's beauty and fame are intimidating. So is the intelligent gaze she turns on me. She gives me her whole attention, as if I'm the most important person in the room. It's flattering yet disconcerting. I feel like a novice actress about to match wits with an expert.

"My question is about the photograph of Robin that appeared in the newspapers," I say. "Why didn't you give the press a more recent one?"

"We haven't any recent ones. Taking pictures has become difficult as Robin gets older—he won't sit still." A weary, harassed look comes over Lady Alexandra's features. "What can that have to do with finding him?"

I hesitate to ask whether Robin has been dead for the six months since the photograph was taken. If my suspicion is off target, it would be cruel to voice it.

"Any little fact may turn out to be important," Hugh explains.

"Did Robin have any medical problems?" I ask.

"No. He's a perfectly healthy, perfectly normal child." Lady Alexandra bursts into a fit of weeping. "Oh, God, if he's not brought back to me soon, I'll die!"

Tabitha hurries to her and offers her a handkerchief. I wonder whether Lady Alexandra wants to halt this particular line of questioning.

The dark man says, "Excuse me, Lady Alexandra. We're ready for the séance."

Now I notice the round table with six chairs, placed in the center of the library, and the candle burning in a silver holder atop it. The music has stopped, and people are grouped around the table, actors awaiting their cue. A strong feeling of aversion twists my mouth into a grimace.

Lady Alexandra composes herself, touches the dark man's arm, and says to Hugh and me, "This is Raphael DeQuincey. He's the best medium in London."

DeQuincey strokes his sleekly pomaded black hair and says, "Well, maybe not the *best*." His voice is fluty, affected. Dark, lustrous eyes animate his gaunt, handsome face; loose black clothes accentuate his slenderness and pale complexion. "But I've a certain *rapport* with the spirits."

"He's going to ask them if they've any information about Robin," Lady Alexandra says.

When I was sixteen, I consulted a medium who claimed to be an exiled Russian princess. After pocketing my money, she closed her eyes, moaned, and delivered a message from my father. She said he'd told me that he was at peace, he loved me, and we would meet again in heaven someday. I immediately knew she was a fraud: my father would never utter such platitudes! To this day, I detest mediums because they exploit bereaved, vulnerable folks.

DeQuincey asks Hugh and me, "Would you like to join the circle?"

"No, thank you." Now that I know my father was alive when the medium delivered his message, I've more reason to think spiritualism is claptrap.

"We'd be delighted," Hugh says, contradicting me.

I stay because I can tell he thinks we might learn something, even if not from the spirits. There are six of us; the other people have vanished like extras whose walk-on parts in the drama are finished. DeQuincey assigns us our places—Lady Alexandra at his right, Tabitha at his left, Hugh between Tabitha and me. On my left are Humpty Dumpty and the soprano.

"I'm Sir Ogden Wilberforce, director at the Drury Lane Theatre," Humpty Dumpty says, "and this is Dame Judith Langmuir, from the Royal Opera."

"Isn't this exciting?" Dame Judith says with a pleasurable shiver.

DeQuincey closes the door and the thick tapestry curtains. The room plunges into darkness. I can't see my companions; the light from the candle barely reaches the table's perimeter. DeQuincey seats himself. "Join hands with those of the persons beside you."

Hugh grasps my left hand, Sir Ogden my right. Sir Ogden's hand is thick and moist. I can discern the faint shapes of everyone's hands forming a circle around the table. I wonder what DeQuincey is charging Lady Alexandra for this farce.

DeQuincey's voice emanates from the darkness: "Let us purge the negative thoughts from our minds and create a *hospitable atmosphere* for the spirits." Air swirls; the candle's flame flickers. Either there's a draft in the room or DeQuincey is blowing on the candle. "Oh, spirits, are you here?" DeQuincey intones.

A hush engulfs the library. I can't hear any noise from outside. The paneled ceiling, heavy curtains, and shelves of books must have an insulating effect, but unease creeps into me.

Three loud, sharp knocks break the hush.

Everyone jumps.

"Welcome, spirit." Elation fills DeQuincey's voice. "Please tell me who you are."

Knocks come in rapid, irregular rhythm. DeQuincey must have some sort of noisemaker on his person. "It's Ludovico, one of my guides to the spirit realm. He was an Italian composer who died in 1768."

Musical notes ripple. Goose bumps rise on my skin. The others gasp. *Someone is playing the piano.* Hugh's and Sir Ogden's hands crush mine. As the invisible musician plays rapid, discordant runs up and down the keys, I decide that the piano must be a mechanical one. DeQuincey must have left the circle, and Lady Alexandra and Tabitha are in on the act. But I feel my companions' fear; it's contagious.

"Signor Ludovico, is Robin Mariner in your world?" DeQuincey asks.

The music stops; the echoes fade. More knocking rattles my nerves. "He says no," DeQuincey announces. "Robin is not among the dead."

"Thank God!" Lady Alexandra exclaims.

"Tell me where Robin is," DeQuincey pleads. "Give me a sign."

The table lurches. An involuntary gasp escapes me as the others at the table cry out. The table levitates and spins. I grope around under it with my foot but detect no hidden mechanisms. DeQuincey says, "Take me to Robin."

The table lands with a thump. DeQuincey shudders, and the sensation passes through our joined hands like a current of electricity. He howls. His voice sounds strangely, alarmingly disembodied.

"I hear him!" DeQuincey's voice wafts to us as if from above. Then comes the sound of a baby crying.

"Oh, God, it's Robin!" Lady Alexandra bursts into loud weeping.

It sounds so real. Maybe it's ventriloquism. DeQuincey says, "Show me where Robin is."

Hugh tightens his grip on my fingers. "Do you see that?"

A dim light shines some ten feet from us and high above the floor. An image wavers in it—the blurry face of a child. I'm astonished even though I know it can't be Robin. I've seen the same phenomenon before, but how could DeQuincey have managed it?

"Robin, can you hear me?" Lady Alexandra calls frantically. "It's Mama." The face vanishes into the darkness. "Don't go!"

"He's touching me!" Sir Ogden cries.

I feel pats on my head and back. The sensation of little hands is so real, so eerie, that I shriek even though I know it must be a trick.

"I feel him too." Lady Alexandra moans. "Robin, come back!"

"There's water all around him." DeQuincey's voice is breathless, exultant. "He's in a boat . . . on a river . . ."

DeQuincey yelps—a surprised, frightened sound. There's a scuffling noise, a clatter, muffled shouts, and a crash. The people with me clamor in confusion. "What's going on?" Dame Judith asks.

"Unhand me!" DeQuincey shouts amid thuds and grunts.

"The spirits are attacking him!" Lady Alexandra sounds on the verge of hysterics. "Somebody help him!"

Hugh and Sir Ogden let go of my hands and rise.

"I gotcha!" a triumphant, familiar voice yells.

Shock launches me to my feet. I grope through darkness, and my hand touches a rough tapestry curtain. I pull it back, and daylight sears my eyes. I blink at the spectacle before me. DeQuincey lies on his stomach, huffing and struggling, at the bottom of the spiral staircase. Mick straddles DeQuincey's back. I look at DeQuincey's chair at the table. Up from it springs a stranger who superficially resembles DeQuincey. He grimaces in embarrassment, then bolts.

"A double," Hugh says.

The double must have been hiding somewhere, and he sat at the table after DeQuincey closed the curtains.

Mick climbs off DeQuincey and points to the gallery. "I caught him up there. He was makin' baby noises and doin' hocus-pocus."

Hugh laughs. "You exposed the charlatan. Good work."

DeQuincey stands and straightens his clothes, flustered and indignant. Dame Judith marches over to him. "You tricked us." She smacks his chest. "The nerve of you!"

Sir Ogden, pale and shaken, wipes his perspiring forehead with a handkerchief. "I knew it couldn't be real."

"It was real," DeQuincey huffs. "I saw Robin in a boat on the water."

"Come on, man. You were caught red-handed," Hugh says.

"All right, so I added a few tricks. I do communicate with the spirits, and they do show me things, but nobody will believe me unless there's some, well, *hocus-pocus*." DeQuincey glares at Mick. "I could have located Robin if you hadn't interrupted."

"Mick, what were you doing here?" I ask.

"I was explorin' the house, and I saw people in here movin' things around. I was curious, so I sneaked in and hid there." Mick points to a cupboard between the bookshelves. "After the ghost session started, I heard somebody go up the stairs, and I followed him, and you know the rest."

I climb the stairs, see an object on the floor of the gallery, and hold up the telescoping metal rod with a small, stuffed glove at the end. "This is how he touched us and played the piano." I sniff, smell smoke, and find a metal box with a glass lens at the end of a cylindrical protrusion. "Here's a magic lantern. He used it to project a picture of a baby's face."

"I was only trying to help. I *can* help." DeQuincey's lustrous eyes burn with zeal.

"You'd best leave town before Sir Gerald hears that you swindled his wife," Hugh says.

DeQuincey extends clasped hands to Lady Alexandra. "Please believe me."

Lady Alexandra stands rigid, her complexion drained of color. Then she turns to Tabitha and says in a flat voice, "Tell the police to search every boat on every river in England."

Mick, Hugh, the others, and I stare in surprise. DeQuincey smiles with relief while Dame Judith says, "My dear, you can't be serious."

Lady Alexandra raises her voice at Tabitha. "What are you waiting for? Go!"

Tabitha scurries out the door. Lady Alexandra says, "I felt Robin's presence during the séance. He's alive. I know he'll come back to me soon." Her arms curve as if cradling her child. She beams her famous smile at the medium. "Mr. DeQuincey, I can't thank you enough."

DeQuincey tugs his lapels and smirks at the rest of us.

"Every boat on every river?" Mick says, astounded.

"That would be a tremendous waste of time," Hugh says.

Although I know what it's like to yearn for somebody so much, to cling to even the thinnest, falsest hope of a reunion, I warn Lady Alexandra, "While the police are busy chasing a fake clue, they could be missing real ones."

"Shut up!" Lady Alexandra turns on us, suddenly ablaze with fury. "Get out of my sight! Never come near me again!"

11

"I'm sorry for bustin' things up," Mick says.

In need of fresh air and a chance to talk without being overheard, he and Hugh and I are outside Mariner House, strolling under a pergola built atop a brick arcade at the bottom of the garden. Pillars support wooden beams from which wisteria, climbing roses, and grapevines hang. Balustrades along the broad walkway guard the fifteen-foot drop to the lower level of the hill.

"That's all right," I say. "You proved DeQuincey is a fraud."

"Do you think Lady Alexandra really believes in him?" Hugh asks.

"She might." If the medium I consulted years ago had tossed me a clue to my father's whereabouts, I probably would have run myself ragged chasing it. "But I do think that when I asked her about the photograph of Robin, she wasn't telling the truth."

When I fill Mick in on my theory that Robin died months ago, he reacts with awe and excitement. "You think Lady A killed him?"

"Why would she?" Hugh is skeptical even though she's a suspect in whatever misfortune has befallen Robin.

"If there was something wrong with Robin, maybe she didn't want him," I say.

Hugh winces at the reminder that his own mother cast him off because of his "wrongness." I bite my tongue too late.

"I bet she did kill him," Mick says. "She musta snuck him out of the house at night and buried him out there." He gestures at the scenery. Directly below us are kitchen gardens and a glass greenhouse. Beyond them, the wooded hillside descends sharply to more woods and the mist-shrouded heath. "And then she pretended he was kidnapped so nobody would know what she done."

Hugh raises his eyebrows, startled by Mick's certainty. "We've all heard of women killing their children, but it's a bit early in the game to jump to the conclusion that Lady Alexandra murdered Robin."

Mick's face takes on a bitter expression I've never seen before. "What's wrong?" I ask.

He bends and scoops up some dried seedpods that have fallen from the hanging vines. "My ma left when I was six. She ran off with some bloke. Didn't even say good-bye." Mick hurls pods one by one over the balustrade. "I thought it was my fault." He stares at his empty hands. "If I'd been a better kid, maybe she wouldn't have gone."

"I'm sorry," Hugh and I murmur in unison. We're appalled that Mick blames himself for his mother's departure, just the way I once blamed myself for my father's—and because we too left Mick without a word. He must have thought we didn't want him! I could hit myself for being so insensitively cruel.

"Yeah, well." Mick's face reddens with embarrassment. "It was a long time ago."

"Maybe Lady Alexandra does have Robin's blood on her hands," Hugh says. "*Out, damn'd spot!*" He pantomimes scrubbing his hands.

Mick smiles at Hugh's clowning. "I'll pump the servants for dirt on Lady A."

My own mother did me a terrible disservice when she lied about my father being dead. I begin to understand that all three of us have brought our histories to this investigation, and it's complicating an already difficult job. "Mick, we need to be objective."

"I will," Mick says, "but I think she done Robin in, and I'm gonna nail her." He runs ahead toward the mansion.

I think of Sir Gerald and wonder uneasily if I'm the one whose objectivity is deficient. "Mick could be right. Maybe we should be looking for a grave."

Hugh frowns into the distance. "I think we're getting off track. If Robin is alive, something bad could happen to him while we spend our time investigating his supposed murder."

"That's a good point." I've no solid evidence that Robin's photograph was taken postmortem. "We should focus on rescuing Robin."

#

We borrow a carriage from the Mariner estate and spend the day riding along the streets of Hampstead, stopping at farms and villas around the heath and houses and shops in the town center to question the locals about the night of the kidnapping. None saw any of the Mariner household members or could provide any clues, and everyplace we went, we learned that the police had already been there and interviewed the same people.

At seven o'clock in the evening, riding back to the Mariner estate, Hugh says, "Well, we dug up proof of one thing: the police are doing their job."

"But they've failed to pick up Robin's trail, and so have we. It could mean he was dead long before the night of the supposed kidnapping."

"Don't write him off yet." Hugh's manner is suddenly sharp, combative. "I'd really like to save the poor little boy."

I suddenly realize that this investigation is more than a job to Hugh. His life must seem so empty since he lost his family and social set, and Mick and I can't fill the whole void. He needs a purpose to give his existence meaning, an accomplishment to prove his worth. Rescuing Robin Mariner would fill the bill.

None of the family or guests joins us at table that night. They must have chosen to eat in their rooms. Alone except for the servants, Hugh and I dine sumptuously on braised leg of lamb with haricots, wine, and raspberry jam tarts. When we leave the dining room, we see Tabitha coming down the grand staircase. Her manner is furtive with an air of excitement. Hugh and I look at each other, then follow Tabitha along the deserted passage in the central wing of the mansion. The few gas lamps burning cast pools of dim light between long stretches of shadow. A draft whistles, voices drift from somewhere, and floors creak. Tabitha looks over her shoulder, and we flatten ourselves against the wall. It's dark enough that she doesn't see us. She hurries down a staircase. We wait a few moments, then descend to a gigantic ballroom. The many crystal chandeliers aren't lit, but the ballroom sparkles like an underwater cavern in which luminous fish swim. On the walls, tall arches separated by marble pilasters converge toward the distant, invisible end. The arches on one side contain windows that overlook a terrace; on the other side, mirrors reflect light from gas lamps on the terrace and magnify the room to even greater proportions. The chandeliers also glint with reflections; their crystal pendants tinkle in the cold drafts that sigh through the air.

The ballroom appears empty. I don't see Tabitha anywhere.

Hugh puts his finger to his lips, and we tread softly to mute the sound of our footsteps on the polished parquet floor that glimmers like a frozen lake. Amid the echoes that fill the ballroom, I hear whispers. I glimpse a dark shape in one of the windows, framed by the arch some fifteen feet from us. The shape separates into two human figures—a man and a woman. As Hugh and I stand concealed in the shadows, the man says, "It's been too *long.*"

His fluty voice is instantly recognizable, as is his tall, slender physique. It's Raphael DeQuincey.

"I've missed you so!" Tabitha says breathlessly. "To see you when other people are around and not be able to touch you—"

The two figures merge again as DeQuincey embraces and kisses Tabitha. I watch in astonishment. When I saw them together this morning, they'd given no hint that they're lovers. I wonder if, at the séance, Tabitha knew it wasn't DeQuincey's hand she was holding.

"I waited for you in the summerhouse this afternoon," DeQuincey says. "Why didn't you come?"

"I couldn't get away from her. She made me redo her hair, and massage her back, and read to her, and on and on as usual until she finally went to sleep." Tabitha moans. "I hate her. Oh, God, I hate her!" Tabitha's agonized voice echoes across the ballroom.

She's talking about Lady Alexandra. I had no idea that Tabitha resented her servitude. Her meek facade concealed a world of emotions.

"So do I," DeQuincey says. "I have to smooch her bottom ten times for every penny of Sir Gerald's money that she pays me."

They must have bonded over their hatred of Lady Alexandra. There seems no other reason the slick, handsome DeQuincey would fall for mousy Tabitha.

"I never should have run away to London with her when we were girls." Tabitha laughs, mocking herself. "We were going to be actresses. But she had talent, and I didn't. The worst thing is, I think she knew it all along. She brought me with her to be her slave!"

"I know, darling. It wasn't fair to you." DeQuincey's sympathetic tone barely hides his impatience; he wants to resume making love.

"When she became successful, I thought she wouldn't need me anymore, and I could leave. But she said, 'Nobody else can take care of me the way you do. Besides, where would you go? How would you live?'" Bitterness edges Tabitha's voice. "She's never paid me wages. I had no money. Our parents were dead;

I couldn't go home. She said that if I left, I was on my own."
The words gush from Tabitha as if from a bottomless reservoir
of grievances. "When she married Sir Gerald, I asked for a
pension so that I could be independent. He's so rich, he could
have afforded it, and he could have hired a hundred servants
for Alexandra. But she said she couldn't bear to depend on
strangers, and he said that if she wanted to keep me, he wasn't
going to interfere. He's as beastly as she is!"

Tabitha's voice turns ragged with tears. "After Robin was
born, I asked them again. I told them I hoped to meet someone and marry and have my own baby. But they said no. They
don't care if I'm lonely and miserable and I die a childless
old maid!"

I see that Tabitha has abundant reason for her ill will
toward Lady Alexandra and Sir Gerald. Did she act on it by
kidnapping their son?

"But you *did* meet someone," DeQuincey says. "Yours
truly." He kisses her hair. "If you hadn't stuck with Alexandra,
you wouldn't have met me."

"Yes. It was the happiest day of my life when you asked
me to dance at her winter ball." Nostalgia gentles Tabitha's
voice; she touches his cheek. "Do you know that it's the one-
hundred-twenty-fifth-day anniversary of that night?"

"Yes, I know," DeQuincey says, fond but impatient.

A new question arises in my mind: If Tabitha kidnapped
Robin, is DeQuincey in on it?

Tabitha pulls away from DeQuincey, folds her arms, and
gazes out the window like a prisoner yearning for the freedom
beyond the bars of her cell. "One hundred twenty-five days
since we fell in love, and how many more will it be before we
can run away together to marry and start a new life?"

He catches her hand, draws her back to him. "It won't be
long. I promise."

She resists his embrace. "But you've been saying that
since—" He smothers her words with a kiss. "After everything

that's happened, how—?" Their clothes rustle as DeQuincey caresses her. Tabitha moans. "Oh, God, I want you so much!"

Hugh and I cringe with embarrassment. *Are they going to continue in front of us?* I think of my own furtive lovemaking with Barrett, and I'm aroused in spite of myself.

Tabitha reluctantly separates from DeQuincey. "I have to go, or Alexandra will come looking for me. If she should find out about us . . ."

As she scurries away, Hugh and I step into the next arch so she won't catch us spying. DeQuincey utters a sigh of thwarted desire, then follows. Hugh whispers, "I'm going to see what he does next," and hurries after DeQuincey.

Leaving the ballroom, walking down the dark passage through the central wing, I ponder the ramifications of the scene I just witnessed. Previously I'd been doubtful that Tabitha, Lady Alexandra, or Olivia had kidnapped Robin. I believe the kidnapper also murdered the lovers in the dinosaur park, and I can't imagine the women capable of that. But Tabitha's affair with DeQuincey suggests a new, disturbing possibility. Maybe Sir Gerald was wrong to deduce that one individual in his household was solely responsible for the kidnapping. I picture Raphael DeQuincey waiting outside Mariner House while Tabitha brings the swaddled baby to him. I imagine him bludgeoning Noel Vaughn and strangling Ethel Norris. But if he and Tabitha conspired to kidnap Robin, and they sent the ransom note and collected the money, then why have they neither eloped nor returned Robin?

Maybe Robin died after he was kidnapped, while he was in the custody of Tabitha, who hates his parents.

I climb the grand staircase, heading for my room. At the top, I glance out the window and see the foreshortened figure of a man appear on the terrace below. The lamps outside are dim, a bowler hat covers his head, and a long coat with a cape over his shoulders disguises the shape of his body. Then he turns and looks up at the house, as if to see if anyone is watching him. I recognize him in the moment before I step away from the window to avoid his notice.

It's Tristan Mariner.

When I peek outside again, he's striding away from the mansion. Light flares from a lantern he carries. Then I'm racing down the stairs and out the door, spurred by curiosity. When I reach the rectangular pool, Tristan is far ahead of me; all I see of him is the lantern's small, bobbing light in the darkness. I follow. He suddenly drops from view, as if the earth swallowed him. I quicken my pace. A thin crescent moon floats amid stars behind the mist that veils the sky, but I don't see the flight of stone steps until almost too late. I teeter at the brink. As I cautiously descend, I hear Tristan's footsteps. I find myself on the ground under the brick arcade on which Mick, Hugh, and I strolled beneath the pergola. In the distance, Tristan's lantern moves through the kitchen gardens. I wonder if he too is secretly meeting someone.

He slips through a gate in a wall, and I follow him along a trail that winds downward through woods so dense that I can hardly believe we're only a few miles from central London. It's so cold that I'm shivering; I wish I had my coat. The path curves, the terrain levels off, and the trees ahead glow in the moonlight that fills an open space beyond them. I stop at the edge of the woods. I hear water lapping. The wind rustles through grasses that fringe a long, broad pond whose gleaming black surface ripples with silver reflections. On the opposite bank, the triangular silhouettes of three pine trees stand like black spears arranged on end in descending order of height. Tristan stands near the pond, holding up his lantern. I suddenly remember that Hampstead Heath is a popular place for suicides. Many dead bodies are found in its ponds every year. My breath catches. Is Tristan going to drown himself?

He walks into the pond. I don't want him to know I followed him, but I can't let a man die. I start toward him. Instead of sinking below the water, Tristan walks atop its surface. Amazement halts me. Then I see the wooden dock beneath his feet. Tristan stops at the end, sets down his lantern, and stands immobile for a long time while I fear that he's going to dive in. If he does, I can't save him; I haven't been swimming since I was a child. Should I go for help? Could I find my way back to Mariner House in the dark?

Tristan sinks to his knees. Head bowed, he clasps his hands together under his chin and silently prays. I watch, torn between relief that he hasn't jumped in the water, fear that he will eventually, and puzzlement. He prays for at least half an hour. Then he clambers to his feet, picks up his lantern, and turns. I hide in the woods before he can spot me. He passes so close by me that I can clearly see his expression—so bleak with misery and different from his usual cold, haughty one that he seems a stranger.

12

Hugh and I meet in the dining room at seven o'clock the next morning, when the servants are setting out breakfast. We're the first ones there. We intend to catch Tristan and Olivia Mariner before they can escape again.

"What did Raphael DeQuincey do after he left the ballroom?" I ask quietly as I finish my toast.

"He went straight to his room." Hugh drains his teacup and rubs his sleepy eyes. "I loitered outside the door until I heard him snoring."

"I saw Tristan last night."

"Oh?" Hugh is suddenly wide awake.

I describe the trip to the pond. "What do you suppose he was doing?"

"Maybe it was a religious ritual." Hugh's voice is waspish. "There was no church handy, so he went out in nature to commune with God." He looks up. "Speak of the devil."

Tristan enters the dining room and serves himself coffee. He wears riding breeches, boots, and jacket. When he sees us rise from our seats and approach him, he doesn't look pleased.

"Good morning," Hugh says in the tone of a man challenging another to a duel.

Tristan nods coldly in response.

"Sarah and I missed you yesterday," Hugh says. "We'd like to talk to you."

"Sorry. I've an engagement." Tristan doesn't sound sorry. He drinks his coffee standing up.

Olivia joins us. "He's going riding with me." She's in breeches and boots too, her curly hair tucked under a cap. Trim and slender-hipped, she would look like a boy if not for her full bosom. "Lord Hugh, why don't you and Miss Bain come with us?"

"I'm sure they have better things to do," Tristan says.

"The only item on our agenda is finding your little brother, Robin," Hugh says. "I should think you'd be interested in helping us."

"I've no information that would be of any use to you."

Olivia grazes at the sideboard, nibbling a slice of bacon here, a sausage there. "Do come, Lord Hugh!" She bats her long eyelashes at him and licks the grease off her lips. "We can get to know each other better."

Tristan aims a warning glance at her. "Don't be foolish, Olivia."

I think he's afraid she'll tell us something he doesn't want us to learn.

Olivia smiles like a mischievous child playing with fire. "I'll ask Daddy if they can come. I'm sure he'll give his permission."

Tristan slams down his empty cup, obviously exasperated because if he doesn't take us along, Sir Gerald will learn that he's refusing to cooperate with our investigation and be angry. He looks down his nose at us. "Have you ever ridden a horse?"

"I spent my childhood riding around the country estate," Hugh says.

"Miss Bain?"

"No." There's no country estate in my past, and I'm leery of horses. I've spent my life avoiding being trampled, kicked, or bitten by those that pull carriages and cabs around London.

"It's so easy to learn," Olivia says.

Hugh glances at me, and I nod reluctantly. If I want to talk to Olivia and Tristan, I've no choice but to go. Hugh says, "We'd be delighted. Thank you. We'll just fetch our coats."

I'm almost hoping to find Tristan and Olivia gone when we return, but they're waiting for us in the foyer. Olivia takes Hugh's arm and marches him outside. Tristan, his handsome face dark with displeasure, accompanies me. The morning is bright, fresh, and cool. Birds sing in the trees along the path down the hill to the stable. The stalls contain more horses than I've ever seen in one place. Breathing the rank smells of hay and manure, I wonder if I should change my mind.

A groom brings a black horse for Tristan and a tan one for Olivia. While he helps Hugh select a horse, Olivia flits along the rows of stalls, opens a door, and says, "Old Jasper will do nicely for you, Miss Bain. He's as steady as a rock."

The huge horse she brings me is dark brown with a black mane. When the groom puts a saddle and bridle on him, he stands tamely, but if eyes are mirrors of their owner's soul, then Jasper's soul is wild, alien, and unfathomable.

One of Sir Gerald's guards brings a long trunk. Tristan opens it to reveal four guns with long barrels. "We thought we'd do a bit of shooting on the heath. Have you ever fired a gun?"

"Many times. Show me the side of a barn, and I'll hit it smack-dab," Hugh says.

"No," I say.

"Shall I teach you, Miss Bain?" Olivia asks.

The thought of going out on the heath with these two dangerous people while they're armed with guns scares me. "No, thank you." I doubt that I could manage a gun while riding a horse for the first time.

Tristan, Hugh, and Olivia easily lift themselves onto their horses. Olivia sits astride like the men. They carry their guns in holsters. The groom helps me up. I feel awkward in the sidesaddle, as if I'm about to slip off. As we ride out of the stable, I clutch the reins. Olivia shows me how to turn Jasper and how to make him speed up, slow down, and stop. I've no confidence that I can control him. Fortunately, he follows Tristan and Hugh out the gate and down a path through the woods.

Tristan and Hugh are such expert riders that they look like centaurs, while I bounce with Jasper's every step.

Olivia laughs. "You'll be saddlesore tonight, Miss Bain."

She's impetuous, inconsiderate, and rude, and I dislike her. "How kind of you to warn me, Miss Mariner." I remind myself that personal feelings toward the suspects won't make my job easier.

"Here's another warning." Animosity flashes beneath Olivia's merry humor. "Don't make a fool of yourself over my father. Women are always throwing themselves at him, and he only picks the beautiful ones."

I'm hot with shame to think that she noticed my attraction to Sir Gerald, angry because she misinterpreted it as desire. "Here's my warning for you," I retort. "Your nasty, childish behavior is driving your father away. If you want him to love you, you'd better grow up."

We glare at each other like two girls having a spat. I'm even more ashamed at stooping to her level when I should have maintained my professional detachment. *Why did I let her get under my skin?*

Olivia says primly, "My relationship with my father is none of your business. You'd better stick to finding Robin."

I seize the chance to do just that. "Where were you when Robin was kidnapped?"

"I was in the game room, playing billiards with Tristan."

I'd like to know if Tristan would give the same answer, but he and Hugh are too far down the slope. "Where is the game room?"

"In the north wing on the first floor. So we didn't see or hear anything."

The path narrows and slopes down the hill. We have to ride single file, and as Jasper carries me ahead of Olivia, I think of the dance teacher she said she stabbed. The skin on my back prickles. This time, she has a gun instead of a nail file. Hugh and Tristan have disappeared around a curve in the path. Their voices drift back to me. When we emerge from the woods at the bottom of the hill, they're waiting for us, their faces stiff with mutual hostility. Tristan leads the way along a road, then through a gap in a wooden fence to the sunlit moor. We ride four abreast. Clouds cast moving shadows on the tall grass and the blooming foxgloves and daffodils. The wind flutters loose strands of hair under my bonnet. The sweet scents of greenery and earth remind me of my childhood photography expeditions with my father. I remember us walking hand in hand through meadows. Then I recall meeting Sally and her mother and the horror of learning that my father had another family. I feel a thump in my heart, like a lid slamming shut on my small trove of happy childhood memories.

Honking noises herald a flock of geese flying across the sky toward us. We stop, and Hugh says to Tristan, "If you don't mind my asking, how is Sir Gerald's estate divided in his will?"

Tristan's expression says he does mind, but he speaks in a deliberately calm voice. "His will makes adequate provision for Lady Alexandra, Olivia, and myself. There are bequests to other people, but the bulk of his fortune goes to Robin."

"Robin is the heir?" Hugh sounds surprised.

Tristan gazes at the sky and aims his rifle. "That's correct."

"You're the elder son. Why aren't you the heir?"

"I was until Robin was born. Then my father changed his will. He doesn't approve of my choice of profession. He expects Robin to take over the Mariner business someday."

"What happens if Robin dies?" Hugh asks.

"I inherit his share of the fortune. Unless Father has another son."

If Robin isn't found alive, Tristan stands to gain the most.

"Going into the church hasn't exactly stood you in good stead with your father," Hugh says. "Did you really have a calling? Or did you become a priest because you knew you couldn't outperform him in business?"

Even after witnessing their clash at dinner, I'm shocked by his rudeness.

Tristan barely glances at Hugh, but his cheeks redden; Hugh's barb has pierced vulnerable flesh. "You're a fine one to criticize another man's relationship with his father. Yours has disowned you, hasn't he? You're not exactly a credit to your family."

Hugh flinches. He bites his lip, and his eyes brim with shame and anger because Tristan has hit him where it hurts most.

A sudden blast shatters the air. Startled, I cry out. A goose plummets from the sky, feathers trailing, and plunges into the grass.

"Ha!" Olivia triumphantly holds her gun aloft.

"Good shot," Hugh says politely.

She laughs. "I had a good teacher." She turns to Tristan. "Aren't you proud of me?"

Tristan smiles faintly. I think Olivia fired the gun to interrupt the conversation that put him in a bad light. I'm about to ask him what he was doing at the pond yesterday when Olivia says, "Lord Hugh, I'll race you to the woods!"

Galloping away, she looks over her shoulder and flashes a coy smile at Hugh. Jasper suddenly launches himself toward Olivia as she speeds across the moor. I'm so surprised that all I can do is cling to the reins, trying to keep my seat in the saddle while the horse's hooves pound the grasses that blur away beneath me. I'm terrified because I'm moving faster than I've ever moved. But suddenly I stop bouncing, and I rise and fall with Jasper's gait. My body has somehow found his rhythm. I feel like I'm riding Pegasus. The sensation of flying is exhilarating.

Instead of stopping at the woods, Olivia disappears through a gap between the trees. Jasper rockets after her. The woods swallow us, and we barrel along a path like a leafy green tunnel. I don't know where we're going or what lies ahead. My fear resurges. The terrain is uneven; roots and stones jut up from the ground. Olivia has vanished. Then I hear hooves pounding toward us from my right. Olivia and her horse burst from the woods, and Jasper balks. It slows him down, but it jolts me off balance. I shout as I fly out of the saddle and the reins slip through my hands. My left foot catches in the stirrup as I fall. My ankle twists before it wrenches free. I land hard on my back, shaken and gasping.

Astride her horse, Olivia looms over me. "Miss Bain, are you all right?" Mischief glints beneath the concern in her expression.

I glare at her and push myself upright. "You did that on purpose."

"I honestly didn't," Olivia says, all wounded innocence. She springs from the saddle and reaches down to me. "Let me help you up."

I don't believe her. I swat away her small gloved hand and push myself to my feet. My twisted ankle hurts. Olivia starts to walk back to her horse, but I grab her arm, and when she tries to pull free, I hold on. "You don't care for Robin, do you?"

Sudden fear shines in her huge brown eyes, although I can't tell whether it's because I've picked up on her dirty secret or because I'm bigger and stronger than she is, and I could hurt her before she could shoot me with her gun. "I love Robin. He's my darling baby brother." Her tone is honey laced with acid.

"You must have been the darling baby once. But now your father can't wait to get rid of you. Are you jealous of Robin?"

There's a disturbing commonality between Olivia and me. No matter that Sir Gerald is present and Benjamin Bain gone; both of our fathers replaced us with new children.

Olivia's expression turns petulant. "I'm not going to listen to this."

"Did you think that if Robin weren't around, your father would love you again?" I tighten my grip on her arm. If Sally had never been born, would my father have come back to me? I'm just as jealous as Olivia is. "Is that why you kidnapped Robin? *Where is he?*"

"That's nonsense!" Olivia twists free of me. "I didn't kidnap Robin. I've no idea where he is. If you don't shut up, you can get back into the saddle by yourself or walk home."

It's a long way back to Mariner House, and I doubt I could make it on my sore ankle. Shaken by my own insights, I let Olivia help me climb onto Jasper. As she rides ahead of me through the woods, a gunshot blares. I hear a man's scream, filled with pain and terror.

Alarm strikes my heart. "Hugh!"

"Tristan!" Olivia cries.

We gallop across the moor. I see their horses by a grove of trees, but not the men. Olivia reaches the grove first and jumps off her horse. I haul on the reins to stop Jasper, clamber down, land on my sore ankle, and teeter. Now I see Hugh sitting under a tree with Tristan standing beside him. Hugh's right hand is clasped against his own left shoulder, his fingers wetly red with blood and his face pale and blank with shock.

My heart sinks. Olivia cries, "What happened?"

I see the gun on the ground beside Tristan. "You shot him!"

Tristan doesn't answer. His gaze is dark with turbulent emotion. Hugh gasps out, "It was an accident."

"An accident," Tristan echoes.

He sounds as if he doesn't believe it himself. The atmosphere between him and Hugh vibrates with electric tension, but I've no time to get the truth out of them. I turn to Olivia. "Go fetch a doctor!"

Standing motionless, Olivia turns her wide, confused eyes to Tristan, who also doesn't move. Angered by their refusal to help, I kneel beside Hugh and unbutton his coat and shirt. When I ease them off his shoulder, he groans in pain. I dab the wound with my handkerchief, trembling with fear, wondering if what I think happened really happened. Did Tristan and Olivia just try to kill Hugh and me?

Tristan glances at the wound. "It's just a graze. The bullet didn't go in. He'll be all right." He sounds as detached as if he's talking about a broken machine. I look up at him. His face now wears an expression of studied indifference.

"Let's get him to the house."

13

As Tristan helps Hugh climb onto the horse, his mouth twists as though touching Hugh is repugnant. Then he rides ahead, leaving Olivia to escort Hugh and me. Olivia is subdued, perhaps frightened by the shooting, perhaps thinking of what mischief to make next. When we arrive at the stable, Tristan is nowhere in sight. John Pierce slouches against the wall, hands in the pockets of his brown leather jacket, an unpleasant smile on his sunburned, scarred face.

"Tristan told me about the accident." Pierce sounds glad rather than sorry it happened. "Are you able to walk back to the house?"

"Certainly." Hugh grimaces in pain as he dismounts. "How about you, Sarah?"

When I slide off my horse, I stagger because my ankle hurts, but I'm more concerned about Hugh. "He needs a doctor."

"Tristan said the wound is minor," Pierce says. "Tabitha can fix him up. You too."

I don't want us nursed by an amateur who's a suspect in the crime we're here to investigate. "I insist on a doctor. There must be one in town that you could send for."

"If Tabitha thinks the doctor is necessary, she'll send for him," Pierce says.

"Where is Sir Gerald?"

"At his bank."

We're at the mercy of the suspects.

At Mariner House, Pierce takes us to a room equipped as an infirmary with a hospital cot, glass-fronted cabinets that hold medical supplies, and an examining table. So many people live or work at the estate that it must need a place where they can receive first aid for injuries. Tabitha joins us, wearing a white apron over her brown frock. I think of her lovemaking with Raphael DeQuincey. Today her plain face is set in pensive, tired lines.

As Pierce departs, he says to Hugh and me, "I told you to resign. You should have listened."

Tabitha addresses Hugh with quiet authority. "Sit on the table, please. Take off your coat and shirt."

When Hugh obeys, she doesn't seem uncomfortable in the presence of a half-naked male stranger or flinch at the sight of his blood. I've seen so much blood that I'm not squeamish, and I've seen Hugh nude before, but the scars on his upper arm and breast—souvenirs from Jack the Ripper—are reminders of his vulnerability. I'm afraid that coming here was a terrible mistake.

Tabitha dips a cloth in alcohol and cleans the bullet wound while Hugh looks away and clenches his jaw. She seems competent.

"Where did you learn nursing?" I ask.

"From my mother. She took care of our family and the men who worked on our farm."

I wonder if she's nostalgic about the farm and regrets leaving it. Her manner reveals nothing. I think of her grudge against Lady Alexandra and wonder if she has something more serious to regret.

Tabitha applies salve and a bandage to Hugh's wound, then pours medicine from a bottle into a measuring cup. "Here's some laudanum for the pain."

If Tristan would shoot Hugh and Olivia knock me off my horse to get rid of us, would Tabitha resort to poison? Before

I can warn Hugh, he takes the cup, says, "Thanks," and swallows the medicine.

"You should go to bed," Tabitha says.

"I'll wait while you tend to Sarah's ankle." Hugh obviously doesn't want to leave me on my own.

"I'll be all right. You can go." I must speak with Tabitha, and he still looks pale and shaky. I just hope nothing bad happens to him while we're apart.

After Hugh leaves, I sit on the table and remove my shoe. I'm self-conscious as I raise my skirt, peel off the brown wool stocking, and expose my thin white leg. A lady doesn't show her bare legs, and nobody—not even Barrett—ever sees mine. The thought of Barrett fills me with guilt. Tabitha gently palpates my swollen ankle with her fingers, and I grit my teeth at the pain.

"It's just a sprain," Tabitha says. "It should be fine in a day or so." She fetches a roll of white cloth, cuts off a strip, winds it snugly around my ankle, and secures it with a pin. "Do you want some laudanum?"

"No, thank you." It will put me to sleep, and I need to stay alert. After I put on my stocking and shoe and slip off the table, Tabitha hands me a wooden crutch, but I'm not ready to leave. "Why are you so afraid that Lady Alexandra will find out you're having an affair with Raphael DeQuincey?"

Tabitha's breath catches. "How did you know about it?" she whispers.

"I saw you together last night."

Shame and fear join the dismay on her face as she realizes what I saw them doing. "Please don't tell my sister!" She clasps her hands in entreaty.

I feel an unexpected kinship with her because I too am engaged in a secretive love affair. "What would happen if Lady Alexandra found out?"

"She would be furious!"

If Inspector Reid were to learn that Barrett has been seeing me behind his back, he wouldn't be so much furious as delighted to make use of the knowledge. "What could Lady Alexandra do to you?"

"She'd make sure Raphael and I never see each other again." Tabitha is shaking; her pale-blue eyes brim with tears.

Reid once tried to expel Barrett from the police force. He might try again, to hurt both of us, and he might succeed. But although the threat scares me, I don't feel as helpless as Tabitha thinks she is. "How could Lady Alexandra separate you?"

"The same way she did years ago when I met a man. She made me choose between him and her. If I'd chosen him, she'd have cut me off without a penny. And he wasn't well off. He couldn't have supported me."

I can't forget that Robin Mariner is missing, perhaps dead, and Tabitha may be responsible, but I also can't help feeling sorry for her. "Why not leave Lady Alexandra and marry Mr. DeQuincey? If you both work hard, you can make a life for yourselves together."

Tabitha stares as if I've suggested they fly to the moon.

"Other women do it all the time. They don't have rich relatives to depend on." My mother and I scraped by after my father disappeared, and I've always earned my own living. Despite the hardships, I enjoy my freedom.

"Oh, but Raphael doesn't want me to suffer. He wants to be able to take care of me before we marry."

Perhaps DeQuincey wants the fun of an affair but not the financial burden of a wife. A medium who tricks bereaved people would have no scruples about leading Tabitha on.

"Last year, a grateful client gave Raphael three hundred pounds. He was going to use it to move to Bath. His business would be better there. I was going with him." She wipes her wet eyes. "But the money was stolen. We couldn't go. I'm afraid we'll never be married." Tabitha seems to recollect that I'm a detective, not a confidant, and she gasps. "I shouldn't be telling you this!" Ducking her head, she scurries from the room.

While I hobble up the grand staircase on my crutch, I mull over the story I just heard. Tabitha thinks three hundred pounds would have freed her from Lady Alexandra. Sir Gerald paid a ransom of a thousand pounds for Robin. If Tabitha's story is true, then it confirms the idea I had when I eavesdropped on her and DeQuincey: they're still here because they didn't collect the ransom, which means they didn't kidnap Robin. And unless she's more talented at acting than she lets on, I think she was telling the truth.

#

Hugh's room is an *Arabian Nights* fantasy. It has mosaic walls of blue, white, and gold tiles and a blue geometric-patterned carpet. A brass fretwork chandelier hangs from chains attached to the ceiling. Hugh, dressed in white silk pajamas, sits in the bed, whose padded headboard is framed by an arch cut into a lattice screen. The quilt that covers him and the pillows that prop him up gleam with gold and silver fabrics. Swags of gold-tasseled ivory satin drape the windows. An alcove contains a platform upholstered in blue velvet and strewn with multicolored cushions. Surrounded by all this splendor, Hugh looks like an invalid sultan.

"What happened out on the heath?" I ask, sitting on a chair that must have been built as a sultan's throne.

"I told you, it was an accident." Hugh yawns, drowsy from the laudanum.

"I don't believe it."

"Don't make such a fuss over nothing."

I stare, incredulous. "You could have been killed."

"Well, I'm still kicking. End of story."

"It's not the end as far as I'm concerned." His habit of being flippant at the wrong times has never seemed so annoying. "Why did Tristan shoot you?"

"He didn't mean to," Hugh says, annoyed by my persistence. "He was reloading his gun, and it went off. I was in the way."

Still skeptical, I tell him what happened when I chased Olivia. "I think she tried to kill me. Just as I think Tristan tried to kill you."

"I think you've lost your marbles."

He's not usually so rude, obtuse, or defensive. This investigation is bringing out the worst in him. "You made Tristan admit that he stands to gain from Robin's death," I remind Hugh. "He doesn't want you to find out that he's the one responsible for kidnapping Robin."

"Tristan doesn't care about Sir Gerald's bloody fortune. He took a vow of poverty. If he inherits, he'll give the money to his mission in India."

I'm unconvinced. "Is that what he told you?" When Hugh nods, I say, "Did you ask Tristan where he was during the kidnapping?"

Hugh sighs in exasperation. "I didn't get around to it. But he wouldn't have hurt Robin. He wouldn't hurt anyone."

I can't believe he's so determined to be so gullible. "How do you know?"

"Some of us are better at reading people than others," Hugh snaps.

His jab at me hurts. I don't want us to quarrel, but I have to say, "What about the man Tristan killed during the boxing match?"

The silver-and-gold quilt rustles as Hugh stirs uncomfortably. "It was an accident."

My patience is fraying, my temper heating up. "Another accident. What an unfortunate coincidence. Did you ask him what he was doing at the pond last night?"

Hugh shrugs. "Sorry."

It's not like Hugh to drop the ball. I remember the tension in the atmosphere after the shooting. "What happened between you and Tristan before he shot you?"

"Nothing." Hugh's gaze meets mine with deliberate, defiant effort. "What happened between you and Olivia while you were alone together?"

My cheeks flush at the memory of our conversation and my unpleasant intuitions about myself. I lower my eyes.

Mick runs into the room, breathless with anxiety. "Hugh! I heard you was shot! Are you all right?"

"I will be if everyone would just let me rest." Hugh looks pointedly at the door, then slides down in the bed and pulls the quilt over his head.

#

Mick and I take another stroll beneath the pergola. We go slowly because of my sprained ankle and crutch. Clouds gather above the heath, obliterating the sun that shone so brightly this morning. Wind rustles the hanging vines. When I tell Mick about the "accident," he doesn't buy Hugh's story either.

"I'll talk to Hugh later," he says. "Maybe by then he'll be ready to rat out Tristan."

"Did you ask the servants if something is wrong with Robin?"

"Yeah. They don't know because they ain't seen him in about six months."

"If Robin had been living here all that time, surely someone would have seen him." My suspicion grows.

"He was kept in his room, and nobody but Sir Gerald and Lady Alexandra and the nurses were allowed to go in there."

"Didn't the servants think it was strange?"

"Not really. Lady A told everybody it was because Robin was delicate, and there's lots of diseases goin' around."

Cholera, typhoid, measles, and tuberculosis are contagious and kill many children. "I suppose it could be true."

"Yeah, well, I think he wasn't normal, and Lady A did away with him. And then she covered it up by pretendin' he needed to be kept apart from everybody."

Another idea disturbs me even more. "If Robin has been dead for six months, and there was no baby in the nursery all that time, then Lady Alexandra isn't the only person who knows it. So do the nurses."

"And so does Sir Gerald," Mick says. "He'd have had to be in on the act."

I immediately rise to his defense. "If he were covering up Robin's murder, he wouldn't have hired Hugh and me. It would have been wiser for him to pay us for the photograph of the man in the dinosaur park and dismiss us."

"Maybe he thought you'd go pokin' around anyway and wants you under his thumb." Mick adds, "You told me to be objective. Same goes for you."

I'm just as eager to think that Sir Gerald is on the level as Hugh is to think the same of Tristan, and nothing I've said has changed Mick's mind about Lady Alexandra. That all three of us are unfortunately lacking in objectivity bodes ill for our investigation.

The sky darkens; the air thickens with the smells of earth and marsh. Across the heath, gray clouds spill into the distant hills. Raindrops splash the vines hanging from the pergola. Mick and I turn back toward the house, which now seems the dangerous repository of more secrets than I at first imagined.

"If there is a cover-up, then Lady Alexandra and Sir Gerald probably aren't going to admit it," I say.

"Yeah. That leaves the nurses." Mick's brow furrows in thought. "The afternoon nurse was fired—she's gone. The morning nurse is an old battle-ax. When I tried to chat her up, she brushed me off like I was a fly. The night nurse is younger. Her name is Lottie. Maybe she'll talk."

14

The inclement weather and my sore ankle prevent me from roving the Mariner estate in search of people to question and clues to Robin's whereabouts. I sit in the red brocade armchair in my room and prop my foot on a teak stool, but I can't bear to waste a whole afternoon. Maybe I could develop the photographs I took yesterday. They may contain clues I didn't notice at the time. My bathroom should suffice as a temporary darkroom.

When I open my trunk of photography equipment, I discover that its lock is broken. Someone has pried into my belongings. The tools, trays, and bottles I carefully packed are all a jumble. Stacked under them are flat cardboard boxes of unused negative plates and photographic paper. They're all sealed except the one at the bottom. I pull it out and remove the large envelope I hid there. The flap I sealed has been torn open. I slide out my photograph of my father in the dinosaur park. I sit on the bed, awash in troubling realization.

Somebody in the Mariner household has seen the photograph.

Whoever it is knows that Hugh and I were in the park the day of the murders and the ransom exchange. If it's the kidnapper, then he—or she—must fear that we know who killed the lovers and collected the ransom money and it's only a matter of time before we tell Sir Gerald.

We're in even more danger than I thought.

I wedge a chair under the knob of my door, then steal into Hugh's room through the connecting door and do the same for him. He's asleep in bed; he doesn't wake. Then I sit in my armchair, study the photograph, and think about the twenty-four years that my father has been gone. So much could have happened to him during that period. He was with his second family for a little more than a decade of it; the rest is a mystery. I wish I knew more about his second disappearance. Maybe it would provide clues to where he went, but I parted with Mrs. Albert and Sally on such bad terms that I doubt they would tell me anything. Then it occurs to me that I know just as little about his first disappearance. All I know is that my father didn't come home and my mother said he'd died in a riot. Perhaps my childhood is like my photograph of the dinosaur park—it contains details that I failed to notice at the time or forgot. If I were to revisit the scene of my childhood, perhaps I would remember them. I've never done it because Clerkenwell harbors painful memories of losing my father, but now that my search for Benjamin Bain has become intertwined with my search for Robin Mariner, I can't avoid it any longer. Tomorrow I must go back to Clerkenwell.

#

I don't expect Hugh to come downstairs for dinner that night, but he does. His color is better, he's impeccably groomed, and on the surface he's his normal, cheerful self, but I feel coldness directed toward me. He's not happy about our difference of opinion concerning Tristan Mariner. The only other person who joins us in the dining room is Sir Gerald. The nude marble statues along the walls observe us silently from their niches as we eat. On the dark terrace outside the window, haloes of mist glow around the gas lamps. Again I wonder whether Sir Gerald played a role in Robin's abduction. I watch him with the cautious scrutiny of a deer presented with a wolf whose sheep's clothing has torn enough for the fangs to show through.

"I heard about the accidents," he says. "Are you all right?"

He looks as strong and hale as ever—remarkably well for a man whose child has been missing for seventeen days. I can't help speculating that he's done away with Robin and feels no remorse. But maybe he was even more vigorous before Robin was kidnapped. Maybe the man beside me isn't a kidnapper but a diminished, grieving shadow of himself. I'm aware that I'm making excuses for Sir Gerald, trying to allay my suspicions.

My suspicions don't abate the thrill of excitement that his presence stirs in me.

"Right as rain," Hugh says nonchalantly.

I start to say they weren't accidents, but Hugh kicks my shin under the table. "Terribly clumsy of Father Tristan," he says, "but these things happen. I once went to a fox hunt where a gun misfired and killed the vicar."

Indignant because he's making excuses for Tristan, I frown at Hugh. Now I understand why he came down to dinner; he wants to prevent me from airing my idea that Tristan tried to kill him.

"Bad luck," Sir Gerald agrees. If he suspects that the shooting was deliberate or that we're hiding something from him, he doesn't let on.

"I think Olivia deliberately knocked me off my horse," I say.

"Another of her pranks," Sir Gerald says. "Sorry. I'll have a word with Olivia."

The maid serves us mulligatawny soup, fragrant with curry. Hugh eats moderately. Sir Gerald shovels it in as if stoking his body with fuel. It's delicious, but once again I have little appetite.

"Anything else to report?" Sir Gerald asks.

"Last night—" Before I can describe Tristan's visit to the pond, Hugh kicks me again.

"Last night, we happened upon a steamy love scene between Tabitha Jenkins and Raphael DeQuincey," Hugh says.

Sir Gerald chuckles. "I wouldn't have thought it of her."

Hugh relates the conversation we overheard. "Tabitha and DeQuincey could have kidnapped Robin for the money." He sounds too eager to cast suspicion on them and away from Tristan.

"But if they had the money, they wouldn't still be here," I say.

"The ransom money is collected, and Tabitha and DeQuincey are suddenly in the wind? Wouldn't they think someone would put two and two together?" Hugh gives me a narrow smile; he thinks Tristan is the only reason I'm poking holes in our case against Tabitha and DeQuincey. I haven't told him about my talk with Tabitha. "They would wait awhile, so it wouldn't look suspicious." He addresses Sir Gerald. "I recommend that you have them followed. They might go check on Robin, wherever he is."

"Good idea, but a little late," Sir Gerald says. "I've had everybody under survcillance since I found that toy rabbit on the stairs."

Hugh and I exchange a glance, suddenly united in our dismay. What else hasn't Sir Gerald told us? I see a guard lurking outside the dining room and wonder if the suspects aren't the only ones under surveillance.

"Not that it's done any good," Sir Gerald continues. "Whoever has Robin is being careful not to lay a trail to him. But maybe he'll slip up."

The main course arrives—duckling ragout in onion and thyme gravy with parsnips and peas—and we eat in silence that vibrates with unspoken thoughts. Then Hugh says, "We were looking at the photograph of Robin and Lady Alexandra that appeared in the newspapers, and we wondered—" His face registers pained surprise; I kicked his shin.

"We wondered who took it," I say.

Sir Gerald regards us with narrowed eyes; either he's noticed that something is off between us or he's displeased by my trivial question. "It was a photographer at the hotel on the Riviera where my wife took Robin last winter. I don't know his name."

Distrust curdles the food in my stomach. I'm afraid something happened to Robin on the Riviera and he never came home.

The maid removes our plates and serves lemon pound cake with white icing, topped with lemon slices. Sir Gerald waves away his dessert and tosses his napkin on the table. "Anything else to report?"

Hugh and I avoid looking at each other as we shake our heads.

#

"Why didn't you want me to tell Sir Gerald about your theory that something was wrong with Robin?" Hugh asks.

We're standing beside the rectangular pool, just beyond the light from the house. The fountain tinkles, and the rippling water reflects a pale moon snared in a net of clouds. The statues and topiary trees are dark, indistinct shapes, and I can barely see Hugh's face.

"Because if I'm correct, then Sir Gerald is in on the cover-up." And I'm afraid to confront him, afraid of his reaction, afraid of what we might learn. Shivering, I clasp my arms against my chest. The night is cold and damp, but now that we think we're under surveillance, we can't talk inside the house.

"Right," Hugh says. "Woe betide us if we look under rocks that he doesn't want looked under. But here's a more immediate problem. We've collected bits of information that don't add up to anything. Sir Gerald is disappointed."

"I know." The thought of disappointing him upsets me. "If this keeps up, he'll fire us." In addition to losing the money and our chance to rescue Robin, I would mind lowering myself in Sir Gerald's estimation. I don't want to make matters worse between Hugh and me, but I have to say, "You shouldn't have cut me off when I tried to talk to Sir Gerald about Tristan."

Hugh's response is quick and defensive. "I didn't want him to think Tristan shot me because he kidnapped Robin and doesn't want me finding out."

"But maybe he did! Besides, Sir Gerald has a right to whatever information we collect. He's paying us for it."

"Well, if that's the case, then you should have told him your theory about Robin's photograph."

His rejoinder stings. "But it's just a theory."

"So is your idea that Tristan tried to kill me. You weren't there."

"So tell me. What really happened?"

"Nothing."

Our harmony is disintegrating. Aware that I must be careful of what I say next, I hesitate before I voice my suspicion. Knowing about Hugh's sexual inclination doesn't make it easier for me to talk about. "Are you attracted to Tristan?"

Hugh expels his breath in an angry snort. "Do you think I'm that stupid?"

I'm angry too—at his resistance to sharing facts that might be critical to our investigation and to protecting himself. "Are you?"

"I draw the line at falling for someone who has nothing but contempt for me." Hugh speaks with injured dignity. "Give me some credit, Sarah."

Although I want to believe him, I'm doubtful. I'm also afraid Tristan will try to hurt Hugh again. "You shouldn't be alone. I'll ask Mick to sleep in your room."

"For God's sake, I don't need a baby-minder!"

I can't force Hugh to exercise caution, but I can offer a reason that might persuade him that he should. "While you were asleep, I discovered that someone has broken into my trunk and found the photograph I took in the dinosaur park."

Hugh is silent for a moment as he absorbs the news. "You think it was the kidnapper."

"Yes. And whoever it is knows we were there the day the ransom was collected and Noel Vaughn and Ethel Norris were murdered. It could be Tristan. You have to be careful!"

"The best way to protect ourselves is to solve the case," Hugh declares.

"Well, I've made some progress." I tell him about my conversation with Tabitha in the infirmary. "I don't think she and DeQuincey kidnapped Robin."

Hugh jams his hands in his pockets and stares at the rippling water in the pool. He obviously doesn't like that I've narrowed our list of suspects, increasing the probability that Tristan is guilty. I don't like the growing strife between us, the disunity that's undermining our investigation. The sooner we solve the case, the better—and not just for Robin's sake. I broach my idea of going to Clerkenwell.

Hugh turns to me, and his smile flashes in the dim moonlight. "Sarah, that's a marvelous idea. I knew that creative mind of yours would come up with a plan."

"Then you think I should go?" I'm reluctant to leave him and Mick at Mariner House.

"Take the first train tomorrow. If Sir Gerald asks where you are, I'll tell him you're following a lead on the mystery witness from the dinosaur park. It would be the truth."

I'm about to ask if he wants me gone so that he needn't listen to me harp on Tristan, but the sound of light, rapid footsteps interrupts me. Hugh puts his finger to his lips. A woman in long, full skirts runs gracefully down the right-hand set of marble stairs that lead from the upper terrace. Light glints on her fair hair. It's Lady Alexandra.

Hugh pulls me behind a conical topiary tree. At the bottom of the stairs, Lady Alexandra walks to a bench that's set against the stone retaining wall that supports the upper terrace, about thirty feet from us. She looks around, paces back and forth, and then sits on the bench. A minute later, John Pierce saunters down the left-hand flight of stairs and perches on the bench beside Lady Alexandra. Gas light from the terrace shines on his sandy hair and her piled blonde tresses, but their faces are in shadow, and they're both dressed in dark clothes. This gives the eerie effect of two disembodied, featureless heads floating in the mist. Their voices are clearly audible.

"To what do I owe the honor of this meeting?" Pierce's tone has a sarcastic edge.

"I just wanted to talk to you, John." Lady Alexandra's voice is softer, uncertain. "It's been so long."

"Two years, eight months, and five days since you told me it was over."

I look at Hugh; he raises his eyebrows. We're both surprised to learn that Pierce and Lady Alexandra were once a couple.

Lady Alexandra reaches toward Pierce. "You're still bitter." Her inflection mixes sympathy with reproach. "I'm sorry."

Pierce slides farther away on the bench. "It's a little late to pretend you care about my feelings."

"Of course I care! We once meant everything to each other."

"*Once.*" Pierce utters a hard laugh. "Until I introduced you to Gerald."

We're even more surprised that Lady Alexandra jilted Pierce in favor of Sir Gerald. Hugh whispers, "Why didn't Sir Gerald tell us?"

I shake my head, disturbed to think that Sir Gerald deliberately withheld the fact.

"It wasn't like that!" Lady Alexandra protests. "You and I had been growing apart before I met Gerald. It was just a matter of time until—"

"You've a talent for rewriting history," Pierce says. "We were still engaged when you met Gerald, but you saw a chance to do better."

Lady Alexandra's head bows in apparent shame. "You make me sound so mercenary."

"I'm just calling a spade a spade. You've never been in love with Gerald. All you wanted was his money and a title."

"That's not true!" Indignation raises Lady Alexandra's voice.

"He's never been in love with you either," Pierce says. "All he wanted was a trophy, like those animals from his hunting trips. Neither of you mind hurting other people as long as you get what you want."

His grudge against Lady Alexandra obviously extends to her husband; he's not the loyal servant he seemed.

"John, I'm sorry I hurt you." Lady Alexandra sounds plaintive, contrite. "It's been weighing on my conscience all this time. I asked you to meet me so I could beg for your forgiveness." She leans toward him and presses her lips to his cheek.

Pierce violently shakes her off. "Save the act for the stage. What is it you really want?"

Lady Alexandra's manner undergoes a swift transformation. "All right. I'll spell it out." Her voice is harsh, imperious. "I want Robin back."

"What are you talking about?" Pierce demands.

There's a flurry of motion as she grasps the front of his coat. "Take me to wherever you're hiding him. Let me bring him home."

"But I haven't got him." Astonishment inflects Pierce's voice.

"Please! I won't tell Gerald. I just want my child!"

Pierce pulls away from Lady Alexandra and says in disbelief, "You think I kidnapped Robin."

"John, you've punished Gerald and me enough—you've gotten your revenge. Now it's time to give Robin back."

"I didn't kidnap Robin." Pierce sounds offended by the very idea. "I don't know where he is."

I don't know whether to believe him. His grudge is ample motive for the crime.

"You'd be smart to give Robin back before it's too late." Lady Alexandra's manner turns hostile, aggressive. "Haven't you figured out why Gerald hired those private detectives? It's because he thinks someone in this house is responsible for the kidnapping."

"Of course I figured that out."

The suspects are onto us; they probably were from the start.

"But if Gerald thinks Lord Hugh and Miss Bain can find out who took Robin, then he's fooling himself," Pierce says. "They couldn't find their own behinds in the dark."

Hugh bristles at the insult.

"Even if they were competent, I've nothing to hide. I'm innocent." Pierce's shadowy hand points at Lady Alexandra. "But I'm not so sure about you."

"What are you saying?" Her voice is cautious.

"Maybe you took Robin yourself."

"How can you suggest that?"

"Don't play ignorant," Pierce says. "You never wanted children. You told me so when we were engaged."

Lady Alexandra hurries to object. "But I changed my mind when I learned I was expecting."

"You said children would interfere with your acting career. I think you got tired of playing the devoted mother and wanted to go back on stage, so you sent Robin away."

A cry of indignation bursts from Lady Alexandra; she jumps to her feet. "I love Robin! All I want is to have him safe in my arms. How dare you?"

"But he couldn't just disappear. There needed to be an explanation. So you pretended he'd been kidnapped." Pierce rises, the better to throw her accusation back in her face. "The mother of the famous kidnapped baby—your best role."

"You bastard!" Lady Alexandra flies at Pierce, beating him with her fists.

He grabs her wrists, forces them down. As she shrieks and fights him, he bends his head and kisses her. They struggle together. Then he shouts, releases her, and touches his mouth; she's bitten him. As Lady Alexandra staggers away and runs up the stairs, Pierce mutters, "Bitch!" He stalks past us, then vanishes into the darkness of the garden.

"I'd say either of those two is a likelier culprit than Tristan," Hugh says with smug satisfaction once they are both gone. "Either could have broken into your trunk and seen the photograph. Or it could have been Sir Gerald himself." Hugh strides toward the house, calling over his shoulder, "I'm for bed. Have a good trip to Clerkenwell tomorrow."

I'm disturbed to realize that whether Tristan is guilty or not—and whatever happened before the shooting—Tristan has come between Hugh and me. He's a threat to more than just the future of our detective agency. Now I'm all the more afraid of finding my father. If it leads to proof that Tristan is responsible for Robin's kidnapping and the murders, it could destroy my friendship with Hugh.

15

After breakfast the next morning, Mick carries my satchel out the front door of the mansion while I hobble on my crutch. My ankle is better today but still sore. I've requested a carriage to take me to Hampstead Heath station, and we wait for it under the columned portico. The weather is cloudy, and a cold drizzle chills me.

"Sure you don't want me to come with you?" Mick asks.

"I'd rather you keep an eye on Hugh."

Mick nods, then turns to greet someone who has come out of the mansion to hover near us. "Hullo, Lottie." He says to me, "This is the nurse I was tellin' you about."

Lottie is perhaps sixteen years old, with light-brown hair cut in a fringe across her forehead and wound in a braided roll at the back. She wears a white apron over a gray frock, and her face is wholesome rather than pretty. She smiles at Mick, and her pink cheeks turn pinker. When Mick introduces me, she curtseys.

"I understand that you took care of Robin at night," I say.

Before I can ask any questions, Lottie's smile vanishes and her eyes take on a hunted look. "I'm not supposed to talk about Robin. I better go." She scurries into the house.

"She's hidin' something," Mick says. "I'll keep after her, but I'd hate to get her in trouble."

"Maybe I'll find my father soon, and he'll tell me something that will lead us to Robin, and we won't need to get Lottie in trouble." The new day has revived my hopes.

A carriage draws up. Mick helps me in, hands me my satchel, and says, "Good luck."

When I board the train to Clerkenwell, I begin a journey that I've avoided for twenty-four years. Apprehension solidifies like a cold, malignant weight in my stomach. While the train rumbles toward London proper, the moist air congeals with smoke from the factories into fog so dense that I can't see beyond the warehouses that border the tracks. I feel as if Hugh, Mick, and Mariner House are part of a world I only imagined.

When I emerge from the train at Clerkenwell station, the fog is saturated with a familiar smell—yeast and sugar from the breweries. Nostalgia pierces my heart. With my satchel in one hand, gripping the crutch with the other, I cross the Green—a misnamed long, paved expanse through which carriages and wagons roll. I recognize the Palladian structure of the Middlesex Sessions House and the pointed tower of St. James's Church in the distance, but much else I see has altered since my childhood. Small ancient houses have given way to large, modern brick buildings. The cardboard factory has been replaced by a lodging house and tobacconist's shop. Many clockmakers', jewelers', and cabinetmakers' workshops are gone, their sites now occupied by warehouses, a glass company, and a saw manufacturer. A new establishment—the Red Star Coffee and Cocoa House—has sprung up next to the Crown Tavern, where my mother sent me to fetch my father on the day he went missing.

Since that day, so much has happened that I couldn't have imagined then. The child I was wouldn't have believed that eventually she would learn that Benjamin Bain wasn't dead, that he was a suspect in one crime and a possible witness to another. Even less would she have believed that she would become a private detective hired to solve a famous kidnapping case.

I walk to the drinking fountain at the center of the Green. I once stood here to watch the thousands of people who gathered to hear speeches and demand reforms. I remember raucous shouting, lit torches, waving banners, and burning effigies. Now the Green is quiet on this foggy day, populated only by shoppers and tradesfolk. My memory of Clerkenwell is like a photograph that I tried to preserve by never returning, as though storing a fragile print between sheets of tissue paper. All these years, I've dreamt of returning home to happier times, and now I'm faced with the fact that it's impossible. Too distraught to take photographs with my miniature camera, I walk through the Green, my head down, afraid that someone will recognize me even though I've grown up and many of my former neighbors must be dead. I try to convince myself that no matter what my father may or may not have done, I've nothing to be ashamed of. In Clerkenwell Close, my heart pounds as I near my family's home.

Instead of the small terraced houses I recall, here are blocks of brick tenements. I'm like a girl in a fairy tale who's found her way back to an enchanted land where she once lived, only to find the magic spell broken. All trace of my family, my past, has been obliterated.

I don't know for certain where Ellen Casey's body was found, although I have an idea. The day after my father disappeared, my mother and I walked along Farringdon Lane, looking for him. We passed a road construction site, and I saw a bouquet of flowers laid on a pile of earth. I went to pick it up, but my mother said, "Don't touch that!" Now I find the site covered by buildings and railroad tracks. I picture a red-haired girl lying lifeless on the dirt. I feel as though by excavating the past, I'm betraying my father, but he instructed me to look for the truth.

How will I know when I see it?

Feeling faint and parched, I trudge back to the Green and enter the Red Star Coffee and Cocoa House. The room is fragrant with steam from the coffee urns. As I approach the counter, where two women are serving customers, a girl runs out from behind it and stops short of me. She's about twelve years old, freckled, with red-gold braids and calm gray eyes. My heart stops.

It can't be Ellen Casey, but the likeness is astounding.

One of the serving women comes to stand behind the girl. Her rusty hair is piled atop her head, her gray eyes are framed by crow's-feet, and her freckled skin is chapped. Another chord of recognition strikes. I speak a name I didn't know I remembered.

"Meg?"

Ellen Casey's younger sister looks wary, then flabbergasted. "Sarah?"

Meg smiles, as if she too remembers how we used to dress up in costumes and my father would photograph us. Dismay immediately erases her smile, and she puts her arms protectively around the girl. No matter that we were once best friends; the memory of her dead sister is between us, personified by her daughter, who looks just like Ellen.

"I'm sorry," is all I can think to say. Sorry for her loss, sorry for springing myself on her.

"There's no need to apologize." Meg's voice still has the Irish lilt I remember. "*You* did nothing wrong."

I feel worse, not relieved. She bears me no ill will, but she thinks my father is guilty.

"Run along back to school, now, Bridget," she tells her daughter.

The girl obeys with a curious glance over her shoulder at me. Meg gestures toward my crutch. "How'd you hurt yourself, Sarah?"

"I fell." Even if I were at liberty to reveal the circumstances, they would sound too fantastical to believe.

"Where've you been all these years?"

I can only shake my head. After my father disappeared, my mother and I moved from one cheap lodging to another; she must have wanted to prevent anyone from getting to know us and connecting us to my father's alleged crimes.

"Why'd you come back?" Meg asks.

I have to say something. "I didn't know about Ellen . . . about my father . . . until last week."

Meg looks astonished, then knowing. "Ah. Your mother kept it from you." She gazes after her daughter. "I 'spose I'd have done the same."

My throat spasms as I swallow emotions.

"You're as white as a ghost. I thought you were one at first." Meg looks around the room. "We can't be talking here. Folks have long memories." Her tone softens; she was always kind. "You'd better come to my house."

She speaks to the other serving woman, making some excuse to leave. Then she takes me to one of the new tenement blocks in Clerkenwell Close. The second-floor flat is small and cluttered yet pleasant. Meg talks while she makes tea in the kitchen. "I married Gerald Logan. Remember him? He works at the brewery. So do our two sons. Bridget's our youngest." She sets steaming cups on the table along with a plate of buttered bread and sits across from me.

I sip the hot, strong black tea and nibble the soda bread, whose taste is familiar; it's her mother's recipe. I remember it from visits to the Casey home.

"What about you, Sarah? You married? Any children?"

"No." I think yearningly of Barrett. He too seems a part of a distant, unreal world.

"Where do you live?"

"In Bloomsbury."

"What've you been doing with yourself?"

"I'm a photographer." I decide not to tell Meg about Hugh and our private detective agency because my unconventional life might put her off.

Meg's sandy eyebrows rise. "Your father was a photographer."

There's no avoiding the subject. "The police started investigating him again." I don't mention the circumstances, which would provoke questions that I mustn't answer. "That's how I found out."

"You poor thing." Meg regards me with genuine sympathy. "It must have been an awful shock." Then she frowns, puzzled. "But if you didn't know about Ellen at the time, then what did you think happened?"

I tell her my mother's story about the riot in which my father supposedly died.

Meg nods. "She tried to protect you." When I tell her that my mother is dead, she says, "I'm sorry," then, "She wouldn't have wanted you to come back. Why did you?"

To avoid telling her about the kidnapping investigation and breaking Sir Gerald's confidentiality agreement, I divulge my personal reason. "I can't believe my father is guilty. I was hoping to find something to show it wasn't true."

"I suppose that if it were my pa . . ."

But Meg's sympathy is strained, like fragile lace stretched too tightly. I can't blame her. The Caseys must have taken some comfort from thinking that they knew who had killed Ellen even if he'd gotten away with it, and now here I am, hoping they're wrong.

"Does everyone think my father was guilty?" I ask.

She looks down at her teacup. "Nobody wanted to live in your house after you and your ma moved out. It was empty for years. Then it burned down."

Maybe someone set fire to the house to exorcise the evil taint left by my father. I can't help rising to his defense. "Just because he was the last to see Ellen alive, it doesn't mean he killed her. The police were out to get him because he organized marches. They could have framed him."

"That isn't why we thought he'd done it." Meg raises her eyes, which are filled with regret. "It was his pictures of Ellen."

"So he photographed her. What does it matter? He took pictures of you and me too."

A queasy look flickers across Meg's face. "Not that kind of pictures. The others."

"What others?"

She hesitates, then rises. "I'll be back in a minute."

She leaves the kitchen. I hear her rummage in the bedroom, and she returns, holding something behind her back. She looks at once sad and defensive. "Ma kept this. I found it among her things after she died." Meg lays an enlarged photograph on the table in front of me.

The image has the soft luminosity of the landscape pictures my father took when we went on photography expeditions. Ellen Casey sits in a chair; her back is arched, her left knee is raised. Her ankle rests on her right thigh, and her hands are clasped behind her head. Her eyes are eyes closed, her moistly shining lips parted. She's dressed in a white blouse, dark skirt, and ribbed wool socks. The skirt is hiked a little too high; the blouse strains a little too tightly across her budding breasts. It's a beautiful portrait of a girl becoming a woman. I'm filled with admiration for my father's artistry and joy at seeing an example of his work that I didn't know existed.

"It's the only picture there is of Ellen," Meg says. "That's why Ma didn't tear it up."

It's the last likeness taken of Ellen before mortality claimed her. My joy gives way to alarm, for I understand how this picture looked to everyone who saw it after Ellen was raped and murdered.

"I'm sorry, Sarah," Meg says.

My father's image of Ellen is innocent compared to the boudoir pictures that I myself once took of women in Whitechapel, but I'm horrified because it could mean that my father had an improper interest in young girls. My mind teems with questions. Why was there no mention of this photograph in the police reports? Wouldn't the police have presented it as evidence of my father's guilt?

Meg fidgets with her apron strings. "Sarah . . . did your father ever . . . *touch* you?"

He held my hands as he taught me how to use a camera, he hugged me often, and he kissed me when he tucked me into bed at night. That's not what she means. "No!" It's the truth, and I'm appalled by her suggestion.

"That's good," Meg says, relieved.

But the fact that my father never violated me isn't proof that he didn't rape and murder Ellen. I can't bear to look at his photograph of her. I turn it over, then see the initials, *B. B.*, penciled on the back. The picture is an original print made by my father, not a copy. "How did your mother get this?"

"My uncle was one of the coppers that searched your house," Meg says. "He took them."

I remember the police traipsing through our rooms. "You mean there were others like it?"

"The others were worse." Meg doesn't need to explain; I know she means Ellen was posed with some, perhaps all, of her clothing removed. "My uncle brought them to our house the day of Ellen's funeral. The whole family was gathered 'round. When they saw the pictures, there was a big to-do. The others were thrown in the stove. This is the only one left."

"So your uncle never turned in the photographs to his superiors." That's why none were in my father's police file.

"My parents didn't want anyone else seeing them. It would've ruined Ellen's reputation." Meg looks at the floor.

I experience a stab of premonition. "Meg, what haven't you told me?" She starts to turn away, but I rise, grab her shoulders, and say, "What happened to my father? Do you know?"

Her staring eyes are like gray marbles rimmed with white, her freckles dark against her suddenly pale skin. She's afraid of me; she's no longer sure I'm not as evil as she thinks my father was. "My pa and my uncles swore to get revenge for Ellen. They went out that night," she whispers. "The next day, it was all over the neighborhood—your father was missing."

Is that why my father left—not for fear of the police, but because the Casey men were after him? Did my mother know?

Meg pushes me away. "I don't know if they did anything to him, and I can't ask them because they're dead." She lifts her chin and says defiantly, "But if they killed him, it would've served him right."

#

I find myself on the train bound for Hampstead with little recollection of how I got there. The carriage is cold, its swaying motion nauseates me, and I tremble as I gaze out the window at the foggy streets and relive my conversation with Meg. It's little solace knowing that the Casey men didn't, as Meg thinks, kill my father that night. The local people, not just the Caseys, believe he's guilty, and I remember my mother crying as she tore up his photographs, burned them in the stove, and smashed negative plates with a poker while I begged her to stop. Did they include erotic ones that my father had taken of other young girls? I remove from my satchel the photograph I took in the dinosaur park, and I stare at the shadowy figure making a viewfinder with his hands.

Look for the truth . . .

Is the truth that my father didn't like being photographed himself because the camera might have revealed the blackness in his soul? Am I the daughter of a monster?

If my father skipped town before the Casey men could get him, did they keep looking for years afterward? Is that why he disappeared on Sally and her mother as well—because they finally caught up with him? Is he dead—lying in an unmarked grave somewhere—or still a fugitive?

16

By the time I arrive at the gates of Mariner House in a hired cab, the fog has spread from London and engulfed the heath, as though I've brought it with me. The reporters, photographers, and gawkers outside the gates huddle in their mackintoshes. At the mansion, I see Lady Alexandra at luncheon in the dining room with her friends. I'm faint from hunger, but I need to tell Hugh what happened in Clerkenwell.

"Miss Bain," Lady Alexandra calls. I pause, surprised that she's speaking to me after she told me never to come near her again. "May I have a word?"

I'm still shaken by what I've learned about my father, but I mustn't pass up an opportunity to further my acquaintance with one of the suspects in Robin's kidnapping. When I approach Lady Alexandra, she says, "Please help yourself to some food first."

I fill a plate with bread, cold ham, and cheese from the buffet. When I return to Lady Alexandra, her friends have left, and we're alone. I lean my crutch against the table and cautiously seat myself opposite Lady Alexandra. Today, she's regal in a periwinkle-blue frock that flatters her fair coloring but draws attention to the bluish shadows under her eyes. Her smile is strained.

"Please allow me to apologize for my deplorable behavior at the séance," she says.

"Of course."

Moments pass while she picks at a hard-boiled egg on her plate and I eat. "What progress have you made in your investigation?"

I'm surprised by her question because none of the other suspects have asked; either they don't think we've found out anything that matters or they don't care. "I'm afraid I can't tell you. You would have to ask your husband."

"He won't tell me anything." She sighs with frustration. "He just says I mustn't worry, he has everything under control."

Although I wonder if she's afraid we've dug up evidence against her, I can't help feeling sorry for her. During the weeks when my father was first missing, I desperately wished for news of his whereabouts. It must be even worse to be a mother whose child is missing. But I can't forget that Robin was secluded in the nursery for six months before his kidnapping and Lady Alexandra may be part of a conspiracy to hide the fact that he's been dead all this time. And I see another reason not to take her at face value.

"If you're so eager to find Robin, then why haven't you told the police that you think John Pierce took him?" I ask.

Lady Alexandra reacts with the same shocked gasp as Tabitha did when I told her I'd seen her with Raphael DeQuincey. "How did you know?"

For the first time, the resemblance between the sisters is visible. It quickly vanishes because Lady Alexandra is angry instead of scared. "You spied on me! Are you really here to find Robin, or are you looking for dirt to sell to the newspapers?"

I'm angry too. My ankle hurts, Hugh has a gunshot wound, and I've just discovered new reasons to believe my father is guilty of rape and murder. Lady Alexandra's accusation is insulting, and I refuse to be cowed. "If you're trying to distract me from noticing that you haven't answered my question, it's not working. Why didn't you tell the police about Mr. Pierce?"

Her anger yields to misery. "I couldn't." She lowers her eyes and her voice. "I—I still have feelings for John. If I'm wrong about him, I don't want to get him in trouble. Even if I'm right, I don't want him punished as long as I get Robin back safe and sound." She raises her anxious gaze to me. "Are you going to tell Gerald?"

"I work for him. I can't withhold information." I'm uncomfortably aware that I haven't told him about my father or my suspicion that Sir Gerald himself was responsible for Robin's kidnapping.

"But if Gerald were to think John kidnapped Robin—if he knew how I feel about John . . ." Her face blanches; she seems too terrified to name the consequences. She reaches across the table and grasps my hand. Her hand is cold, delicate-boned, but strong. "Miss Bain, I must ask a favor of you."

"What favor?" I pull my hand away and flex my fingers. Their tips are red from the pressure of Lady Alexandra's grip.

"Find out if John has Robin. If he does, then tell me before you tell Gerald or the police."

To collude with Lady Alexandra behind Sir Gerald's back would be unprofessional, and I distrust her motives. Does she really think Pierce has Robin, or is this an attempt to direct my suspicion onto him? Does she really care for him, or does she want him blamed for the kidnapping so that she won't be? But I can't help putting myself in her place. In the unlikely event that I thought Barrett had committed a crime, wouldn't I want to be certain before delivering him into the hands of the law? And I'm protecting my father by not telling the police what I know about him.

"I'll think about it—if you'll answer a question."

"Of course," Lady Alexandra says eagerly. "What is it?"

"Have you been inside my room?"

Lady Alexandra frowns, perplexed. "No. Why do you ask?"

I can't tell whether she's lying and it was she who broke into my trunk. But I sway toward believing her, and not only because I can't help sympathizing with her. She couldn't have known I'd overheard her conversation with Pierce, and she couldn't have planned in advance how to react when I confronted her about it, but her speech and manner were such as I would expect from an innocent woman. Unless Lady Alexandra is as good at script-writing on the spur of the moment as she is at acting, she was telling the truth.

#

Now I have even more to tell Hugh, but when I knock on his door, there's no answer, and the door is locked. I experience a cold trickle of foreboding. I rush into my room and try the door that connects it with his. It opens.

"Hugh?" The room is dark, with a musky, sweaty, feverish smell. "Are you all right?" I grope my way to the window, find the curtain cord, and pull.

Light floods the *Arabian Nights* room. Two figures in the bed under the lattice arch bolt upright. One is Hugh. The other is Tristan Mariner. The gold-and-silver quilt falls away from their naked chests. They're as horrified to see me as I am to see them together.

"Sarah," Hugh says in a strained, hoarse voice. "Can you give us a moment?"

I retreat to my room, shut the door, and pace while I listen to scuffling noises and low, agitated voices from Hugh's room. Hearing his door to the passage open, I hurry out my door just in time to meet Tristan. He's fully clothed, his black hair is tousled, and he looks mortified. He's clutching something in his hand. It's his white priest's collar. Without a word, he stalks down the passage and disappears down the back stairs. I go in my room and knock on the connecting door to Hugh's.

"Come in," Hugh calls.

He's dressed and groomed; the aroma of bay rum shaving lotion masks the smell of sex. Before I can speak, he raises his palms and says, "It's not what you think."

"How can it be anything else?"

"I mean, it wasn't just an impulsive roll in the hay." Hugh sinks onto the cushioned platform in the alcove, his gaze focused on some troubling inner vista. "There've been so many men, I've lost count—I don't even remember all their names. But there's never been anyone I felt close to, who I thought was worth the risk of seeing more than a few times." Hugh looks up at me. "Do you understand what I mean?"

His face wears the same daft, starry-eyed expression that I see in my reflection in the mirror after I've been with Barrett. My heart plummets as I nod and sit beside him. "You're in love with Tristan Mariner."

Hugh's cheeks color; elation swells his chest. "I never thought it would happen. I never thought I would find someone who actually makes me glad that I'm what I am."

"Oh, Hugh." I wish I could be happy for him, but he's fallen in love with the wrong person at the worst time. "Tristan is not only a priest but a suspect in the kidnapping of his own brother," I remind Hugh, "and he could also be a murderer."

"I never thought he did it," Hugh declares, "and now I know for sure that he's incapable of hurting anyone."

I'm too shy to speak bluntly and say that sex can trick you into thinking that you know a person and make you believe he's good because you don't want to think that someone who's touched you intimately is evil. "There was the man he killed during the boxing match."

"There was no boxing match. That's just the official story. Here's what really happened: When Tristan was in the army in India, he became friends with a fellow soldier. They weren't lovers, but they were on the verge. The men in their regiment got wise to it. One night they attacked Tristan and his friend. They beat his friend almost to death before Tristan managed to fight them off. One of them died of his injuries—Tristan ruptured his kidney." Hugh sounds proud, gratified. "It was self-defense."

"It couldn't have been self-defense when he shot you."

Hugh sighs. "All right, I'll tell you what happened. You and Olivia rode off and left us alone. The attraction between us was so strong, I felt as if my blood was on fire. When we reached that grove of trees, we jumped off our horses, and suddenly we were kissing. I don't know who made the first move. God, I've never felt anything like it."

The awe in his voice brings back my memory of the first time Barrett and I kissed. My body goes warm and liquid at the mere thought.

"Then he pushed me away. He was furious. He called me a sinner and a perversion of nature. I said, 'If I'm a sinner and a pervert, then so are you, because you want it as much as I do.' I moved toward him, and he aimed his rifle at me and said, 'Don't come near me!' He was shaking so badly, his finger nudged the trigger."

Now I see two reasons why Tristan might have deliberately shot Hugh—to eliminate the object of his forbidden desire and prevent Hugh from exposing him as Robin's kidnapper. "So then you fell in love."

"Not then. I fell in love the minute we first met. I just didn't realize it until he came to my room this morning."

I didn't realize until many weeks later that I'd fallen in love with Barrett at first sight. The initial antagonism between us had been just a smokescreen created by fear and denial. "I warned you not to be alone with Tristan."

"He apologized for shooting me," Hugh says, defiant. "He explained that it was the first time he'd ever been intimate with a man, and he was upset. And when we kissed again, he didn't resist."

Hugh's smile, lit with an inner radiance, is dazzling. I realize that I've never seen him truly happy until now. My heart is heavy because I feel obligated to deliver unwelcome news for his own good. "You have to break it off with Tristan."

"I knew you were going to say that. But I can't. Don't you see I've been waiting for this all my life?"

"How does Tristan feel about you?"

"The same."

"Did he say so?"

"Not in so many words. We didn't have time for many words." Hugh smiles, reminiscent and secretive.

It feels cruel, but I have to say, "He could be using you."

A sardonic laugh bursts from Hugh. "You sound like a granny warning a farmer's daughter about the lecherous carnival barker."

"You sound like you're so blinded by love that you haven't bothered to examine Tristan's motives," I retort.

"He sinned against his church and God just to have it off with me?" Hugh's bluntness makes me cringe. "It's not like that." Afire with his need to convince, he leans toward me. "Sarah, I swear. This is real."

"No, not just to . . ." I balk at repeating it. "He might have been trying to distract you from finding out that he kidnapped Robin."

"He wouldn't. He didn't. Look, Sarah, I know you mean well, but if you can't accept—"

Fear is an icy, bone-deep pain, like the moment before my hands go numb from the cold on a winter day. Have I pushed Hugh into choosing between me and Tristan, the man he thinks is the love of his life?

"Hugh! Miss Sarah!" Mick bursts into the room, panting with excitement. "Robin's been found!"

17

"Where is he?" I ask as I limp on my crutch down the passage with Hugh and Mick.

"On Hampstead Heath," Mick says.

After the eighteen-day search for Robin, and the sightings reported all over London, he's been located so close to home.

Hugh claps his hat on his head and shoves his arms into his coat sleeves. "Who found him?"

"Don't know," Mick says. "I was eatin' lunch in the servant's hall, and the butler came in with the news. I didn't wait to hear anymore. I ran straight up to tell you."

Hurrying down the grand staircase, I ask, "Is Robin alive?" That's all I care about; never mind that we won't earn the reward or that our employment with Sir Gerald is over.

"Was the kidnapper caught?" Hugh asks.

"Beats me," Mick says.

"Exactly where is he?" I ask.

"Don't know, but everybody's goin'. We'll just follow the crowd."

The foyer is empty, the door ajar. We race outside, down the steps. Mist hangs heavily in the air. By the time we've traversed the grounds, my shoes are soaked from puddles left by yesterday's rain, and my armpit hurts from the crutch digging into it. The only people at the gates are two guards. On the narrow, zigzagging road that descends the hill, we join the mass exodus from Mariner House. Older servants plod breathlessly at the tail end. We pass these and, farther down the slope, the younger servants, grounds keepers, guards, and folks whose roles I can't identify; there must be over a hundred. Now we come upon reporters armed with notebooks and pencils and photographers lugging cameras and flash lamps. They chatter excitedly; their long vigil outside Mariner House is about to pay off.

"You go on ahead," I tell Hugh and Mick. My ankle throbs; I'm winded.

"Look!" Mick points down the road at a horse-drawn wagon that contains a tour guide lecturing through a megaphone to a group of customers. Mick and Hugh support me while I limp toward the wagon.

"It's our lucky day. We're about to see history being made," the guide tells his customers.

"We're joining your tour," Hugh says, boosting me aboard. He and Mick scramble up after me.

"Hey! You didn't pay!" the guide says.

Hugh tosses coins to him, and we sit on the hard wooden floor. Two carriages ahead of us turn onto the main road. The wagon follows, and we emerge into open moor. Fog obscures the terrain beyond the hedgerows. The parade soon veers down a different road that curves around the hill. Woods surround the road. The carriages stop on the verge, and Sir Gerald helps Lady Alexandra and Tabitha from the first one; the second disgorges Raphael DeQuincey, Sir Ogden, Dame Judith, and others. The tour guide and his customers jump from the wagon while Hugh and Mick help me climb out.

Sir Gerald leads the rush through the woods along a gravel road that's too narrow to walk more than three abreast. The road descends as it snakes between trees. Water drips from the foliage. Lady Alexandra leans on Sir Gerald's arm. Her anxious murmur and his soothing voice drift back to us. Her friends, close behind her, whisper among themselves. I hobble between Mick and Hugh. I hear other footsteps crunching the gravel behind us and agitated conversation. Everyone spills out of the dim woods onto a grassy bank that fronts a large, irregularly shaped pond edged with reeds. The water is flat and dull, like tarnished silver. On the right stands an old wooden boathouse. On the left, a rowboat is pulled up onto a stone ramp that slopes down to the water. Near the ramp, a man holding a fishing rod stands apart from a small crowd of people who are gathered in a circle, staring down at something on the ground.

The scene is as grim as a funeral. It tells the terrible story.

"Oh, no," Hugh says.

"My baby!" Lady Alexandra cries.

She runs toward the crowd, which parts to let her through. Now I see the small shape lying on the grass, covered with a drenched pale-blue blanket. Fist-sized stones, scattered around the body, must have been wrapped in the blanket and tumbled out when the fisherman brought it ashore. Lady Alexandra moans while Tabitha and Dame Judith restrain her. Sir Gerald strides toward the body, kneels, and draws back the blanket. His back is to me; I can't see his expression, and he's blocking my view of the body, but his posture sags.

"It's Robin." His voice sounds older, tired, and drained of strength.

With all his wealth and power, he couldn't rescue Robin, can't bring him back to life. Sorrow for him swells in me, washing away my previous suspicions in a flood of salty tears. I wish I could console him, but he doesn't even know I'm here.

The crowd exclaims. Lady Alexandra bursts into agonized sobs that echo across the water. As Tabitha and Dame Judith try to soothe her, she collapses on the ground.

Hugh sighs; Mick curses under his breath. Guilt torments me. I've failed Sir Gerald. I should have worked harder, should have been a better detective; I should have found Robin before this happened.

Explosions suddenly erupt amid blazes of white light. The photographers are aiming their cameras at Robin's body,

setting off their flash lamps, taking pictures. Sir Gerald staggers to his feet. In the moment before he pulls the blanket over
Robin, I glimpse the wet, darkened blond curls, the small,
gray, waxen face. I think of the photograph of Robin and
Lady Alexandra. When it was taken, he wasn't dead; it was the
last mortal likeness of him.

Sir Gerald turns on the photographers and shouts, "Get the
hell out of here!"

The reporters swarm around him, yelling questions. I
belatedly notice uniformed policemen among the crowd.
Even as instinctive fear of the law shoots through me, my eyes
follow the sparks that spew skyward from the flash lamps. It's
something I do automatically when I take pictures—I watch
the sparks to make sure they don't land on me and set my hair
and clothes on fire. The sparks divert my attention to the landscape. In the distance, I see a dock that extends into the pond
and three conical pine trees on the opposite bank. Recognition stuns me.

At the same moment, I see Tristan Mariner standing not
twenty feet away. Olivia clings to his arm. Tristan is staring
at Hugh, who starts toward him as if drawn by the pull of
gravity.

I clutch Hugh's arm and whisper, "This is the pond where
I followed Tristan that night!" We took a different route, and
in the darkness, I didn't see the boathouse or the ramp.

Hugh pauses, turning to me in confusion. Tristan averts
his gaze as coldly as if he and Hugh were strangers. I say, "He
knew Robin was in the pond. That's why he came here!"

"*No.*" Hugh stares at me in shock and disbelief. "It
can't be."

"He must have put Robin in the pond himself; that's how
he knew. He wanted to see if the body had resurfaced."

Hugh's aghast face is as white as after Tristan shot him. He
grabs my arm and says in a fierce whisper, "Don't tell anyone."

"I'm not going to protect Tristan!" I think he's not only
the kidnapper but a murderer.

"Sarah, please," Hugh says urgently. "If you care about me, keep quiet."

Mick tugs my sleeve. "Miss Sarah!" He points at the police, who are tussling with the photographers.

I know Barrett is here the moment before I see him. Now Barrett sees me, and his expression fills with shocked bewilderment. I'm horrified, for more reasons than I can name, to have him find me here.

"Stand back!" another police officer yells at the crowd, which is growing as more reporters and gawkers arrive. "This is a crime scene."

It's Inspector Reid.

My first instinct is to protect Mick. I whisper to him, "Run!"

"I'm not leaving you and Hugh." His eyes betray his fears of losing us and of the law.

Steeling myself, I push him so hard that he stumbles. "Go! Before Reid sees you!"

The moment before Reid's glance swivels in our direction, Mick bolts into the woods. He's adept at hiding and the heath is big, so I'm fairly confident that the police won't find him.

Reid's jaw drops. "Sarah Bain? Lord Hugh Staunton?"

Barrett exclaims, "What are you doing here?"

I could say I happened to be in the area, heard that Robin had been found, and came to see. It's not actually a lie. But Barrett frowns; he knows me too well. He can tell I'm thinking about how to skirt the truth.

"We're on a case," Hugh says.

"What case?" Barrett asks, incredulous.

Remembering the confidentiality agreement, I look around for Sir Gerald. He's within earshot, talking to a man who carries a black medical bag—the police surgeon.

Doubt vies with suspicion on Barrett's face. "Are you investigating the kidnapping?"

My guilty silence is my answer.

"Them and every other two-bit private detective in London," Reid says with a sneer at Hugh and me. "Where the hell have you two been? Half the police force is looking for you."

Puzzled, I look to Barrett. "Why?"

Barrett seems too outraged to speak. Reid says, "You may recall that a man and woman were murdered in the dinosaur park at the Crystal Palace."

The image of the victims resurfaces from the depths of my memory, where the events since I moved to Mariner House had pushed it. I see Ethel Norris's bruised neck and her tongue caught between her teeth, and Noel Vaughn's bloody, caved-in head. I swallow, fighting nausea.

"What about it?" Hugh asks.

Reid grins with ugly triumph. "You two are the prime suspects."

Hugh and I look at each other, shocked to learn that our unfinished business has been following us like an invisible bloodhound and has finally bitten us. "We didn't even know the victims. We weren't there when they were killed," I protest.

"That's not quite true, is it?" Reid's nasty grin broadens. "Witnesses at the Crystal Palace saw a devilishly handsome blond swell and a thin, plain woman with a camera follow the victims outside. When I heard that description, I said, 'I'll bet my mother's life I know who that is.'"

I'm alarmed to realize that while we were watching Vaughn and his lady, other people were noticing us. "We didn't kill them!"

"We were on a job, photographing an adulterous husband with his mistress," Hugh says.

Now Barrett looks angry because when I told him about the murder scene I'd happened upon, I neglected to reveal my connection with the victims.

"I don't believe it." Reid glances toward Robin's corpse, which is hidden by the police guarding it. "Well, this day isn't a complete disaster—I've found you, and I'm going to get the truth about the Ripper murders as well as the dinosaur park murders if I have to dig it out of you with my own shovel. You're under arrest."

My heart sinks. Our time for reckoning with the past is finally here.

"Arrest them," Reid orders Barrett. "Take them to Newgate."

I'm terrified because I was locked inside the notorious prison when Reid had me arrested last fall. I don't want to go back. Hugh looks terrified too—he knows what men of his kind suffer at the hands of the wardens and other inmates. I turn a pleading gaze on Barrett.

He's not so angry that he would throw me in jail. He says to Reid, "There's no evidence that Miss Bain and Lord Hugh committed the murders."

Reid grimaces in disgust. "Are you sticking up for them? Don't tell me you're still sweet on Miss Bain." The glance Barrett involuntarily casts at me is anything but sweet, yet intense with personal feeling. Enlightenment flashes in Reid's eyes. "You've been seeing her all this time. She's your girl."

Barrett looks just as alarmed as I am to have our relationship exposed at the worst moment. He flushes and says, "They don't have to go to jail. We can question them at the station."

"Oh, for crying out loud." Exasperated, Reid calls to three other constables, points at Hugh and me and orders, "Take them to Newgate."

My temper suddenly explodes. Last autumn, Reid terrified me, tormented me, threatened my friends, and delivered us into the hands of Jack the Ripper. I'm not going to cooperate meekly now. When a constable reaches for me, I hit his knee with my crutch. He yells in pain. Hugh punches the constable who's tried to seize him. Reporters flock to us.

"Inspector Reid, who are these people?"

"Why are you arresting them?"

"Are they connected to the kidnapping?"

A constable grabs me from behind, tears the crutch from my hand. I scream, stomp on his feet, and kick my heels against his shins. Hugh yells as more constables beat him with their nightsticks. He falls. A photographer thrusts his camera at my face. Exploding flash powder blinds me. The constable wrestles me to the ground, pulls my arms behind my back, and locks handcuffs around my wrists.

"Break it up!" shouts Sir Gerald's angry voice.

As my vision returns, I see his guards wade into the fray and shove reporters and photographers aside. I'm lying on my stomach on damp, muddy grass with a constable kneeling on my back. The guards pull him off. I didn't expect Sir Gerald to protect me, and I'm fervently grateful.

More constables are heaped on top of one another. The guards haul them away to reveal Hugh lying curled up, motionless, handcuffed. I roll over and kneel beside him. "Hugh!"

He sits up and says, "I'm all right," but his nose is bleeding.

We stagger to our feet and find ourselves with Sir Gerald and Inspector Reid at the center of a circle of spectators who include John Pierce, Tristan, Olivia, Raphael DeQuincey, reporters, police, guards, photographers, and servants. I hear Lady Alexandra sobbing over Robin while Tabitha, Sir Ogden, and Dame Judith try to comfort her. Tristan stares at Hugh. Everyone else is watching the drama between Sir Gerald and Inspector Reid.

His face dark with fury, Sir Gerald grabs Reid by the lapels. "My son's just been found dead, and you start a riot? What the hell?"

Reid wrenches himself free, angry to be put in the wrong. "My apologies, Sir Gerald. I didn't mean any disrespect." He glares at Hugh and me. "They resisted arrest."

"Why are you trying to arrest my detectives?" Sir Gerald demands.

Astonished, Reid says, "*Your* detectives? They're working for you?"

"Yes. I hired them to find Robin."

Reid laughs. "Now I've seen everything."

I steal a glance at Barrett. He looks wounded and betrayed as well as furious. I feel so guilty, I can't meet his eyes. I should have told him despite the confidentiality agreement.

"I'm sorry you wasted your money on these two swindlers," Reid says.

Sir Gerald responds in the level, controlled manner of a flint-hearted businessman negotiating with an opponent. "What is it you think they've done?"

Reid tells him about the murders at the dinosaur park. "Now that you don't need their services any longer, I'll take them off your hands." He snaps his fingers at the constables.

They move in on Hugh and me. We're too weary, sore, and defeated to resist again. Our big case, for which we had such high hopes, has ended in tragedy. The prospect of a terrible incarceration in Newgate looms, and when Reid is done with us, we'll surely hang.

"No, you don't," Sir Gerald says. "They're staying."

Hugh and I gape, astonished that he still wants us. Reid huffs, "With all due respect, Sir Gerald, this is police business. You've no right to interfere."

"We'll see about that. I'll just have a word with the prime minister."

Offended because Sir Gerald's influence trumps the police's authority, Reid says, "So I should just let them go free? They're liable to skip town."

I don't know whether Sir Gerald thinks we're innocent or guilty; he doesn't look at us. He tells Reid, "I'll keep them under guard at my house."

Reid frowns, reluctant to give us special treatment, afraid of Sir Gerald going over his head and costing him his job. "I'll need to interrogate them."

"Whenever you want."

"Keep them someplace where they can't talk to each other."

Sir Gerald looks more like an iron statue than a grief-stricken father of a drowned child. "Anything else?"

"They're troublemakers. If anything bad happens while they're in your custody, don't say I didn't warn you." Reid stalks away, calling to his men, "Clear the spectators from the crime scene. Start looking for evidence."

Barrett gives me one last angry, betrayed look before he joins the other constables.

"Thanks, Sir Gerald," Hugh says as a constable removes our handcuffs. "We owe you."

Sir Gerald glances at his wife weeping over their son's body before he gives us a bleak version of his crafty smile. "You'll pay me back eventually."

18

Locked in my room, the key confiscated by Sir Gerald's guards, I call to Hugh through the connecting door, but there's silence on the other side. The guards must have put him in a different room. I remove my coat and bonnet, take them to my bathroom, and wash off the mud. Then I stand by the window. The fog has thickened, it's getting dark, and I can't see anything. The vibrant reds and costly exotic furnishings in my room seem to mock me, a prisoner in this place where I've never belonged.

An hour passes. I hear doors opening, footsteps, and voices in the distance. I wonder where Hugh is. I only hope Mick went home. And where is Barrett? My fear that I've lost him is so agonizing that I double over, clutch my chest, and moan. Has he washed his hands of me? If he has, I can't blame him. Even if he hasn't, he can't stop Inspector Reid from grinding Hugh and me under the wheels of justice.

The clock in the hall chimes six o'clock. A knock at the door raises my hopes that Sir Gerald has come to set me free; but it's only a guard who lets in a maid carrying a covered tray. She leaves it on the table. Shaky from hunger as well as fear, I eat bread, cold roast beef, mulligatawny soup, and lemon cake from last night. Either Robin's death has lowered the Mariner culinary standard or the cook has deemed leftovers good enough for the prisoners. I'm grateful for the animal comfort of the food, knowing that this may be my last decent meal. When I'm done, I'm calmer but exhausted from the long, disturbing day. Before I can lie down for a nap, there comes another knock at the door. I spring to my feet.

It's John Pierce. I'm not relieved to see him instead of Reid. He steps into the room, closing the door, his manner quiet and businesslike. "Inspector Reid is on his way to interrogate you and Lord Hugh. I have a carriage and driver waiting outside to take both of you to the station. I'll distract the police so you can get away."

Astonished, I say, "Why would you do that?" He never liked us, he thinks we're swindlers, and I would have thought he would be glad to see us in the hands of the law.

"Because I don't think you killed those people." His certainty isn't flattering; it's obvious that he thinks Hugh and I are too soft to commit murder. If he only knew. "Because somebody once helped me when I was in a similar position."

I frown, distrusting his goodwill. Pierce explains, "After the Civil War, I worked on a barge on the Mississippi River. A woman was murdered in a town in Tennessee where it docked. The police suspected me. I didn't kill her, but I was a stranger and a drifter. They hunted me, and I barely managed to jump a train. It was a cold, rainy night, and all I had was the clothes on my back. There was another man riding in the freight car. He shared his food with me, and when the police stopped the train at the next station, he distracted them while I ran away. I don't know why he helped me. I never saw him again. This is my chance to repay the favor."

The story has the resonance of truth, but I think Pierce isn't above using his personal experience to manipulate me. "Do you really want to help us, or are you afraid we'll tell Reid something that will make him think you put Robin in the pond?"

Pierce acknowledges my accusation with a humorless smile. "I didn't kill Robin. When he was pulled up from the pond, I was as surprised as anyone. And you shouldn't look a gift horse in the mouth."

"Lady Alexandra thinks you did," I say.

Surprise raises Pierce's eyebrows.

"She accused you last night in the garden."

Pierce grimaces, enlightened and displeased. "So you were eavesdropping. If you stayed for the whole conversation, then you also heard me accuse Alexandra. I think she killed Robin."

"She has an alibi. She was with Tabitha. You haven't."

"You're wasting time. Reid will be here any minute. Do you want to go or not?"

As much as I'd like to evade Reid, I say, "No, thank you." I don't know that Pierce didn't murder the woman in America; I have only his word for it. Maybe he'll have the driver take Hugh and me to a remote place and kill us so we can't talk. At any rate, if we go on the lam, Reid will interpret it as evidence that we're guilty of the murders in the dinosaur park.

Pierce shrugs. "Suit yourself. By the way, Sir Gerald said to remind you to abide by the confidentiality agreement."

Dismay turns the food in my stomach to burning acid. "But this is no longer just a matter of who kidnapped Robin. Why doesn't Sir Gerald want Hugh and me to cooperate with Inspector Reid and tell him whatever we know?" I can't help hoping that if I cooperate with Reid's inquiry into Robin's death, he'll go easier on Hugh and me regarding the murders in the park. "Doesn't he want Robin's murderer caught?"

"Just keep quiet," Pierce says. "If you don't, you'll wish you'd accepted my offer."

As he opens the door, I say, "Wait. Please tell Sir Gerald I'm sorry I didn't find Robin before he died." I don't know whether I'll have a chance to tell him myself.

Pierce regards me with contemptuous mirth. "The police surgeon said Robin was in the pond for at least two weeks, probably since the night he was kidnapped. The cold water kept his body from decomposing. By the time Sir Gerald hired you, it was too late to save him. You were nothing but a waste of money."

He leaves before I can ask him if he was the one who broke into my trunk.

#

I stand watching the door, twisting my hands. My heartbeat accelerates as minutes tick by. I hear footsteps in the passage, then the door opens. I drop my hands, square my shoulders, and brace myself.

Reid strides in, and I glimpse two constables behind him before the door clicks shut. His narrow-eyed gaze surveys the room, and he chuckles. "Living in the lap of luxury, I see. Must be a cushy job, working for Sir Gerald."

The quality of his anger and hatred toward me has changed, as if his will has compressed them into a tight space within him. The possibility that he could explode at any moment is more frightening than his usual overt rage. I'm alone in my bedroom with my enemy, this man who has the power to hurt me in ways more personal than striking me. Resisting the impulse to cower, I glance around the room at vases and figurines, anything I could use to defend myself.

Reid smirks as if he knows what I'm thinking. He drags a fragile teak chair into the center of the room, away from potential weapons. "Sit down, Miss Bain."

I obey, knowing he could force me. I stare him in the eye, my courage fortified by my own hatred.

Reid pulls the red brocade armchair so close to me that when he sits, our knees touch. "How'd you and Staunton dupe Sir Gerald into hiring you?"

"I'm not allowed to say. I signed a confidentiality agreement." For the first time, I'm glad I did; it's an excuse behind which I can hide all manner of secrets. I mustn't tell him about the photograph I took in the dinosaur park or my search for my father.

"Fine." Reid's lack of objection makes me wary. "We'll talk about the murders in the park. They happened before you started working for Sir Gerald, so your agreement doesn't cover that."

A chill of apprehension runs through me. *How did he know?* I can't imagine that Sir Gerald told the police. Maybe it was somebody else from Mariner House? But there's another disturbing possibility. "Where is Hugh? What have you done to him?"

"Don't worry." Reid's unpleasant smile says he wants me to worry. "You can see him as soon as we're finished talking."

He also wants me to think Hugh spilled all the beans. I don't believe Hugh would have done it willingly. Panic creeps along my nerves.

"Why were you and Staunton following Noel Vaughn?" Reid asks.

I want to believe Reid doesn't already know the answer. Maybe Hugh didn't talk. But maybe he did, and Reid is checking his story. If I tell Reid about our case, maybe he'll see that Hugh and I had no reason to kill the couple and a jury would be unlikely to convict us; maybe he'll leave us alone. "His wife hired us because she thought he was cheating on her, and she wanted proof."

"So you spied on Vaughn for a couple of weeks." Reid names the places we followed Vaughn. "But he was a good boy."

No one except Hugh and I knew everywhere Vaughn went, except Vaughn himself; we never reported in that much detail to his wife. My fear burgeons because I think Hugh told Reid about the case for the same reason I'm telling him—to get him off our backs—and it didn't work. Cold perspiration dampens my armpits.

"Then you saw him with Ethel Norris at the dinosaur park. You photographed them in the act."

I'm frantic to know if Hugh is all right, desperate to escape whatever Reid has in store for me. "Yes. Then we went home."

Reid gives me a chastising look. "That's not what your partner says. Vaughn caught you spying. He was furious."

"Yes. He yelled at us. We left."

"You're leaving out the part where Vaughn chased you and Staunton. He tried to take your camera and smash the negative plate."

I stare, astonished. "*What?*"

Reid's teeth flash through his mustache in a wolfish grin. "So you hit Vaughn on the head with an iron bar. Ethel Norris started screaming. You strangled her to shut her up."

"That's not what happened!" Outrage fills me.

"It is, according to Staunton."

"He didn't say that! He wouldn't!" But I suppose that if he were subjected to torture, he would say anything to make it stop.

"I'll spell it out for you," Reid says. "Staunton is telling one story. If you want to tell a different one, here's your chance."

Now I see what Reid is doing. "You're trying to play Hugh and me against each other. It won't work." Even if Hugh crumbled under duress, even if he incriminated me, I shan't incriminate him. "We spied on Noel Vaughn, we took photographs, and we went home."

"Staunton sold you out. He doesn't deserve your loyalty." Reid's patronizing manner doesn't quite hide his impatience.

"And if I say Hugh is the murderer? Then what? You'll let me go?"

Reid smiles, shrugs, and spreads his hands, as if to say "*Yes, it's that simple*" without actually committing himself.

I shan't fall for that. "Hugh didn't kill those people, and neither did I."

Angry frustration shows through Reid's smile like fire through a window of a burning building. "Either Staunton goes down, or you do. It's your choice."

Folding my arms, I glare at him to hide my terror. I brace myself for curses, threats, and blows.

"I'll let you think it over," Reid says. "In the meantime, you can tell me what you've discovered at Mariner House."

Unbalanced by the sudden change of topic, I stammer, "The confidentiality agreement—"

"Ah, yes, the confidentiality agreement." Reid regards me with pity. "Your determination to protect Sir Gerald is admirable, but how much longer do you think he's going to protect you? You didn't solve the kidnapping. Robin is dead. You're no use to Sir Gerald. He'll cut you loose any minute now."

I press my lips together, afraid that I'll vomit, that Reid is right. Our time at Mariner House is running out, and the threat of Newgate looms.

"So." Reid's eyes twinkle; he perceives my thoughts. "Tell me about Sir Gerald's nearest and dearest. Who would you like to start with—Lady Alexandra, Tristan, or Olivia? John Pierce or Tabitha Jenkins?"

Comprehension rattles my already overtaxed nerves. Reid thinks Robin's kidnapping was an inside job, and he suspects members of the Mariner family. "You don't owe them anything," Reid says. "If they were in your position, they would rat on you quicker than I could count one, two, three."

He also aims to kill two birds with one stone. He wants to pin the dinosaur park murders on Hugh and me as well as solve Robin's murder, and he thinks I have information he needs. I'm reluctant to give up my information and not only because of the confidentiality agreement. I still believe that the same person who kidnapped Robin also committed the murders. Providing an alternative suspect in the murders might help me exonerate Hugh and myself, but I feel a certain loyalty to Sir Gerald as well as fear of his wrath. And Reid is capable of misinterpreting evidence and sending an innocent person to jail while the real criminal goes free. I hold my tongue.

"I'll make you a deal," Reid says. "You give me the dirt on the Mariner family, and here's what my report about the murders in the dinosaur park will say: Noel Vaughn and Ethel Norris attacked you and Staunton. There was a fight, and you two killed them in self-defense. You won't be charged with their murders, and I'll see that you don't even spend time in prison for obstructing justice."

It's a trick. He'll never let us go unpunished. "No," I say, stubborn even as my voice cracks.

Reid rises and stands over me, his gaze so hostile that I have to force myself to meet it. I smell his sweat, see his nostrils flare. My heart pounds, and my stomach churns.

"You have until tomorrow morning to change your mind." His voice is tight with his effort to control his temper. "If you don't, the deal is off the table, and I'll see you in Newgate."

The door slams behind him, and the key turns in the lock.

19

The roar of a crowd and the tramping of footsteps penetrate the darkness under the black cloth that hangs from the back of my camera and covers my head. The image in the viewfinder is a blur of motion—a parade of men, their faces smeared with soot. They carry burning torches and wave signs. I can smell the smoke, but I can't read the messages painted on the signs or understand the words the men are chanting. Effigies with wax heads, skewered on pikes, whirl above the parade. Along the roadside are mobs of people yelling and shaking their fists. They swarm into the parade, and it explodes into a brawl. I swivel the camera on its tripod, looking for my father.

Bricks and bottles fly through the air. A baby's high-pitched crying rises above the noise. Police constables invade the scene in the viewfinder. Fear assails me because they're after my father. I crank the bellows of my camera, trying to bring the scene into focus. The constables shout as they beat someone with their nightsticks. I can't see who, but I know it's my father; I can hear his pleas for mercy through the clamor of cursing. Desperate to rescue him, I fling the black drape off my head.

The marchers, police, the mob, and my camera are gone. I'm alone in a garden at night. Marble statues pose amid flowerbeds. Smoke veils the moon, and the woods in the distance are on fire. I hear the baby crying. It's Robin Mariner, calling my name. I turn to see the ivy-covered brick wall of a mansion. A ladder leans against the wall beneath a window on the second floor. Robin's cries emanate from the window. I grasp the ladder, lift my skirts, and climb. At the top, I crawl through the window into a dim room that's empty except for a crib. There lies baby Robin, swaddled in a blanket. I pick him up, and he cries as I carry him along a dark passage and down a flight of stairs. Something falls from his blanket, a little toy rabbit with white plush fur and pink glass eyes. I hear footsteps racketing down the stairs behind me and angry shouts.

They're after me.

Robin vanishes from my grasp. I'm riding sidesaddle on a horse through misty woods. I clutch the reins as the horse gallops faster, too fast. A gunshot blasts nearby. Hugh shouts, and I smell the smoke from the burnt powder. Olivia, on horseback, bursts upon me. I'm jolted off my mount; I'm falling.

Even as I scream, my feet land on solid ground. I'm standing beside a pond that gleams silver under a gray sky. People from the march wave fists, signs, and torches at me; they shout threats. My hands are yanked behind my back. Inspector Reid's voice says, "You're under arrest."

I can't see Reid or Robin Mariner, who's still calling to me. Near the pond lies the drenched, lifeless body of a little girl with red braids—Ellen Casey. Hard, cold steel cuffs lock around my wrists. I raise my eyes skyward in hope of divine salvation.

Two great winged beasts—each with the body of a lizard, a serpent's neck, and a beak full of sharp teeth—swoop down upon me. Flames char their ribbed yellow wings; smoke darkens the sky. I scream as Robin cries, the crowd hurls bottles, and glass shatters.

Coughs erupt from me, convulse my body, and waken me from the nightmare. Every breath I take wheezes painfully. Thick, hot, bitter air burns my lungs. The room glows with a hazy, flickering orange light. I'm choking on smoke, lying surrounded by flames that devour the white silk canopy over my bed. Tangled in the heavy white quilt, I kick until I'm free of it and roll off the bed, landing with a painful thud. Flames snake across the Chinese carpet toward me as I cough and wheeze, too breathless to move. My vision blackens at the edges.

"Sarah, Sarah!" It's not Robin calling me; the voice is deeper and louder now. It belongs to Mick. The window shatters. Cold, damp, fresh air revives my fading consciousness even as the flames around me blaze brighter. Mick crawls through the broken window. He hurries to the door and tries the knob; it's locked. He bangs on the door and yells, "Fire! Help!"

Nobody comes. Mick runs to me and lifts me up. I've never been happier to see anyone, but I fear for his life as well as mine. "Mick, why didn't you go home?" I gasp the words out between coughs.

"Good thing for you, I didn't." Staggering under my weight, he carries me to the window. "I been hidin' in the woods. After it got dark, I snuck back to the house to look for you and Hugh. I saw the fire."

"Where's Hugh?"

"I dunno. We'll find him later." Coughing and gasping, Mick heaves me onto the windowsill. "We gotta get out."

I'm lying on my stomach with my legs dangling into the cold night and the rest of me still in the flaming room. Mick pushes my hand out the window and clamps it around something hard, thin, and knobby. "Climb down the vines."

"I have to save my cameras!"

"There's no time."

I slither down the brick wall, my fingers clutching at the ivy, my feet scrambling for toeholds. My eyes sting and water from the smoke. My vision is blurred, and I can barely see Mick in the window above me, silhouetted by the flames behind him. The ivy leaves are wet and slippery, and the stems I'm clutching peel away from the bricks. I scream as I fall.

A bush catches me in a nest of sharp twigs. Mick shinnies down the wall, agile as a monkey, and lifts me out of the bush. We collapse on wet grass. I'm exhausted, my skin sore from scratches, and my sprained ankle throbs, but gulps of fresh air cleanse the smoke from my lungs, and the coughing subsides.

"We gotta get help before the house burns down," Mick says.

Clambering to my feet, I see another second-story window lit by flames. The room must be two doors from mine. "Look!" I point. "Hugh is in there!"

I don't know how I know, and Mick doesn't ask. He runs toward the window. Panting, I hobble after him. The fog is so thick that I can't see the far end of the house. A man suddenly appears out of the fog and darkness, blocks our path, and says, "Who goes there?"

He's one of Sir Gerald's guards. He carries a rifle in a sling over his shoulder.

"Fire!" Mick shouts, pointing.

The guard runs to the house and unlocks a door. Then we're hurrying up a flight of dimly lit back stairs, bursting into the second-floor passage, which is hazy with the smoke seeping out from beneath the doors of my room and Hugh's. The guard rings a mechanical bell that's mounted on the wall, and its loud clangs echo through the house. Suddenly, the passage is full of guards and police constables. Servants come lugging pails. Mick and I run to Hugh's room and bang on the door, shouting, "Hugh!"

There's no response. A guard pushes us aside, unlocks the door, and opens it. A blast of heat, smoke, and firelight sends us reeling away. The carpet is a sea of crackling flames around the bed where Hugh lies, his eyes closed and mouth open, veiled by smoke. Horrified, I lunge toward Hugh, but Mick pulls me back. Servants dash pails of water on the burning carpet and drench the bed. Constables rush in and carry Hugh out. Mick and I follow them to another room, where they lay Hugh on the four-poster bed. Motionless in his dark-blue silk pajamas, Hugh is as limp as a rag doll, his face unnaturally pink. I touch his cheek. It's hot from the fire. The constables open the windows to let in fresh air. I can't see Hugh's chest rise or fall or hear any breath from his parted lips.

"Hugh!" I cry in terror.

Mick grabs Hugh by the shoulders, shakes him, and yells his name. Hugh stiffens as though electrocuted. His mouth sucks air with a rasping, squealing sound. He begins to cough so violently that his body heaves up from the bed. Mick and I sob in relief while the constables haul Hugh into a sitting position and pound on his back. He gasps, retches, and hacks up phlegm.

"God, I have the mother of all headaches," he says in a hoarse voice; his green eyes are watery and bloodshot. "What the hell happened?"

"That's what I want to know," says John Pierce.

Now I notice the other people in the room, which is furnished like a boudoir in the palace of Versailles with ornate gold furniture, porcelain vases, and other art objects. Pierce, Tristan, Olivia, Lady Alexandra, and Tabitha hover by a painted mural that depicts ladies in white wigs and Marie Antoinette–style gowns playing tag in a formal garden. They're all fully dressed, all wide awake. As they regard Hugh, Mick, and me with consternation, I become aware that I'm in my white cotton nightgown, my hair hangs in two frizzy braids, and my feet are bare. My heart is still pounding from residual terror; I'm still shaken by our close call.

"Miss Bain's and Lord Hugh's rooms caught on fire," a constable explains.

"How did the fires start?" Tristan asks. He's looking everywhere but at Hugh, whose gaze is riveted on Tristan.

"They must have left candles burning and fallen asleep," the constable says.

"No, I didn't!" I've never done such a careless thing in my life, and I'm horrified that the police think I almost burned Mariner House down.

"Neither did I," Hugh says, gasping. "And even if I had, wouldn't it seem strange that Sarah did it at the same time?"

"Them fires was no accident," Mick says. "When I broke into Miss Sarah's room, I smelled kerosene. Somebody musta poured it under the door."

I was too preoccupied with saving myself and Hugh to wonder how the fires started or why only in our rooms. I stare at Mick, astonished.

"That's a serious accusation," Pierce says coldly.

"There was no kerosene smell in either room," the constable says. The other policemen mutter in agreement.

"That's because it burned away before you got your fat arses over here!" Mick says.

"Watch your mouth, boy!" the constable says.

Olivia smirks as if she finds the situation amusing. Lady Alexandra covers her nose with her hand and says, "The smoke is making me ill." Tabitha, meek and worried, accompanies her out of the room.

Mick turns to me. "Miss Sarah, somebody in this house tried to burn you and Hugh to death!"

Wariness appears on the faces of Pierce, Olivia, and Tristan. I glance at a porcelain clock on the bureau: it's two thirty. What were they doing up so late?

"That's enough," the constable says to Mick, then turns to Sir Gerald's guards. "Lord Hugh can stay here, but we need someplace else to put Miss Bain."

I clutch Hugh's hand and say, "I'm not leaving him!"

"Neither am I," Mick says.

"Where is Inspector Reid?" I ask. Although he wouldn't jump to take my side, surely he won't ignore the possibility of arson.

"He's off duty for the night," the constable says. "His orders were to keep you two separated."

"He wants us hanged for murder," I say. "If we're burned to death first, he won't thank you."

"Good comeback, Sarah," Hugh says with a hint of his usual humor.

The constable looks weary, harassed. "I'll put our men on guard outside your doors."

"Like we should trust you coppers," Mick says, "after you let Jack the Ripper get away with killin' six women."

The police glower at Mick; their failure to catch the Ripper is still a sensitive spot. I say, "Sir Gerald should be the one to settle this. Where is he?"

"Daddy went to town to arrange Robin's funeral." Olivia sounds put out because her father deserted her in favor of what she considers trivial business. "He's staying at his London flat."

So Sir Gerald is the only Mariner household member who wasn't home when the fires started.

"I'm in charge while my father is gone. Let them stay together," Tristan says to the constable. "Tell Inspector Reid that I'll take responsibility." He speaks in the same detached manner as he did after he shot Hugh.

"Very well," the constable says, glad to have the decision taken out of his hands.

Tristan leaves the room with Olivia. Neither of them looks at Hugh, Mick, or me. John Pierce scrutinizes us with narrow, hostile eyes before he too departs.

#

I'm freezing in my thin nightgown, but I can't close the window because Hugh needs fresh air. Before the police lock us in the room, I persuade them to let the servants bring our baggage and find spare clothes for Mick, whose own clothes are wet and dirty from hiding in the woods. My wardrobe and Hugh's arrive saturated with smoke but intact. My leather trunk, satchel, and pocketbook protected the miniature camera, lenses, the photograph of my father, and other articles inside them, but my large camera and my enlarger didn't fare as well. Their cases are charred and water damaged, and their lenses are cracked. I'm so upset, I have to remind myself that we're lucky to be alive.

While I tuck Hugh into bed, Mick goes in the marble-and-gold bathroom to put on his clean, dry clothes. When it's my turn for the bathroom, I run hot water in the tub, undress, look in the mirror, and wince at my hollow, bloodshot eyes and the red scratches on my skin. I soak until the water cools, then dress, braid my hair, and find Hugh and Mick asleep in the bed. I leave one gas light burning and sit in a white-and-gold silk armchair to guard Hugh and Mick, but I'm so tired that I doze until a knock at the door rouses me.

According to the clock on the mantle, it's five twenty in the morning. A constable lets in Olivia, to my surprise. She brings a teapot, cups, and a covered platter on a tray. She whispers, "I thought you and your friends might be hungry."

"Thank you. That's very kind of you." I am grateful; we could probably starve as far as anyone else in Mariner House is concerned, but her kindness seems out of character.

Even as I suspect her of ulterior motives, she sets the tray on a table and says, "Can I talk to you?" She points to the bathroom.

It's not wise to be alone with a person who might have tried to burn me to death, but surely she wouldn't hurt me while the constable is outside, and I'm interested to know what she wants. I join Olivia in the bathroom and close the door. She perches on lid of the latrine, I on the edge of the tub. She looks tired and pale, but her eyes spark with nervous energy.

"I came to tell you that Mick is right—somebody set those fires," she says.

Surprise jolts me because she didn't say so earlier. "Who?"

"First, you have to promise you'll tell Inspector Reid."

"Why don't you tell him yourself?"

Olivia fidgets with her hair, which is in wild, crackling disarray. "Because Daddy ordered everyone not to talk to the police."

I wonder again why he's not cooperating with them. "Why don't you tell your father, then? I should expect he'd want to know who set fire to his house."

"Because he won't want to hear." Olivia pauses, draws a breath, then releases the words on a forlorn sigh. "Because it was Alexandra."

I've heard so many stories since I came to Mariner House that I won't take this one without a grain of salt. "How do you know?"

"Before the fires started, I happened to look out my window, and I saw Alexandra hurrying toward the house. She was carrying what I thought was a basket. I wondered what she was doing out so late. Now I know it was a can of kerosene. She must have been fetching it from the shed." When I don't reply, Olivia looks wounded. "Don't you believe me?"

I counter with a question of my own. "You don't like your stepmother, do you?"

Olivia shrugs. "No. I admit it. But why should I like her? She doesn't like me. She acts as if I don't exist. It's been that way since she married Daddy."

Come to think of it, I've never seen Olivia and Alexandra exchange a word or even a glance.

"I was thirteen. I was at boarding school in France when Daddy sent for me. I was so excited." Olivia's eyes sparkle with remembered happiness. "But when I got home, he said he was getting married the next day. He only brought me home because if his daughter wasn't at the wedding, it wouldn't look right." Olivia sounds as disappointed as she must have felt. "I didn't meet Alexandra until the wedding. She barely spoke to me. Daddy was so busy showing her off to everybody, he didn't pay any attention to me either. I was so upset that I drank too much champagne. I got drunk and sick, and Tristan had to take care of me. Afterward, Daddy said I was a disgrace and sent me back to school. When Alexandra had a baby, it was Tristan who wrote to tell me. Daddy let me come home for Robin's christening, and then he sent me away again." Olivia is crying now; tears redden her eyes.

I can't help feeling sorry for Olivia. She suffers from her father's abandonment year after year, like a chronic illness, while for me the loss of my father was a brutal but swift cut, like an amputation. But I still don't trust her. "So you wouldn't mind getting your stepmother in trouble." Maybe she's trying to incriminate Lady Alexandra and get herself off the hook for Robin's murder as well as the fires. Maybe she thinks that if Lady Alexandra and Robin were both gone, she might regain Sir Gerald's love. "Why should I believe you?"

"Because I wouldn't say it unless it were true." Olivia sniffles and wipes her eyes with the back of her hand. "It would upset Daddy. He doesn't want to think Alexandra is bad. And I don't want Daddy to be upset."

"Why do you care how he feels? He treats you so cruelly." Even as I speak, although it's true, I feel uncomfortable about criticizing Sir Gerald.

Olivia regards me with surprise. "Because I love him."

It hasn't escaped my notice that I'm a fine one to talk. My father is by all accounts a rapist and murderer, and I still love and want to protect him. "If I tell Inspector Reid that you've accused Lady Alexandra of setting the fires, Sir Gerald is sure to hear about it."

A cunning smile brightens Olivia's face. "You could say that *you* saw her with the kerosene can."

"You're asking me to lie." I'm indignant, as though lying isn't a habit for me.

"It wouldn't be entirely a lie. Alexandra tried to kill you and Lord Hugh. What difference does it make who saw her?"

"Inspector Reid would be more likely to believe you than me. You should tell him that you saw Lady Alexandra."

"Sarah?" Mick whispers outside the bathroom door. "Who are you talkin' to?"

"Oh, forget I said anything," Olivia says, peeved. "But if Alexandra tries to kill you again, and she succeeds, it's your own fault." She flounces out of the bathroom and bedroom. Mick is munching on biscuits and cheese from the tray she brought. Hugh awakens with a fit of coughing. After it subsides, he asks, "What's going on?"

I pour tea for us and relay Olivia's story. The food and the hot, fragrant India tea restore my strength and lift my spirits, but I can't forget that Hugh and I are murder suspects or that the day will bring Inspector Reid back to interrogate us. I don't know where I stand with Barrett, and we're trapped in Mariner House with an arsonist.

"I believe Olivia," Mick says. "Lady A tried to kill you and Hugh because she thinks you know too much."

"I'm sure someone thinks so. It could have been any of the others," I say.

Hugh looks skeptical. "Supposing we did know who the kidnapper is, wouldn't whoever it is think we'd have told Sir Gerald already?"

"Maybe he thinks we're stringing Sir Gerald along, taking his money for as long as we can," I say.

"Yeah, and our time is about up," Mick says.

"Well, here's more evidence that it's not Tristan," Hugh says. "He didn't let the police separate us."

"Maybe he wants to keep us together so he can kill us all at once," I say.

Hugh slams his teacup down on the bedside table. "Oh, for Christ's sake, stop making up reasons to blame Tristan for everything!"

I hate to resume our quarrel, but I have to say, "He shot you. He could have set the fires."

"So could Olivia. She knocked you off your horse. And she's just come to you with a story that a blind fool could see is an attempt to send you down a garden path."

Mick crumbles his biscuit, uneasily caught in the middle. "It weren't Sir G. He ain't home. My money's on Lady A."

I haven't the heart to remind him about objectivity, for I'm relieved that Sir Gerald has an alibi. "It could have been Tabitha or Mr. Pierce," I say for the sake of keeping the peace. After our brush with death, my friendship with Hugh seems doubly precious.

"Well, whoever tried to kill you must be real disappointed you're still alive," Mick says. "We better find out who it is before they try again."

20

The sound of men's voices in the passage wakes me. I sit up straight in the chair in which I dozed off. Hugh and Mick are fast asleep. Sunlight and cold air stream through the open window. As the doorknob turns, I jump from my chair, crying, "Hugh! Mick! Wake up!"

Mick, instantly alert, leaps from the bed. Hugh stretches, coughs, and groans before he swings his legs over the side of the bed and shakily stands. The door opens, and Inspector Reid strides in. He looks so furious that I'm afraid he's going to arrest Hugh and me. Mick puts himself between us and Reid, spreads his arms, and says, "You ain't takin' them anywhere."

"You're right. I'm not." Reid jerks his chin at Hugh and me. "You're free to go."

My relief quickly crumbles under a sense that things are far from good. Hugh says, "Not that I want to look a gift horse in the mouth, but how come? Yesterday you were so sure that we were murderers."

Reid's mustache is straggly at the ends, as if he's been gnawing them in frustration. "You've got an alibi."

"Who is it?" I ask, hardly daring to believe.

"A grounds keeper at the Crystal Palace. He was in the dinosaur park that day and saw you and Staunton leave. He also saw Noel Vaughn and Ethel Norris. They were still alive when you left."

I understand why Reid is furious; he thought he'd solved the crime and was about to get his revenge on us, and now he has to start over from scratch. I'm amazed that there was yet another person we didn't notice at the park.

Delighted, Hugh grasps Reid's hand and shakes it. "You proved we're innocent. Thank you from the bottom of my heart."

"Don't thank me," Reid says, pulling his hand away and wiping it on his coat. "Thank Miss Bain's sweetheart." He aims a dirty look at me. "Yesterday PC Barrett sneaked over to the Crystal Palace. He beat the bushes until he found you an alibi."

I'm thrilled to learn that Barrett didn't forsake me.

"Don't be such a bad sport, man," Hugh says. "This witness could be a lucky break for you too. Maybe he can lead you to Robin's kidnapper. Did he see the ransom exchange?"

"Oh, now you want to talk about the kidnapping." Reid grins as if he's maneuvered us into a corner. "So tell me what you know about the Mariner family."

We're silent, bound by the confidentiality agreement and loath to trust Reid.

"Changed your mind? Well, in that case, pack up and go home."

Mick plants his feet wide and his hands on his hips. "You can't kick us out. We're working for Sir Gerald."

Reid sets his sights on Hugh and me. "If you know what's good for you, you'll hand in your resignation. Didn't you almost get burned to death last night? And if that's not enough reason"—he jabs his finger at our faces—"if you poke your nose in my investigation again, not even God will be able to save you." He storms out of the room.

Hugh and I are speechless for a moment, intimidated.

"We're not gonna knuckle under to him, are we?" Mick asks.

"I should say not." Hugh coughs strenuously, then says, "We have to find out who killed Robin."

Mick grins. "Yeah!"

I sense that justice for Robin isn't Hugh's only concern; he wants to stay at the estate so that he can be near Tristan and prove that he isn't the kidnapper and killer.

"First, a hot bath to steam my lungs clean." Hugh shuts himself in the bathroom.

"Keep an eye on him," I tell Mick. "Don't leave him alone."

Opening the door, I find myself face-to-face with Tristan Mariner, his hand raised to knock. He drops his hand and steps backward, alarmed to see me. I shut the door and advance on him, forcing him to back away down the passage.

"Stay away from Hugh," I say. "You've done him enough harm."

"Miss Bain." Although he's dressed in full clerical garb, Tristan seems ill at ease, bereft of his usual haughty dignity. "It's you I came to see. Please allow me to speak with you."

We stop at the end of the passage, which is deserted except for the two of us. "I suppose you're going to ask me not to tell anyone that I caught you and Hugh together?"

He bites his lip, and his handsome face flushes, but he holds my gaze. "Whether you tell or not is up to you. But whatever you do, you should consider the consequences."

"Are you threatening me?" After last night, I'm afraid of Tristan and everyone else in Mariner House, but anger makes me bold. "Did you set the fires? Did you try to kill Hugh and me? Are you here to tell me that if I don't keep quiet, you'll try again?"

"No. I didn't. I came to talk to you about my sister."

I frown, surprised because I evidently read him wrong. "What about Olivia?"

"I apologize for her behavior the day we went riding."

"You needn't," I say, wondering what he really wants. "Olivia's the one who knocked mc off my horse."

"She didn't mean to hurt you."

"That you know of."

Tristan rakes his hand through his black hair. Not even after I caught him with Hugh did he seem as distraught as now. "Olivia can't help how she is. She's had a difficult life." Before I can say I'm aware of that because of what she told me last night, Tristan says, "Her mother was mentally unstable."

Like mother, like daughter.

"Vittoria had fits and delusions. She once attacked the conductor at the opera house because she thought he was trying to murder her. My father didn't know how serious her condition was until after they were married. He thought she was just a volatile, temperamental opera singer. But she became worse after Olivia was born." Tristan relates this story in the grave, hushed tone that I imagine he would use during confession. "When Olivia was three, my father had to put Vittoria in an asylum. That's where Vittoria committed suicide."

I remember Olivia at dinner, saying her mother had killed herself with poison.

"Olivia had been our father's pet, but after her mother died, he couldn't bear to look at her. I think her mother was the only woman he ever truly loved, and Olivia is so much like her. He thinks she inherited her bad blood. He left her in the care of nurses and governesses, who let her do whatever she wanted just to keep her quiet. I tried to comfort her and guide her, but I'm twelve years older, and I was mostly away at school, then the army, then the seminary. She misbehaves to get our father's attention. It's the only way she knows how."

Tristan's expression softens with pity and tenderness for Olivia. He suddenly seems more human, less formidable. I remember that he too lost his mother, and I suppose the tragedy they have in common bound him and Olivia together despite the difference in their ages. I wish I'd had an older brother to protect me and care for me after my father disappeared. My antipathy toward Tristan lessens as I perceive something of what Hugh must see in him—compassion and generosity behind his arrogance. But I can't quite bring myself to trust him beyond doubt.

"Why are you telling me this?"

"Because I don't want you to think Olivia is an evil person," Tristan says. "She isn't. She's just immature and reckless and unhappy."

Maybe Tristan isn't evil either. That Hugh fell in love with him must mean he has virtues besides his looks. But I also wonder if he knows that he and Olivia are suspects in Robin's murder and he's told me these things to make himself appear noble and innocent and her deranged and guilty. "Or maybe you want me to believe the exact opposite of what you said."

He bends a long, somber look on me. "Just remember what I said, Miss Bain. Whatever you do, consider the consequences. And you should warn your friends."

He strides away down the passage, leaving me to wonder again whether he just threatened to kill us.

I go looking for Barrett and find him in my burned room. There, the smoke smell is strong, pungent, and sickening. The drenched, soggy ashes of the Chinese carpet lie on scorched floorboards. The bed is black, burned down to the mattress stuffing, and the wallpaper hangs in charred tatters. Barrett stands by the window, whose curtains are completely burned, gazing outside. My heart leaps; I'm so glad to see him. At the sound of my footsteps squishing on the wet floor, he turns. His expression is tight-lipped, unfriendly. He raises his eyebrows, waiting for me to speak first.

My spirits descend. "Thank you for finding an alibi for Hugh and me."

"I was just doing my job." Barrett's tone is as cold as his gaze.

I feel guilty because I lied to him. I love him so much, and I can't bear for us to be at odds. "Please don't be angry." My emotions are still fragile from my brush with death. Tears sting my smoke-irritated eyes.

"Why shouldn't I be angry? You say you're going to Nottingham to visit a sick friend, and then you turn up here. How am I supposed to feel?"

"I'm sorry. Sir Gerald—"

"Shove his confidentiality agreement! Who's more important to you—Sir Gerald or me?"

Although dismayed that he should question my love for him, I remember how hesitant I was to express it. "You are, of course."

Barrett narrows his eyes in disbelief. "But you knew that if you took the job, you would have to lie to me, and you took it anyway."

He's right, but I leap to my own defense. "It wasn't like that. When Hugh and I met Sir Gerald, things happened so fast, I barely had time to think."

"You had time to think about the murders in the dinosaur park. You told me that you just happened onto the crime scene. Inspector Reid thought I'd known all along that you and Hugh were there and I was covering for you, but I was completely blindsided!"

Imaging his shock and mortification, I feel terrible. "I'm sorry. Hugh and I thought it wouldn't be fair to Mrs. Vaughn if we told the police about her husband." My excuse is just a cover for the real reason I didn't tell Barrett why I went back to the park.

"The fact is, there's always somebody or something more important than being honest with me." Barrett grimaces in self-disgust. "I should have known. Last fall you kept secrets from me, and I'm a fool for believing you wouldn't do it again just because we're— " He throws up his hands. "Hell, I don't know what we are."

Fear seeps into the well of my guilt. Have I offended him so badly that he no longer loves me? But I'm also angry because he won't try to see my side, because my love for him gives him the power to hurt me, and because I know that his every complaint against me is justified.

"I'm sorry I lied to you." I'm genuinely remorseful. "Please forgive me." I try to sound dignified instead of as if I'm begging.

Barrett regards me as if I've missed a point that should have been obvious. "It's not a matter of you apologizing and me forgiving. It's this." He grabs my shoulders and turns me to face the drenched wreckage. "You and Hugh took a job that you had no business taking. You got in over your heads with somebody dangerous." His hard, hectoring tone batters me like a club. "You could have ended up burned to death in that bed. And you don't understand that the reason I'm so angry is that I care about you!"

I pull away and face him. His eyes shine with tears. My own anger melts, but as I reach for him, he backs away, hands raised.

"Don't try to get around me by making love to me."

"I'm not!" My cheeks burn with embarrassment that he would think me so devious. "I just want us to be the way we were before."

"Then be honest. Tell me everything."

Even though I'm aware that our relationship is at stake, I hesitate. My habit of secrecy is of much longer duration than just the six days since I signed the confidentiality agreement and more entrenched than my trust in Barrett.

"For God's sake, Sarah!" Exasperation raises Barrett's voice. "You don't owe Sir Gerald or his family your loyalty. One of them tried to kill you and Hugh."

His common sense pierces my defenses, erodes my justification for keeping him in the dark.

"Why are you protecting them?" Barrett looks thunderstruck as an answer occurs to him. "Is it Sir Gerald? Are you and he—?"

"No!" I'm horrified that he would think it, ashamed because my feelings for Sir Gerald aren't entirely neutral. Now I have to come clean, or Barrett won't believe that I've been faithful to him. "All right. I'll tell you everything. But not here."

#

After I don my coat and hat, Barrett and I walk down the grand staircase. I don't need my crutch, but my ankle is still sore. The foyer is dim, its windows shuttered and the chandelier swathed in black crape. Candles burning in silver candelabra provide the only light. Inside the parlor, the heavy curtains are closed. The mirrors, paintings, and mantels are also swathed with black crape, and more candles flicker. People dressed in black surround a little white coffin. The sweet, heavy scent of roses and lilies mingles with the smell of burning wax. Quiet weeping and murmured condolences echo. Servants wearing black armbands usher in more black-garbed ladies and gentlemen through the front door. Carriages are lined up along the driveway as other visitors arrive. It's Robin Mariner's wake.

Barrett leads me outside. The sun is a hazy white globe floating in the chill mist. I can still smell smoke from the fires. We walk in silence across the garden. Barrett's profile is like stone; he doesn't touch me or look at me. An eternity separates us from our last time in my bed. How I regret taking the job with Sir Gerald! Robin was already dead then; Hugh and I couldn't have saved him. I also regret spying on Noel Vaughn because if Hugh and I hadn't been in the park that day, we wouldn't be in this fix now, and I wouldn't have learned that my father probably murdered Ellen Casey.

We descend the hill to a section of the grounds I've not seen before. In a woodland clearing stands a folly with a circular stone base enclosed by fluted white columns, topped with a round dome, and surrounded by grass in which daffodils and hyacinths bloom. Barrett stoically waits for me to speak.

I take a deep breath, as if preparing to dive into shark-infested waters. After I tell Barrett about the toy rabbit dropped on the stairs the night of Robin's kidnapping, I reveal everything I've learned about Tristan and Olivia Mariner, Lady Alexandra, John Pierce, Tabitha Jenkins, and Raphael DeQuincey. I include my theory that something was wrong with Robin and his parents covered it up. Barrett listens intently; his stern expression gives no hint of his thoughts. Unnerved by his scrutiny, I describe Tristan's nighttime trip to the pond and my conversations with Lady Alexandra, Pierce, Olivia, and Tristan. Guilt needles my conscience as I think of Hugh. When I'm finished, I feel lighter, euphoric—as if I've cast off a heavy burden I'd been carrying—but sick too, as if I've gorged on poisonous fruit.

Barrett doesn't speak, and his expression doesn't change. The distance between us is greater, not less. My sick feeling worsens. "What are you going to do now?"

"I'll tell Inspector Reid what you told me. He'll take it from there." Barrett's aloof manner says he hasn't forgiven me. "You and Hugh and Mick had better go home before Reid catches you hanging around here." He starts to walk back toward the mansion.

We can't part like this. I'm afraid but also angry. After I've betrayed Sir Gerald's trust, broken my own word, and jeopardized my friendship with Hugh, Barrett is brushing me off. "Wait! I told you everything. Why are you still mad?"

Barrett turns on me, his eyes so full of revulsion that I let go of him and step backward. "'Everything?'" He shakes his head. "I think there's a lot you left out."

Guilt roils my stomach because he's right. I feign innocence. "What else could there be?"

"Let's start with why you went back to the dinosaur park the day after you spied on Noel Vaughn and Ethel Norris."

I can't tell Barrett that I went to look for my father. He would have to tell Inspector Reid, and Reid would launch a manhunt for Benjamin Bain, who is not only the fugitive prime suspect in Ellen Casey's murder but a possible witness to the dinosaur park murders and the collection of Robin Mariner's ransom.

"I went back to photograph the dinosaur models."

Scorn twists Barrett's mouth; he doesn't believe me. "How did you and Hugh get Sir Gerald to hire you?"

"Hugh's father knows Sir Gerald. He introduced us." That, at least, is the truth.

"And Sir Gerald just up and decided to hire two amateur detectives with no credentials?"

It sounds preposterous, but I say, "Yes." I can't tell Barrett about the photograph of my father. And now I become aware of another, more personal reason that's holding my tongue. Barrett has been a policeman much longer than he's been my lover, and he might think I'm contaminated by my father's crimes—spoiled goods, unworthy of his respect or affection.

The skepticism in Barrett's gaze turns to disappointment laced with pain. "Oh, Sarah."

He gave me a chance to make matters right between us. I lied, and he knows it. But I couldn't have done otherwise. Twisting my hands, with my stomach churning and a craven, beseeching smile on my face, I wait for his response.

"I can't do this anymore." Barrett's voice wobbles. "I love you, but I can't trust you, and I can't be with somebody I can't trust."

Alarm seizes my heart. I move toward Barrett, arms outstretched. "Please don't do this!"

The resolve in his expression halts me. "It's over, Sarah."

My pride demands that I accept his decision with dignity, but my anguish is so great that I can't stifle my sobs. Now that I've finally lost him, I realize how much I love him—much more than I ever thought.

Barrett regards me with a mixture of pity and resentment. "Why are you so upset? You never really wanted to marry me. You could've been honest about that, if nothing else."

Then he's gone.

21

I want to lie down on the ground amid the daffodils and hyacinths, bury my face in the cool grass, and mourn. My fear that every man I love will abandon me is reality. Because I dared to search for my father, he's more lost to me than ever, my memory of him tainted by what I've learned about his past. And my own recklessness and dishonesty have driven Barrett away.

But I can't give in to the impulse, for I won't be the only person to suffer from the consequences of my actions. I must warn the others. I run toward the mansion, ignoring the pain in my ankle, wheezing from the smoke that still permeates my lungs. When I burst into the room where I left Mick and Hugh, Mick is finishing the cheese from the tray Olivia brought last night, and Hugh is buttoning the collar of his clean white shirt, his hair damp from his bath. They look at me in surprise.

"Sarah, what's happened?" Hugh says.

I lean on the closed door, as if to keep out the horsemen of the apocalypse. "I told Barrett."

"Told him what?" Mick says.

"Everything we've learned about the Mariners."

The concern in Hugh's expression turns to disbelief. "Including Tristan?"

I nod unhappily.

"You know how I feel about him, and you threw him to the wolves!"

"I'm sorry. I didn't want to." I try to reason away my guilt. "But we couldn't go on protecting him or the others."

"Not after one of them tried to set you on fire," Mick says, although obviously reluctant to take sides. "She's right. If she hadn't told Barrett, I would've."

Hugh regards Mick with disgust. "And here I thought you were the last person to condone snitching to the police."

Here comes a quarrel that could carry us beyond reconciliation, and Barrett must be reporting my information to Reid at this very moment.

Mick takes command. "No more time to talk. We gotta run." He grabs my satchel and pocketbook, thrusts them at me, and tosses Hugh his coat and hat.

"I have to pack my things first," Hugh says.

"Better to get out with the clothes on your back than stick around for the shit to hit the wind," says Mick.

I abandon my big camera and my enlarger; they're probably unfixable. As we head down the passage toward the door to the back stairs, two police constables call, "Stop!"

Inspector Reid must have sent them after us. As Mick hurries us down the grand staircase, loud, angry voices erupt from the parlor. Servants gathered by its doorway peer inside. We join them, like gawkers irresistibly drawn to a train crash. The guests at the wake have retreated to the perimeter of the candle-lit room. In the center, near Robin's coffin, Lady Alexandra stands facing Inspector Reid, Barrett, and two constables.

"You've no right to interrupt the vigil for my son," she says in her clear, ringing stage voice. She's dressed in opulent mourning garb—a full-skirted black gown trimmed with crape ruffles, a sheer black veil over her blonde hair, and a heavy, gleaming jet necklace.

"I have every right," Inspector Reid says in his most authoritative tone. "This is a murder investigation, and I'm in charge."

I glimpse Lottie among the servants and Tabitha Jenkins and Raphael DeQuincey among the guests; they're watching the drama with rapt attention.

"I refuse to talk to you without my husband present," Lady Alexandra says.

Barrett spots me, and his gaze briefly meets mine. His expression is bland, impersonal. My chest aches as if my heart is physically broken.

"Where is Sir Gerald?" Reid says. "I've some questions for him too."

It's clear that Barrett has told Reid what I said, with the result that Reid has turned the focus of the police's investigation onto the Mariner family.

"My husband is in town," Lady Alexandra says.

"Well, then, you can cool your heels until he gets back." Reid addresses the constables: "Take Lady Alexandra and Miss Jenkins to their rooms. Lock them in."

Tabitha clutches her throat; her eyes widen with fright. Lady Alexandra huffs with indignation.

The front door opens, and two constables enter the foyer with Tristan and Olivia. The siblings are in coats and hats; Tristan carries two suitcases, and his face is dark with anger above his white collar. Olivia's hands are cuffed behind her back, and she struggles against the constable who pushes her into the parlor while the other constable escorts Tristan.

"We caught them at the train station," the constable tells Reid as Olivia tries to kick him.

"Let me go, you bastard!" Olivia shrieks.

Tristan notices Hugh. Emotion flashes in his eyes before he averts them. Hugh keeps his expression carefully blank, but I hear him draw a tremulous breath.

"Well, well," Reid says with sardonic amusement. "They tried to fly the coop."

"Not so," Tristan says coldly. "I was escorting Olivia to her new school."

I remember that Sir Gerald said he meant to send Olivia away to a finishing school as soon as one was found for her, but the timing is suspicious.

"What a convenient excuse," Reid says.

"When Daddy hears about this, he'll kill you!" Angry tears sparkle in Olivia's eyes.

"Your rich daddy can't protect you now. You're a murder suspect." Puffed up with conceit, the working-class man who's gained the upper hand over his social superiors, Reid points at Tristan, Lady Alexandra, and Tabitha in turn. "So are you."

Gasps of shock arise from the servants and guests. Lady Alexandra exclaims, "Are you accusing me of murdering my own child? How dare you!"

Tabitha's anxious gaze seeks out Raphael DeQuincey. He blanches with fear.

"It wasn't one of us," Tristan says coldly. "Robin was murdered by a stranger who climbed up a ladder to his room, carried him down it, and drowned him in the pond."

"The very same pond where you recently made a secret midnight expedition," Reid says. "What a coincidence—or was it?"

The color drains from Tristan's face. He looks around, as if wondering who told Reid about his visit to the pond. I feel Hugh glare at me.

"New evidence has come to light," Reid says. "We now suspect that Robin's kidnapping was an inside job."

Amid another wave of astonished exclamations, Olivia stops struggling. Wariness fills her eyes. Tabitha reaches out her hand to DeQuincey, who sidles toward the back door that leads to the terrace. His panicky gaze is riveted on Inspector Reid.

"What new evidence?" Lady Alexandra demands.

"Robin's favorite toy rabbit," Reid says. "Didn't you wonder where it went?"

Lady Alexandra shakes her head, bewildered.

"It must be at the bottom of the pond," Olivia says.

"It was found on the back stairs the night Robin was kidnapped," Reid says. "The kidnapper dropped it there as he carried Robin out of the house. The kidnapper was somebody who lives here. The ladder was planted afterward to make it look like somebody from outside had taken Robin."

Everyone stares at Reid in shock except Barrett, who's watching me. When our gazes meet, he averts his eyes and compresses his mouth.

"Where did you get that absurd theory?" Scorn withers Tristan's voice.

"From Sir Gerald. He found the toy rabbit."

"Gerald didn't tell me anything of the sort," Lady Alexandra protests. Tristan and Olivia nod in agreement.

"He didn't share that little gem with me either. Only his private detectives." Reid jerks his thumb at Hugh, Mick, and me. "They were kind enough to pass it along."

We band closer together, targets of hostile stares from the company. Tristan's look at Hugh is the same look that Barrett gave me when he learned I was investigating the kidnapping. Hugh tries to conceal his misery behind his most dignified, aristocratic manner.

"Even if the kidnapping was an inside job, why are you accusing us?" Tristan asks. "We're not the only people who live in Mariner House."

The servants stir in consternation that Reid dispels by saying, "The servants have been cleared. That leaves the four of you, plus Sir Gerald and John Pierce."

"It wasn't me," Lady Alexandra hastens to say. "I was with Tabitha when Robin was taken."

"And Olivia and I were together." Tristan puts his arm around his sister.

"We'll be taking a long, hard look at those alibis," Reid says. "One of you wasn't where you said you were. One of you was stealing Robin out of his crib, weighing him down with rocks, and drowning him in the pond."

"That's ridiculous!" Lady Alexandra cries. "I would never have hurt my baby."

"You might have if there was something seriously wrong with him and you didn't want to be the mother of a baby who was less than perfect."

Confronted with my theory about Robin, Lady Alexandra looks suddenly frightened—proof, albeit intangible, that my theory holds water.

"You're just trying to put the blame on us because you haven't been able to find the real killer," Tristan says, but he sounds shaken.

"The 'real killer' would have had a motive for wanting Robin dead. Such as inheriting Sir Gerald's fortune. Oh, but aren't you now the heir apparent?"

Tristan rubs his hand over his mouth. Olivia blurts, "Tristan didn't do it."

"So maybe you did," Reid says. "Maybe you thought that with Robin gone, you would be Daddy's little girl again."

Olivia stares him in the eye and pouts.

John Pierce steps forward from among the crowd of guests. I didn't notice him earlier; I can't tell if he's been there all this time or just sneaked in. "The ransom note was posted from Shoreditch on April eleventh." This is a piece of information that Sir Gerald didn't give Hugh and me. "Sir Gerald has been tracking our movements since the night of the kidnapping." Pierce seems to have known this all along, but I can tell from their startled expressions that it's news to Lady Alexandra, Tristan, and Tabitha. "We were all at Mariner House that day. None of us could have sent the note."

"Maybe the note was a hoax," Reid says. "Or maybe one of you wanted to bilk Sir Gerald and had help from someone on the outside."

Raphael DeQuincey bolts from the parlor, jostles past the servants, and runs out the door that leads to the garden. Tabitha cries, "Raphael, wait!"

"Was that the medium?" Reid says to the constables, "I want him for questioning."

The constables run after DeQuincey. Amid the general clamor, Tabitha calls, "Raphael, don't leave me!"

As she tries to follow him, Lady Alexandra grabs her arm and demands, "What's gotten into you?" Tabitha sags to her knees and bursts into tears. Lady Alexandra gapes at her in disbelief. "*You and Mr. DeQuincey. . . ?*"

The front door opens, and Sir Gerald strides into the foyer. "What's going on here?" he demands.

Hugh, Mick, the servants, and I step aside to let him enter the parlor. There, he beholds the police, the weeping Tabitha, the handcuffed Olivia, and the mute, shocked guests.

"Gerald!" Lady Alexandra flings herself into his arms. "Thank God!"

The changes that the past twenty-four hours have wrought in Sir Gerald shock me. Purplish bags underscore his blood-shot eyes, and new lines carve his coarse skin, as if his body is taking the brunt of his grief over Robin's death. But his manner is still imperious as he says to Reid, "Why are you bothering my family? Shouldn't you be looking for my son's killer?"

"That's exactly what I'm doing," Reid says. "They're the suspects. But you knew that."

Sir Gerald immediately turns to Hugh and me; he's deduced that we've talked to the police. His gaze darkens with angry reproach. Guilt shrivels my insides.

"He said you found Robin's toy rabbit on the stairs." Lady Alexandra casts her pleading gaze up to her husband. "Tell me it isn't true!"

Sir Gerald looks grim; he doesn't answer. Lady Alexandra cries, "No!" She pushes away from him and sobs. Tristan and Olivia regard their father as if he's betrayed them. Pierce's expression is deliberately neutral.

"You should have told me at the start." Reid's manner is censorious, resentful. "Instead, you let my squad chase around London for almost three weeks, investigating false tips and wasting our time. We'd still be in the dark if your detectives hadn't spilled the beans."

Reid aims a dirty look at Hugh and me. He's furious because we withheld information, because I told Barrett instead of him. But it's not Reid's fury that concerns me most. Hugh, Mick, and I face Sir Gerald as if we're three backstabbers caught with bloody knives in our hands. I think of the business rivals he's destroyed, the rebellious slaves he shot, and I look around, hoping for rescue.

Everyone watches us, rapt with suspense and not about to intervene. Inspector Reid smiles, malevolently eager to see me get my comeuppance. Barrett frowns and takes a step toward me, perhaps because he still cares about me, more likely because of his instinct to protect the weak from the strong. I should warn him not to put himself between me and Sir Gerald, who won't spare anyone who gets in his way.

"I'm sorry," I say.

Sir Gerald doesn't seem to hear me. The anger leaves him as though it's unneeded ballast he's jettisoning from a ship. His gaze, now as opaque and inscrutable as during our first meeting, focuses on some distant horizon invisible to everyone else.

"You can go." Sir Gerald speaks in the cursory manner with which he dismissed Hugh's father from his office.

I'm too astonished and hurt to feel relieved. It's as if Sir Gerald thinks I'm so insignificant that punishing me isn't worth his time. Everyone else is silent and still, blank-faced with puzzlement.

Mick nudges Hugh and me and whispers, "Let's go before he changes his mind."

22

"I thought Sir Gerald would have our heads," Mick says as we walk down the road leading away from Mariner House, past carriages filled with passengers arriving for Robin's wake. "Why didn't he?"

Hugh snorts in derision. "It wouldn't have put the cat back in the bag."

I'm still trying to make sense of my emotions. I knew I was nothing to Sir Gerald but hired help, and the fact that I failed to live up to his expectations shouldn't bother me this much. "Maybe he thinks we know something that we haven't told the police and letting us go was a bribe to keep us quiet."

"So we've been bought off?" Mick says, half flattered, half resentful.

"Better bought off than strung up by our thumbs." In a foul mood, Hugh stalks ahead of Mick and me.

I feel scant relief that we've escaped punishment from Sir Gerald. I've handed the police a packet of evidence against the Mariner family, and I have no control over how they use it. This could be my old nightmare from last fall come again—that my actions bring harm to someone.

"We mustn't leave yet," I say.

Hugh calls over his shoulder, "What choice do we have?"

At the gates, I see guards letting in more carriages, the crowd outside larger than ever. Reporters, photographers, and curiosity-seekers have come to view the aftermath of Robin's death. I stop. "We have to find out who killed Robin." I also want to make it up to Sir Gerald for betraying his trust.

"Just how are we supposed to do that?" A spell of coughing overcomes Hugh. When it's finished, gasps heave his chest, and his eyes are red and watery "All the suspects are in there." He points at Mariner House. "We're out here."

"I don't know," I admit.

"Inspector Reid won't want us pokin' around," Mick says.

"But we can't leave everything up to him," I say. Reid tried to pin the murders in the dinosaur park on Hugh and me, and his investigation into Robin's murder is a chance for another miscarriage of justice.

"Sarah. It's over." Hugh is impatient, exasperated. "Face the facts."

He's suffered the worst of all of us from our time at Mariner House, just as he suffered the worst during the Ripper case. It's no wonder he wants to quit. But I can't quit, and I can't solve Robin's murder by myself.

"Inspector Reid might decide Tristan murdered Robin," I say. "Don't you want to prove he's as innocent as you think he is?"

Although it's an obvious, deplorable attempt at manipulation, I'm desperate enough to try it. But Hugh only gazes solemnly at me with his haunted red eyes. "Maybe I was wrong about Tristan. He and Olivia tried to run away. That rather suggests he's guilty."

I feel bad for Hugh, no matter that I have continually tried to rid him of his blind faith in Tristan. I think of my father, in whose innocence I still desperately want to believe.

Hugh walks out the gates and hires a carriage driver who's waiting for customers. As he climbs into the carriage, he calls to Mick and me, "Are you coming?"

My chances of accomplishing anything at Mariner House are slim. I don't want to part from Hugh while we're at odds, and I'm afraid to let him go alone. The memory of his suicide attempt last fall still haunts me. But I have a duty to bring justice for Robin Mariner and to protect the innocent. And now that I've lost Barrett, I must salvage something from the wreckage of my life.

"Go with him," I tell Mick.

Torn between conflicting loyalties, Mick says, "Fitzmorris will be with him when he gets home. I can't leave you here alone. I'll stay too."

"Suit yourselves," Hugh says.

The carriage bears him out of sight. Newly aware of the magnitude of my love for him, gripped by a fear that I'll never see him again, I have an urge to run after Hugh.

"Come on," Mick says, heading toward Mariner House. "The sooner we solve this, the sooner we can go home."

#

As we backtrack along the road that leads to Mariner House, Mick asks, "What are we going to do when we get there?"

This is an all-too-familiar situation; our plan doesn't extend beyond the immediate next step. "We'll have to improvise."

"For starters, let's avoid them." Mick points to armed guards stationed along the road.

We cut across the grounds, circling the mansion, whose solid brick bulk appears impenetrable. Its windows gleam like hostile eyes watching us. Our route takes us down the hill, below the brick arcade that supports the pergola, to the out-buildings. As we steal past a barn, two police constables round the corner.

"Hey! You're not supposed to be here."

We're already running in the opposite direction. My ankle throbs. The constables' footsteps pound after us. Mick pulls me down a narrow passage between two barns, past a fenced yard that contains sheep. The constables, hot on our heels, yell, "Stop!" We reach the brick wall that encloses the estate—a dead end. I look over my shoulder and see the constables almost upon us. We're trapped. They'll take us to Inspector Reid, who will surely send us to jail for trespassing, interfering with a police investigation, and any other charges he can dream up.

"Hurry!" Mick turns right, yanking me with him.

We run for some fifty feet parallel to the wall, then slip through a gate just as the constables arrive there. On the other side, a narrow path borders the wall. Below the path, the wooded hillside slopes steeply toward the heath. We plunge down the hill, which is covered with slippery dead leaves, and I lose my footing. My hand tears free of Mick's, and I tumble head over skirts until a tree stops me with a jarring thud against my back. Dizzy and breathless, I hear the constables laughing uproariously.

Mick skids down to meet me. "Miss Sarah, are you all right?"

As he helps me to my feet, my head spins, my back hurts, and my legs wobble, but nothing seems badly damaged. "Yes."

"Good riddance!" the constables shout.

They're apparently not going to desert their post to chase us, but they've shown me the futility of my hope of sneaking into Mariner House. The sky has darkened. Water pelts the leaves of the trees and splashes on me; it's raining again. "Maybe we should just go home."

"Don't give up yet," Mick says.

As we circle the estate through the woods, he wanders around in search of something. I'm too dispirited to ask what. We finally stop at a point some twenty feet downhill from the surrounding brick wall and closer to the road below. Here, a section of the slope is steeper, almost vertical, as if a big slice had been shaved off the hillside. Roots from trees above and a thick mat of vines hang over the incline. Mick walks onto a rocky ledge that fronts the slope, lifts the vines, and reveals an iron door that's about six feet high and painted with green-and-brown splotches to blend in with the scenery.

"How did you know about that?" I ask, surprised.

Mick grins. "I learned a few handy things from the servants."

"What is it?"

"A secret escape route from the house. Sir Gerald built it in case his enemies come after him." When Mick grasps the door by its handle and pulls, it swings back smoothly on oiled hinges. The dark tunnel behind it exudes a cold draft that smells of earth. Mick steps across the threshold, takes a box of matches from his pocket, and beckons.

I do not want to go in there. I do not like dark, unfamiliar spaces. "Don't the guards know about this?"

"Yeah, but they don't know we know," Mick says. "They won't look for us here. And they won't tell the coppers. It's supposed to be a secret."

A secret shared by the servants and who else? Summoning my courage, I follow Mick into the tunnel. It's high enough for a man to stand upright in but so narrow that we'll have to walk single file. The sides and ceiling are shored up with wooden beams. The sight of oil lamps strung along the walls doesn't relieve my fear. Mick strikes a match, lights the first lamp, and pulls the door shut. The lamp's flame glows weakly in the darkness. Mick precedes me along the tunnel, striking more matches, lighting more lamps as he goes, pushing away the darkness ahead of us a few feet at a time. Tree roots dangle from the ceiling like gnarled, ghostly fingers. The tunnel zigzags as it snakes uphill, so I can't see the lamps we've left behind us. I'm afraid they'll burn up all the air. Panic quickens my breath; I feel faint.

"I'm starved," Mick says. "When we get to the house, I'm gonna sneak in the kitchen and steal us some food."

I hear the whispery sound of dirt and pebbles sliding, and I imagine the great weight of the hill collapsing onto the tunnel, crushing us to death. After minutes that seem like eons, Mick lights the final lamp and says, "Ha!"

We've reached the end of the tunnel—an iron door that must lead to the cellar of Mariner House. My relief quickly gives way to fear of what awaits us on the other side. Mick tries the knob, then rattles and thumps on the door. He turns to me, crestfallen. "It's locked."

23

I awake suddenly in complete darkness. I don't know where I am. Panic-stricken, I grope around me while my heart hammers as if trying to break out of my chest. My fingers touch the hard dirt surface I'm sitting on and the rough planks at my back. My eyes adjust to the darkness, which isn't as complete as I thought. A faint, thin vertical strip of gray light illuminates Mick, lying curled up beside me asleep. Relief calms me. We're in Sir Gerald's escape tunnel, near the secret exit to the woods. We extinguished the lamps and decided to wait out the day here and then make another attempt to breach Mariner House at night.

I rise, stretching my stiff, sore muscles, and push the iron door open wider. Cold, damp wind filters into the tunnel. Outside, black trees sway beneath a cobalt sky studded with thousands of stars that are never visible in foggy, smoky, gas-lighted London proper. The full moon dazzles among them like a silver coin surrounded by silver dust. I slept the whole afternoon. My stomach growls; I've not eaten since last night.

I shake Mick until he rouses. "It's time."

Mick yawns, stretches, and stands. "God, I could eat a horse."

We emerge from the tunnel, blinking in the moonlight, shivering in the cold. Darkness has transformed the woods into an enchanted forest from some nightmarish fairy tale.

They're alive with creatures rustling through the underbrush, owls hooting, wings flapping, wind rustling the trees, and disembodied voices calling. As we grope our way up the hill, I see Mariner House rising from within the brick walls that surround the estate, aglow with light from its windows like a haunted castle. I wonder if Inspector Reid has solved Robin's murder. I wonder if Barrett is still at Mariner House and whether he's thinking of me. Missing him is a raw wound in my heart.

"There's a pit here," Mick says. "Watch your step."

We inch our way down the slippery side of a cleft in the hillside, perhaps four feet deep and six across. At the bottom, as we wade through dead leaves, a muffled shriek freezes me in my tracks. Up from the leaves rises a shape. Hunched over, grunting and panting, it looks like a bear. We yell and scramble up the side of cleft. The thing at the bottom collapses. Now I see two spread arms, two bent legs—it's a man. Lank dark hair frames his ashen face. His slender body heaves as his breath rasps through his gaping mouth. His eyes are black pools of terror that gleam with reflected moonlight.

"It's Raphael DeQuincey!" I say.

The medium raises himself on his hands and left knee and tries to crawl out of the cleft, dragging his right leg. He collapses again and sobs.

Mick and I look at each other in astonishment. "Have you been here since this morning?" I ask DeQuincey.

"Yes," he says between gasps. "I couldn't get *away*. There were too many *police* chasing me."

"What's wrong with your leg?" Mick asks.

"I fell into this pit. I think it's broken. It hurts so much, I can barely move. I had to cover myself with leaves to hide from the police." DeQuincey moans in agony. "Help me get out of here. *Please!*"

DeQuincey wouldn't be in this predicament if I hadn't talked to Barrett, and I don't think he's guilty of anything except performing fake séances. "We'll help you," I say. "Mick, we must take him to a doctor."

Before I can climb into the pit, Mick says, "Wait. Here's our chance to get the straight goods from him." He asks DeQuincey, "Did you kill Robin?"

"No!"

"Then why did you run from the coppers?"

"If I'd let them grill me, it would have come out."

"What woulda come out?"

"I can't tell you. It'll make me and Tabitha look bad. You'll think we kidnapped Robin and killed him, and you'll tell the police."

"No, we won't," Mick says.

"How do I know I can trust you?"

"You got a choice?"

Footsteps crunch twigs on the hill above us. There I see a moving spot of light—the flame of a lantern. It's too dark to tell whether the person is a constable or one of Sir Gerald's guards.

"Better talk fast," Mick says to DeQuincey.

DeQuincey expels a sigh of capitulation. "Tabitha and I sent the ransom note."

Fresh amazement renders me speechless. I'd ruled out the possibility that they were involved in the kidnapping.

Mick snorts in disbelief. "You admit you sent the ransom note, and you expect us to believe you didn't kidnap Robin?"

"It's true! We didn't! Somebody else did!" Frantic to convince us, DeQuincey says, "Tabitha was with Lady Alexandra when Robin was taken. I was in Grosvenor Square, holding a séance for my client Mrs. Webb at her house. You can ask her and her friends. *They'll* tell you."

I recover my voice. "If you and Tabitha didn't kidnap Robin, then why did you send the note?"

"We needed money to go away together. Two days after the kidnapping, Tabitha got the idea of the ransom note. We weren't greedy—all we asked for was a thousand pounds. That would have been plenty to set me up in business in Bath, and Sir Gerald wouldn't have missed it," DeQuincey says, as if that excuses their actions. "When I wrote the note, I said to leave the money in the dinosaur park because I used to live near there and I know my way around. It seemed like the *perfect* solution."

Mick nudges me. "What d'ya think?"

My intuition says DeQuincey is telling the truth. "I think the only thing he and Tabitha are guilty of is taking advantage of Robin's kidnapping by extorting money from Sir Gerald."

"Yeah . . ." Mick says reluctantly.

"But if the police find out, they'll pin Robin's murder on us." DeQuincey's voice slides up to a shrill, panicky pitch. "And if they start beating up on me, I'll roll over and confess." He adds sheepishly, "I'm a coward."

Although his story has failed to reveal the identity of Robin's murderer, I realize that he may be able to solve other mysteries. "There was a double murder in the dinosaur park on the day you collected the ransom. Were you a witness to it?" Next I'll ask him if he saw my father.

DeQuincey moans, writhes, and clutches his broken leg. "I don't know anything about a double murder. Tabitha and I weren't there. We didn't collect the ransom."

"You passed up a thousand pounds?" Mick says, incredulous. "Why?"

"We got cold feet because we were afraid that Sir Gerald would set a trap, and when we came to get the money, his goons would jump out of the bushes and catch us."

Disappointment crumbles my hope of finding my father. No matter what he's done, I need to hear his side of the story, but I've arrived at another dead end.

"You ain't much of a criminal mastermind," Mick says in disgust.

"No. I'm not." DeQuincey drops his fluty, theatrical accent. "I'm just Joey Fenton, a cobbler's son from Hackney, trying to make a dishonest day's living. I've told you everything." More footsteps approach, and he hushes his voice. "Now help me!"

The guards or police are coming closer to us. I'm revolted by DeQuincey's actions, but I won't have Robin's murder blamed on him while the real culprit goes free. "All right," I say. We'll take him to a hospital and figure out what else to do later.

Mick and I skid down to the bottom of the pit, crouch on either side of DeQuincey, drape his arms around our necks, and lift. He's heavier than he looks; my knees buckle, and my ankle twinges. Leaning on us, he hops one laborious step at a time up the side of the pit, dragging his broken leg, sucking air through clenched teeth. I listen for footsteps between the sounds of the wind in the trees and carriage wheels on the road. When we're finally out of the pit, DeQuincey suddenly goes limp and crumples to the ground.

"He's fainted," I say.

Mick slaps DeQuincey's cheeks. DeQuincey rouses, crying, "Don't hit me!"

He faints twice more while we struggle down the hill. Somehow we reach the road. By this time, I'm exhausted and wet with perspiration, and my back and my sprained ankle are sore. Mick is breathing hard. DeQuincey trembles and groans as he hops slowly between us along the road that separates the hill and the heath. The moonlight paints the moors in ghostly shades of gray. It's at least a mile to Hampstead village. I don't know how we'll make it. Still short of breath from smoke inhalation, I can't bear DeQuincey's weight for much longer. I wonder if the police are guarding the train station, watching for the fugitive.

DeQuincey groans so loudly that I don't hear the hoofbeats until they're thundering on the road directly behind us. A male voice shouts, "Police! Stop!"

Terror freezes my blood. I turn as light spills over us; I blink in the glare of lanterns attached to two horses ridden by mounted constables.

"Run!" Mick drags DeQuincey and me toward the woods.

One of the constables blocks our path, saying triumphantly, "Hey, I found the runaway medium. You owe me a crown." The other, maneuvering his horse behind us, protests, "I saw him first."

Both constables jump off their horses, and the first says, "Raphael DeQuincey, you're under arrest."

"Don't let them take me!" DeQuincey cries in terror, then he faints again.

Too exhausted to defend him, Mick and I ease him to the ground. "He didn't kill Robin," I say.

"How do you know?" the first constable asks. "Who are you people, anyway?"

His partner laughs. "Well, I'll be darned. It's Sarah Bain and her street urchin."

"What are you doing with DeQuincey?" the first constable asks.

"We found him in the woods," Mick says.

"What's the matter with him?"

"His leg is broken," I say. "We were taking him to the hospital."

"Inspector Reid told you to get lost. What are you doing here?"

Reid will be angry enough to hear that we disobeyed him, never mind that we planned to sneak into Mariner House. Ignoring the question, I say, "Mr. DeQuincey is innocent," and I explain about the ransom note.

The constables exchange skeptical glances. The second one says, "We'll take him back to Mariner House and let Inspector Reid be the judge."

Mick whispers to me, "We gotta get out of here."

"I can't leave Mr. DeQuincey," I whisper back. There's no one at Mariner House to defend him and Tabitha from Inspector Reid.

"What about them?" the first constable asks the second, pointing at Mick and me.

"We'll take them in too."

"Miss Sarah, come on!" Mick tugs my arm.

"You go. I'm staying."

The second constable says to us, "You're under arrest."

"Arrest?" Mick's voice echoes my dismay. "What for?"

"Aiding and abetting a fugitive," the second constable says. "Inspector Reid can bring other charges against you if he wants."

24

I ride back to Mariner House on one of the horses, my hands cuffed behind my back, like a queen captured by an invading army. Mick, also handcuffed, trudges beside me while the constables guard us. The unconscious Raphael DeQuincey is slung facedown over the other horse like a sack of grain.

The driveway outside the mansion is empty except for a single large black carriage, its two horses, two footmen, and driver. The lights in the windows look sinister and inhospitable. I wonder what else has happened here today. It seems that Mariner House is my destiny to which I'm fated to return again and again and never escape.

When the police help me down from the horse, I'm so stiff and sore, so tired and weak from hunger, that I can barely stand. A fit of coughing wracks me, and Mick thumps my back until I spit up phlegm laced with smoke. As the police unload DeQuincey, he regains consciousness and moans. Guards escort Mick and me into the mansion; the constables follow, supporting DeQuincey. In the foyer, a few gas sconces are lit. The crape-shrouded chandelier hangs like a heavy black moon. The door to the parlor is closed, but I can smell incense, candle wax, and flowers. Men's raised voices issue from the dining room.

"This is extortion!" It's Inspector Reid; he sounds furious.

"It's my emergency protocol," Sir Gerald says.

His voice is ragged but calm. My heart thumps at the sound of it. Maybe Barrett wasn't so wrong to think I've given Sir Gerald a place in my affections.

"In the event that I'm detained by the authorities anywhere in the world, the funds in the Mariner Bank are automatically frozen," Sir Gerald says.

"The home secretary and the prime minister have been receiving telegrams and visits all day from frantic account holders demanding their money." The third man has a gruff, Scottish-accented voice.

"Not to worry," Sir Gerald says. "Now that my family and I have been released from house arrest, the funds will be unfrozen."

Apparently the police have been holding and questioning the Mariners all day.

"He's got us over a barrel, Reid," the Scotsman says. "I have to shut down your interrogation."

I admire Sir Gerald's nerve and his determination to protect his family, but I'm appalled by his tactics, and I don't want to think it's really himself that he's protecting.

The guards and constables, Mick, DeQuincey, and I reach the dining room door. The dining room has become the police's makeshift headquarters. Chairs are pushed back from the table, which holds a disarray of teacups, half-eaten sand-wiches, and full ash trays. The air smells of tobacco smoke. The statues, draped in black cloth, peer down as if in disapproval at the three men facing off by the table. The constables hesitate, reluctant to interrupt. Reid is in shirtsleeves, hair tousled as if he's been raking it with his hands, and his bloodshot eyes blaze with anger. Sir Gerald looks tired but smug. Reid speaks to the Scotsman, whom I've never seen before.

"With all due respect, Chief Commissioner Monro, you're making a big mistake," Reid says. "One of these people is a murderer. Just give me a little more time with them. I'll get a confession."

"You're out of time," Commissioner Monro says. He's about fifty years old with a wiry physique and a military bearing. Short gray hair recedes from his high round forehead; his luxuriant gray mustache curls up at the ends. He has the bronze complexion typical of men who've served in India. His clothes—a black suit coat, gray trousers, and starched white shirt—are immaculate and precise, like a soldier's uniform. I recall that he replaced Sir Charles Warren, who resigned in 1888 at the height of the Ripper investigation.

"Thanks, James. I knew you would see reason," Sir Gerald says.

"But they're flight risks," Reid protests. "The son and daughter had tickets for passage on a ship to Marseille."

Maybe Tristan did try to escape; maybe he really is guilty. But I can't ignore the possibility that Olivia, who was with him, could be the true murderer.

"Better hurry and make an arrest before they can abscond," Commissioner Monro says.

"How am I supposed to do that?" Reid demands.

"You're the detective; you figure it out."

"You mean, I'll take the fall if the case is never solved." Reid's tone is acid with rancor.

Monro shrugs. Sir Gerald says, "Now that we've got this settled, the police can leave my house."

The tobacco smoke in the air triggers another coughing fit. My coughs draw the men's attention to me. Reid says, "You again? What the hell?"

"We caught them on the road trying to help the medium escape," the first constable explains as he and his partner drop DeQuincey in a chair.

Reid's anger turns to astonishment. "Well, I'll be."

He, Commissioner Monro, and Sir Gerald stare down at DeQuincey, who looks worse than he did in the moonlight. His face is sickly white, marred with bruises and bleeding cuts, awash in sweat and mud. His wet black hair is plastered to his forehead, leaves cling to his garments, and he moans in pain.

"He killed Robin," the second constable says.

"You mean, he confessed to you?" Reid's expression combines incredulity and dismay. He obviously doesn't want to believe that a subordinate solved the case.

"Well, not exactly. He told them." The constable points at Mick and me. "*She* told us."

"No, he didn't," I say. Reid, Sir Gerald, and Commissioner Monro turn to me. The smile lines on Monro's face indicate a genial nature, but his expression is severe. His eyes are bright blue, his gaze penetrating. "Mr. DeQuincey said that he and Tabitha Jenkins only sent the ransom note."

"That's all!" DeQuincey sobs and gulps. "We didn't kidnap Robin. We didn't kill him. We didn't even collect the damned money!"

"Of course you didn't." Reid's sarcastic rejoinder sounds a little flat, as if he's repeating words he's said to hundreds of criminals who've denied their guilt.

"So it was Tabitha." Sir Gerald speaks with cautious relief, as if he's testing the idea, less than certain.

"What are you waiting for?" Commissioner Monro asks Reid. "Here's your chance to end this sorry business." He seems ready to believe that DeQuincey and Tabitha are guilty.

Reid hesitates, frowning. I sense that he's recalling how he tried and failed to pin the Ripper murders on my innocent friend Mr. Lipsky. His rash ambition got him suspended from the police force, and he surely won't want to make the same mistake in another high-profile case. He says to the constables, "Fetch Tabitha Jenkins. We'll see what she has to say."

Sir Gerald halts them with a raised hand. "Your men don't have the run of my house anymore. I'll do it."

He leaves the room, and as his brisk footsteps mount the stairs, DeQuincey keens, "Tabitha! I'm sorry! Forgive me!"

"Wish I could stay," Commissioner Monro says to Reid, "but the home secretary is waiting for a report."

After Monro departs, Reid turns on me. "Why were you hanging around here?"

"I wanted to know what was going on," I say in lieu of admitting I was afraid he would pin Robin's murder on the wrong person. "I believe DeQuincey. I think that all he and Tabitha did was send the ransom note after someone else killed Robin."

Reid looks askance at me. "Thanks for your amateur interpretation." He jerks his chin at one of the constables. "Uncuff her and the boy."

The constable obeys. Mick and I flex our sore wrists. The steel has left red indentations in my flesh. Reid says, "Go home. Stop meddling. If I have to tell you again—"

The sound of quick footsteps rackets down the staircase. We turn to see Lottie in the doorway, breathless and wide-eyed. "Miss Tabitha is dead!"

I'm speechless with shock and disbelief. Mick exclaims, "What? How—?"

"Tabitha!" Arms outstretched as if to rescue her, DeQuincey lunges out of his chair. He sprawls on the carpet, bursts into sobs, and pounds the floor with his fists. "Oh, God, no!"

Reid curses, bolts from the room, and yells at the constables to stay with DeQuincey. Mick, Lottie, and I charge up the stairs after Reid. In the passage in the south wing, Olivia stands by an open door from which the sound of weeping emanates. Clad in a long white nightgown with puffed, lace-trimmed sleeves, her long, curly dark hair uncombed, she looks like frightened child. Reid pushes past her into the room. The doorjamb is splintered where the lock was forced. Mick and I stop at the threshold, and my gaze quickly takes in the room, which is smaller than the one I stayed in, with plain wooden furniture and subdued colors. Barrett stands at one side of the bed, Sir Gerald between Lady Alexandra and Tristan at the other. Tristan holds a rosary and murmurs prayers, his head bowed over Tabitha.

"All-powerful and merciful God, look kindly upon your servant Tabitha Jenkins, and by the blood of the cross, forgive her sins."

Barrett and Sir Gerald look stunned. Lady Alexandra has one hand gripped around the bedpost for support, the other clapped over her mouth. I smell the sweet, unexpected aroma of chocolate before my attention locks onto the figure on the bed. Tabitha lies diagonally across the counterpane in a grotesque, contorted position—her back arched like a bow, her buttocks and thighs raised some ten inches off the bed. Her peach-colored nightgown and gray wool wrapper are twisted around her stiff legs, the toes of her bare feet tightly curled. Her arms are bent, her hands balled in fists. Her white nightcap has fallen off, and her two ash-blonde braids splay from her head like exclamation marks. Her face is a ghastly mask of agony—bluish complexion, pale eyes bulging, flared nostrils, jaws clenched. Her exposed teeth have bitten through her tongue.

Mick gasps in horror. My own horror is laced with bewilderment. *What could have done this?* Brown liquid has drooled from Tabitha's mouth and splattered the bed linens. At first I think she must have vomited, but then I see that the brown trail leads down the white dust ruffle to the carpet. There, a brown stain surrounds an overturned blue china cup. It's spilled cocoa, the source of the chocolate smell.

"Deliver her now from every evil, O Lord; bid her eternal rest, and let your perpetual light shine upon her soul forever and ever. Amen." Tristan crosses himself.

"What the hell happened?" Reid demands.

Barrett's grim gaze flashes to me for an instant before he says to Reid, "The door was locked. When I knocked, Miss Jenkins didn't answer, so I broke in. I found her like this."

"How did she die?" Reid sounds puzzled; he's never seen death like this before either.

"It looks like she took poison." Barrett moves to the bedside table and points at a small bottle made of clear glass with a cork stopper. Mick and I steal farther into the room, the better to see. The bottle contains white granules. The white label bears an illustration of a skull and crossbones between the words "Strychnine" and "Poison" printed in black. Barrett points at the cup on the floor. "She must have put it in her cocoa."

"She committed suicide?" Reid is astonished.

So am I. In my dealings with Tabitha, I observed no sign that she would take her own life. But maybe she was so heartbroken because DeQuincey ran out on her that she wanted to die.

Sir Gerald lifts a sheet of white notepaper that had been lying on the table beside the poison bottle. "Here's the note." He hands the paper to Reid.

I see the two words handwritten on it in blue ink: *I'm sorry.*

Lady Alexandra dissolves into sobs. "It means she killed Robin! Oh, God, I didn't know she hated me so much that she would kidnap and murder my innocent child!"

Sir Gerald puts his arms around her. An angry scowl darkens his face.

"She tried to repent of one sin by committing another." Tristan's tone combines sadness with reproach.

"More likely, she wanted to avoid being hanged for Robin's murder." Reid adds, "When I interrogated her, she acted like she was hiding something. Now it's obvious she was trying to protect herself and DeQuincey."

He seems ready to believe in the scenario that the evidence suggests. I feel stirrings of relief—I myself would like the case solved, even with such a horrible ending. And if Tabitha and DeQuincey are guilty, then Sir Gerald isn't. But now that my initial shock has passed, I perceive something wrong. "Tabitha and DeQuincey couldn't have kidnapped Robin. She was with Lady Alexandra. He was in Grosvenor Square."

Barrett and Reid frown as if I've thrown a wrench into their machine. Then Lady Alexandra says, "She wasn't with me."

Surprise replaces the displeasure in Barrett's and Reid's expressions. Sir Gerald holds his wife away from him and stares, incredulous, into her face. "You lied to the police? And to me?" He speaks as if the latter is her more grievous offense.

Lady Alexandra wipes her streaming eyes. "Yes. Tabitha didn't have an alibi; she was alone in her room. We were afraid the police would think she took Robin. So I lied to protect her." Lady Alexandra sees Barrett and Reid's disapproval and cries, "She's my sister! We've stood by each other all our lives! If I'd known, I never would have lied for her!"

Although still displeased, Sir Gerald, Reid, and Barrett nod in understanding, but I see another problem. "You were Tabitha's alibi," I say to Lady Alexandra, "but she was yours too. Where were you when Robin was kidnapped?"

Lady Alexandra doesn't flinch at my hint that she could be responsible for her son's murder. "I was in the ballroom, rehearsing for the private plays we have during the summer," she says promptly. "Lottie can vouch for me. She was there watching."

Mick gulps, then coughs as if he's swallowed the wrong way. Everyone looks toward the passage, where Lottie is standing. Her eyes widen, and she shrinks back, dismayed to be put on the spot. She glances at Lady Alexandra and nods vigorously.

"Well," Reid says, "that closes the case." He seems at once relieved because he won't be blamed for Robin's murder going unsolved and disappointed because he can't take credit for a solution.

"Congratulations," Sir Gerald says with a tinge of irony.

Reid tucks Tabitha's suicide note into his pocket, then says to Barrett, "Send the body to the morgue and Mr. DeQuincey to Newgate." On his way out the door, he turns to me. "Thanks for giving us the goods on the suspects and finding DeQuincey. I thought I'd never say this, but maybe you're worth the air you breathe."

25

Reluctant to leave Mariner House, unable to believe the case is closed, I loiter in the driveway. Mick has wandered off somewhere, but he soon joins me. Then Barrett and two other constables emerge from the mansion with Raphael DeQuincey. They load him into a carriage while he struggles and screams, "We didn't kill Robin! Please don't take me to jail! Oh, God, somebody save me!"

The other constables climb in with him, and the carriage rolls away. I feel sick because I've just witnessed the terrible miscarriage of justice I feared.

Barrett walks over to Mick and me. "The show's over. Why don't you just go home?"

His voice is frosty. The woeful disappointment I feel tells me I've been hoping we could mend our relationship. I force myself to address the more important business. "I don't think it is over. I don't think Tabitha poisoned herself."

Barrett eyes me with more annoyance than surprise, as if he'd been expecting me to make more difficulties of some sort. "Why don't you?"

I'm so tired, weak from hunger, and upset that the effort necessary to marshal my thoughts is tremendous. "Because Tabitha's death is too convenient for the Mariners. It gets them off the hook for Robin's murder. One of them must have put the poison in her cocoa."

"I think it was Lady Alexandra," Mick says.

Barrett shakes his head, pitying us for what he obviously thinks is our delusion. "The door was locked. The key was in the lock inside. I had to break the door down. Nobody could have gotten into the room to poison Tabitha."

"Maybe they brought her the cocoa and she let them in," I say. "Where were Sir Gerald, Lady Alexandra, Tristan, Olivia, and John Pierce tonight, before she died?"

Barrett folds his arms, refusing to be drawn into further discussion.

"Lady A lied when she said she and Lottie were together when Robin was kidnapped. So did Lottie." Mick sounds grieved by her betrayal of his trust. "She told me before that she was in the servant's hall with the cook and the butler."

That explains Mick's and Lottie's reactions earlier to Lady Alexandra's claim. "Lady Alexandra would have been familiar with Tabitha's handwriting—they were sisters," I say. "She could have forged the suicide note."

Incredulity permeates Barrett's expression. "So you think Lady Alexandra killed Robin too?"

"There was something wrong with Robin," Mick says. "She killed him because she didn't want him."

Barrett groans. "Not your half-baked theory about Robin's photograph again."

I still believe in my theory, but it's obviously not going to convince Barrett. "If Lady Alexandra didn't poison Tabitha, someone else did. Tabitha was a poor relative, not a Mariner family member by blood. If someone had to be sacrificed to protect Sir Gerald or his children—"

"Tabitha was the perfect scapegoat," Mick concludes.

Barrett responds with a sardonic twist of his lips. My persistence is only pushing him further into denying the validity of my allegations. I employ the only means that might sway him. "I was right about Jack the Ripper. You didn't believe me when I first tried to tell you who he was."

"Don't throw that in my face. Just because you were right that time doesn't mean you are now."

His anger and resentment toward me are affecting his judgment. "I'm not asking you to take my word that Tabitha and DeQuincey are innocent. I'm asking you to investigate and make sure there's not been a mistake."

"That's Inspector Reid's call, not mine. And he's satisfied that Tabitha and DeQuincey are guilty. So is Sir Gerald."

I wonder if Sir Gerald really is satisfied. I can't believe he would be blind to other possibilities. "Maybe if you talk to Inspector Reid . . . ?"

Barrett chuckles disdainfully. "Reid's not going to reopen the case on my say-so. Not after he thought he had you and Hugh for the murders in the dinosaur park and I proved you didn't do it."

That was the second time Barrett saved our lives and strained his fraught relationship with Reid. I shouldn't expect more from him than that, but I can't give up on finding out the truth about Robin's murder. "Please! I beg you!"

I reach for Barrett, but he impales me with a wary, calculating gaze, as if I'm a cutthroat he's met while patrolling the streets. "What's the real reason you're pushing me to help you prove that Tabitha and DeQuincey didn't kill Robin?"

How I wish to believe they're kidnappers and murderers so I needn't feel guilty about Tabitha's death or DeQuincey's arrest! "I gave you evidence against them. I'm responsible for making things right." There's still time to save DeQuincey, but there's nothing I can do for Tabitha except exonerate the man she loved.

Distrust narrows Barrett's eyes. "Or maybe you're just a bad sport because you were fired before the case was solved. Maybe you're trying to keep it open just so you can worm your way back into it and wring some more money out of Sir Gerald."

Offended by his accusation, I can only sputter.

Mick leaps to my defense. "That's an insult to Miss Sarah." He grabs Barrett's collar, raises his own fist. "Take it back!"

I pull Mick away from Barrett. "I would never do such a thing! Don't you know me better than that?"

Barrett's expression turns solemn, regretful. I can tell he's remembering the last time we made love, the day he asked me to marry him. "I once thought I knew you."

I'm furious that he thinks me capable of such mercenary behavior, but then I recall what I've learned about my family's past. If my father raped and murdered Ellen Casey, then I'm the child of a monster. Maybe I am a bad sport who doesn't want to accept that Tabitha and DeQuincey are guilty and I'm wrong. Maybe being a bad sport is only the least of the hidden flaws in my character. What others might I have inherited from my father?

Barrett speaks to me in a cold manner that wounds my heart. "You found DeQuincey. You helped solve the case." This is how he'll speak to me from now on if ever we chance to meet. "So you didn't earn the reward—tough luck." He turns and strides into the mansion.

#

I'd hoped that the end of the investigation would give Barrett and me a second chance, but it's distressingly clear that Barrett doesn't intend for us to reconcile.

Mick and I trudge down the road away from Mariner House, I carrying my satchel, outcasts not worthy of a ride to town. A few gas lamps dimly light our way. I'm glad we're going home, but when I think of Hugh and wonder what he's doing and feeling, my spirits sink lower. I fear for him, and I wonder if our friendship is another casualty of our investigation.

A shrill cry accompanies a pattering of footsteps behind us. "Mick! Wait!"

I turn to see Lottie running and waving. I stop, but Mick walks faster. Lottie hurries past me and trots beside Mick. "I have to talk to you."

"*I* don't want to talk to *you*." Mick jams his hands into his pockets and scowls at the ground. "You lied for Lady Alexandra."

"I didn't have a choice! If I hadn't gone along with her, she'd have fired me."

"Yeah? Well, now that Robin's dead, you're out of a job anyway."

Lottie pants as she explains, "My mother was in an omnibus accident. She's paralyzed. I'm supporting her and my two younger sisters. If Lady Alexandra gives me a bad reference, I'll never get another job."

As I catch up with them, Mick halts and faces Lottie. They're standing in the light from a gas lamp, and I see the anger in his expression give way to sympathy. "Oh. Well. I get it."

Lottie sighs with relief. "I'm so glad you're not mad."

I feel sorry for her because it's obvious that Mick means more to her than vice versa.

"But I think Lady Alexandra killed Robin, and you helped her get away with it and pin it on Tabitha and Mr. DeQuincey," Mick says.

Tears glisten in Lottie's eyes. "I'm sorry."

"'Sorry' don't make up for the fact that Mr. DeQuincey's gonna be hanged while the real killer gets off scot free." Mick's voice is gentle but reproachful.

"Oh, no!" Lottie clasps her throat as she weeps. "I like Mr. DeQuincey. He was kind to me. So was Miss Tabitha. This is all my fault!"

"No, it isn't." Since I myself deserve much of the blame for these circumstances, I can't let Lottie accept the burden of guilt. "And we don't know for sure that Lady Alexandra has done anything wrong besides lying about where she was when Robin was kidnapped."

"*I'm* sure," Mick says.

"We have no proof," I remind him, "and we can't be certain Tabitha was murdered."

Lottie smiles with tentative relief, but Mick frowns. "Well, somebody did Robin in, and you and I both think Tabitha didn't off herself. But now that Sir Gerald's dumped us, and the coppers won't listen to us—what do we do?"

"We find out who killed Robin and Tabitha, and we bring evidence to Inspector Reid. He'll have to listen to us then."

"So how are we gonna do that?"

Without access to Mariner House and the suspects, it does seem impossible.

"I'll help you if I can," Lottie says, eager to make amends.

I feel suddenly light-headed and disoriented, as though time has spun backward. Suddenly it feels as if it's my first morning at Mariner House, and the only clue I've discovered is a photograph of a mother and child. "Perhaps you can help," I say to Lottie, "by telling us about Robin."

Lottie touches her fingers to her lips; her eyes grow round with fear. "But Sir Gerald and Lady Alexandra—"

"They don't have to know you talked," Mick says. "We won't rat on you."

"Well, all right." Lottie still looks uncomfortable with breaking her employers' rule. She seems more desirous of getting herself back in Mick's good graces than of preventing a miscarriage of justice, but I can't afford to care about her motives. "Robin was"—she searches for words—"not normal."

"'Not normal,' how?" Mick asks.

"He was limp, like a rag doll. He couldn't sit up, and his body would jerk and tremble. He couldn't walk; he couldn't even crawl. When I fed him, I had to hold his head so he could eat and drink. Most babies start talking by that age, but Robin only made noises like an animal, and he didn't seem to understand anything you said to him." Lottie shakes her head sadly. "The poor little boy."

So the photograph didn't lie, and there was something seriously wrong with Robin, which included mental retardation. "Is that why he was kept out of sight and the nurses were ordered not to talk about him?" I ask.

"Yes. I think Sir Gerald and Lady Alexandra were ashamed of him. I heard them talking one night in Robin's room when they didn't know I was there. He said he couldn't have anyone know his son wasn't normal, and she was afraid people would blame her for Robin's problems. They said it would've been better if Robin had never been born."

"See?" Mick says with grim triumph. "I told you Lady A didn't want him."

"But that goes for Sir Gerald too." My heart sinks as my suspicion of Tristan, Olivia, and John Pierce weakens and the evidence against Robin's parents burgeons. Did Sir Gerald or Lady Alexandra fake a kidnapping and drown Robin, like lions killing a defective cub? Who is the monster?

"Maybe they were in on it together," Mick says.

The idea that both parents conspired to kill their child seems even more atrocious than if one of them acted alone. "When did Robin's problems start?"

"I started working for the Mariners when he was a week old. He was already limp and shaky. I knew something was wrong because I've taken care of other babies. But it didn't show that much until he got older."

"That explains why there were no recent photographs of Robin," I say. His parents stopped having him photographed when his condition became obvious. "Could nothing have been done for him? Did Sir Gerald and Lady Alexandra ever consult a physician?"

"Oh, yes. Sir Gerald brought in one from the hospital in Bolshover Street. Dr. Kirkland, his name was." Lottie smiles briefly, as if at a pleasant memory. "I was there while Dr. Kirkland examined Robin."

"What did the doc say was wrong with Robin?" Mick asks.

"I don't know. Lady Alexandra sent me away before Dr. Kirkland told her and Sir Gerald."

"What treatment did Dr. Kirkland prescribe?" I ask.

"None, as far as I know."

"Robin's condition must have been incurable." My heart sinks deeper. "That would be all the more reason for Sir Gerald and Lady Alexandra to get rid of him."

Lottie looks dismayed at the thought. "But they're important, respectable people! They wouldn't drown their baby!"

I think of the guards patrolling the Mariner estate. "Sir Gerald must have people to do his dirty work."

"So what if Sir G or Lady A killed Robin? We can't prove it," Mick says morosely. "We can't even tell anybody why we think they did."

Lottie bows her head, taking Mick's words as a reproach for putting her family ahead of justice for Robin. I hasten to say, "It's all right, Lottie. Even if we did tell, it probably wouldn't do any good. Sir Gerald is so powerful that he and Lady Alexandra could get away with murder even if they'd been caught red-handed." I'm afraid it's true, and I can't reproach Lottie while I'm putting my father ahead of justice for Ellen Casey, protecting him even though he's probably a rapist and murderer.

Lottie licks tears that have trickled onto her lips. "Well, I'd better get back to the house. Lady Alexandra will be wondering where I am." She turns to Mick. "Will I ever see you again?"

"Yeah, sure," Mick says, looking uncomfortable. He only cultivated her to get information, and it's clear that he's just realized she has feelings for him. As we walk toward the gates, he says, "When we get home, we'll ask Hugh how to solve Robin's murder. He always has good ideas."

But I don't know if Hugh will want to help. The only thing I know for sure is that although the police's investigation of Robin's death may be over, ours is beginning anew.

26

It's past eleven o'clock at night when our train grinds to a weary halt at St. Pancras station. On the platform, Mick and I meet a lone newsboy hawking papers. "Read the latest about the Robin Mariner murder! The funeral is at St. Paul's tomorrow at two o'clock!"

"The press won't have heard that the murder is officially solved," I say to Mick.

"When they do, the papers will be full o' lies."

I'm more certain than ever that Tabitha and DeQuincey are innocent, but Tabitha's reputation will be ruined posthumously, and how can DeQuincey get a fair trial in court after he's deemed guilty by the public?

At the house, Fitzmorris lets us in. "Where have you been?" he asks, glancing anxiously behind us. "Is Hugh with you?"

"No." Apprehension stabs me.

"We thought he was here," Mick says.

"He came back this afternoon," Fitzmorris says. "He was in a terrible state—coughing, pale and shaky, and smelling of smoke. I asked him what had happened, but he refused to tell me. After he changed his clothes, he went out. He wouldn't say where."

I think of the other times when Hugh has gone out alone, and I fear for his safety. What evils might he fall prey to at the hands of unscrupulous men who would take advantage of him in his vulnerable condition?

Fitzmorris notices Mick's and my bedraggled appearance, and the worry lines on his face deepen. "What's happened to you? Sarah, what's going on?"

He asks if we're hungry, and when Mick admits we've not eaten today, he cooks us supper. In the kitchen, we gratefully devour fried sausages and bread, washed down with hot tea while we talk. When we're finished explaining, Fitzmorris is shocked into grave silence, and I feel guiltier than ever on Hugh's account.

"I'm sorry," I say. "I never should have let Hugh get involved with the kidnapping case." Fitzmorris has worked for the Staunton family for thirty years; he's as much an older brother to Hugh as a valet, and there's nobody who loves him more. "I should have told Sir Gerald no."

"It's not your fault," Fitzmorris says with a wry smile. "When Lord Hugh sets his mind on something, wild horses can't stop him."

Knowing that about Hugh doesn't ease my guilt. Nor does remembering that Tabitha Jenkins is dead because giving my information to the police likely drove Robin's murderer to poison Tabitha and fake her suicide. And Raphael DeQuincey must be in prison now, awaiting his trial, which will surely and wrongfully end in a death sentence.

Mick pushes his chair back from the table. "I'll go look for Hugh. I know some places he might be."

Although nighttime London is dangerous even for a former street urchin who knows it well, I don't try to stop Mick and neither does Fitzmorris. We all want Hugh found before he comes to harm.

#

After a sounder sleep than I expected, I awake at eight o'clock in the morning. I feel refreshed, invigorated, and filled with new hope. As I wash and dress, my problems don't seem as impossible to solve. I hurry to Hugh's room, certain he must have returned.

But his room is empty, the bed not slept in, and when I go downstairs, I find Fitzmorris alone in the kitchen. "Lord Hugh isn't back," he says as he pours tea for me. "Neither is Mick."

Now I'm afraid for both of them, and if I'm to find out who killed Robin and Tabitha and save DeQuincey from a wrongful execution, I shall have to begin on my own.

#

The hospital in Bolshover Street is near Regent's Park, about a mile from Argyle Square. It's a large redbrick building, and a plaque over the entrance reads, "Royal Orthopedic Hospital." Two relief sculptures flank the window above the plaque—a boy leaning on a cricket bat and a girl holding a bouquet of flowers. When I pass through the door, I find myself in a large, marble-walled hall like a waiting room at a train station. Patients or visitors sit on benches. I approach the desk, where a nurse in a white uniform and cap sits.

"I'm here to see Dr. Kirkland."

"Have you an appointment?"

"No," I say, then lie, "Sir Gerald Mariner sent me." I feel bad about going behind his back, but I must discover the truth even if it's detrimental to him.

Another nurse escorts me to the second floor, along a wide corridor past wards filled with patients—all children, many with casts on their legs, lying in the rows of beds. Nurses and doctors massage crippled limbs or exercise them with weights. I pity the children. If Robin had lived, would this have been his fate?

I hear laughter, shouts, and a clattering racket in the distance. A man in a wheelchair zooms around the corner and straight toward me. "Catch me if you can!" he calls over his shoulder. Two little boys, also in wheelchairs, laugh with glee as they follow close behind him, trailed by children hobbling on crutches or braces.

The nurse with me cries, "Look out!" We jump out of the way before we're run over.

The man speeds past me. Tall and lanky, he has fluffy white mutton-chop whiskers. His head is bald except for a fringe of red hair. The boys overtake him and startle a nurse who's carrying a tray of medicines. She shrieks and drops the tray. The man narrowly avoids hitting an orderly pushing a cart. One boy reaches the far end of the passage and yells, "I won!"

The man and the other boy coast to a stop as the other children cheer. My escort leads me to the man and says in a fond, amused tone, "Dr. Kirkland, you really shouldn't encourage them to make mischief."

He's the doctor that Sir Gerald consulted about Robin. He smiles and says, "Sometimes mischief is the best medicine." His long, mobile face is only slightly wrinkled; he's younger than I first thought—in his fifties, perhaps. With his white beard, red bow tie, striped vest, and old-fashioned gray frock coat, he looks like a character from Mr. Dickens's *A Christmas Carol*.

"There's someone here to see you," the nurse says and introduces me. "Miss Bain was referred to you by Sir Gerald Mariner."

Dr. Kirkland looks up at me. The expression in the blue eyes beneath his fluffy white brows is intelligent, friendly, and surprised. "A pleasure to make your acquaintance, Miss Bain." He shakes my hand without rising from the wheelchair, and I realize with a shock that he wasn't using it just for play; he's crippled. "We can talk after I finish making my rounds."

I accompany him as he wheels himself down the corridor and visits the patients in the wards. Even the most afflicted children brighten when he approaches them, and those who are mobile follow him as if he's a kindly Pied Piper. Now I understand why Lottie smiled when she mentioned him.

When we're seated in his office, a small room where stuffed animals sit on the shelves with medical books and the paper-strewn desk holds a jar of penny candy, Dr. Kirkland says, "Who is the patient? Your child or a young relation?"

He thinks I'm here to obtain treatment for someone. I can't lie to this nice man. "There's no patient. I came to ask you for information about Robin Mariner."

Dr. Kirkland's expression turns grave at the mention of his patient who'd been kidnapped and murdered. "I'm sorry, but I can't discuss my patients." He seems a man who rarely gets angry, but his good humor toward me has lessened. "Exactly what is your connection to Sir Gerald?"

"I'm a private detective. Sir Gerald hired me and my partner to find Robin." I hurry to explain myself before Dr. Kirkland orders me to leave. "The police think Tabitha Jenkins—Robin's aunt—and her friend Raphael DeQuincey were in on the kidnapping together and they killed Robin. Tabitha is dead. She was poisoned. Mr. DeQuincey has been arrested."

Dr. Kirkland regards me with astonishment and disbelief. "I've heard nothing of this. It wasn't in the newspapers."

"It just happened last night. But I don't think Tabitha and Mr. DeQuincey killed Robin. I want to find out who did."

Mystified, Dr. Kirkland shakes his head. "What significance can Robin's medical condition have?"

"Maybe none. I'm grasping at straws. Robin's condition is a secret that never came to light during the police's investigation. There may be others. If I can uncover them all and put them together, perhaps they'll reveal the truth about his murder."

Dr. Kirkland's fluffy brows draw together in a skeptical frown. "Does Sir Gerald know you're here and why?"

"No."

"How did you learn that Robin was a patient of mine?"

To protect Lottie, I say, "I heard talk at Mariner House," and then confess, "I'm no longer working for Sir Gerald. But I can't wash my hands of this while a man's life is at stake. And I believe that whoever killed Robin also poisoned Tabitha Jenkins." Desperation makes me lean forward and ask what I've no right to ask. "What was wrong with Robin?"

Disconcerted by my intensity, Dr. Kirkland leans back from me. "Surely you see how this looks: a stranger walks in off the street and asks me for information about a patient—information that's confidential, I must add. Why should I believe what you say? Why should I even believe you're who you say you are?"

"You don't have to believe me. But if you keep silent, an innocent man may be hanged while the real murderer goes unpunished. Are you willing to risk the chance?"

Dr. Kirkland strokes his whiskers and frowns. "I suppose not. And you already seem to know something of Robin's condition." He hesitates while I twist my hands in a fever of suspense. "Robin had Little's Disease. Have you ever heard of it?"

I shake my head.

"Little's Disease was named for William James Little, the surgeon who founded the Royal Orthopedic Hospital. I studied under him." As I wonder whether Dr. Kirkland took up this particular field of study because he's crippled himself, he explains, "It seems to be a disorder of the brain. There's no way to ascertain what kind. Despite the advances in science, the brain is still a mystery." Dr. Kirkland taps his finger against his bald pate. "The symptoms usually appear within the first two years of life. They range from involuntary movements, flaccid or stiff limbs, and seizures to blindness, deafness, and mental impairment."

Some of these symptoms match Lottie's description of Robin.

"They can be mild or severe." Dr. Kirkland says sadly, "Robin's symptoms were severe."

"What causes Little's Disease?"

"We don't know, but it's often associated with injuries to the child's head during birth or illnesses in the child or mother."

It must be terrible to have a child so afflicted. My heart goes out to Sir Gerald and Lady Alexandra even though I suspect that one or both of them murdered Robin. "Is there a cure?"

Regret clouds Dr. Kirkland's blue eyes. "Not at present. There are treatments, though. We can provide canes, crutches, braces, and wheelchairs that enable the patients to move around. We can stretch stiff limbs with splints. We can administer sedatives to calm the seizures. We can perform surgery to reposition malformed joints, lengthen contracted tendons, or cut the nerves to spastic muscles."

The surgery sounds like torture. I can't help thinking that whoever killed Robin may have done him a favor. Perhaps Sir Gerald and Lady Alexandra didn't kill Robin to get rid of him but to spare him years of suffering.

"Little's Disease is a chronic condition that doesn't improve with age," Dr. Kirkland says. "Robin would have been crippled, unable to walk, talk, or take care of himself all his life."

"How did Sir Gerald react to the diagnosis?" I ask.

"He's unaware of it, as far as I know."

"But I thought he consulted you? I thought he was at Mariner House when you examined Robin and you spoke to him afterward." That was the impression I'd gleaned from Lottie.

"No. I've never met Sir Gerald. It was Lady Alexandra who consulted me and invited me to Mariner House. After I examined Robin, I reported my diagnosis to her. Sir Gerald was away. I doubt that he even knows of my existence. That's why I was surprised when the nurse said he'd referred you to me."

Either Lottie had mistakenly assumed Sir Gerald had called in Dr. Kirkland or Lady Alexandra had deliberately given her the wrong idea. "Are you saying Lady Alexandra didn't tell Sir Gerald that Robin had Little's Disease?"

"That's correct. And she made me promise not to tell him. I respected her wishes."

So Lady Alexandra kept secret from Sir Gerald the news that Robin's condition was incurable.

"Later, I realized I shouldn't have promised," Dr. Kirkland says. "A father has a right to information about his child. But at the time, Lady Alexandra was devastated by the news. She cried so hard that she couldn't breathe, and she had heart palpitations. I had to give her a sedative. She said she couldn't bear to watch Robin grow into an adult but never be normal, to always have to hide him from the public."

Dr. Kirkland shakes his head regretfully. "I suggested sending him to an institution. Some parents aren't able to cope with a handicapped child. I was fortunate. I contracted poliomyelitis when I was six, but my parents loved me and treated me like an ordinary boy and taught me that I could do anything I wanted. Of course, my handicap wasn't as extreme as Robin's—I can walk with crutches when I need to, and it didn't affect my mind. I'm sad to say that institutionalization is a common practice for families with children like Robin."

"Why didn't Lady Alexandra send Robin away?" I ask.

"She said Sir Gerald would never agree to it. According to her, he thought Robin's ailment was a temporary phase, and he would be furious if he even knew she'd consulted me."

My relief is massive. Sir Gerald hadn't lost his hope that Robin would be normal someday and therefore had no reason to exterminate the child. He's innocent after all; my trust in him was neither undeserved nor misplaced.

"I never saw Robin again," Dr. Kirkland says. "Two weeks after I diagnosed him, he was kidnapped."

27

"I won't say, 'I told you so,'" Mick says smugly. "Lady A drowned Robin so she wouldn't have to put up with him for the rest of her life."

We're sitting in the kitchen, and I've just relayed the information I gleaned from Dr. Kirkland while Fitzmorris cooks lunch. Hugh is still missing after more than twenty-four hours, the longest he's ever been gone. I envision him lying unconscious in a bathtub in some hotel, his wrists slit and the water turning red from his blood. Mick and I are glad of something to talk about besides Hugh, but we're listening for the sound of him at the door.

"Sir Gerald isn't in the clear yet," I say, determined to be more objective from now on. "Dr. Kirkland assumed that Lady Alexandra never told him Robin had Little's Disease, but we don't know it for a fact. Sir Gerald is a proud man, and an abnormal child must have been difficult for him to stomach."

"Yeah." Mick looks disappointed to think he could be wrong about Lady Alexandra. "And it would've been cheaper to drown Robin than stash him in a fancy hospital."

"I'm sure Sir Gerald could spare the money. He would have been more concerned about his public image. Maybe he thought the secret would come out even if Robin was far away in a hospital." I realize that while the new evidence casts a bad light on Sir Gerald and Lady Alexandra, it's also cause for reconsidering the other suspects. "I wonder if anyone else at Mariner House knew about Robin's diagnosis. If Olivia did, she'd have had less reason to be jealous of him. And Pierce might have thought that Robin's disease was enough punishment for Lady Alexandra and Sir Gerald."

"But I don't see what difference it makes with Tristan," Mick says. "If he wanted Sir Gerald's dough, Robin had to die, no matter what shape he was in."

The sound of familiar steps above us launches Mick, Fitzmorris, and me out of the kitchen and up the stairs. In the foyer, we see Hugh toss his hat at the rack and miss.

"Thank heaven, you're back, my lord!" Fitzmorris says as he picks up the fallen hat.

"We were so worried," I say, tearful with relief.

Shrugging off his coat, Hugh turns to us. His eyes are sunken and bloodshot with dark, puffy circles underneath. His haggard face is rough with stubble. When he hangs his coat on the hook, he loses his balance and braces himself against the wall. A haze of alcohol fumes surrounds him. He's naked from the waist up except for the bandage covering the bullet wound on his arm; he's lost his jacket and shirt. My relief turns to dismay.

"Where were you?" Mick demands. "I looked all over."

"Drowning my sorrows." Hugh slurs his words. "With company that's more congenial than I can get here."

My heart sinks; he still hasn't forgiven me for telling the police about Tristan. And I can smell, in addition to the liquor and the stale vestiges of his bay rum shaving lotion, the harsh odor of unfamiliar cologne. He's been with a man—or men. He could have been caught by the vice squad, arrested for crimes against nature, and sentenced to two years of hard labor in prison.

"Why are you back so soon?" he asks me. "I thought you were going to solve Robin Mariner's murder and one-up the police."

I'm angry at Hugh for turning on me, at Tristan for coming between us, and at myself for letting things get so out of hand. "The police's investigation is over."

"Really," Hugh says with a dreary lack of interest. When Mick describes Tabitha's supposed suicide and DeQuincey's arrest, Hugh smiles faintly at me, as if to say, *I told you it wasn't Tristan*. Then he turns and unsteadily climbs the stairs.

"My lord, shouldn't you have something to eat?" Fitzmorris calls.

"I'm knackered. I'm going to bed."

My temper pushes aside my concern for Hugh. Following him up the stairs, I say, "You can't just bow out of this!"

"Watch me."

"I'm not the only one who agreed to work for Sir Gerald, and I'm not the only one who dug up evidence on the suspects. You ought to help me finish what we started."

"I'm finished with the detective racket." Hugh stumbles and grasps the banister for support. "Anyway, you just want another go at Tristan. You're determined to frame him for Robin's murder."

"That's not true!" But I can't forget my conversation with Barrett, and I wonder again about my own motives. My anger flares hotter at the thought that Hugh could be right about me, the monster's daughter. "Why are you so determined to protect Tristan? He doesn't care about you."

"Thanks, Sarah. Rub it in," Hugh says with bitter sarcasm. "I could ask that about you and Sir Gerald. You've bent over backward to make excuses for him, and he threw you out like a pregnant parlor maid."

I gasp in wounded indignation. "It's not the same thing."

"You're right. It's worse. I think Tristan is the love of my life. You think Sir Gerald is your father."

"*What?*"

"You've laid the unvarnished truth on me, so let me return the favor. You want Sir Gerald to be innocent because you want your father to be innocent. You feel guilty because you didn't look hard enough for your father when he went missing, and you're trying to make up for it by selling yourself out to Sir Gerald." Hugh taps his head with his finger. "You've got the two of them mixed up in your mind."

His accusation is so unexpected, ludicrous, and cruel, I'm too flabbergasted to counter it. "Why should you get to drink and carouse and feel sorry for yourself while Mick and I struggle on alone? It's not fair!"

Mick calls plaintively, "Let's not talk about this anymore."

Hugh stops at the top of the stairs and faces me. Anger blazes in his red, swollen eyes. "I'll tell you what's not fair. I could have told the police about your father, but I didn't, because I knew it would hurt you, and we were friends, and I was loyal to you. But you told them about Tristan even though I begged you not to. Where was *your* loyalty?"

He turns, stalks into his room, and slams the door.

My temper cools as quickly as it ignited, leaving me devastated. My knees buckle, and I sit on the stairs. Mick sits beside me, awkwardly pats my hand, and says, "Don't worry, Miss Sarah. He'll come around."

But Hugh's words echo in my ears: *You think Sir Gerald is your father.*

"In the meantime," Mick says, "you and me can keep at it together, can't we?"

We were *friends*. Our investigation has cost me Hugh as well as Barrett. But Mick looks so anxious that I force a smile as I nod. His friendship and our hope of solving Robin's and Tabitha's murders are all I have left.

#

At one thirty in the afternoon, Mick and I weave through the noisy crowds that jam the streets around St. Paul's Cathedral. Robin Mariner's funeral is a momentous event for a public enthralled by the story of his kidnapping and murder. The cold, drizzly afternoon hasn't deterred spectators from turning out in hordes. Newsboys shout, "The police caught Baby Robin's killers! One dead, one in jail!" Drawings of Raphael DeQuincey and Tabitha Jenkins grace the front pages of the newspapers. Peddlers do a good business in beer, meat pies, pickled oysters, and souvenirs—postcards, teacups, and boxes of candy bearing painted pictures of the photograph of Robin with Lady Alexandra. Many people wear black clothes or black crape armbands. I wonder if the public will ever know the secret about the little boy who so many prayed would be found alive, for whom so many now grieve.

Mick and I plow along in the wake of other people moving in the same direction. The crowds grow thicker. Carriages and horses clog the lane on the west side of St. Paul's. The enormous baroque structure of white masonry walls, columns, and towers rises from a sea of humanity. Its high, majestic green dome dissolves into the rain and mist. Photographers stand ready with cameras on the steps that front the cathedral's entrance. Gilded ropes strung on brass posts mark off a wide aisle down the center of the steps. At the bottom, and all around the cathedral, police constables hold back the crowds. Mick and I are crushed up against the base of the statue of St. Christopher. I stand on tiptoes in a futile attempt to see over the heads that block my view in all directions.

"How are we gonna find Sir Gerald in all this?" Mick asks.

The funeral is our chance to tell Sir Gerald what I learned from Dr. Kirkland. Although he probably won't welcome the news that we think his wife killed their son, tell him we must. He paid me to find out who kidnapped Robin; I feel a duty to finish the job, and he has the power to convince the police that they've arrested the wrong person. But I'm not eager to see him. Since my quarrel with Hugh, I've mulled over what he said, and after trying hard to deny it, I've had to admit that it's true.

It also explains my puzzling attraction to Sir Gerald.

I cast Sir Gerald as a stand-in for my father. I fell prey to the illusion that Sir Gerald, who embodies paternal strength and protectiveness, filled the void in me that my father's absence left. I wanted him to be innocent, as if that could negate my father's guilt. Now I'm ashamed that I was so blind to the workings of my own mind. I thought Hugh was cruel to set me straight, but he did me good even though he spoke in anger. I owe him a tremendous debt.

A commotion stirs the crowd. A phalanx of policemen's helmets and gentlemen's top hats bobs above the crowd, moving toward the cathedral. Craning my neck, I see the funeral party and guests—hundreds of people, all dressed in black—mount the steps. Photographers aim their cameras; flash powder ignites in explosions of white light, fiery sparks, and sulfurous smoke. The crowd buzzes with excited conversation as spectators point out the important politicians, merchants, and theatrical stars among the funeral party. At its head, Sir Gerald escorts Lady Alexandra, her face hidden by a black hat with a veil. John Pierce, Tristan, and Olivia follow them. Mick and I are immobilized by people tightly packed around us.

As the funeral procession streams into the cathedral, the crowd breaks through the police cordon and swarms up the steps, jostling the photographers and knocking over cameras mounted on tripods. Police yell, brandishing nightsticks, but they're vastly outnumbered. The crowd carries Mick and me with it. People push against me, feet trod on mine, and elbows jab my face. I stumble on the steps, and Mick pulls my hand.

"Hurry!" he cries. "This is our chance!"

The last members of the funeral party are entering the open doorway between the tall white columns. We and hundreds of other people stampede in after them before the door slams shut. Inside the cathedral, the vast, cold, echoing space is filled with the sweet smells of flowers and incense. Gold ornamentation on walls, columns, and the high ceiling gleams in the dim light from candles and gas lamps. The nave seems a mile long, its floor inlaid with a diamond pattern of black and white marble and lined with rows of chairs. Midway along its length, under the windows that circle the base of the dome, stands Robin's white-draped coffin on its bier, surrounded by floral bouquets and wreaths. There, the priest, bishop, and other church officials greet the funeral party. While ushers show guests to their seats, policemen chase out the trespassers.

"Over here!" Mick urges me through one of the archways that border the nave. We run up the outer corridor for some twenty feet, then duck between two rows of vacant chairs. We crouch, hiding, until the other trespassers have been ejected and the police are gone. Then we walk up the aisle, but a man blocks our way before we reach Sir Gerald. It's Inspector Reid, wearing black civilian clothes. My heart sinks.

Reid eyes Mick and me with exasperation. "What are you doing here?"

"We have to speak with Sir Gerald," I say.

"Of all the nerve!" Reid says in a low, furious whisper. "This is no time to bother Sir Gerald and his family." He seizes us by the arms and starts to march us down the aisle.

"Let go!" Mick cries, so loudly that his voice echoes throughout the cathedral. "We got somethin' important to tell Sir Gerald. It's about Robin's murder!"

Guests and funeral party turn in our direction. Sir Gerald strides toward us, saying, "What's the problem?"

"Trespassers," Reid says. "They're just leaving."

Sir Gerald recognizes us and frowns. Behind him, John Pierce stares coldly, Lady Alexandra lifts her veil to see us, and Tristan puts a protective arm around a pale, subdued Olivia. Disapproval radiates from the clergy and the guests. I flush, but Mick has no inhibitions.

"Tabitha Jenkins and Raphael DeQuincey didn't kill Robin," he announces. "We know who did."

The crowd murmurs in astonishment, Sir Gerald's frown deepens, and I shush Mick. Wild claims aired in public aren't going to convince Sir Gerald, and Reid isn't going to let us stay long enough to substantiate them. We had better keep silent and wait for another occasion than incur ridicule that will set Sir Gerald's mind against us.

But even as Reid drags us toward the door, Sir Gerald says, "Wait. I'll handle this." Beckoning to Mick and me, he walks through an archway.

Reid reluctantly releases us. We follow Sir Gerald downstairs to the crypt. The vast space is honeycombed with thick stone columns and arches. Our footsteps clatter on the mosaic floor. The air is cold, damp, and reeks of the cesspools that under lie London. A few gas lamps shine like weak stars that don't illuminate the darkness enough for me to see to the far ends of the crypt. Sir Gerald leads us to an area where I discern the hulking shapes of tombs that contain England's illustrious dead. I hear dripping water, faint murmurs from the crowd upstairs, and skittering noises, perhaps from rats.

Sir Gerald turns to face us. At last I truly see him for what he is—not a stand-in for my father, but a virtual stranger. He takes his watch from his pocket and glances at it. "The service starts in ten minutes." His voice is as cold as the air. "You'd better talk fast."

He's about to bury the son I now believe he didn't murder. My father disappeared to avoid punishment for the murder he likely committed. It's as though I've been looking at a photograph that I thought was a double exposure of the same man, and now I see that it's of two different men who bear no resemblance to each other. My attraction to Sir Gerald is gone, but my fear and awe of him remain. Tense with misgivings, I tell him about Lady Alexandra, Dr. Kirkland, and Robin's diagnosis.

His eyes gleam like I imagine a tiger's would in the jungle at night. Mick and I back away from the anger in them. "I terminated your employment," he says. "My family isn't your business any longer."

I'm surprised because he doesn't seem surprised by my news. Now I understand why he agreed to talk to us in private—he didn't want the people at the funeral to hear any secrets we might voice about his family. "You already knew?"

"Yes." His voice is flat, controlled. "My wife told me."

Mick and I exchange disconcerted glances. "When did Lady Alexandra tell you?" I ask. The timing matters because if Sir Gerald knew before the night Robin was kidnapped and murdered, then the crimes could be his doing.

Sir Gerald ignores the question. "You've got five minutes left. Was there anything else you wanted to say?"

Mick blurts, "We think Lady Alexandra killed Robin because she didn't want to be saddled with a feeble-minded cripple for the rest of her life."

I wince because he's worded our suspicion so crudely as well as accurately.

"If you breathe one word of this, I'll sue both of you, and Lord Hugh Staunton, for slander." Sir Gerald's quiet voice hisses with menace.

"It ain't slander if it's true," Mick says, frightened yet defiant.

Sir Gerald chuckles. "I'll win in court. I'll take every penny you have, and you'll go to the poorhouse."

I feel my terror resonate through Mick; we know he's right. What chance would we have against him? And everyone knows that life in the poorhouses is hell—squalid conditions, meager food, and backbreaking manual labor. Aghast that we've endangered Hugh as well as ourselves, I'm nonetheless puzzled by Sir Gerald's reaction.

"When you hired us, you were so determined to find out who kidnapped Robin," I say. "Why are you satisfied to put the blame on Tabitha and DeQuincey when there's even a chance that they're innocent and the wrong person will be hanged?"

"I believe they're guilty."

His voice rings with less than complete conviction. I press my point. "Lady Alexandra lied when she said she was with Lottie the night Robin was kidnapped. She took away Tabitha's alibi—and created a new one for herself—after Tabitha was dead and couldn't contradict her. She set Tabitha up to take the blame for Robin's murder."

"She did it to save her own neck," Mick chimes in. "She probably poisoned Tabitha, besides."

"I won't listen to any more accusations against my wife." Sir Gerald turns and walks toward the dim light that emanates from the stairwell.

Mick and I hurry after him. "But you yourself suspected Lady Alexandra," I say. "The day you hired us, you seemed willing to let her take the consequences if we found out she was responsible for the kidnapping. Why are you protecting her now?"

Even as I ask the question, I wonder if it's really Lady Alexandra he's protecting. Perhaps he, not his wife, is the monster who killed his defective child.

Sir Gerald pauses below the first stair and turns. The light illuminates his face, which is stoically impassive. "My wife is expecting."

Shock stuns us speechless. This is the last development I could have foreseen, but it explains so much.

"She's almost three months along." Now Sir Gerald's voice rings with masculine pride. "Her condition's delicate. Any upset could be dangerous."

He's protecting the baby as well Lady Alexandra. That's why he's willing to let Tabitha and DeQuincey take the blame for Robin's murder. Maybe he's even convinced himself they're guilty so that he needn't think the woman who's carrying his child is. That's why he was so quick to put a stop to our investigation, pay us off, and cut us loose. Lady Alexandra's pregnancy represents a fresh start for him—a chance for a son who doesn't have Little's Disease, a new heir that he needn't hide from the public.

I was replaced by Sally, Olivia by Robin, and now Robin by a new baby. Sir Gerald and my father have something in common after all.

Sir Gerald points his finger at us. "If you make a public accusation against Lady Alexandra and she loses the baby, its blood will be on your hands."

28

When Mick and I get home, we find a distraught Fitzmorris waiting. "Lord Hugh went out again," he says.

Mick doesn't volunteer to look for him this time. While we eat a supper of cold meat, bread, and pickles, we commiserate about our clash with Sir Gerald.

"Lady A is gonna get away scot-free," Mick concludes glumly. "And if we rock the boat, Sir G will cook our goose."

I'm forced to admit that Hugh was right. "It's over," I say, despite my disturbing sense of unfinished business. "Raphael DeQuincey will hang." And there will be no justice for Robin.

That night, after Mick is in bed, I go upstairs to the attic. Rain patters on the roof as I unearth two suitcases from among the old furniture and other cast-off items. I take the suitcases down to my room and remove my clothes from the cupboards. As I fold dresses and undergarments, Fitzmorris comes to the door.

"Sarah, are you leaving?"

I swallow the lump in my throat before I turn to him. "Yes."

His expression is filled with concern. "Why?"

"I can't stay here. I've taken too much advantage of Hugh's hospitality, and now that we're"—my voice breaks—"not friends anymore . . ."

"But surely you'll make up?"

I shake my head, unable to face Hugh again and see the hostility in his eyes where there was once affection. "It's best that I leave now."

"But where will you live?"

"At one of the hotels by St. Pancras station. Until I can find a room in a lodging house."

"Sarah, please don't go," Fitzmorris says. "Lord Hugh loves you and needs you. He's just so upset that he's forgotten."

I can't forget that involving Hugh in my troubles last fall ruined his life and almost got him killed. He would be better off if we'd never met. My lips tremble, and I press them together as I close the suitcase.

"At least wait until morning."

I sigh and nod. I don't really want to trudge through the cold, wet night to sleep in a cheerless hotel room. I take the other suitcase downstairs to my darkroom. There's little to pack besides the extra tools, trays, negative plates, and photographic paper I didn't take to Mariner House. I sort through my exposed plates and printed enlargements. Because I don't want a reminder of Hugh's and my high hopes for our detective agency, I throw the plates and prints of my photographs from the Crystal Palace into the kitchen wastebin without looking at them. I pack the best pictures I took around London and in my studio; they'll serve as my portfolio when I apply for work at the big photography companies. I come across a portrait of Hugh, and my heart aches at the sight of his mischievous smile. I put it in the suitcase with my photographs of Mick, Catherine, Fitzmorris, the Lipskys, and my father, his shadowy figure in the woods near a daffodil-strewn graveyard.

A tear drops on my father's picture. I wipe it off with my hand. As I carry the suitcase out of the kitchen, the top print in the wastebin catches my attention.

It's the one I took by the glass fountain in the Crystal Palace—the shot that failed to capture Noel Vaughn and Ethel Norris because someone bumped my camera. My heart thumps as I unexpectedly recognize someone among the strangers gathered around the fountain. I take the photograph out of the wastebin and study the tall, slender, dark-haired man dressed in black. I didn't notice him on the day I took the picture because I didn't know him at the time.

He's Raphael DeQuincey.

#

The next morning, I join a long queue of people outside Newgate Prison, the granite dungeon that occupies an entire city block by the Old Bailey courthouse. The day is cold, the mist laced with eye-stinging smoke from the factories. Carriages in the street splash through puddles left by last night's rain. As we inch toward the visitor's entrance, I shiver, recalling my own brief but terrible incarceration last autumn. We climb a short flight of steps, walk along a dim passage, and emerge in a courtyard surrounded by prison wards that rise three stories high. Inmates shout greetings, pleas, and obscenities to us from the barred windows. The queue ends at the guards stationed near the visiting box—a big iron cage with a slanted roof, built against one wall. I see prisoners inside the cage facing visitors who stand on the outside. They talk and argue; they press their hands together and kiss through the metal grating between the bars of the cage. When I finally reach the front of the queue, I tell the guards I'm here to see Raphael DeQuincey.

"Yeah, everybody and his brother wants a gawk at the scum who killed Robin Mariner," one guard says as the other searches my satchel for weapons, liquor, and other contraband while a female warder pats me down. He points to a group of people standing by a door opposite the visiting cage. "You can wait over there. The next tour starts in a few minutes. That'll be ten pence."

I'm disgusted because the guards are showing off DeQuincey as if he's a freak at a carnival but glad I'll be able to see him. I hand over the money and join the group, which includes reporters and photographers. Soon a guard leads us into the jail, single file through a dim labyrinth of corridors paved with flagstones. I'm last in line, and when we stop, the people ahead of me murmur in awe, horror, or glee. Flash powder lights up the corridor as the photographers take pictures. The reporters call out,

"Mr. DeQuincey, what have you to say for yourself?"

"Which of you put Robin in the pond—you or Tabitha Jenkins?"

"Are you sorry?"

I hear whimpering, the only response. At last it's my turn. A thick, iron-studded door stands open. I peer into a narrow cell that has stone walls and an arched ceiling. In the light from the single barred window, I see a man curled on the wooden bed. His right leg, in a thick white plaster cast, protrudes from beneath the blanket that covers him. DeQuincey's hair is shaved on one side where a blood-stained bandage covers his scalp. Dark bruises circle his eyes, and red cuts mar his pale, gaunt face. His left front tooth is missing. Whimpering and grunting, he seems more animal than human.

"What happened to him?" I ask the guard.

"The other prisoners beat him up. That's why he was moved to solitary confinement."

The man who allegedly killed Robin became a punching bag for his fellow inmates and, I suspect, the police and guards. I feel guilty because my information contributed to his imprisonment, but then I recall that my photograph proves he was at the Crystal Palace on the day of the ransom exchange and murders. Perhaps everything I thought I knew about the kidnapping is wrong, and DeQuincey is where he belongs.

"Time's up." The guard herds people down the corridor.

"If you let me talk to him alone, I'll pay you ten more pence," I say.

The guard considers me with a sly, lewd expression. He must think I'm among those women who are attracted to criminals. "Make it a half crown, and you get fifteen minutes."

After the coin exchanges hands and the guard escorts the group outside, I enter the cell and say, "Mr. DeQuincey?"

He gazes at me without recognition. His white, trembling hands creep out from the blanket and pull it tighter around himself. The last two fingers on his left hand wear splints and bandages. His right wrist is chained to the bed. He blinks, trying to focus on me. "Who are you?"

I hope the injury to his head hasn't damaged his wits. "Sarah Bain. We met at Mariner House."

Fearful awareness creeps into his expression. I look around the cell and see a water tank, basin, and a chamber pot in the corner, a shelf by the window that holds a Bible, and a wooden stool. I pull the stool close to the bed and sit by DeQuincey. Then I reach in my satchel, pull out my photograph of him, and hold it in front of his face.

"I took this on the day of the ransom exchange. You said you weren't at the Crystal Palace, but there you are." I point him out among the people admiring the glass fountain.

A spark of horror glints in DeQuincey's eyes. He understands what I'm telling him. His bruised, puffy lips form the word *no*.

"You lied. You said you and Tabitha didn't go to collect the ransom money, but you actually did." I shake the photograph at him before I replace it in my satchel. "This is proof."

DeQuincey shakes his head, winces in pain, and gingerly touches the bandage on his scalp. "Not Tabitha."

His meaning sinks in. "You mean you went to the dinosaur park alone?"

"She didn't know." DeQuincey sounds eager to defend Tabitha.

"Because you didn't tell her?"

"Yeah. We decided not to go, but . . ." Tremors ripple through DeQuincey, and I wonder if he's ill or the beating damaged his nerves. "I kept thinking about the thousand pounds. I couldn't resist," he says sheepishly.

"Where's the money now?" The logical question springs to mind despite the fact that the money is the least of my concerns.

DeQuincey's body twitches convulsively. "Hell if I know. I didn't take it."

Confused, I say, "But you just admitted you went to the dinosaur park."

"Went there, yeah. Took the money, nope."

I begin to realize that there's more to this story than my photograph of DeQuincey suggests. "What happened at the park?"

Sudden anger sharpens his gaze. "Hey. I remember who you are." He points a wobbly finger at me. "You're Sir Gerald's lady detective. You and the boy found me in the woods and broke my leg. Then you turned me over to the police." He recoils under his blanket like a snail into its shell. "I'm not talking to you anymore."

"We rescued you after you broke your leg," I say. "The police caught us."

"Yeah, well, that's not how I remember it."

Maybe the beating did damage his mind. "I'm trying to rescue you now," I say, although if I learn that he was involved in Robin's murder and the fires that almost killed Hugh and me, I'll gladly forsake him. "Tell me what happened. It's your only chance to save your life."

DeQuincey's expression turns forlorn. "There's no saving me. I'll be meeting the rope-maker's daughter soon."

"Then why not tell me anyway? You can't make things worse."

"That you know of," he retorts.

It's an odd thing to say, and it hints that the truth is odder than I can imagine. "So you're soon to be hanged, and Tabitha is already dead. What could be worse?" The answer occurs to me. "You're protecting someone. Who is it?"

DeQuincey chews his lip, torn between his will to remain silent and an urge to confide. Dissolving into tears, he says, "I've a wife and two boys."

"*You're married?*" Here's something else that Tabitha didn't know about DeQuincey. "I thought you and Tabitha were planning to elope."

"That was what she wanted. She didn't know I already had a wife and family." Shamefaced, he says, "I couldn't think of a way to tell her."

I'm outraged on Tabitha's behalf. "You could have said, 'I'm married. We can't be together,' and walked away. Instead, you led her on. You're a greedy, selfish cad!"

"Don't you think I know it?" DeQuincey says woefully. "But I cared about Tabitha. I really, truly did."

He doesn't say he loved her, and his remorse doesn't excuse him or lessen my outrage. "If you really, truly cared about her, you wouldn't have involved her in your scheme to profit from Robin's kidnapping."

"The ransom note was her idea too," DeQuincey protests.

"Then you must have planted the idea in her mind. I doubt she was cunning enough to think of it all by herself."

"Well, now I'm left to take the whole blame."

"Poor you." I regard him with disgust.

How I would like to believe that Tabitha's death and his arrest are his fault! If he hadn't romanced Tabitha, there would have been no love scene in the ballroom for Hugh and me to witness, and nothing for me to tell the police about Tabitha and DeQuincey. I'd like to believe that DeQuincey deserves his sorry fate. But hanging is too extreme a punishment for seducing a willing woman and sending a ransom note to the parents of a child that somebody else kidnapped and murdered. Besides, it was my choice to talk to the police.

"I'm going to die," DeQuincey wails. "My wife will be a widow, and my children will be fatherless. They don't deserve this!"

His fate and his family's are at least partially my responsibility, like him or not. "So you're protecting your family. Has someone threatened them?"

DeQuincey doesn't reply, but his gaze shifts and his Adam's apple jerks.

"Was it Sir Gerald?" I feel the chill of encroaching distress. Sir Gerald would surely make it his business to uncover the dirty laundry of any person who associated with his wife. If he or Lady Alexandra murdered Robin, what better use for his knowledge than to force DeQuincey to take the blame? "Did he promise you that if you keep quiet, your family will be safe?"

"Not Sir Gerald!" DeQuincey blurts. I'm relieved, but he trembles harder, with panic, because he's admitted that someone has indeed threatened his family to buy his silence.

"How can you be sure this person will keep his word? How are you going to protect your family after you're dead?"

"I never thought of that." DeQuincey bursts into sobs. "I don't know what to do!"

"The only way you can make sure they're safe is to exonerate yourself," I say. "I'll help you, if you tell me everything."

I'm far from certain my help will save him, but he grasps at this only available straw. "I sneaked out of Mariner House without telling Tabitha, and I went to the dinosaur park. Our ransom note told Sir Gerald to leave the money in a hollow tree at two o'clock. I got there half an hour early, so I hid in the woods and waited. About ten minutes later, I saw John Pierce coming with a valise. He put it in the tree and left. I waited a few more minutes to make sure he was gone. I was just heading for the tree when I heard footsteps. I thought, 'Bloody hell, a trap!' I ran back in the woods. I was so scared I almost wet myself. Then I saw Pierce coming back. He walked straight to the tree, and he took the valise and left again."

Pierce stole the money. But of course he's the logical person to have done so; he was there, and he had the opportunity. If DeQuincey hadn't changed his mind about collecting the ransom, no one would have been the wiser.

"Why didn't you tell Lady Alexandra and Sir Gerald?"

"Pierce would have denied it. It would have been his word against mine, and who would believe me?" DeQuincey utters a woeful laugh. "I've got a police record for theft. Besides, nobody except Lady Alexandra, Sir Gerald, and Pierce was supposed to know about the ransom. If I'd admitted being in the park, Sir Gerald would have assumed it was me who kid-napped Robin and sent the note."

I surmise that Pierce knew about DeQuincey's secret family because he'd been the one who investigated him for Sir Gerald. "So it was Pierce who threatened your family."

"Yeah."

"But how did he know you were there that day?"

"I told him."

"*Why?*"

"It was a chance to make up for losing out on the ransom. I went to Pierce and said I'd seen him steal the money and that unless he gave me half of it, I would tell the police."

My mouth drops even though I already knew how rash DeQuincey is. "You blackmailed Pierce."

"I thought I was so smart," DeQuincey says ruefully. "At first it seemed like I had Pierce where I wanted him. He was all upset. He's been paying me twenty pounds a week."

Pierce must not have been confident that the police wouldn't believe DeQuincey. Maybe he had kidnapped and murdered Robin and therefore was afraid that if the police learned that he'd taken the ransom money, such incriminating evidence would be enough to get him hanged. Maybe he thought five hundred pounds a small price to pay for DeQuincey's silence.

"When did he threaten your family?" I say.

"After you caught me in the woods and we were back in Mariner House." DeQuincey explains, "When Lottie said Tabitha was dead, everybody ran upstairs to see, but I couldn't because of my leg. Pierce came and told the constable to leave us alone for a minute. Then he said that if I didn't keep my mouth shut about him, he would kill my wife and boys."

While Mick and I and the others were gathered around Tabitha, another drama was taking place unbeknown to us. It's as if I've been looking at a photograph of Mariner House and the gruesome scene in Tabitha's room is visible through the win-dow, but the window of the dining room, where Pierce threat-ened DeQuincey, was curtained. Pierce must have realized that because DeQuincey was now on the hook for Robin's murder, paying him blackmail would no longer suffice to buy his silence.

"I told Pierce that I would talk and he would be arrested before he could get to my family. But he said he had people ready to do it if I ratted on him," DeQuincey says miserably. "I couldn't take the chance that he was bluffing." He apparently cares about his family even though he took up with another woman. "So then Pierce offered me a deal: if I would take the blame for Robin, he would support my family after I'm dead."

"And you agreed? You trust Pierce?" I can't believe it.

DeQuincey shrugs. "I'm not so smart, right?"

Not only did Pierce coerce DeQuincey into taking the blame for Robin's murder, he tried to scare Hugh and me into quitting our investigation. I'm growing more certain not only that he's Robin's murderer but also that he poisoned Tabitha and faked her suicide. And now I see that an additional crime can possibly be laid at Pierce's door.

"Was there anybody else in the dinosaur park with you and Pierce?" I ask.

"No," DeQuincey says.

As I sigh in disappointment, he says, "Wait. I forgot. When Pierce was leaving, he bumped into some people. A man with a red-haired tart. They were kissing."

Noel Vaughn and Ethel Norris. My hope revives. "What did Pierce do?"

"Beats me," DeQuincey says. "That's when I skedaddled."

He didn't see Hugh and me. He also didn't see my father. It's a letdown, as is the fact that although I think Pierce killed the lovers, there's no evidence to prove it. The only possible witness to their murder is my father, who's still missing.

"I've told you everything," DeQuincey says. "Are you going to get me out of here?"

"Yes." But I've no idea how to use my evidence to free him or deliver Pierce to justice.

29

Upon my return home, I hear Hugh's voice in the parlor. I'm relieved that he's back but afraid to face him because we parted on such bad terms. I find him reclining on the yellow silk-covered chaise longue and Mick seated on the sofa by the fire. Hugh looks clean and neatly groomed and dressed. The gaze he lifts to me is lucid and somber.

Eager to forestall another quarrel, I say, "I'm moving out." I don't want to go, but I'd rather leave voluntarily than have him evict me. "I'll just fetch my baggage and be on my way."

Hugh springs up from the chaise and grasps my shoulders. "Sarah, please don't leave." His eyes are filled with regret and shame. "I want to apologize for treating you so harshly. I've been a complete bastard. Will you forgive me?"

His heart is too kind to sustain his grudge. My heart overflows with so much love for him that tears blur my eyes. "I'm the one who should apologize to you."

Hugh waves away the notion. "I spent last night walking for miles around the city, just thinking. By the time I lumbered home this morning, I understood what had happened—I went head over heels for Tristan Mariner, and then I blamed you for my unhappiness while you were only trying to watch out for me. I shouldn't have said that about your father."

His gaze softens with the affection I've missed so much. I'm fervently glad he's not mad at me anymore. "But you were right about my father. And I could have been more tactful."

"Well, it's in the past. I'm just hoping that I haven't lost one of the few true friends I have in the world." Apprehension clouds Hugh's gaze. "I haven't lost you, have I, Sarah?"

"Of course not." I swallow a sob. "I've been so afraid I'd lost you."

As we smile at each other, Hugh holds out his arms. I awkwardly step into and return his embrace. Although we've shared an intimacy that's rare for a man and woman who aren't a couple, we've never expressed our love this physically. The warmth of his body, the smell of his bay rum shaving lotion, and his cheek against my hair are such a comfort after my distressful experiences. But I remember that the last man to embrace me was Barrett, and Hugh pats my back while I cry. I feel his body heave; he too is crying for love lost.

When we're finished, we step apart and wipe our eyes. Mick is slouched on the sofa, embarrassed by our display of emotion. Hugh clears his throat and says, "Now that that's over, back to business. How do we find out who really killed Robin?"

I'm glad he's decided not to quit our detective agency and glad I'm able to say, "I think I already know."

Hugh and Mick exclaim in surprise. "How'd you find out?" Mick asks.

I sit beside Mick while Hugh reclines on the chaise longue, and I describe my visit to DeQuincey.

"So it was John Pierce," Hugh says. I can tell that he'd been afraid it was Tristan and he's glad to hear otherwise.

Now that the heat of the moment when I heard DeQuincey's story about Pierce has passed, seeds of doubt germinate in the cold light of reason. "There's no proof that Pierce murdered Robin. The only thing DeQuincey saw Pierce do was take the ransom money."

"That Pierce is so determined to send DeQuincey to the gallows is proof enough for me," Hugh says.

I'm aware that Pierce's guilt isn't the only bone of contention between Hugh and me. We're still arguing for and against Tristan's innocence. "Understand that even without absolute proof, I'm ready to believe Pierce murdered Robin, Tabitha, Noel Vaughn, and Ethel Norris, but I'm afraid the police won't be."

"Yeah," Mick says. "They think they've already got their man."

"Inspector Reid would be more furious at us for meddling again than ready to trust anything we say," I point out.

"We could tell Barrett first," Hugh says. "Maybe he can help us convince Reid."

"He won't." Anguish pains me as I think of Barrett.

"Why not?" Hugh asks. "I know you two are on the outs, but Barrett is an honorable fellow who wouldn't want the wronged man hanged."

Unable to bear describing my hurtful conversation with Barrett, I say, "DeQuincey isn't a credible witness. He has a police record. Barrett would probably think DeQuincey made up the whole story about John Pierce to save himself."

"But we can't just sit on the information," Hugh says. "And I still want to solve this case." His eyes light with the same enthusiasm as when we began our investigation.

"So do I." After all that our investigation has cost us—my illusions about my father, our broken hearts, and my photography equipment—fulfilling our original purpose would be fair enough compensation.

"Fortunately, the police aren't our only recourse," Hugh says. "We'll tell Sir Gerald."

#

The train to Hampstead thunders through the night. Vapor condenses and drips down the window beside the seats where

Mick and I sit opposite Hugh. It's so foggy that all I can see outside are the lamps on posts along the track. We waited until night to return to Mariner House, when Sir Gerald is likely to be home. This journey seems a negative image of my first one to Mariner House—darkness instead of daylight, dread instead of high hopes. I think we all feel a sense of inevitability, as if fate has steered us toward whatever will happen there tonight. Tonight will see the end of everything, for better or worse.

"Do you think Sir Gerald will believe us?" Mick asks.

"Let's not jinx ourselves by speculating," Hugh says with a smile. There's a sparkle to him that I've not seen since before Robin's body was found in the pond.

"First things first," I say. "We have to get there."

At nine twenty on this cold evening, we're the only passengers who get off the train at Hampstead Heath station. The high street is empty of pedestrians and traffic, the shops closed. Lights shine from two public houses, where I suppose any reporters in the neighborhood have taken refuge. A lone carriage for hire waits by the deserted green. We hurry to it and climb in. "Mariner House," Hugh calls to the driver.

As we ride through town, I peer at the shop windows and see that the photographs of Robin and Lady Alexandra have been replaced by newspaper front pages bearing an illustration of Raphael DeQuincey behind bars. I shiver. Hugh and Mick are silent, infected with the same unease as myself. We gaze out at the fog that renders the heath beyond the fences and hedgerows invisible. As we ascend the hill, the woods envelop us like a mythical forest, which parts to let the hero walk in and then seals off the path behind him. Water drips from the trees, and branches scrape the carriage's roof. I fight the notion that we'll never return from Mariner House.

"We can still change our minds," I say, recalling that Hugh said the same thing during our first trip.

"Couldn't pay me enough to turn back," Mick says.

"Ditto." Hugh leans forward as if to make the carriage go faster.

I think he's not just eager to tell Sir Gerald that John Pierce murdered Robin—he hopes to see Tristan as well.

Before we reach the summit of the hill, Hugh tells the driver to let us out. The night smells of wet earth. The darkness is total between the lamps on posts spaced at wide intervals. We bypass each one and aim for the next, like ships at sea following lighthouses along the coast. We walk until we see several men standing by the gates of Mariner House. Voices and laughter drift toward us. Two of the men are wearing police helmets. The others are Sir Gerald's guards.

"We can't just waltz up to them and ask to see Sir Gerald," Hugh whispers. "We're *personae non gratae*, excuse my Latin."

"We better use the tunnel," Mick says.

"What tunnel?" Hugh asks.

I explain about Sir Gerald's secret exit. "But the door inside the house is locked."

Mick grins. "Not now, it ain't. I unlocked it before we left last time, just in case."

So that's what he was doing when he wandered off that night.

"Good thinking." Hugh claps Mick on the shoulder. "Onward!"

Mick glances at the dark woods and says to me, "We need the light."

I open my satchel and remove the small metal lantern. Mick lights it with a match from his pocket and carries it while we trudge through the woods. Beyond the high brick wall, Mariner House is a black hulk with few lighted windows. I hear footsteps in the distance and see lights from other lanterns flickering between the trees—Sir Gerald's guards patrolling. Twice, they come so near that Mick has to extinguish the lantern and we huddle in the darkness until they're gone. More than an hour later, we haven't found the entrance to the tunnel.

"It's here somewhere," Mick says.

Every tree, every stretch of hillside, looks alike. We're tired and cold, and my feet are soaked; Hugh and I muffle coughs from our smoke-irritated lungs. At last Mick says, "Ha!" He's located the steep, rocky slope overhung with vines. He opens the iron door and shines the lantern into the tunnel.

"Are you sure it won't collapse?" Hugh asks.

"It only needs to hold up 'til we're inside the house," Mick says.

"Somehow that doesn't reassure me," Hugh says, but he follows Mick and me into the tunnel.

Although Mick lights the first few oil lamps strung along the walls before he extinguishes our lantern and closes the door, the tunnel seems even darker than the first time. The night seems to add an extra weight that presses down on the ceiling. As I follow Mick up through the zigzagging tunnel and pause while he lights more lamps, behind me Hugh's breathing grows labored, and he coughs constantly. I'm afraid someone in the house will hear or our passage will bring down the tunnel. I try to calm myself with the idea that Sir Gerald must keep the tunnel in good repair in case he has to use it himself. Not a moment too soon, we reach the far end. Now I'm more afraid of what awaits us on the other side.

The door opens easily. Hugh whispers, "Thank God," as we step into a stone-walled passage.

Moments later, we're stealing past the kitchen, pantry, and scullery. The house seems deserted, too quiet. Climbing the back stairs, I feel uneasy because I don't know where John Pierce is. If we run into him, he'll surely prevent us from seeing Sir Gerald. "Let's try Sir Gerald's office," I whisper.

"I know where it is," Mick says.

He leads us to the second floor of the south wing. The passage is dark except for gas lamps burning at the entrance to the mansion's central wing and a faint glow from a doorway at the end. Mick points to the doorway. We tiptoe to it and cautiously step inside. The large room, paneled with wood and furnished with leather chairs and sofas, is illuminated by a fire burning in the hearth at the right and dim gaslight from an alcove at the left. A faint smell of decay underlies the odors of wood and smoke. Now I see a bear standing eight feet tall on its hind legs and a tiger whose fangs are exposed in a snarl. On the walls are dozens of mounted heads—deer and elks with branching antlers; a rhinoceros like an ugly, leathery unicorn. I remember the tour guide mentioning Sir Gerald's hunting trophies. The office is quiet and still except for the crackling of the fire. Curtains on the windows are open; darkness presses against the panes. I think Sir Gerald must have stepped out. As I wonder where to look for him, I hear grunting, panting noises.

My heart lurches. Hugh and Mick stiffen. Through my mind flashes the notion that one of the beasts is alive. The sounds are coming from the alcove, and we move toward it, irresistibly curious. Zebra skins spread on the floor muffle the noise of our footsteps. Gold and jeweled artifacts glitter in the glass cases; a statue of a Japanese warrior poses in full armor. These, and the other treasures I barely glimpse, must be souvenirs of Sir Gerald's travels. On each side of the entrance to the alcove stands an upright elephant tusk, long and curved and sharp-pointed. The alcove contains a desk with a window behind it and bookshelves on either side. In the dim light from a green-shaded gas lamp suspended from the ceiling, Sir Gerald sits with his head resting on his folded arms amid papers, ledgers, a bottle of brandy, and a half-full glass. His shoulders quake, and his grunts and pants sound like those of a wounded animal.

He's crying.

We watch, fascinated; it's as though a titan has crumbled. Sir Gerald is grieving with the age-old grief of every bereaved father who's just buried a child. I wonder if my father ever grieved over losing me when he left me forever. Sympathy for Sir Gerald wells in me, and I wonder what else he might be grieving about. His knowledge that the people close to him

are so untrustworthy and his relationships with them so love-
less that one of them murdered his son? The idea that his son's
own mother could be the killer? He and my father aren't the
same person, but they're both a mystery to me.

Sir Gerald senses our presence and raises his head. His face
is swollen and mottled from weeping. He wears a dressing
gown and nightshirt, and his hair is disheveled, as if he rose
from his bed because he couldn't sleep and sought refuge here
among his mementos of better times. He looks appalled and
furious that anyone should see him like this.

"How did you get in?" Sir Gerald sits upright. Strength
visibly floods back into him as if by an act of sheer will, and
he appears to grow larger before our very eyes.

I'm reminded of a dragon or other mythical beast, tem-
porarily subdued during a battle and rising again, invincible.
We're too intimidated to confess that we used his secret tunnel.

"What are you doing here?"

Finding my voice, I stammer, "I needed to talk to you.
About Lady Alexandra."

"You came to throw more mud at my wife?"

Hugh steps in. "What she's trying to say is, we no longer
believe it was Lady Alexandra who murdered Robin."

A gulp bursts from Sir Gerald. It's the sound that a drowning man might utter when he sees a life preserver tossed to
him. Although Sir Gerald stood by Lady Alexandra, he must
have been terrified that his wife, who is pregnant with their
new child, was a monster who'd destroyed their son. I'm as
glad to allay his terror as I am ashamed that I contributed to it
when I accused Lady Alexandra.

"We think we know who really did kill Robin," I say.

"Why should I believe anything you say? You keep changing your mind, pointing your finger at one person after
another." But Sir Gerald can't hide his desire to hear us. He's
lost his discipline over his emotions, his ability to play his
cards close to his chest. The brandy bottle on his desk is almost
empty, and he smells of liquor. He's drunk, and I think he's

also in the throes of a mental breakdown that started when Robin was kidnapped and that he's held at bay until now.

Mick speaks up. "Here's why you should listen to us: you want the truth, and nobody else is gonna give it to you. If you throw us out you'll be always wondering."

Sir Gerald looks at Mick, and I remember the first time they met and Sir Gerald took to him. "All right. I'm listening. Who is it?" His expression warns me that I'd better be right this time.

"Excuse me, Sir Gerald." John Pierce speaks from behind us, at the door.

Alarm sizzles through me and widens Hugh's and Mick's eyes. We didn't hear him coming. Now we'll have to accuse Pierce to his face, and it will be his word against ours.

"The guards spotted prowlers outside the estate." Pierce has seen Hugh, Mick, and me, and his face registers surprise, then disapproval. "You're the prowlers."

Sir Gerald silences him with a raised hand and says to us, "Who killed Robin?"

"We were just about to speak of the devil," Hugh says, pointing at Pierce.

30

Sir Gerald stares, uncomprehending, first at Hugh, then at Pierce.

"Yeah, it's him," Mick says. "He killed Robin."

"That's bosh!" Pierce's scorn isn't quick enough to conceal the alarm that flickers in his eyes. "Sir Gerald, I warned you about these people. They're trying to bilk you again."

A watchful stillness comes over Sir Gerald. I imagine him as a hunter in the jungle, waiting to shoot the tiger. "John, I've never asked you, but I'm going to now." His voice is very quiet. "Did you kill Robin?"

Pierce laughs, but the sound is breathy with fear. "Of course not. It was Tabitha and Raphael DeQuincey."

Sir Gerald squints as if trying to discern whether the movement he sees in the jungle is the tiger or just the wind. I realize something I should have at the start: the outcome of the murder investigation depends more upon what Sir Gerald is willing to believe than upon the actual truth. He, with his power and influence, is the ultimate judge. This is our one chance to prevent a miscarriage of justice.

"You took the ransom money," I say to Pierce.

Even as the alarm flares brighter in his eyes, Pierce appeals to Sir Gerald. "She's lying. I left the money in the hollow tree. Tabitha and DeQuincey took it."

"You thought nobody saw you take it, but somebody did," Hugh says.

"That couple who were fooling around in the dinosaur park? They couldn't have talked because I—" Realizing too late that his reaction put a lie to his denials and his words are tantamount to a confession, Pierce looks aghast.

"You murdered Noel Vaughn and Ethel Norris," I say. "They were witnesses. You couldn't let them live." Other mysteries unravel before my eyes. "You broke into my trunk and saw my photograph of them. You knew Hugh and I were at the park, and you thought we'd seen you too. That's why you wanted to sneak us out of Mariner House—so we couldn't tell the police. And after I said no, you tried to burn us to death."

"I don't know what she's talking about," Pierce blusters.

Sir Gerald bangs his fists on the desk, leans across it, and points at Pierce. "You kidnapped my son. It was you who you sent the ransom note. You took my money after you killed Robin. You never meant to give him back!"

Pierce recoils and wipes his mouth with a trembling hand. "All right—I took the money. But I didn't send the ransom note, and I didn't kidnap Robin." He obviously hopes that if he admits to a lesser offense, he won't be punished.

Sir Gerald beholds him with a mixture of realization and contempt. "You still have a grudge against me because I married Alexandra."

"Taking the money was good enough revenge on both of you." Pierce surely knows better than to let his triumph show, but he can't resist. He shrugs. "It didn't make any difference to Robin—he was already in the pond by then. Somebody else put him there."

"*You* put him there! After I picked you off the docks in bloody Jamaica and gave you a good job and a home. You shit-faced, traitorous bastard!"

"A job as your slave." Decades' worth of pent-up resentment spews from Pierce. "A home where I'm at your beck and call twenty-four hours a day and you fuck the woman you stole from me."

"If not for me, you'd have nothing. And you murdered my son!"

Their mutual hatred is ugly to see, but Mick, Hugh, and I exchange relieved glances because things have gone better than we expected; Sir Gerald is convinced, and it won't be long before DeQuincey is freed from jail. I only regret that it's too late to save Tabitha.

"The police are outside," Hugh says to Sir Gerald. "With your permission, we'll fetch them. They can arrest Mr. Pierce."

"That won't be necessary." Sir Gerald opens the top drawer of his desk. His hand comes up holding a pistol.

My breath catches. Hugh's jaw drops. Mick exclaims, "Whoa!"

"I'll send this blackguard to hell without any help from the hangman." Sir Gerald staggers out from behind his desk and points the gun at Pierce.

Pierce backs away, his face a picture of disbelief. "You can't shoot me."

"Just watch." Sir Gerald is trembling; fresh tears leak from his eyes as his grief reverberates through his anger.

Suddenly I understand why Sir Gerald hired Hugh and me, why he didn't tell the police the kidnapping was an inside job, and why he made us sign the confidentiality agreement. He intended to avenge Robin with his own hands, and if we saw him commit cold-blooded murder, we would be too beholden to him—and too afraid of him—to object, let alone tell anyone.

Pierce stumbles backward. The blood drains from his complexion, leaving it as yellow-white as polluted snow. His fearful gaze is riveted on the pistol as Sir Gerald takes aim at his heart. Contradictory impulses urge me to flee but root me to the spot. Although Hugh and Mick look terrified, they don't move either. We're loath to watch Sir Gerald kill Pierce, but we're responsible for this scene, obligated to witness it. I want to close my eyes, to spare myself the sight of blood and death, but I also want to see justice done.

As Sir Gerald cocks the pistol, a sob convulses him. His finger fumbles on the trigger. Pierce lunges at Sir Gerald. He grabs the gun with both his hands and yanks it upward. The gun points at the ceiling as the men stagger, bump the furniture, and fight for control of the weapon. Bellowing with murderous rage, Sir Gerald rams his left fist into Pierce's ribs. Pierce yells in pain, but he doesn't let go. The gun swings in wild arcs, pointing down, sideways, and at us.

"Get down!" Mick drops to his knees, pulling Hugh and me with him.

As we crawl toward the door, there's a loud bang, the sound of glass breaking, and the smell of sulfur. I scream, turn, and see the jagged hole in the window behind Sir Gerald's desk. The rush of cold air from outside fans the fire in the hearth into a blaze. Pierce and Sir Gerald fall in a tangle of legs. They thrash on the floor and shout obscenities.

Frightened voices and rapid footsteps clamor throughout the house. People who heard the shot are coming. Sir Gerald lies under Pierce, bucking and flailing, trying to throw Pierce off him. While his right hand holds the gun over his head, he punches Pierce's face with his left. Pierce clings to Sir Gerald's wrist and bangs his hand on the floor in an attempt to make him release the gun. I have to help Sir Gerald. His attempt at cold-blooded murder has banished the vestiges of my personal feelings for him, but his life wouldn't be in danger if not for me. Clambering to my feet, I look around for a weapon. Hugh and Mick hurry toward Pierce and Sir Gerald, but someone rushes past them, crying, "Daddy!"

Olivia, in a white night dress, her curly dark hair like a cloud around her shoulders, throws herself on Pierce's back. She claws his head, grabs his hair and pulls as she shrieks, "Stop it! Leave my father alone!"

Then Tristan is in the room. He grabs Olivia by the waist, pulls her off Pierce, flings her aside, and reaches for the gun. With a mighty bellow and heave, Sir Gerald rolls over onto

Pierce. Tristan is caught in the battle like a man on railroad tracks spun up in the wheels of a train. Olivia screams.

The frenzy is over so fast, I can't see what happened. Pierce is on his feet, the gun in his hand. Sir Gerald and Tristan are on the floor, struggling to rise, panting and disheveled. Pierce aims the gun at them. Bloody lines mark his cheeks where Olivia scratched him, and he gasps for breath. "Don't move, or I'll shoot."

Sir Gerald raises himself on hands and knees. He roars as he vaults at Pierce, whose finger is on the trigger. "No!" I cry. Tristan grabs Sir Gerald around his legs.

"Gerald!" Lady Alexandra hovers near the door, blonde hair streaming to her waist, clutching the throat of her crimson satin housecoat.

The room is now full of other people, mostly servants. Lottie is among them, open-mouthed with fright. As Pierce backs out the door, Sir Gerald wrenches himself free of Tristan and charges after Pierce. Mick, Hugh, and I—and everyone else—follow. Two guards with rifles hurry up the passage toward us. Sir Gerald points at Pierce and yells, "He killed Robin! Shoot him!"

Lady Alexandra gasps as she beholds Pierce. "Oh, God. It really was you. I was right."

I think she lied about Tabitha not only to protect herself but because she wanted to believe that Tabitha, not Pierce, was guilty. But everything I heard her say to Pierce in the garden that night and about him to me later was real, not an act.

The guards aim their rifles at Pierce. Olivia puts her fingers in her ears. She looks thrilled. I'm glad help has arrived, though dismayed that death still seems inevitable. Hugh stares at Tristan, who doesn't seem to notice him. All Tristan's attention is for Pierce and Sir Gerald.

Lady Alexandra flings herself at Pierce, shrieking, "You killed Robin!" She beats his chest with her fists. He pushes her away, and she falls on the floor. He moves so suddenly that I don't know what he's up to until a second later, when he's holding Lottie with her back to him, his arm tight around her waist, the gun barrel jammed against her temple. He says to the guards, "Drop your weapons, or she dies."

Shock paralyzes everyone else. Whistles shrill faintly outside. The police must have heard the gunshot; they're coming. Lottie whimpers, her eyes round with terror. Mick cries, "Lottie!" and lunges to rescue her. Hugh and I hold him back.

Sir Gerald roars, "Shoot him! That's an order!"

"I can kill her before you can kill me," Pierce says to the guards.

They look at Sir Gerald, at each other, at Lottie. They lower their rifles and let them fall to the floor. Relief floods me.

"Good," Pierce says while Sir Gerald sputters in helpless rage. "Now I'm going, and if you try to stop me, I will kill her."

As he walks Lottie down the passage, she cries, "Help!"

Sir Gerald advances on them, but Olivia throws her arms around him. "Daddy, you mustn't. He'll shoot you."

"He killed my son. I'm not letting him get away with it!" Sir Gerald struggles to free himself from Olivia. She's stronger than she looks, clinging tightly.

"I'll kill you myself!" Lady Alexandra sobs as she crawls after Pierce.

Tristan grabs her skirts to stop her. Mick pulls away from me. "I gotta save Lottie!"

He runs after her and Pierce. Hugh and I follow. I call to Pierce, "The police are outside. They won't let you escape."

"They will unless they want her blood on their hands."

Lottie sobs, straining away from the gun pressed to her temple. "Mick, help me, please."

We reach the grand staircase, and Pierce forces Lottie down it. "Keep that boy away from me, or I'll shoot him," he tells Hugh and me.

Hugh bounds down the stairs ahead of Mick. "Let's talk this over, Mr. Pierce. How far do you think you can get, dragging this poor girl?"

Pierce laughs, a sound both sardonic and strained. "Far enough." He's halfway down the stairs with Lottie.

"Let her go, you bloody pig!" Mick yells.

Lottie stumbles descending the last few steps, but Pierce holds her upright. They cross the dim foyer with Mick, Hugh, and me in pursuit while other servants watch fearfully from the landing above us. Pierce drags Lottie to the French doors at the back of the foyer.

"Open them," he says. When none of us obeys, he thrusts the gun hard against Lottie's temple. "Do it!"

"Go to hell," Mick says, but he opens the doors. We follow Pierce and Lottie out to the terrace. The wind is rising; it chills my face and flaps my skirts. The sky is clearing, and the gibbous moon shows its cratered face through tatters of mist. Lottie shivers and sobs while Pierce forces her across the terrace and down the stone staircase. As we pursue them onto the pavement that surrounds the rectangular pool, two round bright lights suddenly emerge from the shadows in the topiary garden. They beam from lanterns that dangle from the arms of two guards. The guards aren't the same ones who disobeyed Sir Gerald's order to shoot Pierce, but they must have heard about what just happened. They aim their rifles at Pierce.

"Drop your weapons," Pierce says. "Let us pass, or I shoot her."

The guards advance, their expressions impassive as they sight down the barrels of their rifles. Either they don't care about Lottie or they think they can bluff Pierce into surrendering. Pierce frowns, and his finger twitches on the trigger.

Mick looks imploringly at Hugh and me. Hugh says, "Mr. Pierce, it's over. Surrender."

The only sounds are the wind, the tinkling of the fountain, and Lottie's sobs as Pierce stares the guards down. He must know that his choices are making his stand now or facing the hangman later. Mick, Hugh, and I stand by helplessly, anticipating the storm of gunfire.

Footsteps clatter across the terrace above us. I turn to see Tristan Mariner run down the staircase. He positions himself between Pierce and the guards, in the line of fire. Facing

Pierce, he spreads his arms to hold the guards back. Hugh inhales a sharp gasp. The guards lower their rifles. Tristan, breathless from exertion, ignores everyone except Pierce. "Let the girl go." His handsome face is flushed, his expression cautious yet determined. He taps his fingers against his chest. "Take me instead."

"Your sacrifice won't be necessary, Father," Pierce says with a mocking laugh.

Tristan moves toward Pierce. "I'm a better hostage than she is."

Hugh whispers, "Oh, God, no."

"Don't come any closer." Pierce's eyes flash with suspicion; he thinks Tristan has some scheme to thwart his escape.

"They know you killed Robin. They'll shoot you." Tristan gestures at the guards behind him. "They don't care if they shoot the girl too. Neither will anybody else. She's nobody. But they won't shoot me." Tristan stops inches from Pierce and Lottie. "I'm Sir Gerald Mariner's son. Nobody will hurt you if I'm with you and my life is at stake."

Pierce neither moves nor changes his obstinate expression, but I sense his thoughts shifting. "Take off your coat," he orders Tristan.

Tristan unbuttons and removes his black coat, drops it on the steps, and stands in his shirtsleeves and priest's collar.

"Raise your hands," Pierce says. "Turn around, slowly. Then turn your pockets out and pull up your trouser legs."

"I'm unarmed," Tristan says, complying.

Although I'm relieved for Lottie, my hopes sink as I realize that Tristan actually intends to go with Pierce, and he has no means of defending himself. Hugh says, "Tristan." He sounds moved as well as horrified by Tristan's heroics. "Don't."

If Tristan hears or cares that Hugh is worried about his safety, he doesn't let on. Pierce beckons, and Tristan moves closer. In one quick, deft motion, Pierce thrusts Lottie away and pulls Tristan against him like a shield. Lottie runs sobbing to Mick and throws herself into his arms.

"Throw your weapons in the pond," Pierce orders the guards.

Two rifles splash and sink. Pointing with his toe at the ground a yard from himself, Pierce says to one of the guards, "Put your lantern there." The guard grimly obeys. Pierce lets go of Tristan, jams the pistol against his back, and picks up the lantern. "Let's go."

We watch, speechless and appalled, while Pierce marches Tristan into the darkness. "Tristan will try to capture Pierce," Hugh says in a voice that quakes with fear. "He'll be killed. I have to save him." Hugh bolts after Pierce and Tristan.

"Hugh, no!" Afraid he'll be shot while trying to rescue Tristan, I run after Hugh.

"I'm coming too." Mick leaves Lottie and runs after me.

One of the guards chases Hugh while the other heads off Mick and me. Mick is still carrying the lantern we brought, and he swings it at the guard. As the guard dodges, Mick yells, "Go, Sarah! Help Hugh."

Mick veers across the lawn. The guard can't chase both of us; he hesitates, then goes after Mick. I race past the fountain in pursuit of Pierce and Tristan. It's dark beyond the radius of the glow from the lamps on the terrace, and I bump into a marble urn. Ahead I see a light moving in the direction of the staircase down which I followed Tristan the night he went to the pond. Pierce must be taking the same route out of the estate. Then I'm caught in a glare of light. Ear-splitting whistles accompany my first glimpse of three police constables carrying lanterns.

"Police! Stop!" they shout.

I run for the cover of the topiary trees. The constables pound after me. Maybe they don't know what's happened, but they saw me fleeing the mansion and probably assume I'm the person who fired the gun. I can't stop to explain. The moonlight guides me between the dark pools of shadow cast by the conical and spherical trees. Panting, I come up against a brick wall. The police shout at one another, "Did you see where she went?" "Over there!" I feel my way along the wall until

I find a gate. On the other side, the path that skirts the wall is deserted, the forested hillside quiet except for the wind rustling the leaves, dark except for the moonlight. I hurry along the path until I find another that leads downhill. Whether Pierce intends to walk out of London or catch a train, he'll have to get off the hill first. Maybe I can intercept him at the bottom. I hear more whistles, more shouts, as I plunge down the path through the woods. They seem to be coming from every direction. I don't know how many police or guards are out here. I don't know whether Hugh is safe or what I'll do if I find Pierce and Tristan.

I trip on branches and fall twice before I reach the path's end. Bruised, sore, and sweating despite the cold, I come out on the road at the bottom of the hill. To my left, perhaps thirty feet away, two figures are crossing the road. Keeping to the edge of the woods, I steal up the road after them. They disappear into the woods on the opposite side, and I experience moments of frantic anxiety before I locate the path they took. At its end, the landscape is as scarred, blighted, and alien as the surface of the moon that casts ghostly light over it. This part of Hampstead Heath was once mined for sand and gravel for building railways. Gusting wind whips tears into my eyes, and I can barely see the flame of Pierce's lantern as I follow it along bare, sandy slopes that descend to swamp-edged craters filled with glittering black water.

The calls and whistles are faint now, distant. Much as I don't want to be alone with Pierce and Tristan, I hope Hugh isn't also on their trail and about to do something reckless.

The light vanishes into a grove of stunted trees. I hurry to catch up. Beyond the trees, I cross another road to more woods. The path through them is a dark, windblown tunnel. I've lost Pierce and Tristan. If I go for help, they'll surely be far away by the time I return. I'm not even sure I can find my way back to Mariner House.

"Stop right there." Pierce's voice comes from the darkness ahead of me.

31

My heart jumps. I freeze, terrified that Pierce has spotted me. He'll shoot Tristan, and there will be another death on my hands before he shoots me too.

"You're not going to talk me into surrendering to the police, Father Tristan," Pierce says. "You may as well save your breath."

He's speaking to Tristan. I clutch my chest, faint with relief that he's unaware of my presence. As I tiptoe toward the men, the forest thins out. Ahead is an open space in a broad, shallow depression where moonlight shines on a carousel and striped tents in a deserted midway. It's the Hampstead Heath fairground. Instead of carnival music, I hear the wind flapping the flags on the roof of the carousel. A lawn slopes toward stalls that contain the refreshment stands and shooting galleries. Benches are ranged along the top of the slope. A lantern flickers beside the nearest bench. There Pierce and Tristan are slumped with their backs to me; I hear them panting. Exhausted by their flight, they've stopped to rest.

"I'll help you convince the police that you're innocent," Tristan says.

He's trying to trick Pierce into turning himself in.

"Ha. Why would they believe you?"

"Because it's a fact. You didn't kill Robin." Tristan speaks with such conviction that if I didn't know better, I would think he was telling the truth.

"Well, if you really believe that, it makes two of us."

"I'll hire a good solicitor to defend you in court." Tristan sounds more eager to help Pierce than afraid Pierce will kill him.

"Thanks." Sarcasm inflects Pierce's voice. "We both know it doesn't matter what the court decides. Sir Gerald thinks I'm guilty, and his opinion is the only one that matters."

"Let me talk to him," Tristan pleads. "I'll convince him that all you did was steal the ransom money."

Pierce chuckles. "I underestimated you. You're doing exactly what your father would in your position—trying to dupe me."

I can't save Tristan and capture Pierce by myself. I hear the distant calls and whistles and silently urge the police to come.

"I'm not trying to dupe you. I'm trying to save you."

"Sir Gerald could pull it off, but you haven't his talent for manipulating people. You're an inferior chip off the old block."

"He'll see reason after he calms down," Tristan says with dogged persistence. "If you return the ransom money, he'll forgive you."

"Better stick to peddling Christianity to the heathens. Sir Gerald never forgives anyone for anything. I'll use the money to get out of England."

"Where will you go? My father has a long reach."

"It's a big world, and I know of places where even he won't find me."

"By now the police have mounted a search for you. Can't you hear the whistles?" Tristan says. "You won't get out of London."

"Not with you slowing me down and trying to sabotage me." Pierce reaches down, picks up the lantern and stands. "This is where we part company."

Tristan jumps to his feet. "I'm going too. Without me, you're dead."

I don't understand why he's not glad to be released. Alarm catches my breath because Pierce will vanish before the police come.

"I'll take my chances." Pierce walks into the woods toward me, the lantern in his left hand, the gun in his right.

I hide behind a tree while Tristan hurries after Pierce and stands in front of him. "Either I go with you," Tristan says, "or you can shoot me now."

Without hesitation, Pierce aims and cocks the gun. Tristan lifts his chin and squares his shoulders like a man facing a firing squad. I can't keep quiet any longer. "They're over here!" I shout. "Help!"

The men turn toward the sound of my voice. Then Pierce cries out as if in pain and astonishment. His knees buckle, the gun and lantern drop from his hands, and he falls facedown. Behind him stands Olivia.

I gasp in shock. Olivia, who must have followed us from Mariner House, is wearing an unbuttoned mackintosh over her white nightdress and galoshes on her feet. With her bare, mud-streaked legs and the leaves caught in her wild hair, she looks like a vagabond. Her eyes sparkle; her exultant smile beams.

"*Olivia?*" Tristan says.

Bewildered by the turn of events, I stumble over to Pierce. He moans, twitching on the ground like a hooked fish. The lantern has rolled a few feet away, and it's too dark to see what Olivia did to him. Then he goes still and silent.

"I got him!" Olivia sounds like a child who's won a game. "He can't hurt us now. See?" She kicks Pierce in the ribs with her heavy boot. He neither moves nor makes a sound.

"Olivia, what have you done?" Dread fills Tristan's voice. He kneels beside Pierce.

The pelt of footsteps and the sound of coughing precedes the arrival of Hugh. Mick is with him, carrying the lantern; they're both winded from running. "Thank heaven," I cry, relieved that they weren't shot or arrested.

"Sarah!" Hugh sees Tristan on the ground, and the relief in his expression turns to alarm. He halts abruptly, as if he's slammed into a wall. "Tristan. Are you hurt?"

Tristan raises a hand, warding Hugh off. Mick says, "Where's Pierce?" Then he spies the body on the ground and shines his lantern on it. The thick leather-covered hilt of a knife protrudes from Pierce's back. Wet red blood gleams around the base of the steel blade. "Gorblimey!"

Olivia stabbed Pierce. Hugh and I gape, dumbfounded.

Tristan feels Pierce's neck for a pulse and looks up, his eyes filled with disbelief and horror. "He's dead."

I'm too stunned to be glad that the danger is past and Robin's murderer delivered to justice. Hugh murmurs, "All's well that ends well."

Staggering to his feet, Tristan clutches his heart as if he's the one who's been stabbed. Olivia slips her hand through his arm. "Let's go back to the house. I have to tell Daddy I killed Mr. Pierce." She smiles at Hugh, Mick, and me, pleased to have an audience. "Daddy will be so proud of me!"

I'm astonished by her self-centered reaction to killing a man. I'm ashamed of my relief that Hugh, Mick, and I didn't need to do the honors ourselves.

Tristan puts his hand over Olivia's, but he doesn't move. His face is white, rigid.

"What's the matter?" Olivia asks. "Mr. Pierce deserved to die. He killed Robin."

Tristan turns a sorrowful gaze on her. "No, Olivia. He didn't."

The shock of Pierce's sudden, violent death has impaired my wits; I don't understand why Tristan is denying that Pierce is guilty, why he's behaving so oddly.

"Of course he did." Olivia sounds like a little girl whose brother is spoiling her treat. "That's why Father tried to shoot him. That's why he ran away."

Tristan shakes his head. "I'm not going to lie anymore."

Enlightenment strikes me with the force of a punch in the chest. Tristan is confessing that he himself killed Robin. That's why he sounded so certain Pierce was innocent.

"Oh, God." Hugh's voice is hoarse with the pain of betrayal and heartbreak. "It was you after all."

Now I also understand why Tristan took Lottie's place as Pierce's hostage. He'd sinned by committing murder, and he wanted to atone. When Pierce was about to shoot him, he didn't resist because he would have rather died a martyr than lived with his guilt.

"Tristan, no!" Olivia recoils from him as if he'd slapped her.

"I can't go on protecting you." Tristan regards her with tender pity. "Not after this." He gestures at Pierce's corpse.

"But you promised. It was your idea to tell Father and the police that we were playing billiards together when Robin was kidnapped. You said nobody would ever know."

My ideas about Robin's murder undergo another shocking alteration. Tristan lied to protect Olivia, not himself.

Mick stares, incredulous, at Olivia. "*You* killed Robin."

Hugh exhales in relief. I'm stunned because although I never trusted Olivia, my suspicions had focused on the other suspects. Olivia had become lost in the shuffle of evidence and conjectures.

Olivia faces Hugh, Mick, and me. "I didn't mean to kill him." She seems more defiant than repentant. "It was an accident."

"You sneaked into the nursery, kidnapped Robin from his crib, carried him to the pond, weighted him down with rocks, and drowned him," I say. "How can you call that an accident?"

Tristan rises to the defense of the little sister he's always protected. "That's not how it happened. She didn't go to the nursery to kidnap Robin."

"I wanted to see why Daddy and Alexandra kept him hidden," Olivia says.

"She was just curious," Tristan says.

"I thought there must be something wrong with Robin. And there was." Olivia's lip curls with revulsion. "He was little and puny and crooked."

I envision her bending over the baby in the crib and her surprise when she discovered the secret that Robin's parents had tried to conceal.

"When I said, 'Hello, Robin, it's your big sister, Olivia— remember me?' he made grunting sounds, like a pig. And this was the child that Daddy made such a fuss over." Jealousy embitters Olivia's tone. "The one he loved more than me."

Mick, Hugh, and I are silent, fascinated to hear the story.

"Then Robin started having spasms. He was stiff and shaking all over, and his face was twisted. I didn't do anything to him. I didn't even touch him! He started bawling. I was afraid Alexandra would hear, and she would catch me in the nursery and tell Daddy, and he would be angry. So I picked up a pillow and held it over Robin's face."

"She was only trying to muffle the noise." Tristan's look at Hugh, Mick, and me begs us to believe it.

"When I took the pillow off his face, he was dead." Olivia shrugs. "I must have pressed too hard."

"She suffocated him by mistake," Tristan says.

I don't think it was entirely a mistake, and I can tell that Tristan doesn't either. "So you dumped Robin's body in the pond, and you put the ladder outside the nursery to make it look as if he'd been kidnapped." Now that my shock has abated, I'm furious at Olivia. "You let Sir Gerald and Lady Alexandra suffer and hope he would be returned. And Raphael DeQuincey is in jail because of you."

My hands clench; I want to strike her on my own behalf as well as theirs. The fire, losing Barrett, and the damage to my friendship with Hugh all trace back to Olivia's selfishness.

"Not because of her," Tristan says. "After Olivia killed Robin, she came to me. She was frantic; she didn't know what else to do. She told me what had happened." He addresses his words to Hugh, as if his opinion is the one that matters most. "*I* disposed of Robin's body and faked the kidnapping." He bows his head in remorse. "I didn't want Olivia to be punished."

"Christ," Hugh whispers. He seems both horrified by Tristan's deceit and awed by the lengths to which Tristan went for the sake of brotherly loyalty.

The night I watched him at the pond, Tristan must have been praying for Robin's soul and God's forgiveness. But his excuses and his remorse don't cut any ice with me. "You were going to let Olivia get away with Robin's murder and Raphael DeQuincey hang for it!"

Tristan faces me, somber and apologetic. "I know that what I did was wrong. My conscience has been torturing me ever since. I'm going to tell the police the truth now."

As he starts up the path, Olivia runs to him and cries, "Don't do this to me! I don't want to go to jail—I don't want to be hanged! Why not just let Mr. Pierce take the blame for Robin's murder? It can't hurt him—he's dead. And everybody thinks he's guilty."

The look Tristan gives her contains reproach as well as sorrow. "I covered up Robin's murder for you. I can't cover up anything else."

Olivia flinches. "There's nothing else to cover up." Her tone is artificially blithe.

I'm flabbergasted to realize, yet again, that there's more to the story than I thought. This case is like a montage of photographs; new ones keep appearing, and I've yet to see the last.

"You poisoned Tabitha," Tristan says.

It's not the idea that astonishes me; I've always thought that the person who killed Robin also poisoned Tabitha, and in another moment, I would have inferred that it was Olivia. It's the certainty in Tristan's voice. How could he know?

Olivia utters a tinkling, nervous laugh. "Don't be silly."

"I saw you climb out of her window just before the police found her dead."

The falsely innocent smile drops off Olivia's face.

"You put the strychnine in the cup of cocoa and brought it to her. She thought you were being nice to her." Tristan speaks in the grieved tone of a man who's solved a puzzle he wishes he hadn't. "You watched her drink the cocoa and take ill. She must have begged you for help, but you let her die. You wrote the note and locked the door so that everyone would think she'd committed suicide."

Olivia's huge, luminous eyes glint with fear. "I didn't do it just for myself. I did it for you. Someone had to take the blame for Robin's murder. Daddy suspected both of us. As long as the murder wasn't solved, he would never believe we were innocent. It had to be Tabitha. She's not family. She didn't matter."

Mick exclaims in disgust. "Did you set the fires too? Did you think it was all right to kill Miss Sarah and Lord Hugh because they don't matter either?"

"I only wanted to scare them so they would stop poking around and go away." Olivia delivers this confession as though the fires were trivial and his accusation merely irritating. She says to Tristan, "Please don't tell Daddy about Robin. He'll be so angry."

"Olivia, you've killed three people. We can't go on like this." Tristan's manner is gentle but firm. "It has to stop tonight."

I remember the conversation we had after the fire. Tristan wasn't threatening me; he was trying to warn me about Olivia. I think he understands that murder has become a habit with her, and if he helps her escape the consequences this time, someday she'll find it worth her while to kill again.

Olivia scowls, walks around Pierce's body, and kicks the dead leaves like a pouting child. "It will stop. Just don't tell."

Tristan holds out his hand to Olivia. "Come with me. I'll talk to the police. I'll make them understand that you're young, you didn't know what you were doing, and they should be lenient. I'll explain to Father that you didn't mean to kill Robin."

"No!" Olivia falls to her hands and knees. Obstinacy tightens her mouth. I think she's about to throw a tantrum.

"If I don't tell, they will." Tristan nods at Hugh, Mick, and me.

As we surround Olivia, Mick says, "The jig's up."

"Come along like a good girl, or we'll have to get rough," Hugh says.

I feel a sense of completion, for although delivering Olivia to justice won't resurrect Robin, Tabitha, or Pierce, and we'll live with our mistakes forever, our investigation is finally concluded. While Raphael DeQuincey may serve prison time for the ransom hoax, he won't hang.

"You won't tell. Because I won't let you!" Olivia scrambles up, holding the gun that she found near Pierce's body.

How badly I misinterpreted her actions, underestimated her determination to avoid the consequences of her crimes. Alarmed, I cry, "Look out!"

As Hugh, Mick, and I reel backward, Tristan shouts, "Olivia! No!"

"If we get rid of them, everything will be all right." Olivia fires at us.

Hugh and Tristan lunge at the same moment that the gun discharges with a flash of light from its muzzle and a bang that reverberates through the forest. Hugh puts himself in front of Mick and me. Tristan shoves Hugh to the ground.

Terror stabs me, and I shout Hugh's name, but I haven't time to find out whether he's been shot. Mick yells, "Sarah, run!" and pushes me.

I hurtle toward the woods. Through the haze of pungent smoke from her first shot, I see Olivia take aim at Mick. He zigs and zags like a boxer avoiding punches. Olivia jerks the weapon from side to side, tracking his movements while she advances on him. Mick pivots to run, trips, and sprawls flat on the ground. Olivia stops inches from him, pointing the gun straight down at his back.

"Mick!" I stumble as I change direction and rush to him. I hear Tristan's urgent voice, but Hugh is dreadfully silent. My momentum sends me crashing into Olivia.

The gun fires. Olivia shrieks as I knock her sideways. I snatch for the gun, but she swings it up and hits my forehead. The explosion of pain is blinding. My vision is a dark haze webbed with white veins. My hands scrabble at Olivia. It's like fighting an invisible cat the size of a human. She's all shrieks and howls, flying hair and wiry, twisting body. Her fingernails claw my face. I swat her, and she screams. I grab at her hair in my futile attempt to find the gun. Her kicks thump my shins. I don't know what's become of Mick and Hugh. I sob because I'm afraid they're dead. All I can do is hold onto Olivia, so that if they're still alive, she can't kill them. Now I feel the gun's hard barrel thrust against my ribs.

Shouts and whistles blare nearby. The police are coming too late.

Gunshots boom like thunder. I scream as the impacts jolt me off my feet. Warm, wet, viscous liquid drenches my face and neck. I fall to the ground, and Olivia lands on top of me. I can't breathe. The sweet, salty, iron-tasting liquid fills my nose, my mouth. Panic and terror surge. I can't move. I've been shot. I'm choking on my own blood. I'm dying.

A confusion of running footsteps and loud, anxious voices surrounds me. Light flares. My vision is red from the blood in my eyes. Through the blood, I see someone standing over me. It's Sir Gerald, holding a shotgun, his face a picture of grim, vindictive satisfaction. He extends his foot, and his boot prods Olivia. Her inert weight rolls off me. I turn my head toward her, and what I see is so terrible that my consciousness blurs at the edges. Half of Olivia's face and neck are a mass of blood, mangled flesh, and shattered bone. Her remaining eye stares at me. Through my nausea and horror, I hear Mick's voice, shrill with excitement.

"He shot her! He musta heard everything she said. He shot her!"

My hands frantically scramble over my chest, my stomach. There's no pain, no wound; the blood on me is Olivia's, not mine. Hugh and Mick are kneeling beside me. I croak out their names, and they moan, "Thank God, thank God."

I'm so glad to see them safe that tears rinse Olivia's blood from my eyes. Then Hugh and Mick are gone, and someone pulls me into his lap and cradles me in his arms. It's Barrett.

"Sarah! No!" His howl of protest echoes to the sky. His face, bent over me, is contorted with grief, his eyes streaming with tears. "You can't die. Come back. Sarah!" He presses my face to his chest, his cheek against my hair, and weeps.

He doesn't know what happened; he didn't notice Olivia. He thinks the blood is mine and I was mortally wounded.

In a moment I'll tell him I'm not dead, but for now I don't speak or move because I'm too breathless and the comfort of his embrace feels too good.

32

The Drill Hall Assembly Room in Hampstead overflows with the noisy crowd that has gathered for the coroner's inquest into the deaths of John Pierce and Olivia Mariner. The audience occupies all the chairs behind the front row, where I sit between Hugh and Mick. The first row is reserved for witnesses who will testify. All the chairs in it except ours are empty. More spectators stand three deep against the walls. At the center of the front of the room is the witness box; to its right, twelve vacant seats for the jury. Two long tables with chairs face each other in the space between the audience and the witness box. Reporters with notebooks and artists with sketchpads sit at one table. The room buzzes with excited conversation.

Hugh leans close to me and whispers, "This is our last chance to get our story straight."

We've gone over our story again and again during the two days since Olivia and Pierce died. We've boiled it down to a simple version of events that we hope will be accepted. But as I behold the witness box where each of us in turn will sit alone and testify, tremors of fear chill me. "I don't think I can do it." I've told many lies during my life, but lying to a court of law is perjury—a crime for which we could go to prison.

"'Course you can." Mick pats my hand and whispers in my ear, "Remember, when they asks you why we went to

Mariner House, you say that DeQuincey sent the ransom note, and Pierce stole the money, and we wanted to tell Sir Gerald."

"Sir Gerald accused Pierce of murdering Robin and pulled a gun," Hugh whispers. "Pierce took Tristan hostage and ran away. We caught up with them on the heath."

"Pierce was dead when we got there," Mick whispers. "We didn't see what happened. Olivia came out of nowhere and attacked you. We don't know why."

"Sir Gerald turned up. He shot Olivia to save you." Hugh whispers, "Simple as A, B, C."

When we received the summons to testify at the inquest, we hotly debated whether to tell the whole truth. Hugh said, "I don't want to get Tristan in trouble for covering up Robin's murder. He saved my life." Mick said, "Me neither. He saved Lottie's life too." And I didn't want to get Sir Gerald in trouble—he'd saved my life when he shot Olivia. In the end, we decided that Olivia and Pierce had both already received the justice they deserved, and nobody need be punished on their accounts. The true story of that night on the heath would be just another secret we would have to keep, along with our knowledge about the fate of Jack the Ripper.

A stir of excitement ripples through the room as two groups of men file in. One group occupies the twelve chairs designated for the jury. The other men take seats at the empty table. Among them are Barrett and Inspector Reid; the others must be the coroner and government officials. The reporters open their notebooks, and the artists take up their pencils. Reid's stern gaze sweeps the audience, then settles on us. A predatory smile flashes under his mustache.

My stomach plunges.

We've no idea how much Reid knows about the events of that night. Before he got to the scene, Sir Gerald sent Hugh, Mick, and me home with two of his guards as escorts. Until today, we've ventured outside our house only once—to call on Mrs. Vaughn and explain what happened to her husband. She grieved violently, but at least she knows that his killer has been delivered to justice, even though there will be no trial or legal retribution. Eventually we'll track down and inform the family of Ethel Norris. For now, we've been living in seclusion, depending on the newspapers for information. London is rife with speculation and rumors, but the authorities have released no statement, presented no official version of the events. Sir Gerald has kept away the reporters and police who've demanded interviews with us. Now it's obvious that Reid thinks we had a hand in Olivia's and Pierce's deaths and can't wait to interrogate us.

I steal a glance at Barrett, whom I haven't seen since that night. His somber face betrays no awareness of me. My anxiety increases because he's sure to testify, and we don't know how much he saw or what he'll say. I look at the empty chairs in our row—apparently, no one is coming to fill them. Sir Gerald, Tristan, and everybody else from Mariner House are absent. We and Barrett are the only witnesses, and if our story doesn't agree with his, that will give Inspector Reid ammunition with which to destroy us. I feel a spate of anger at Sir Gerald. After everything we've been through because of him and his family, he's left us to face the law by ourselves and take the consequences.

The man in the center seat at the table pounds a gavel. The audience quiets. He introduces himself as Dr. Danford Thomas, Coroner for the Central Division of the County of London. He's tall and lanky, bald and bespectacled. "I hereby open this inquest into the deaths of Miss Olivia Mariner and Mr. John Pierce." His expression is pinched and bitter, as if he's just swallowed foul-tasting medicine.

My heart pounds, Hugh coughs into his handkerchief, and Mick jiggles his foot as we wait to hear who will testify first. Dr. Thomas says, "I shall forgo the usual procedure and rule on the case now."

The room erupts into a hubbub of confusion. Hugh and Mick and I look at one another, unsure whether this means reprieve or disaster for us. The reporters call out questions that jumble into cacophony. Barrett and the jurymen look perplexed. Spectators grumble, deprived of the show they expected.

Inspector Reid, crimson with anger, faces Dr. Thomas. "You have to call witnesses. You have to let me question them and the jury hear their testimony. What gives you the right to disregard the law?"

"The authority vested in me by the Crown." Dr. Thomas's voice is tight with disgust. Now I understand why he looks so bitter: he dislikes the situation as much as Reid does. He pounds his gavel, the audience quiets, and he announces, "Olivia Mariner kidnapped and murdered her half brother, Robin Mariner, because she was jealous of him. She poisoned Tabitha Jenkins and stabbed John Pierce because they knew and were blackmailing her. She died of a self-inflicted gunshot wound, having committed suicide due to remorse. The case is hereby closed. The witnesses and jury are dismissed. The inquest is adjourned."

He rises and stalks out of the room, the puzzled jurymen trailing in his wake. The reporters chase him, calling, "How do you know that Olivia Mariner murdered Robin? What evidence says she committed suicide?"

All three murders have been rightfully attributed to Olivia, even though her motives were partially misinterpreted. Hugh, Mick, and I are free to go, our secrets safe. But I barely have time to feel jubilant. As Mick and Hugh propel me from the room, through the mob of departing spectators, Inspector Reid comes charging toward us, his expression savage with fury.

"What do you know about this?" he demands. "What really happened to Olivia Mariner and John Pierce?"

Outside the building, the street is crowded with people awaiting the result of the inquest. Reporters mob Hugh, Mick, and me, yelling questions. Photographers snap our pictures; flash powder explodes around us. Reid grabs my arm and shouts into my face, "Did you kill them?"

His hand is ripped away from me as four of Sir Gerald's guards surround us, clear a path through the crowd, and escort us away. I'm afraid to find out where they're taking us but thankful to escape Reid. I hear him yell, "Damn you!"

The guards lead us down an alley. At the far end stands a large black carriage, whose door opens. Inside sits Sir Gerald.

"Get in," he says. Neatly groomed, wearing a black city overcoat and derby, he seems his normal, brisk self. "I'll take you to the train station."

Although we're loath to brave the crowds, the reporters, and Inspector Reid again, we hesitate. We haven't forgotten the sight of Sir Gerald with his rifle, standing over Olivia's corpse like an executioner inspecting his work. But we know more certainly than ever how dangerous it is to cross him. We climb into the carriage. I sit beside Sir Gerald, Hugh and Mick opposite us. As we ride through Hampstead village, I muster my courage and ask, "Did you rig the inquest?"

Sir Gerald shrugs. "I had a drink with the prime minister."

I'm afraid to ask how he twisted the prime minister's arm. We're in no position to quibble.

With an air of getting down to business, Sir Gerald says, "I wanted to thank you for helping me bring Robin's killer to justice."

Hugh, Mick, and I exchange queasy looks. We've yet to resolve our mixed feelings about Olivia's death. Sir Gerald's shooting her was justice of the bloodiest sort, but perhaps no worse than turning her over to the law. I would rather die quickly by a bullet than endure the ordeal of the walk to the gallows, the noose around my throat, and the time to imagine the snap of my neck breaking. I wonder if Olivia knew that her father shot her. I hope not. If she had, she would have been devastated because he loved her so little that avenging Robin mattered more to him than her life. And I think she would rather have died than see, as I'm seeing now, his complete lack of remorse. I pity her despite the fact that she tried to kill me.

"It was our pleasure," Hugh says with a wince.

We're far from happy about our role in Olivia's death but glad Sir Gerald didn't protect Olivia and help her get away with murdering Robin and Tabitha. If he had, we would have been obligated to oppose him, which would have meant certain ruin for us. Furthermore, denouncing him as a vigilante who took the law into his own hands would be the pot calling the kettle black.

"I'm going to offer you a permanent job," Sir Gerald says. "You'll be my personal investigators, on call whenever I need you." He names a retainer fee that makes our jaws drop. "Effective immediately. The usual confidentiality agreement."

We look at each other, our ambivalence stronger than ever.

"Well?" Sir Gerald says impatiently.

We can't afford not to consider his offer; our prospects are as bleak as before we met him. But although I was wrong about him when I suspected him of murdering Robin, he did kill his daughter in cold blood. I doubt that saving my life figured into his decision to shoot Olivia. He's a monster after all—a monster who bends the law to his own purposes. If we accept the job, what might he expect us to do? What price failure? In retrospect, I see that we didn't exactly solve the kidnapping case; it's more that our mistakes paved the path to the solution.

"Why do you want to hire us?" I ask.

"You don't give up," Sir Gerald says. "I like that."

Now I realize that the minute we stepped into this carriage, we stepped back into his orbit, and the force of it is too mighty to resist. We look at one another, nod, and I answer for us. "We accept."

"Good." Sir Gerald nods as if he too saw our acceptance as inevitable.

He shakes hands with each of us. His grip on my fingers is gentle enough but hard with the strength of a steel trap that could spring at any moment.

The carriage stops outside the train station. Sir Gerald says, "I'll be in touch," and we climb out. We watch him ride away, then exchange leery glances.

"It's like gettin' in bed with the devil," Mick says.

"There'll be hell to pay, sooner or later," Hugh says.

Then his head whips around as if some remarkable sight has caught his attention. I follow his gaze and see, by the village green, a priest. It's Tristan Mariner, hurrying toward us, calling Hugh's name.

"Excuse me," Hugh says, his face suddenly luminous.

He walks toward Tristan. When they meet, they bow like businessmen at a town assembly. But even from a distance, I can see the flush on their cheeks and smiles trembling on their lips and sense the longing they take pains to hide.

"We might as well go home," Mick says with a satisfied grin. "Hugh'll be busy for a while."

My heart swells with joy for Hugh—and envy. He and Tristan are having the reunion that Barrett and I never will.

#

Mick and I arrive in Argyle Square to dense fog that drips with rain and reeks of tarry smoke from the factories. I'm glad to be back, but when we enter the house, tears fill my eyes, and I can barely see to hang up my coat. I've never felt lonelier.

Mick runs to the kitchen to tell Fitzmorris what's happened. I light the fire in the parlor, sit staring into the flames, and try to convince myself that things could be worse. Although I'll always wish I could have prevented Tabitha's death, Olivia Mariner and John Pierce will trouble the world no more. Thanks to Sir Gerald, Hugh and Mick and I have a new livelihood, and I can replace my photography equipment. But my illusions about my father are gone forever. Barrett is gone too. The aching emptiness of loss will never leave me.

That evening after dinner, I'm sitting in the parlor again when Hugh comes home. His face still wears that luminous expression. I raise my eyebrows, asking questions that I'm too shy to voice.

"Tristan will have to quit the priesthood if he wants to be with me." Hugh warms his hands at the fire. "I told him the decision is up to him. I won't ask him to make the sacrifice." Hugh sounds tired, rueful, but at peace. "If he quits, he'll also be giving up his mission. His ship to India sails next month. He'll have to decide by then."

He'll have to decide whether being with Hugh is worth risking exposure as a homosexual, arrest, and imprisonment.

"He doesn't want to leave me and go back to India, but he feels that he should because of Robin," Hugh says. "He colluded with Olivia and covered up the death of an innocent child. He's got a load of guilt to work off."

I can't think of anything to say.

Hugh's smile flashes. "Don't feel sorry for me, Sarah. Things are good with Tristan and me, for now. If he gets on that ship next month . . . well, 'Better to have loved and lost,' et cetera."

He goes upstairs. I'm happy for him and sorrier for myself. As I wipe my eyes, I hear knocking at the front door and Fitzmorris letting someone in. The sound of a familiar step launches me to my feet.

"Sarah?" Barrett stands in the parlor doorway.

His image shimmers in my tears like a mirage. I blink in astonishment. Instinctive caution tamps down my joy.

Barrett's manner is stiff and somber as he says, "Can I talk to you?"

I think I know why he's here. A pulse of dread pounds through my veins, but I nod and compose myself. We sit on the sofa by the fire. The few inches between us seems like miles.

"Is this about the inquest?" I want to get this over with. "Did you come to tell me that you disagree with the coroner's ruling?" Barrett must have seen something of what happened on the heath that night; he must intend to warn me before he tells his superiors.

"No! That's not why." Barrett's color rises. He draws a deep breath and says, "I came to ask you to take me back."

My spirits soar, but I can't believe what I'm hearing. "But why . . . ?"

"When I thought you were dead, I realized I couldn't bear to lose you." His voice shakes, and his keen gray eyes shine with tears. "When I found out you were alive, I realized how much I'm still in love with you, and there's no use trying to pretend I'm not."

I can hardly find the breath to say, "Why did you wait two days to come?"

"Because I was afraid you wouldn't want me. I said some awful things to you. I didn't mean them. I'm sorry." Barrett blinks, swallows, and takes my cold hands in his warm, tense clasp. "Can we start over?"

I want it so badly, I could shout it to the skies. But I know he did mean the things he said, and there was truth in them.

Disappointment eclipses the hope in Barrett's expression. "Shall I go?"

"No!" I clutch his hands as he starts to withdraw them. But even as renewed hope brightens his eyes, I know it wouldn't be fair to let him think that we can pick up where we left off as though nothing happened. I grope for the words to explain. "If we're to start over . . ."

He exhales and smiles with relief. "I'll do whatever you want. Just tell me what it is."

"I need you to understand that there will be things I can't tell you." Those things include information related to the events of that night on Hampstead Heath, my father, and my future work for Sir Gerald.

"That's all right." Ardor sweeps away Barrett's recollection of how infuriated he was by my dishonesty.

"There will always be secrets between us," I warn him.

"I don't suppose any man and woman know everything about each other," Barrett says, eager to make concessions. "I don't care as long as we're together. Sarah—"

Then I'm caught up in his arms, in our desire that has gone unsatisfied for too long. We don't kiss because Hugh, Mick, or Fitzmorris might walk in on us, but we hold each other tight. Tears of happiness leak from my closed eyes, and I silently pray that the next time Barrett discovers I kept a secret from him, it won't be the last, unforgiveable straw.

EPILOGUE

Later that same night as Barrett leaves, I stand by the window and watch him disappear into the rainy darkness. I'm content because I know he'll come back. My troubles have abated, all except for one: somehow I must make peace with never knowing for sure whether my father is a rapist and murderer, never knowing where he is.

Outside the window, a solitary figure steps haltingly into the light cast by the gas lamp near the front walk. It's a young woman in a plain, neat coat and bonnet, huddled under an umbrella. She pauses to look at the house. Her face has my own features, albeit younger and prettier.

It's Sally, my half sister.

I'm astonished because I didn't expect to see her again. She must have remembered that I said I lived in Argyle Square. Jealous anger lashes out from me like a whip. Sally is the child that my father begot, raised, and loved after he abandoned me.

Our gazes meet. She sees my expression, hers fills with embarrassment and fright, and she hurries away. But now that I'm over my shock, I remember my curiosity about Sally, and I can imagine what these days since we met have been like for her. I've had a kidnapping, murders, and a fight for my life to take my mind off that traumatic meeting, but she must have had little else to think of except me. I run out of the house, into the rain.

"Sally, wait!"

She stops and turns. "I shouldn't have come. I'm sorry."

Her eyes fill with tears. They're water dashed on the fire of my anger, and I remember that my father also abandoned Sally. I think this isn't her first time here; she's stood outside the house before, trying to work up the courage to call on me.

"Come inside," I say. "We can talk."

A smile blooms through her tears, and a hard, rough soreness that's been lodged in me since I first met her, like a peach pit in my heart, softens. "Thank you," Sally says with a gasp of relief. "I'd like that."

She joins me in the kitchen and expertly builds up the fire in the stove while I fill the kettle and measure tea into the pot. I imagine her doing this every day at the Chelsea mansion, and I deduce that my father never sent money to her and her mother. She hasn't had an education that would have fitted her for better work.

"Does your mother know you're here?" I ask while we wait for the kettle to boil.

"No. She wouldn't have wanted me to come. But there's something I have to tell you." Sally takes a deep breath. "My proper name is Sarah. My mother never liked it, so I've always been called Sally. The name was his idea. He named me after you. He must have loved you and missed you very much." Sally sighs. "I just wanted you to know."

My eyes sting, and not just because I'm so glad that my father didn't forget me, but for Sally. It must have hurt her to learn that she was, no matter how much he loved her, a replacement for the child he'd lost. Yet instead of hating me for it, she came here to give me this gift.

"Thank you," I say, sadly aware that she's a better, more generous person than I.

Sally nods, shy in the awkwardness of the moment. The teakettle whistles. She lifts it off the stove, pours the hot water into the teapot, and says, "All these years I thought I had no family except my mother, and it's been rather lonely, and . . . well, it would be nice to have a sister."

The appeal in her eyes is irresistible. "I think it would be nice too," I say, to my own surprise. We smile at each other, and I know Hugh and Mick would welcome her as a friend. It seems that another good thing has come of my investigations.

"I also wanted to ask you about that photograph of our father," Sally says. "You took it recently?"

I nod, reluctant to divulge the long, complicated, painful tale.

Sally must perceive my reluctance; she tactfully doesn't press the matter. "At least he's still alive. I was hoping you could tell me something about him. There's so much I don't know."

Moments ago I would have enjoyed throwing what I know like acid in Sally's face; now I hate to repay her kindness with the cruelest tit for tat possible. But I think of how I've been living a lie created by the secrets my parents kept from me, and I decide that Sally deserves to know the truth, no matter how painful for both of us.

"We should sit down."

Facing me across the table, cups of tea in front of us, Sally waits expectantly. I tell her about Benjamin Bain's police record and Ellen Casey's murder. Her face pales with shock. By the time I'm finished describing my trip to Clerkenwell, tears are running down her cheeks.

"He can't have done it!" she exclaims. "He wouldn't hurt anybody!"

She evidently remembers the same gentle, kind man that I do. Her faith in him restores mine. My almost-certainty that he raped and murdered Ellen Casey begins to crumble.

"If he's caught, he'll be hanged!" Sally cries. "What are we going to do?"

"There's nothing we can do. We've no proof that he's inno-cent. We don't even know where he is." Then I reconsider.

Maybe, if we pool our knowledge, it will add up to a clue. "Sally, tell me what happened when he disappeared."

"There's not much to tell. One Sunday, he went out to take photographs. He didn't come home that night. On Monday, my mother went looking for him at the university press, and they told her he'd resigned on Friday." Sally adds, "We stayed in Oxford until our money ran out. Then my mother found us work in London." The tight expression on her face must be the same I wear when I'm keeping a secret. There's more to the story.

"Did anything unusual happen before he disappeared?" I ask.

"How did you know?"

"A lucky guess."

"About a week before he disappeared, he got a letter," Sally says. "I've never seen him so upset. He turned his back on me while he tore it open and read it. Then he ran outside, and I heard him being sick. When he came back, he looked dead white. I said, 'Papa, what's wrong?' He just said, 'Promise you won't tell anybody about this.' I promised, and he burned the letter in the stove."

We'll not speak of the past to anyone, my mother had said after he disappeared, when we moved away from Clerkenwell to start a new life.

"I've never told anyone until now," Sally says. "But maybe I should have broken my promise. I've always thought the letter was the reason he disappeared. If I had told, maybe he'd have been found."

Her expression fills with a guilt that I know too well. I hurry to say, "When he disappeared—the first time, in 1866— I thought that if I had looked harder for him . . ."

Our gazes meet and hold. We share the novel idea that if one of us isn't responsible for whatever happened to our father, then neither is the other. Smiles tremble on our lips as the weight we've borne since childhood lifts from our shoulders.

"Who was the letter from?" I ask.

"Someone called 'Lucas Zehnpfennig.'" Sally spells it. "I read it on the envelope. I remember because it was such a funny, unusual name."

"Who . . . ?" A sudden memory stuns me silent. I'm ten years old, coming home from school, and seated in the parlor with my mother is a strange man. My mother looks uneasy, but the man smiles and says, "Hello, Sarah. I'm Lucas." He says his last name, which is so odd that I giggle. He lifts me onto his lap. "What a pretty girl!" He's stroking my hair when my father comes in. My father is angrier than I've ever seen him. He says, "Go to your room, Sarah." I obey, and I hear my father ordering the man named Lucas to get out. That night, my parents have one of their whispered arguments.

Sally's voice draws me back to the present. "What is it?"

"I think I met the same 'Lucas' when I was a child."

"What a strange coincidence."

I'd forgotten about that day because soon afterward, my father had disappeared and nothing else mattered. "I don't think it was a coincidence. Lucas comes to my family's house, and my father disappears. A letter from Lucas comes to your family's house, and he disappears again?" I shake my head. "I think Lucas had something to do with both disappearances."

"But what?" Sally asks.

"I don't know." But I've a hunch that finding Lucas Zehnpfennig is the key to finding my father and the truth about the past. And find him I will, if it's the last thing I ever do.

ACKNOWLEDGMENTS

Many thanks to Matthew Martz, Sarah Poppe, Jenny Chen, and the whole team at Crooked Lane Books for their enthusiastic efforts on behalf of my work. Also, to Pam Ahearn, my agent, for always being there.